A Gexalatian Tale Series

BOOK ONE

Return to Royalty

E. PAIGE BURKS

Return to Royalty, A Gexalatian Tale Series Book One

Copyright © 2017 by E. Paige Burks. All Rights Reserved.

No part of this publication may be reproduced, stored in a retrieval system or transmitted, in any form or by any means—electronic, mechanical, photocopying, recording or otherwise—without prior written permission from the publisher, except for the inclusion of brief quotations in a review.

For information about this title or to order other books and/or electronic media, contact the publisher:
Infinity Flower Publishing, LLC
infinityflowerpublishing@gmail.com
www.epaigeburks.com

ISBN: 978-0-9984620-0-4 Softcover
        978-0-9984620-1-1 eBook

Printed in the United States of America

Cover and Interior design: 1106 Design

Publisher's Cataloging-In-Publication Data
(Prepared by The Donohue Group, Inc.)

Names: Burks, E. Paige.
Title: Return to royalty / E. Paige Burks.
Description: [Pasadena, Texas] : Infinity Flower Publishing, 2017. | Series: A Gexalatian tale series ; book 1 | Interest age level: 015-018. | Summary: "Nyx Estrella is a princess from Gexalatia, a world on the other side of a portal. Unfortunately, she has no idea. Sent to Lucky, Texas, when she was a baby to protect her from the evil King Paraximus, her biggest concerns are grades and seeing her friends. She has no idea that she possesses magical abilities and that her reality is about to become really strange."-- Provided by publisher.
Identifiers: ISBN 978-0-9984620-0-4 (softcover) | ISBN 978-0-9984620-1-1 (ebook)
Subjects: LCSH: Princesses--Juvenile fiction. | Teenage girls--Texas--Juvenile fiction. | Magic--Juvenile fiction. | CYAC: Princesses--Fiction. | Teenage girls--Texas--Fiction. | Magic--Fiction. | LCGFT: Fantasy fiction. | Science fiction.
Classification: LCC PZ7.1.B87 Re 2017 | DDC [Fic]--dc23

For seventeen-year-old Paige.

"Love what you do and do what you love.
Don't listen to anyone else who tells you not
to do it. You do what you want, what you love.
Imagination should be the center of your life."

— RAY BRADBURY

Special thanks also to my friend, Mark Baacke, who always pushes me to follow my heart; my parents, for always sharing my excitement, even when they're not sure what I'm talking about; my sister, for tolerating my weirdness on a daily basis; my Grannie, for being my biggest fan; and my wonderful husband, for knowing more about Gexalatia than probably even me.

Prologue

100 years ago, the Plains of Aduro.

Everything was chaos.

All along the valley below, the sound of swords and yelling filled the air. Fading beams of sunlight were cast about, setting the cerulean blades of grass ablaze. Blood was soaking into the ground, turning it muddy and ugly. Men and beasts clashed; this would be the last great battle for Gexalatia.

Hairy dog-like monsters used clawed hands to tear into the men that charged down the hill and into the valley. Archers stood at the edge of a cliff, firing into the fray. The monsters, atrox as they were known, fell dead, their hair matted with the gore of those they had slain. The plainsmen of Aduro, the Caelin, sat astride their bird-mounts. The sound of a battle drum sent the raperes charging, their riders shouting as they cut down the atrox and any who bore the crest of Siccita.

Mages stood just beyond the raperes and their riders, weaving spells meant to destroy the atrox. Blasts of Auresi and Acerbi magic charged the air, making it sizzle with the energy they summoned. It did little to deter the hell-spawn as they clambered from fissures which had opened along the plains.

Liana knew that time was drawing short for them. Her army was vastly outnumbered, overwhelmed by the atrox. She knew that soon, if the Siccitan army was not stopped, her dead would begin to rise, turning to cariosus as they were imbued by dark magic. There would be no hope for victory if she allowed that to happen. Cariosus had no sense of sides; they would kill and devour whoever stood in their path. Desperation was rising in her chest as she turned her eyes toward the far side of the valley, where a black dragon was hanging in the air, flapping massive wings. Her desperation turned to fear as she watched a man drop from the dragon's back into the midst of the fight.

Liana knew she had to cut off the evil at its source, and that source was King Paraximus' most renowned and feared general, Jet Lamia. It was by his hands that the atrox clawed their way out of the earth, and it was through his doing that darkness had fallen over the country of Ymber. Peace would be a distant dream until he was cut down.

Gexalatia had seen war for too many centuries now. It was becoming commonplace, something Liana lamented over. Too many good and noble men met untimely deaths; too many sons and daughters came into a dangerous world. But today would be the last day. Liana would make sure of that. She would meet her own death this day, or she would finally stop Jet. There were no other options.

The battle that raged around him was nothing as Jet walked among the pandemonium. Beside him, an atrox roared, ripping into an enemy soldier. Jet watched the beast maul the soldier, tearing chunks of flesh from his body. This battle was no different than all the ones before. The atrox paid him no mind as they ran about him like wild dogs, clearing a path for their leader. It made a dark smirk come to his lips.

The horror of war was nothing to him. He'd stood among scenes such as this countless times, enjoying the dying screams of his victims. He craved the taste of his enemies' blood, but today was special. Today he would have the one life he truly desired.

He turned his dark eyes, looking toward the top of the hill to where three mounts stood. Two soldiers in the green and white of Liana's banners sat astride raperes, which pranced on either side of a thick black warhorse. A small rider sat easily on the horse's back, a hooded cloak pulled low. Jet knew instantly it was her, and satisfaction filled him. This was the moment he'd spent his entire life preparing for.

It was easy enough for him to make his way to her. He met no resistance, her soldiers like paper as he used his hands to tear into them. Jet had always been one for close-quarter combat, using his own brute strength to stop his enemies. He enjoyed the fear that streaked through their eyes, and the scent of their blood on his hands. Even the Caelin were no match for him, their bird-mounts unable to pierce him with their razor beaks.

A Caelin warrior charged at him, swinging a heavy war hammer from his mount's back. Jet threw up his hand, a silver shield forming to block the man's attempted blow easily. He used his free hand to send a blast of searing magic at the rapere, which it managed to dodge with a flap of stubby wings. The blast glinted off the rapere's armor, the chalargentum repelling Jet's magic. Unfortunately, the beast's fluttering unseated its rider, causing him to fall to the muddy ground.

Jet watched the rider scramble to his feet as he released the magic that formed the shield. Sadistic humor shot through him as the warrior leapt to his feet, the rapere feathers in his braids catching the wind. He lifted his war hammer, bellowing a battle cry. Jet smirked as the warrior brought down his hammer and he ducked under it easily, dealing a blow to the warrior's forward arm. He bared his fangs in a delighted grin as horror flashed across the warrior's face, the bones in his arm jutting against his skin. In desperation, the warrior used his good arm to draw a short blade at his belt, but it was too late. Jet caught the blade of the sword, enjoying the feeling of it biting into his palm.

Jet let his eyes shift over the warrior's face, seeing that the colorful oils he'd used to paint his skin with were smudged, smeared with blood. He always wondered, just before the killing blow, what was going through his victims' minds. He liked to imagine their fears and their regrets and what he looked like through their eyes. With an easy motion, he drove his hand into the man's chest, feeling bone and flesh parting around his fingers. The Caelin man's beating heart was racing as Jet wrapped his fingers around it, squeezing it and twisting as he withdrew his hand. It continued to twitch for a long second as Jet held it, watching the man collapse.

Jet shifted his eyes to the hill then, grinning maliciously as the hooded rider urged her horse forward. Her warhorse was strong as it leapt through the battle, racing toward him. The wind caught at her hood, pulling it from her face as she let the cloak fall away from her shoulders, drawing swords from sheaths on her back. She cut down a foot soldier that meant to stop her, her eyes fixed on her target.

Time seemed to stand still as her horse neared Jet and he tossed the chunk of flesh in his hand away. In an easy motion, he waved his hands, forming a Geminaci blade in each one. He twirled the double-ended, hooked blades easily, sparks of Acerbi magic slinging from them like water. He drove them into the body of the horse as it reached him, watching it crash heavily to the ground, its leg severed from its body. He scowled as he realized that she had leapt away, landing a few feet from him.

Her armor was black, her lavender hair braided into plaits down her back. A helmet sat on her head, leaving her eyes bared. Her lilac gaze was calm as she held her curved scimitars, which Jet could see were etched with a Priorae prayer of vengeance.

"Here we are at last," Jet said darkly. He lifted his weapons, ready for her next attack.

Liana said nothing as she gazed at him. Her calm was deceptive; inside, her heart was racing, fear and rage pulsing through her. Jet had certainly done a good job of drawing her out. He'd slaughtered her men and her subjects, driving a knife into the heart of the kingdom of Ymber, just to lure her here to Aduro. He'd destroyed everything he touched, and she was certain that was his plan.

"No words?" he asked, smirking lightly.

Liana noticed that blood was splattered across his face. He didn't wear any armor, only black leather and the bright red mantle of Siccita, which was stained with the blood of her people. His dark hair fell across his eyes, strands pulling from the braid down his back, and his hands were dripping with the blood of his most recent victim. He bared razor fangs in his smile, and she knew she had to stop him here.

Her aura brushed strongly against his as she watched him, darkness pulling her into it. She'd heard stories about the monstrosity that he carried with him, but she'd never seen it firsthand. Even now, she could feel it twisting just underneath the darkness, something more sinister than Jet's own brand of evil.

"What shall I say to the likes of you?" she asked finally, pulling the helmet from her face. Despite being his enemy, Jet could see the beauty that had once lured his father into her clutches.

He tilted his head, something disturbing crossing his eyes. "I've been waiting for you." He seemed genuinely pleased with himself. "I've prepared something. Just for you."

Liana gritted her teeth. She braced as her eyes followed his swift movements, blocking the crushing blow of his Geminaci against her swords. In an easy motion, she twirled her body, swinging both of her blades. She watched as one managed to catch him, slicing into the thick leather doublet that covered his chest.

His black eyes darkened as he touched his sliced flesh, looking at the blood on his fingers. His lips quirked tauntingly. "Do you want the beast to come forward so soon?"

Liana drew a steeling breath. "I have yet to see what you really are," she said, a bitter edge to her voice. "Would you hide your true nature from me?" She arched a delicate brow. "I thought you've been preparing for me."

Her words were enough. Haughtiness crossed his face as he stepped toward her. He twirled the Geminaci, as if he was baiting her, but her plan was already in motion. Liana could feel a presence closing in behind her. She offered Jet a grin, lowering her swords. Realization crossed Jet's face too late as a massive cat lunged from behind her.

In an instant, the huge black monster was on him, her tail whipping fiercely as she dug her talons into his body. They tumbled to the bloody ground, tussling for a moment, a blur of black and red. Liana remained still, watching the exchange. Her heart caught when Jet inflicted a painful wound, causing the cat to fall to the ground. Bakene struggled for a moment to regain her feet, baring massive fangs, a low growl shaking the air.

When Jet moved to his feet, he was bleeding profusely, a bite gouging into his shoulder. He was returning her snarl with equal fervor, having released the Geminaci to press his hand over his wound. He was furious as he stared at her. Liana had tricked him.

The black cat snarled loudly at him, crouching low to the ground. She looked like she was preparing for another strike, but she was forced to brace when Jet lunged at her, digging his claws into her neck. Bakene was strong, twisting and writhing against his grip, but his fury lent him strength, allowing him to hold her down. A strangled yowl left her lips, just as another hairy body leapt toward them.

Dexter, a hulking black wolf, lunged at Jet, driving him from Bakene, allowing a red-haired girl to slide from his shoulder. Sinister, a white wolf and Dexter's mate, was hot on his heels as he pursued Jet, her powerful jowls snapping.

Behind them a tall woman swung a large battle-axe, dispatching an oncoming atrox with a single blow. She grinned as she reached Liana. "Sorry to be late," she said, her northern accent thick. "Atrox are a pain in the ass!" Her sandy hair was bound with a leather tie, her face painted in customary Aife war paint.

Liana frowned at the warrior-woman. "This is no time for jokes, Ungyo," she said softly. "Bring him down." A grimace was on her face as she watched the wolves encircle Jet. He was snarling darkly at them, but his eyes were fixed on her. The monster was stirring once more in his aura, this time pressing to be released.

Ungyo nodded and her smile vanished at the shift in his aura. She lumbered into the fight behind the wolves, preventing any of the atrox from coming to their leader's rescue. The red-haired girl, Otsana, was kneeling beside Bakene, using a healing spell to seal her wounds.

Frustration was seeping into her as Liana realized the most important member of her team was missing, but then she felt him slowly materialize beside her. She turned quickly, surprised when he lifted a hand, striking down an atrox with a golden blast. He smirked at her, smug laughter in his eyes. "You should be more careful."

"You're late," she snapped, watching Kumiho. He was dressed in plain clothes, brown and unassuming, obviously intending to be long gone after the fight was over. He never did anything by anyone's timeline except his own, and he never stepped into battle on anyone's behalf. It'd been a miracle that he had agreed at all.

He offered a sly, foxy grin. "I needed you to seal the illusion," he said. He turned his head, nine golden braids falling over his shoulders. "It will be to our advantage." He lifted his fingers, his golden eyes becoming bright as he touched the bloody edge of Liana's sword.

Liana held her breath as magic suddenly pulsed over the battlefield, freezing the chaos. Men and atrox, mages and raperes were suddenly stilled where they stood, poised in whatever action they had been performing. Jet blinked, confused as he realized the wolves were also frozen, silence filling the air. He clenched his fists, baring a snarl, feeling his own body unable to move. What kind of trick was this?

He drew a sharp breath as the ground suddenly opened under his feet, plunging him into darkness. He summoned his blades as movement returned to him, ready to kill the next person he saw, but the sound of a harp stilled his hand, making his heart lurch in his chest.

"Wake up, sleepy-head," a sweet voice said, calling him from the darkness.

Jet blinked, light pressing against his eyes. His confusion was worse as he realized he was lying in a bed, one that he was familiar with. He sat up quickly, pressing his hand against his face. Had he dreamed the battle?

"Hello, sleepy-head."

Jet turned, seeing a blue-haired woman sitting near balcony doors. She was looking at him from where she sat in front of her harp, her hands poised over the strings. Her pale cheeks were flushed slightly and she smiled softly, shaking her head.

"I didn't think you were ever going to wake up," she said, playing a beautiful melody as her fingers tickled the strings.

Jet moved slowly to stand, his feet bare on the cobbled floor. "You never play when I'm here," he said softly, watching as she closed her eyes, long eyelashes kissing the top of her cheeks as the music moved through her and into the harp.

"I felt like maybe I should today," she said, smiling coyly as she glanced at him.

Jet felt his heart soften at the way she gazed at him. "Savra," he said, brushing his fingers across her cheek.

She let her hands fall from the strings, pressing one over his. "I have something for you," she said then, standing slowly. The thin silk of her nightgown flowed over her legs as she walked toward a bureau, her navy hair falling thickly down her back.

"What is it?" Jet asked, watching her open a box.

"A good luck charm," she said, turning back to him. She was smiling warmly. "Close your eyes."

Jet sighed. "You know I hate these games."

She laughed, the sound caressing Jet's ears. "Just do it."

Jet sighed again, but did as she instructed. He felt her cool fingers grasp his, lifting his hand, sliding cold metal over his ring finger.

"Open," she said.

Jet blinked, looking down at his hand. He frowned, looking back to her. "What is this?" he asked, lifting the gold band.

"A promise," she said, stepping toward him. She reached up, pressing her hand against his face.

Jet lifted his hand, reaching for hers, surprised when he suddenly felt talons against his face. He blinked quickly, feeling lightheaded. "Savra . . ." He staggered backwards, feeling the beast in his chest suddenly twisting, much as it would if he was dying. "What . . ."

Her face began to melt away, becoming furry and ugly. She snarled, falling to the floor on all fours. "You're so stupid," Bakene growled, baring a fangy grin.

Jet's knees buckled and he collapsed to the ground, shaking his head as the fog from the dream began to clear. Once again, the fury of battle filled the air, blood on his hands as he clutched at the cerulean grass. He realized his mind was slow. This had all been a trap.

Rage filled him as he looked up, despite the breathless feeling that was choking him. Something was binding him, magic wrapping tightly around his body and his aura. He could see Liana's team standing around him, the wolves growling as Otsana pointed the tip of her sword at his neck.

"It's over, Jet."

The Limen, Somewhere Near Lucky, Texas.
Morning of Tuesday, December 21, 2010.

THE WIND WAS BEGINNING to pick up, whipping fiercely around a lone figure. A swirling doorway was beginning to open before him, lighting the dark with bright light. He wrinkled his nose against the scent of the world on the opposite side of the doorway. He knew the light was from the sun on the other side.

Liana had warned him that this place was different. It was unlike anything he had ever seen before, and it would take every ounce of his cunning and strength to do what she had tasked him with doing. The thought made him roll his eyes.

After all these years in the dungeon, he didn't feel any different.

Jet drew a steadying breath, pulling the bag on his shoulders tighter.

It was time.

The pushing and sucking of the Limen was cold against his skin. It made him feel like he was covered in goop when the Limen unceremoniously dumped him from inside of it. The air was hot suddenly, much warmer than the frozen winter he'd left behind. Foreign, putrid smells hit his nose instantly, and he fought the urge to cover his face. Golden rays of light were streaming down through the branches of the trees around him.

Jet lifted a hand to shield his eyes, scowling darkly.

Earth was nothing like Gexalatia.

Instead of faded hues of cerulean, the trees were an obnoxious shade of green or brown. The leaf litter around him was dead and brown, and the scent of pine trees was strong as it filled his nose. He could feel his scowl deepening as he took a moment to gather himself. He wasn't surprised when he turned, catching sight of a figure beside him.

"Who are you?" the man demanded, pulling a knife from his belt.

Jet arched a brow at his weapon, unfazed. He stepped toward the man, reaching in his bag to withdraw a palm-sized stone. "From Liana," he said shortly.

The man frowned, clearly surprised. He slowly lowered the knife. Jet let the stone drop heavily into his hand, watching a rune begin to glow brightly.

The man was surprised as light flashed around them, the trees turning into limestone pillars. He blinked as the grass gave way to a velvet carpet, a throne room springing to life around them.

Jet had always admired this type of glamor. It was sophisticated and difficult to master. He stood silently, crossing his arms as the man before him fell to his knees. A woman appeared before them, her violet eyes softening. Lavender hair fell around her shoulders and past her waist, her gown rustling as she took a step forward. A simple golden tiara sat in her hair.

"My dear Seth," she said, smiling gently at him. "It has been too long."

"My Queen," Seth said, keeping his head bowed. "It is quite a surprise to be graced with your presence."

"I apologize for this message coming to you in such an unusual way, but there is much to be said, and not enough time to say it," she said, folding her hands in front of her.

Seth looked up then, moving to stand. "Is everything all right?"

She shook her head, her lavender eyes filling with sadness. "We are running out of time," she said softly. "Paraximus' forces are pushing at our borders, leaving me with little choice." She turned to look at Jet. "I intended to save this for when the time is right, but I fear it will never be. We must act now. That is why I have sent Jet to you."

Seth turned his eyes on Jet, surprise on his face. "You are him?" he asked. "King Paraximus' general? They once called you the Black Terror." Seth looked down, a sign of respect. "It is said the battlefields ran red with the rivers of blood when you walked them."

Jet rolled his eyes, looking away.

"Jet has promised his allegiance to me," the queen said, drawing Seth's attention. "He has sworn his fealty and will do what he must to keep my granddaughter safe."

Seth shook his head, pleading in his eyes. "I don't understand, Highness."

"You do not need to understand Seth," the queen said pointedly. "I have trained and prepared Jet for this purpose. He knows what to do, and all I require is your compliance and help."

Seth bowed at the waist, hearing the slight edge to her sweet voice. "Yes, My Queen," he said.

"Deliver my message to Dorothea," the queen continued. "Training and preparation is to begin immediately." She drew a slow breath, uncurling her hands. "I cannot sustain this much longer." She turned to look at Jet. "Do not forget our agreement."

Jet nodded. "Of course," he said blandly.

She turned back to Seth. "Good bye, Seth, my dear," she said, offering a small smile. "Gods be with you."

Seth bowed, drawing a slow breath when the glamor fell. The stone in his hand fell still, beginning to crumble with the loss of magic. He looked to Jet, his blue eyes still uncertain.

"Well then," he said softly. "I am at your disposal, General."

Jet turned to face him, feeling a deep sigh escape him. "Do not call me that," he reprimanded. Despite the way the title grated on him, he couldn't bring himself to be upset with the man. He felt too disoriented in this foreign place.

Seth nodded once, lifting his eyes to Jet. "Apologies," he said softly. He took a moment to take in the single bag slung across Jet's shoulders. "May I assist you?"

Jet scowled again. "Just take me to the girl!" he snapped. He'd been here for less than a minute and already he was tired of it.

Seth pressed his lips together, uncertainty filling his gaze. "In due time," he said hesitantly. "We need to make preparations." He took in Jet's customary tunic and pants. "You cannot get along in this world without certain things."

Jet fought down another sigh, this time feeling frustration welling inside him. "I don't have much time," he growled. "There are things to be done if the girl is to survive."

Seth offered a small smile. "I am aware of that," he said slowly. "But I know this world." He angled his head. "And I know that you will never gain the Princess' trust unless you allow me to help you."

Jet narrowed his eyes at the man. Clearly he wasn't about to make this easy. Jet had a feeling none of them would, and his frustration began to build once more. This wouldn't be a quick extraction like he'd planned. Dread filled him at the thought of having to spend a year here, but it only made him clench his jaw harder. "Tell me your name again."

"Seth."

Jet shifted his eyes over Seth, taking in his tall frame and curly, brown hair. He was wearing denim jeans and a button-down flannel shirt, much different from the clothes Liana's guard had given Jet. "And what do you know about this place, Seth?" he asked carefully.

"Many useful things," Seth said with ease. "I have been here for many years, keeping watch over the Princess." He turned, indicating that Jet should follow. "I will take you to where you will stay and help you get ready."

Jet scowled, but followed him. He was at a disadvantage, and he knew better than to piss Seth off. He couldn't make it here without Seth's knowledge. Liana had spent the time to teach him what he needed to know, but practical knowledge was something he lacked.

The trees gave way shortly to a clearing. It was odd to Jet how the clearing was cut into a perfect circle, clearly unnatural. He felt his feet still when a black object caught his eyes, glistening menacingly in the sunlight. It looked something like an armor-plated beetle, and what should have been its eyes flashed as Seth walked toward it.

"A machine," Seth said, reading his face. He saw Jet's surprise deepen when he opened a door. "It's called a car."

Jet took a slow step toward it. He realized his heart was racing as he watched Seth. "Car?" he asked. The word was foreign. "Is this a war beast?"

Seth laughed and slipped inside, and the beast suddenly roared to life.

Jet jumped at the sound, feeling his body tense. He watched Seth step out, the beast continuing to rumble as he walked around to the other side. He gave a pull to a lever, causing another door to open.

"Transportation," Seth said then. He inclined his head. "The mortals here are quite adept at building machines to assist them in their everyday lives."

Jet arched a brow, walking toward it. He was surprised to see a rather comfortable-looking chair inside. He pulled his bag from around his shoulders, sinking into the car. He tensed when Seth shut the door, feeling caged suddenly. His eyes followed Seth carefully as he walked around to the other door.

Once he was settled, Seth closed his door. "Put on your seatbelt," he instructed. "I don't want a ticket."

Jet frowned, watching as Seth reached over his shoulder to pull a lash across his chest. He did the same, snapping the clip. Anticipation was crawling down his spine. Why did he need to tie himself down? Was this another way to trap him?

"Don't worry," Seth said, glancing at him. He reached down to move a lever. It clicked several times. "You'll like this."

Jet felt his stomach flip when the car began to move, rolling slowly backwards. He watched as they moved toward a gate, which opened onto a stretch of black. "What is this?" he asked, gripping the door handle when the car bumped onto the pavement.

"A road," Seth said easily. "The humans here use materials to pave their roads." He moved the lever up. "It makes driving so easy."

Jet clenched his jaw when the car began to move forward, eating up the ground with swift speed. It was terribly disconcerting, making his heart race in his chest as the terrain flashed by at an ungodly speed.

"Were you given instruction on how to operate a car?" Seth asked. "Her Majesty said that you were."

Jet forced himself to relax, nodding once. "She gave me a book," he said shortly. After she'd taught him to read the language, she'd given him a small manual to study. She'd said it would be helpful, even though the words seemed like a pile of gibberish to him at the time.

"Good," Seth said. "I'm sure it didn't make much sense to you, but I'll show you what you need to know." He pointed suddenly, the car slowing. "Do you see that sign?"

Jet turned to follow his gesture, seeing a white plaque attached to a pole. He narrowed his eyes. His brain was adjusting quickly, reading the English words. "Speed limit?"

Seth nodded. "That tells you how fast you can drive on this road."

Jet turned to look at him as if he had five heads.

"This gauge tells you how fast you're traveling," Seth said, pointing to the speedometer. "The sign says 65, so that is where I put the needle."

Jet scowled. "You realize that means nothing to me."

Seth offered a smile. "It will."

The ride seemed insufferably long. Despite being used to sitting still for long periods of time, Jet was beginning to regret coming here. He reached into his bag after a moment, producing the paper that Liana had given him. It was smooth to the touch and colorful, the colors having been manipulated into a picture. It was of a blonde-haired girl. Liana had explained that it was a photograph and that the humans here possessed machines that produced these. He didn't understand how that was possible, but he let his eyes drift over her face, memorizing it. If nothing else, she would be the one thing he would know here.

"She is a sweet girl," Seth said suddenly.

Jet looked at him, narrowing his eyes. He didn't respond, seeing that Seth clearly was trying to make conversation.

"You'll like her."

Jet scowled. "I'm not here to make friends with her," he snapped. He could feel himself bristling suddenly. "You forget why I came here."

Seth shrugged then. "I haven't," he said easily. "Perhaps I envy you."

"Why?" Jet asked bitterly.

"I've watched her for many years and never been able to speak to her," Seth said, offering a smile. "You are much more fortunate."

Jet rolled his eyes. He didn't have time for Seth's childish notions of worship. She was nothing but a means to an end.

The Temple of Daya, Celo Cavus, Siccita.

The third day of winter, the 905th year of the reign of King Paraximus Lamia.

December 23, 2010, Earth Time.

THE CHANTING OF PRIESTESSES was a soft thread as it echoed throughout the temple. A silver-haired man entered the empty worship room, kneeling beside a figure. He waited, head bowed for the man beside him to rise slowly.

"What news do you bring me, Aterro?"

Aterro looked up slowly at his king, brushing strands of silver hair from his face. King Paraximus cut an intimidating figure. He was tall with wide shoulders. His dark hair fell down his back, becoming salted with gray hairs with his age. His eyes, dark like a moonless night, cut through Aterro, making him feel bare before his king.

"We have word from Regius Carmen, My King," he said, trying to keep his voice from quivering. "Our informant says that there is turmoil in Liana's courts."

Paraximus' eyes narrowed, the only sign of his displeasure at Aterro's presence. "And this is news why?" The King was well aware of the attack he had ordered on her forces.

Aterro bowed his head, hearing the dangerous tone to his master's voice. "I'm sorry, My Lord," he said, feeling anticipation crawl down his spine. "I thought you should know your plan has come to fruition."

Paraximus turned slowly from Aterro. "Fruition, son of my sister, would be to have the Atturon girls in our hands," he said darkly. He turned away from Aterro, letting his eyes shift to the statue of Daya. Her hands were outstretched, beckoning to her worshipers to come before her with gifts, her face expressionless and solemn. Aterro's interruption was irritating, especially since he brought no good news to Paraximus. He stared hard at Daya for a long moment, fighting the urge to spill Aterro's blood on the temple floor. Surely it would be a better offering to the goddess of supremacy than what he had brought.

"What shall I do, My Lord?" Aterro asked cautiously. He could feel anger swirling in the King's aura, filling him with dread.

"Find the girls. Do not return until you have something worthy," Paraximus growled, turning away from his servant. "Leave me."

Aterro rose slowly to his feet, bowing quickly. He scurried from the room, leaving Paraximus alone. The priestesses had stopped their chanting, the temple filling with deafening silence. Paraximus stepped toward the statue, feeling a stirring of magic. He watched in silence as the head priestess rose from where she was kneeling, turning to face him.

"King Paraximus," she said, her voice echoing hollowly around the temple. "Our Lady commands your submission before her."

Paraximus reached the steps of the dais upon which the statue stood, kneeling slowly. "I will do as she commands," he said, bowing his head.

The head priestess waved her hand, conjuring a mirror. "Our Lady commands you to look," she said. She held the mirror out to him. "She offers you a vision, in exchange for your sacrifice."

Paraximus' eyes shifted from the mirror to the small body lying lifeless on the altar before Daya. He noticed that blood dripped slowly from the altar, staining the floor at Daya's feet. It was said that Daya, the most beautiful of all the deities, required the blood of children to maintain her beauty. She bestowed her favor upon her loyal followers by offering visions, which ultimately led to giving them the power they desired. Paraximus didn't believe in superstitious dragon shit like that, but he knew a secret about Daya's priestesses, one in particular about the head priestess, Mara.

Mara had become the head priestess in a fairly short amount of time, using her ability to conjure images of the past in her mirror to con her way into the folds of Daya's followers. It was clever, hiding her true power and allowing her the riches and station of a priestess. Most of the girls here were born into their position, forced to serve Daya for the duration of their lives. No one chose this life willingly, except Mara.

Paraximus, however, knew Mara's true nature. She wasn't an Acerbi like she pretended to be. No, she was something more sinister and dark, sustained by the blood of children. He had known from the moment he first saw her.

Now, as she gazed at him, her eyes were blank and lifeless. No soul sparked beyond them, and Paraximus sensed a void around her body where her aura should have pulsed. The scent of earth was faintly masked by the incense that burned in the temple. Mara was not even truly alive, her body nothing more than a vessel for demons. She was an Erosi.

Paraximus fought down a smirk at the thought. Erosi were dangerous, controlled by their own bloodlust, but not Mara. He had kept her quite subdued, in exchange for her visions. He could feel the sucking pull of the magic she conjured, watching as the mirror's surface swirled.

He didn't expect to see more than Liana sitting amongst her Council, but what he did see made his breath catch in his throat.

The light of the Limen was bright as it opened, baring a world on the other side. A figure stood before it, a pack on his back. The wind was blowing fiercely around the canyon, but the figure paused, turning to look back before crossing into the light. And then, the mirror swirled, leaving Paraximus staring at his own surprised reflection.

"Are you satisfied with your vision, King Paraximus?" Mara asked vacantly.

Paraximus forced his eyes to Mara's. He was momentarily frozen, uncertain that her vision was true. "Do not presume to deceive me," he hissed dangerously.

No emotion flashed across Mara's face as she straightened. She waved the mirror away, an ugly smile pulling at her face, making her dead eyes seem grotesque. Her teeth were jagged and sharp, the demon seeping through its disguise. "I have shown you what I was commanded," she said, her voice reverberating with the squeal of dark entities. "Now Our Lady requires more from you."

Paraximus gritted his teeth. He'd felt unlike himself lately, as if the Ignotsi magic that coursed through him was beginning to overcome his body. This was Daya's doing, he was certain. "What does she require?"

Mara folded her hands together, the disgusting grin sliding from her face. "The blood of the Atturon girls."

Paraximus scowled darkly. "I need them to harness the power of the Visus."

"You need one," Mara snapped angrily. "The other Daya requires." Her face smoothed, her voice returning to its normal pitch. "She also requires a renewal of your pact, Dark King. Otherwise she will allow your own pride to consume you, and appoint another to do her bidding."

Rage seethed through Paraximus. Demanding bitch of a goddess. She had always been fickle, but she seemed worse than usual. He controlled the murderous ache that flooded his chest, forcing himself to bow his head. It wouldn't do to destroy Mara and lose Daya's favor. "Whatever she asks," he said tersely.

Mara nodded, turning away from him. "Do not forget her kindness, King Paraximus."

He turned his eyes to Daya, whose features seemed to shift, her white, stone lips turning in a light smile. Damn her to hell.

$$3$$

Smith's Grocery, Lucky, Texas.

Friday, December 24, 2010.

THE SKY WAS OVERCAST as Dorothea pulled her truck into the parking lot of the grocery store. She knew it was going to be a cold Christmas. The wind caught at the door of the big pickup as she opened it and slid out.

Dorothea was a small woman and the pickup dwarfed her, making her feel smaller. The door slammed as she pushed against the wind to shut it. Once she made it inside the store, she smoothed her own dark hair from her face. It was early enough in the morning that she was the first one in the store. She forced a cheerful smile as the woman at the register greeted her.

"Mornin' Dee," she said. Makeup was caked heavily on her face, and her lips were painted a bright pink. Her hair was done up tall and pageant-styled above her head.

"Hi Val," Dorothea said. She paused to pull a cart from the line by the register. "It's getting chilly out there."

Val nodded, her face pulling into a heavily wrinkled frown. "Sure ain't good for these old bones," she said conversationally.

Dorothea nodded in understanding. "Any plans for the holiday?" she asked.

"Kids and grandbabies are comin' to the house," Val said, her blue eyes suddenly brightening. "That's always a big enough plan for me."

Dorothea smiled. "How old are they now, Val?"

"Youngest is eight months and the oldest just turned two," she said proudly.

"That's great, Val!" Dorothea said brightly. She shifted her eyes around the store. "I need to get my shopping done so I can get home."

"Oh, of course!" Val said good-naturedly, nodding toward the deli counter. "Got a great deal on cooked chicken for tomorrow."

Dorothea nodded. "I'll look into it . . ."

She was mildly grateful as she pushed the cart away from the register. Val was a sweet woman, but Dorothea didn't really care for her. She was far too chatty, and her face looked plastered on. But her smoker's voice gave her a great tenor on Sunday mornings.

It didn't take Dorothea long to gather the items on her list, and she did pause for a moment at the deli. The baked chicken looked delicious, and it would save her some time in cooking dinner. She took her time in choosing one before turning to the register. She wondered what Val would say about the garlic chicken.

Dorothea came around the end of the aisle, gasping in surprise when she nearly ran into a man coming around the corner at the same time. She was momentarily startled, but then she recognized Seth's tall form and curly brown hair. "Seth?" she asked, her voice soft. "What are you doing here?"

Seth offered a small smile. "We have business to discuss," he said, mimicking her tone. "There has been word from Regius Carmen."

Dorothea's face fell. "Word?" she whispered. "Another message?" This was the news she had been dreading.

Seth nodded. "Pay for your groceries," he said gently. "We'll meet in our usual place."

Dorothea felt like she was in a fog as Seth walked past her, disappearing down the aisle. She pushed her basket forward slowly, turning her eyes to the register where she knew Val would be waiting. She was further surprised to see an unfamiliar man standing beside Val, saying something to her.

Val shook her head, a guarded look on her face. Her eyes shifted toward Dorothea in a nervous way, and the stranger turned his head, following her gaze.

Dorothea felt as if she was going to swoon. The fear that gripped her was enough to make her arms and legs feel like lead, and it washed over her like ice water. She realized a cold sweat had broken out on her brow, and she knew her face was pale. Her knuckles were white around the push bar on the shopping cart. She couldn't move as the man turned to face her.

His eyes were blacker than a moonless night, and they narrowed as he walked toward her. His face was smug as he came within feet of her.

Dorothea felt fury fill her and she forced courage to fill her voice. "What the hell are you doing here?" she ground out.

He arched a brow, seeming surprised to hear English words coming from her. "Is that any way to speak to your superior?" he asked, his own English deeply accented. His onyx eyes narrowed slightly.

"You have no authority here," Dorothea whispered furiously. She could feel the disgust on her face. "I owe you nothing."

Humor flashed across his face, fading into something dark and cruel. "You should make both our lives easier and give her to me, handmaid."

Dorothea gritted her teeth, feeling everything inside her rise up against him. If there was one thing she would never do, it was turn her child over to this heartless murderer. The Sarotian that flowed from her lips was strange on some level. She hadn't spoken her native tongue in twenty years. But the words conveyed more meaning than any English phrase she could have uttered.

"I'd rather die first."

A burning hatred filled his eyes. His own Sarotian words were angry and clipped. "That can be arranged."

"Jet."

Dorothea jumped, realizing her heart was hammering in her chest as she looked over her shoulder, seeing Seth walk toward them. "You brought him here?" she whispered vehemently.

Seth nodded. "We'll talk about it later," he said, his eyes shifting to Jet. "Let's go."

Dorothea watched as those black eyes shifted to her once more, then away. He didn't utter another word as he turned to leave the store, but she read his gaze. This was only the beginning. Once he was gone, Dorothea felt the strength she'd found rush out of her. She was stunned as she stood there, trying to make sense of Jet's presence. What did this mean? Was Nyx in danger? She was trembling as she pushed her cart to the register.

"Everything all right, Dee?" Val asked, her blue eyes concerned. "Looked like things were gettin' a little tense."

Dorothea shook her head. "It's fine, Val," she said quickly, throwing her groceries onto the belt. She didn't know what she would say about the situation. She couldn't possibly explain her life to Val.

Val nodded mutely as she rang up the groceries. She kept stealing glances at Dorothea, seeing how pale her face was becoming. "You need some water, Dee?" she offered gently. "Maybe sit down a sec?" She pressed her lips together and paused. "You look like you seen a ghost."

Dorothea shook her head, trying to regain her composure. "What did he ask you, Val?" she whispered finally. Her head was spinning.

Val frowned. "He asked about Nyx," she said quietly. "Quite a strange accent, too."

Dorothea felt her heart drop to her feet, and she pressed her hands over her face. "Oh God above," she whispered.

"I can call Danny," Val said quickly. She caught one of Dorothea's hands over the register. "Look, Dee, you don't have to tell me about where you came from or what's happening." Her blue eyes were earnest. "We all know you were runnin' from somethin' when you came here."

Dorothea felt tears crowd her eyes.

"But if that man is here for you and your girl, we need to get Danny involved," Val continued.

Dorothea shook her head. The last thing she wanted was to have the sheriff involved in this. There was no way anyone here in Lucky could understand what was happening, and there was no hope of stopping him.

"I can handle it, Val," she said, reaching across the counter for her bags. She needed to go home. She would have to deal with him on her own. She brushed the front of her blouse smooth as she gave Val money. She tried to force the edge from her voice. "I appreciate your help."

Val frowned deeply, but she knew it wasn't her place to pry. "Okay, Dee," she said, sighing. "But know Danny is just a call away."

Dorothea nodded. "Thank you, Val."

The wind was becoming bitingly cold as Dorothea pushed the cart out and loaded her groceries into her truck. Her hands were shaking as she slammed the doors quickly. She knew she needed to talk to Seth and find out what this was about. But she felt a desperate need to check on Nyx. If Jet was here, who else had come through with him? But she couldn't risk going home and leading Jet straight to Nyx.

She threw the pickup into gear, squealing the tires as she pulled out of the lot and hit the highway. Her heart twisted in her chest when a black coupe suddenly slung onto the road behind her, following her closely.

This was it.

She knew where she needed to go, and she sped up the road, turning off the highway onto the road that led toward the old factory. Lucky, Texas, had once been a booming manufacturing town, but as the economy and technology changed, the large factory that once employed so many was shut down. Families were forced to move elsewhere, and Lucky was now diminished and small. It had been that way for many years, and the factory was barely more than a skeleton of a building as Dorothea steered her pickup into the abandoned lot.

The black coupe was hot on her heels, sliding to a stop in the gravel.

Dorothea's hands were shaking violently as she opened the door to her truck, sliding out. She gritted her teeth to stop her jaw from trembling as the dust began to settle, and Seth stepped from the coupe.

Jet followed his lead, sliding out of the passenger side. He was careful to shut the door of the car gently, crossing his arms as he leaned against it. He'd shut it too hard the first time, causing the glass to shatter. Apparently he didn't know his own strength anymore. "I really don't have the patience for this game, wench," he said in Sarotian, his onyx eyes skittering around the abandoned lot. Everything here was so disorienting, leaving him in a permanently foul mood.

"That's enough," Seth said, his voice commanding. Jet shot him a dirty look over the top of the car. The only reason he listened to Seth was because he needed him. Jet knew he couldn't get by on his own.

"I won't take you to her," Dorothea said, her voice strong, despite the way her heart was racing in her chest. "I won't let you kill her."

At this Jet smirked darkly, shaking his head. His black hair fell across his face in wisps. "I'm honored that you would still think of me so highly," he said. He fixed his piercing, soul-sucking gaze on her.

"Give her the letter," Seth said, stepping away from the car.

Jet snarled at Seth over the top of the car. "I'm not a delivery boy!" he snapped.

Seth leveled a look at him. "You took my jacket, and the letter is in the pocket." He wondered if Jet's outbursts would subside or if he'd get used to it. Jet was nothing like he expected.

Jet straightened from where he was leaning against the car, reaching inside the jacket. Bitterness was still swirling inside him.

Dorothea felt her heart catch hard in her chest, and her eyes widened. She saw the humor in Jet's eyes as he pulled a missive from his coat pocket, flipping it out for her to take.

"What is this?" she asked suspiciously. Her eyes took in the wax seal. It was pressed with the Queen's emblem.

"It explains everything," Seth said gently. "I received one as well."

Dorothea took it slowly from Jet's fingers, watching as he sank back against the hood of the car. She pulled at the seal with shaking fingers, her eyes widening as she took in the words written on the parchment. She had to read it over several times to make it make sense. Finally, she looked up at Seth.

"This can't be," she breathed.

"These are the Queen Mother's wishes," Seth said gently, feeling pity streak through him. He had felt the same when he'd first heard the news, but he knew Liana had a plan. She didn't make mistakes.

Dorothea looked to Jet, shaking her head. "I won't agree to this," she said forcefully. She watched as he rolled his eyes.

"You have no say in the matter," he said gruffly. "Now then, you can make both our lives easier and just give her to me."

Dorothea felt a hot surge of anger, both at his tone and at the words on the paper in her hand. This wasn't right. None of this was right.

"I won't give her to you, Jet!" she suddenly yelled. She crumpled the paper in her hands, throwing it at the ground. "I don't know what game you're playing, but there is no way Her Majesty would send a murderer!"

Jet's eyes darkened suddenly. Without a word, he crossed to her, shoving her roughly against the side of the pickup. His hand was tight around her throat. Satisfaction seeped through him as she gripped his wrist, trying to draw a breath.

"Jet, stop!" Seth was on them quickly, trying to pry his hands from around Dorothea's throat. "Let her go!"

"I asked nicely," Jet said softly, his voice like silk. His onyx eyes were murderous. "I will not ask again." He was tired of everyone's petulance. No one told him no, but that's all he'd heard since he'd come through the Limen. He may not have been royalty anymore, but he wouldn't allow them to disrespect him any longer.

Seth felt like he didn't exist as he watched the exchange, his heart pounding in his chest. Doubt began to fill him about the plan. It didn't seem possible that Liana had been able to sway Jet's heart so easily to her side. What if this was a ploy to kill them and Nyx?

A mixture of fear and fury was swirling in Dorothea's chest. Tears were filling her eyes, but she held Jet's gaze. She forced a small laugh.

Jet's eyes narrowed dangerously. "What's so funny, wench?"

"She knows nothing." Dorothea took satisfaction at the surprise that flashed across his face. "I have kept her origin a secret. She's useless to you. She can't even touch Aure."

Rage suddenly creased Jet's brow, and he lifted her, slamming her hard into the side of the truck. A pained cry left her lips as he let go of her, watching her slide to her knees. Unlike himself, Jet knew Dorothea was an Inerse, a true human. She gasped in pain on the ground, bracing herself with her hands. Seth immediately reached for her, shooting Jet a dark glare. Any words he said were lost on Jet.

Everything inside Jet was twisting in a molten rage. That fact made all the difference. It made everything about his job so much more difficult. Liana couldn't possibly think that the girl could survive the journey without any training. Jet knew the enemies they would face, if they were lucky, but if they weren't lucky . . . without any knowledge of her abilities, the Princess was dead. It made him want to slit this woman's throat. It took all of the self-control he had, and then some, just to remain still, watching her sob softly.

His voice was soft and deadly when he finally regained control. "I should kill you," he said. "You don't deserve to live. You've condemned her."

Dorothea shifted her eyes to him. "She will never trust you, Jet," she said through her tears. "I made certain of that." She looked away. "Without me, you will never be able to accomplish your mission."

Jet gritted his teeth then, reaching down to heft her to her feet. "Bitch," he snarled. He bared fanged teeth. "You will help me. Or I will kill you." He released her for a brief moment to catch Seth as he tried to intervene, shoving him away as if it was nothing. His glare was deadly. "Both of you, and take her by force."

Dorothea felt her heart twist in her chest at the thought. She couldn't let that happen. She knew there was only one option. She bowed her head.

"I will help you."

4

The Estrella Residence.

Friday, December 31, 2010.

NYX FLIPPED OFF THE TV, getting to her feet to look out her window. The wind began to blow hard, and she shifted her eyes across the pasture, frowning. That wasn't a good sign. It meant it would be cold tonight at the bonfire.

Nyx stood to press her hands against the glass, feeling the freezing cold pressing back. She pressed her lips together. She didn't particularly like the cold like this.

She looked at the clock, seeing the time. She needed to shower and find something warm and cute to wear. If something like that existed. Mostly there was warm clothing, and then there was cute clothing.

Nyx rolled her eyes at the thought. She needed to make an impression. Randy would be there. Her cheeks flushed lightly as she hopped into the shower, thinking about Randy. She really, really liked him, and she hoped that he would notice her for once.

The water from the shower was hot, but it made the air in the house feel extra cold as she jumped out, wrapping her wet hair in a towel. She pulled on a thick robe and slippers, running to her room and cursing the cold under her breath.

Her closet didn't offer anything good as she pushed through her clothes, hoping something would jump out at her. Instead, it was mostly summer clothing, halter-top blouses and T-shirts.

She sighed in annoyance, settling for a long-sleeved shirt with butterflies. It wasn't full of spark, but it would do. She guessed it didn't really matter anyway, because no one would see it underneath her thick jacket.

Nyx was in the midst of blow-drying her golden hair when she finally heard her aunt come into the house. She set the dryer down and tousled the fluffy disaster on her head, walking down the stairs.

"Hi," Aunt Dee greeted. She was busy putting groceries away, barely pausing to look at Nyx. It seemed like she'd been gone longer than usual, and she was acting funny, a nervousness about her. In fact, she'd been acting funny for a few days now. "I like that shirt. Is that what you're wearing tonight?"

Nyx frowned down at it. "Yeah," she said slowly. Dorothea was flitting around the kitchen like a busy bee, with an urgency that Nyx didn't like. She started to ask if everything was okay when her phone began to ring.

Nyx slid the lock, recognizing her friend's number.

"Hey Anna."

"Hey girl!" There was excitement in Anna's voice. "So I'm about to leave my house to come get you."

Nyx glanced at the clock, frowning. "I gotta finish my hair," she said, turning away from her aunt's weirdness.

"I can wait," Anna said. Nyx could hear the smile in her voice. "Besides, I have so much to tell you!"

Nyx rolled her eyes, walking back up the stairs. "Well tell me when you get here," she said.

"All right," Anna sighed. "Be there soon."

Nyx hung up the phone, shaking her head as she ran up the stairs. She missed the way Dorothea paused, her face falling sadly as she watched her go.

The night was cold when Nyx and Anna piled into Anna's Mazda. It had been a gift for Anna's sixteenth birthday. It smelled like the perfume Anna always doused herself in to hide the barest hint of cigarette smoke from her parents.

"So Randy's definitely going to be there?" Nyx asked as she buckled in.

"Abby said he was," Anna said, her hazel eyes sparkling. She took a moment to put the car in drive, glancing over at Nyx. "I hope that guy we met at the bar comes, too. He's super fine. I would go out with him."

Nyx rolled her eyes, recalling the guy Anna had met two weeks ago. They'd exchanged numbers, but Anna hadn't said anything about him until now. "That's what you said about Brandon, and Jake, and Paul," she said, ticking them off her fingers. "And that one guy that I can never remember his name . . . and they all turned out to be losers."

Anna frowned as she pulled onto the highway. "This is different, Nyx," she said emphatically. "Seth is completely different than any of those other guys."

Nyx shook her head, looking out the window. "He seems like a flirt," she said.

Anna sighed. "Everybody has their flaws."

"Some flaws are just bigger than others," Nyx commented dryly.

The car had just barely had a chance to warm up when they reached the Rogers' ranch. Abby and Melanie Rogers had been hosting the bonfire now for several years, and their parents always did it big. Of course, it didn't hurt that the Rogers family was rich as hell, something about oil money, like the Williams family. Nyx always wondered why she and her aunt had never been fortunate enough to find oil, since it apparently was everywhere around Lucky.

The entrance to the ranch was a big gate, made of stone and an archway that had the Rogers' family brand across it. It was decorated with beautiful Christmas lights, which led the way up the hill to where the ranch house sat. It was decorated beautifully as well, and Nyx could see Christmas trees in the large bay windows.

"God, how can they afford to do this every year?" Anna said, voicing Nyx's thoughts.

Nyx shook her head. "Think Mr. and Mrs. Rogers would want to adopt us?" she asked teasingly.

Anna grinned at her. "Wouldn't that be nice?" she quipped. "New cars every year!"

They pulled up slowly, seeing the other vehicles parked in the distance around the back of the house. The bonfire was just beginning to burn, and Anna followed the dirt road around toward a barn. Nyx felt her heart catch in her throat when she saw Randy's truck. It was parked in the midst of the crowd, and music was pulsing from the big speakers on the back of the truck.

"There's your man . . ." Anna said teasingly, pointing him out.

He was easy to spot, his tall frame in his usual brown coat and his maroon and white baseball cap. He recognized

Anna's car and he made his way through the throng of people toward them.

"Howdy, girls!" he called as they stepped out of the car.

Nyx raised her hand, a big grin crawling across her face. "Hey, Randy!"

Anna shook her head, leveling a look at her friend over the hood of her car.

Nyx ignored her as she pulled her hair out of the scarf she was twirling around her neck. She walked toward Randy, returning his hug when he wrapped her in his big arms.

"You're just in time," he said, releasing her and hugging Anna. "Mrs. Rogers just brought down her famous trash can punch."

"Sweet!" Anna piped. She looped her arm through Nyx's. "Let's go."

Nyx followed her toward the barn, waving at the other people she knew. Most were her childhood friends whom they had gone to school with since they were small. She absentmindedly took the cup Anna handed her, looking down into it.

"Relax," Anna said at the look on her face. "It's water."

Nyx offered her a grin, taking a sip. "Let's go dance or something," she said. Anna would be turning twenty-one in a few weeks, but Nyx's birthday wasn't until October. She knew she could drink here with her friends if she wanted to, but it just didn't seem right. Anna led the way back toward Randy's truck, where they could see Abby and Melanie standing in the bed, swaying to the music.

"Hey Nyx!" Abby said, grabbing her hand and pulling her up. She hugged her. "Haven't seen you in a couple weeks."

Nyx shrugged, swaying beside her. "My aunt's been going through this phase," she said. "Something about I'm not a baby anymore and she never sees me."

Melanie leaned over then, rolling her eyes. "Our mom, too," she said, lifting her cup. She grinned at her twin sister. The song changed to a pulsing club beat, and Melanie's eyes widened. "This is my song!"

Nyx laughed as she and Anna danced next to the twin sisters. It was easy to let the music sweep her away.

Dorothea pulled her coat tighter, trying to ward away the chill that was seeping into her. She couldn't believe that she had agreed to this, and the thought made her stomach flip. She felt sick. She tried not to cringe as a shadow formed silently beside her on the porch.

Silence stretched between them as Jet leaned against the railing. Seth took a seat beside her in the opposite chair.

"If you want my help, there are rules," Dorothea said finally, unable to look at Jet. She heard him scoff.

"Just let me tell her," he said, an edge to his voice. "Enough of your games."

Dorothea shook her head, rounding on him. "My terms, or I won't help you," she said bitterly. She wasn't sure how she managed to remain so firm when every part of her was trembling with fear.

Jet narrowed his eyes, indicating he was pissed, but listening.

"You are only to interact with her on my terms," Dorothea said. She braced as a bitter wind blew against her. "Once I tell her the truth, she will have to know that she can trust you. That is the only way your mission will be achieved."

Jet considered this for a moment. He had a year until the Limen would open again. He wasn't in too much of a hurry, but he wasn't fond of the idea of being friends with her. He focused his gaze on the small woman before him, enjoying the way she was trembling in fear.

"Fine," he said curtly. He pinned her with a glare. "But do not waste my time, handmaid. My patience for you is wearing thin."

Dorothea's brow furrowed and she swallowed thickly. "You can find her down the road," she said, mustering bravery she didn't feel. "She'll be there with her friends, at the bonfire party." She looked at Seth. "She's with Anna."

Jet arched a brow. He expected this wretched servant to cooperate, but not this readily. He looked at Seth, seeing recognition on his face. Clearly he knew this "Anna" girl.

"Thank you, Dorothea," Seth said, rising from his chair. He started after Jet, but Dorothea caught his hand.

"Please, take care of her, Seth," she whispered. "Don't let him hurt her."

Seth offered a gentle smile. "Of course."

They didn't waste any more time with her as they climbed into the car and disappeared into the cold night. Jet was anxious to see what the Princess looked like in person.

The Rogers' Ranch.
Friday, December 31, 2010.

THE CAR CAME SLOWLY over the hill, pausing at the top. The bitter wind blew against the car, making it shake lightly. Down below, the glow of a fire was illuminating the grass. Thumping music floated on the wind, filling the night.

Jet scowled. The humans were acting like a bunch of wildlings. It was below them to behave in such a manner, especially the girl.

"Please be mindful of our agreement," Seth said quietly. He looked over at Jet, seeing his scowl deepen. "If you break my trust, I will not help you."

Jet rolled his eyes. As if he even needed Seth's help. If he wished, he could simply kidnap the girl and hide out until they could cross to Gexalatia. He knew Seth and Dorothea's threats were little more than veiled attempts at maintaining some sort of control over the situation.

"Yeah, yeah," Jet said, waving his hand. "Let's go."

Seth moved the car forward carefully, following the road down to the barn, where the rest of the cars were parked. Once they were parked Seth opened his door and slid out. Jet followed his lead, catching the smell of burning wood on the wind. There was no cover in the open field and the wind was biting as it blew around them. Jet ignored it, though, doing as Seth had instructed and pulling a black leather jacket around his shoulders. Apparently walking around in this weather without a coat would make him look suspicious, or something to that effect.

Jet was finally close enough that he could make out a vehicle, four girls standing in the back. It was easy for him to pick her out. She was the only Auresi among them. He couldn't feel an aura surrounding her like he expected, and it made him frown. If what the wench said was true, the girl had never been able to access her magic. Despite that, there was a warmth about her that he could feel, even from a distance. Curiosity picked at him. He wanted to see her up close.

"Let me do the talking," Seth said, seeing that Jet's eyes didn't leave Nyx. "Once I introduce you, you'll be on your own."

Jet nodded mutely. For some reason he couldn't explain, he felt his stomach curl into a knot. Not even the chaos of battle could make him nervous, so why did he feel this way?

Carefully, he made his way through the crowd, just a step behind Seth. He could feel the stares of the humans around them. Despite being ignorant, somehow humans had an innate ability to recognize danger, even if they didn't know that's what they sensed. Nyx could have sensed him if she wished, but without any training, he knew she wouldn't know what she was feeling even if she did.

Finally, they reached the truck. He watched as she swayed in time to the music, lifting her hands above her head. She was laughing and talking to the girls around her, her blonde hair fluttering around her.

Jet's eyes narrowed as he studied her. Doubt began to fill him. He'd never seen anyone as carefree as she was. He was only mildly surprised when she fixed her eyes on someone behind them.

Jet watched her eyes change, and the scowl pulled at his lips again.

A tendril of something was winding through the air. It was slight, barely anything pushing against his aura, but he felt it. She didn't know what she was doing, luring the poor sap in with her residual strength. Jet could feel it, and he knew the boy behind him could, too. He likely thought it was his own feelings for her, but it was a pretty trick, something that could only affect mortals.

Jet shook his head. Stupid girl. Her magic was very strong, which would ordinarily make her dangerous. His thoughts shifted back to her guardian, turning bitter. She was stupid too, for thinking that the power that flowed through Nyx's veins could be tempered. The handmaid was lucky that Nyx hadn't lost control or done something stupid.

"Seth!" A brunette girl jumped down from the back of the truck, throwing her arms around Seth's neck.

Jet rolled his eyes at the way Seth grinned stupidly, pulling her against him.

"I'm so glad you could make it," the girl said, grinning broadly. Her voice was obnoxious and grating to Jet's senses.

Seth nodded as he released her. "I'm glad you asked me to come," he said pleasantly. He turned his shoulders slightly. "Anna, I want you to meet my cousin."

Jet frowned. He didn't want to be anyone's cousin, let alone Seth's. He tried to look interested as Anna turned her eyes on him.

"Hi," she said, offering a smile and holding out her hand. "I'm Anna."

Jet nodded, reaching gingerly to shake her hand. "Jet," he said shortly.

Anna seemed surprised for a moment, and she glanced up at Seth. "Where are you from, Jet?" she asked.

"Europe," Seth said then, shooting Jet a glance. The accent in his voice was thick still. "A small country in Europe."

"Oh," Anna said. She glanced back at him, offering another friendly smile. "Well, welcome."

Jet nodded slightly. He watched as Anna turned and walked back to the truck, catching Nyx's hand. They exchanged words and Nyx slid down. Her eyes were uncertain as she looked between them. Jet felt his heart lurch in his chest. She was much prettier in person. The photo Liana had of her didn't do her justice. Her blonde hair fell around her face, forcing his eyes to meet her deep green gaze. The smile that pulled at her lips made her face light up in an innocent way. He didn't have a clue what he would say to her.

Nyx caught Anna's hand as she walked to her.

"He's here," Anna said excitedly. She waggled her eyebrows suggestively. "And he brought his cousin."

Nyx wanted to sigh as she jumped down from the tailgate. She followed Anna toward Seth. Nyx thought he was very attractive, and he smiled gently when Anna introduced them. Actually, he was more than attractive. His features were smooth and delicate almost, his skin like porcelain. He was so pretty, he almost didn't look real.

"Nyx, you remember Seth," Anna said, still grinning. "And that's his cousin, Jet."

Nyx looked between them and offered an uncertain smile. "Hey, how's it going?" She felt her chest tighten as she looked at Seth's cousin. He was tall, like Seth, but his black hair and equally dark eyes made him super intimidating. Nyx felt uncomfortable at the way he was almost glaring at her.

Jet said nothing as Seth offered pleasantries. Nyx laughed politely as Seth said something intended to be funny. She exchanged a few words with Seth and Anna, uncertainty crossing her face when Anna caught Seth's arm in hers, pulling Seth away toward the barn. Nervousness began to fill Nyx as she realized that Anna had totally ditched her with this other guy.

Slowly, she turned to look at him, twiddling her fingers. "Did you want something to drink?" she asked, indicating the barn. "Abby and Melanie's mom makes great punch."

Jet shook his head. "I don't drink," he said evenly. He seemed to relax some, but his eyes were still pinning her in an uncomfortable way.

"Oh," Nyx offered a small smile. "I don't either." She stepped closer to him so that she could hear him over the sound of the music. "So, where in Europe are you from?"

Jet crossed his arms. He could feel annoyance flooding him. He wasn't happy about this ruse at all. "Nowhere you've heard of," he said curtly.

Nyx frowned at him then. "Oh." She glanced up, reserve on her face. She was wracking her brain for anything to talk to him about. "How long have you been here?"

Jet turned his head. "I arrived a few days ago." His eyes shifted away from her, and everything about his body language said he didn't want to talk to her.

Nyx nodded slowly, biting her lip hard. She hated Anna. "How long are you staying?" she pressed, watching his face. She noticed that, like Seth, there was something inherently beautiful about him, even his dark eyes. She guessed they were probably a really dark brown, but she couldn't tell in the firelight.

Jet shrugged then, his eyes shifting over the people milling around them. He seemed like he was either doing his best to ignore her, or he was watching everyone carefully. "Until the first day of winter," he said dismissively.

Nyx felt her brow furrow. "What day is that again?" she asked casually.

He turned his eyes on her then, annoyance creasing his face. "You don't know?"

Nyx crossed her arms, feeling exposed suddenly under his piercing gaze. "I can't say I've ever really paid attention," she said slowly. "It's never been important."

Jet sighed in disgust. "I see." He turned away from her.

Nyx frowned at his back, feeling offended. "Where are you going?" she blurted. She'd never had to interact with someone so rude.

"To find Seth." His tone was dismissive as he walked away from her without even sparing her another glance.

She was flabbergasted as she stood there, watching him walk away. It must have shown on her face, because suddenly Randy was beside her, frowning at her.

"What's wrong?" he asked.

Nyx blinked from her stupor, feeling her negative feelings fade away as she looked at him. "Nothing," she said quickly, smiling. "Just Anna's boyfriend and his weird cousin."

Randy glanced toward the barn, to where they'd disappeared. "Is that who that was?"

Nyx nodded. "Yeah, no big deal," she said quickly. She watched Randy shift his eyes back to her, and she felt her cheeks turning red.

"You wanna come with me to get a drink?" Randy asked, tilting his head.

Nyx nodded emphatically. "Yeah," she said quickly. She followed him toward the barn, which was lit and warm. It had been set up with tables and chairs, and there was food laid out, as well as the keg and sodas and a pitcher of pink punch. Melanie's mother was manning the table, offering coffee and cocoa to a few people.

Mrs. Rogers smiled as they neared. "Hey guys," she said brightly. Her blonde hair was pulled into a ponytail. She looked just like her girls, save for a few wrinkles around her mouth and eyes. "Y'all want some coffee or hot chocolate?"

"Yes," Nyx breathed, smiling as she was given a Styrofoam cup. "It's so cold out there."

"Here ya are, sweetheart," Mrs. Rogers said, pouring steaming liquid into her cup. She then turned her eyes to Randy. "Randy?"

"Just some punch," Randy said good-naturedly, picking up a cup.

"All right," Mrs. Rogers said. "If you're drinkin', put your keys in the drinkin' bowl."

Nyx grinned as Randy fished his keys from his pocket, dropping them into a large glass bowl. She watched Randy offer Mrs. Rogers a smile as he turned away from the table and led her to sit on a bale of hay near a floor heater.

"She made me do that last year," he said as they sat. He rubbed his hands together by the heater, turning his eyes on her. "I got too drunk and she made me spend the night."

Nyx grinned as she took a sip of her hot chocolate. "Well that was nice of her," she said. She glanced down at the floor. "My aunt would come unwound if she knew I had gotten drunk." She stole a glance at him. "Were your parents cool?"

Randy nodded. "Oh yeah," he said. "They know I drink, so they didn't mind. Plus, my mom really likes Mrs. Rogers so she knew where I was."

Nyx nodded, attempting another sip from her cup. Her hot chocolate was too hot, and her throat was raw from the first sip. "So, whatcha been up to over the break?" she asked, watching as he lifted his ball cap, brushing his strawberry-blond hair in a nervous way.

"Some deer huntin' with my dad," Randy said, offering another smile. "But you don't look like the type to be interested in hearin' about that."

Nyx felt her heart catch. She knew where this was going, but she played dumb. "So are you signed up for classes yet?" she asked.

Randy looked down, rubbing his hands together distractedly. "Actually, I was going to ask what you were taking this semester," he said carefully. "Maybe we could take a class together."

Nyx widened her eyes in surprise. "Yeah," she said quickly, feeling her heart skip a beat. She could feel her face turning super red. "That would be awesome."

Randy grinned at her. "Cool," he said. He took out his cellphone. "Give me your number so I can text you."

"Okay," Nyx said, trying to hide the huge smile that was pulling at her face. She rattled off her cell number, feeling like the butterflies from her shirt were inside her stomach.

Randy seemed relieved suddenly. "Awesome."

Nyx nodded. "Yeah," she said. She was wracking her brain for something else to say, but her brain was empty suddenly.

Awkward silence fell over them as Nyx tried to keep from jumping up and down and acting like a fool. Inside, her heart was doing flip-flops and her inner self was fist-pumping. She couldn't wait to tell Anna that she'd given Randy her number.

Nyx was grateful when Randy's cousin, Joe, called for him, and she practically ran out of the barn to find Anna. Her heart was racing with excitement when she came around the fire toward the truck. She hadn't seen Anna and Seth or Jet, and she wouldn't have been surprised if Anna and Seth had snuck off to somewhere.

Nyx figured if she couldn't find Anna, she'd just tell Melanie and Abby. She had to tell someone the good news or else she might burst from her happiness. She was mildly surprised when she found Anna leaning against the front of Randy's truck, sucking face with Seth.

Nyx started to turn around and not interrupt, but she couldn't help it as she ran to her friend. "Anna!" She grabbed her arm excitedly. "I have to talk to you. Now!" She offered a small smile to Seth. "Sorry, be right back!"

Anna frowned as she let go of Seth. "Be right back, baby," she said, grinning at him. He nodded, offering a barely concealed grin as he let her go.

Nyx narrowed her eyes at him, seeing his deep blue eyes fixed on Anna as she drug her away. "Okay, first off, you've known this guy for all of five minutes," Nyx said as she and Anna were finally alone. "And second, it was lame for you to leave me with his weird cousin."

Anna shrugged. "Sorry," she said simply. "I just wanted some alone time with him. We've been talking on the phone every night since we met." A small smile pulled at her lips as she looked at the excitement on Nyx's face. "What's going on?"

"Randy just asked for my phone number," Nyx blurted. She giggled when Anna caught her hands, squealing with excitement.

"What for?" she gasped. "Is he going to take you out?"

Nyx shook her head. "He didn't say," she said, unable to shake her grin. "He said he wants to take a class together this semester. But it's probably just so he can ask me out later."

Anna nodded excitedly. "This is so amazing!" she gasped.

Nyx nodded. "I know!"

They giggled like little girls, unaware of the dark eyes that were watching the exchange.

The Alvar Residence.

Saturday, January 1, 2011.

ET WAS SITTING IN A CHAIR, watching Seth as he sat on the couch, a small device in his hands. Seth smiled as the device dinged, his fingers moving across the surface of it. He would wait for a moment and the ding would sound again. Each time, his smile grew a little bigger.

"What the hell are you doing?" Jet asked.

Seth glanced up at him, his smile drooping a bit. "I'm talking to Anna."

Jet arched a brow, irritation flooding him. "How?" he asked. "She's not here."

Seth smirked, holding up the device. Jet could see that there were words across it. "She's sending me messages on my phone," he said simply. "That's how we're talking."

Jet frowned, stepping toward Seth and reaching for the phone. Seth let him have it, watching as Jet turned it over in his hands. "What sorcery is this?" Jet asked.

"Remember how I told you the mortals were good at creating things?" Seth asked teasingly. "This is one of them. It's called a 'mobile phone.'"

Jet handed it back to him, flinching slightly when it dinged. He seemed highly unimpressed.

"We should get you one," Seth said absently as he sent Anna a message back.

"Why?" Jet demanded. "So you can know my every move?"

Seth shook his head. "No," he said slowly, still typing. "So you can get the Princess' number and talk to her. Start to build a relationship." He looked up then, his eyes narrowing slightly. "I never did ask. What did you think of her?"

Jet frowned deeply. "She looks like a young girl." He crossed his arms. "Stupid and immature and incompetent."

Seth arched a brow, trying to decide if he should be offended. "She is our princess. You should show some respect."

Jet scoffed. "She's your princess. Not mine."

Seth was frowning. "A moot point," he said dismissively. "What do you think of her?"

Jet shook his head, pensive suddenly. "She hasn't touched her power yet . . ." he said. "I sensed her aura, but no sign of her strength." He crossed his arms. "She has some residual strength that she must not be aware of." He looked up at Seth. "Did you feel her summoning a charm?"

Seth nodded. "I did notice that."

Jet scowled. "She will need much training, and even then she will not be ready."

Seth shrugged. "You have a year," he said. "She can learn a lot in a year."

Jet smirked bitterly then. "A thousand years would never be enough for her to have the strength to face my father. Not even Liana has even an inkling of the power that he can attain. No one knows what he is capable of."

"And you do?" Seth asked, feeling his chest clench. He hadn't been home in so long. He knew he couldn't possibly fathom what was really happening there.

Jet shook his head, a sardonic smile on his lips. "I've been in prison for the last century. How could I know what he has managed to gain in that time?"

Seth felt his jaw clench. "Either way, we must try."

Jet nodded mutely. That was all they could do. They would never succeed, even with all the trying in the universe.

The Temple of Daya, Celo Cavus, Siccita.

The twenty-second day of winter, the 905th year of the reign of King Paraximus Lamia.

Wednesday, January 12, 2011, Earth Time.

THE TEMPLE WAS SILENT. It was well past midnight. Paraximus stepped toward the dais where Daya's statue stood. Her ever-present smile was taunting as he neared, kneeling before her. "Why have you summoned me here?" he whispered, bowing his head.

The air rippled and shimmered around him before being sucked toward the statue. Paraximus could feel the powerful draw of magic as it rushed into the cold stone like water down a drain. He didn't dare look up as the sound of crumbling stone filled the air. Fear washed over him, chilling him to the bone.

"My king." Daya's voice was harsh, like the scrape of nails across stone. Her presence was oppressive, her aura choking Paraximus.

He struggled to draw a slow breath. He'd stood in Daya's presence once before, and somehow this time felt worse. "Goddess," he said softly, keeping his head bowed. He never wanted to see her empty, grotesque form again.

"Look into my eyes, Paraximus," she commanded, her voice shaking the walls of the temple.

Paraximus drew a hard breath, lifting his head. He fought the urge to wince. Despite being the goddess of beauty, few had seen Daya's true form. She was tall, skin and bones, her hair thin and stringy. She leaned forward to look at him, her eyes empty sockets. Rows of sharp teeth lined her mouth, which had no lips. Her fingers were long and ghastly as she reached out to him, dragging a single razor-sharp talon beneath his chin. Paraximus felt his jaw clench at the contact.

It was said that Daya was born from the side of Aure in the eons before the world was formed. He and his creator twin, Aucer, were locked in fierce battle. Each blow formed the rivers and the mountains and the creatures that walked the land. Aucer formed the serpents and the insects and boiling lava that spewed from volcanoes, the god of chaos. Aure formed the sea and sunshine, the creator of order and peace. Upon the final blow, Aucer struck Aure's side, causing his anger and hatred for his brother to spew forth. From the rotten, putrid blood that poured across the ground Daya grew.

As a pact of peace, the twin creators chose to never fight again, Aucer realizing his chaos could only be tempered by the peace that came from his brother. To seal their pact, they created the Auresi and Acerbi, to bear their magic and keep the world in balance. Little did they know that Daya would slink among the world they created, forcing the balance to shift and become uneven, bringing death and destruction with her. She forced the creation of Inerse, who would eventually be sent to her domain upon their deaths, where they would keep her company for eternity.

"You are slow to do as I ask," she growled, pressing her claw against his neck.

"Apologies, Goddess," Paraximus said, clenching his fists. Every nerve in his body was on fire, his muscles tense to the point of aching. The fear that she inspired in him was staggering. "The situation has become . . . complicated."

"There is no complication," she said, tilting her head unnaturally. "You are capable of crushing Liana, if that is your true desire."

Paraximus looked down. "It is."

"Do not try my patience," Daya growled, withdrawing from him. "You are nothing before me. If I wanted your life, I would take it, and no force could stop me." She smirked despite having no lips to smile with. "You have forfeited your place in Aucer's kingdom. Never forget this."

Paraximus couldn't move as he listened to her drag her distorted form across the dais.

"On the eve of the solstice, I will make the conditions right. You will send your forces through the bay and to Sorona. You will take the girls and bring them to me. I will give you what you seek and take what I am owed."

"And what of my son?" Paraximus asked. "Your vision must have been of some significance."

Daya turned then, slinking toward him. She pressed her gnarled fingers roughly against his forehead, drawing blood. "I will bestow upon you the strength to summon Limens as you please," she said quietly, "but there will be a price."

Paraximus winced painfully as a burst of cold magic shot through him. He gasped as it flooded his body, wrenching at his veins. He could barely stomach the pain as her power coursed through him. It seemed like the pain lasted forever before she withdrew her hand, blood dripping from her fingers. Paraximus gasped for a breath as he watched her lick his blood from her hand. The cold pain continued to linger, a side-effect of her gift.

"You must return to me on the night when Deimos rises and Pistis is hidden in shadow," Daya said. "Just as your son is bound by blood, so too are you. If you fail to come, you will be absorbed by the power you so desperately desire."

Paraximus pressed a hand against his chest, feeling weakened. The cycle of the moons wasn't far away. He would be forced to return to her sooner than he was comfortable with. He glanced up sharply when a form stepped from the shadows. He bared his fangs when Mara appeared.

She crossed silently to Daya, the sucking void of her aura more potent in his weakened state. "Take this," Daya said, motioning to the mirror in Mara's hands. "It will serve as your eyes on the other side."

Paraximus reached up as Mara extended the mirror. It was cold in his hands, drawing on his energy.

"Do not forget my price." Daya stepped back to the crumbled remains of the statue.

"Yes, Goddess." Paraximus bowed his head. The sound of shifting stone filled the air, her oppressive aura dissipating. When Paraximus looked up again, she was gone, reformed into the statue, as was Mara.

He drew a shuddering breath as he looked around, knowing he was alone. The pain in his chest lingered, but it was nothing like it had been in Daya's presence. He moved shakily to his feet, looking at his reflection in the mirror. With his new power he would destroy Liana and he would send his strongest to kill Jet.

The Limen, Somewhere Near Lucky.

Friday, January 14, 2011.

THE SUN WAS BARELY PEEKING over the trees. A swirl of cold magic filled the air, lifting the leaves from the ground. The whisper of wind lifted, forming into a churning portal. The canyon wall began to ripple, giving way to a tall figure unfolding from the previously solid mass. The air was cold, but it was nothing compared to the Gexalatian winter they had just emerged from.

A woman turned, a plaited braid of brown hair falling across her shoulder. A white feather was tucked into her braid. "This must be the right place," she said in her native Sarotian.

Two men stood on either side of her. One was tall with brown hair and blue eyes, while the other was slightly shorter with blond hair and blue eyes. The taller had a sword strapped to his back and the shorter carried a dagger at his hip. Another woman passed through behind them, just as the portal began to ripple and fade. They were all clothed in thin, plated armor, thick leather covering their arms and legs and boots on their feet.

"They came to this putrid world?" the second woman asked. Her hair was short, standing in blue spikes. She brushed a strand from her eyes, which were the same cerulean as her hair.

"What, you wouldn't want to move here, Tanith?" the blond man asked, sneering. "It would probably be too quiet for your tastes."

Tanith scowled at him. "You couldn't live here because there wouldn't be enough women to satisfy you!" she snapped.

The brown-haired man laughed, elbowing his comrade. "Lovers' spat there, Devyn?"

Devyn scowled darkly. "Lay off, Lance."

The first woman turned, a scowl on her face. "Enough of your childish games," she said shortly. "Our King has chosen us for a specific mission." Her hazel eyes narrowed. "I assume you know what the punishment for our failure is."

Tanith scowled, bowing her head. "Apologies, Captain," she said.

The brown-haired woman turned her eyes away. "We must find the General." She looked about the trees around them. "No doubt he will have sensed the power of the Limen that sent us here." She could still feel its ripple through the air, and she knew it would spread for a long time before it fizzled out. The magic Paraximus commanded was no small amount. "Tanith, go with Devyn. Lance and I will search to the north." She turned to look at her followers. "Remember, we are being watched. Let's not fail our King."

Tanith bowed. "Yes, Captain Sophia." She was extremely unhappy about being with Devyn. He was such a selfish pig, and judging from the look on his face, he wasn't fond about being with her, either.

"Meet here in two days' time with what you have learned," Sophia commanded.

The two groups split, vanishing into the early morning.

The Alvar Residence.

Sunday, January 16, 2011.

JET DROPPED FROM THE bough of a tree, watching a deer walk across his path. It didn't seem to notice him as he straightened, his onyx eyes following the twitch of its ears. He could feel a knot forming in his chest, twisting in anticipation. He clenched his jaw, wishing the voice whispering softly in his head would stop. It was distracting.

He glanced up, seeing the faint silhouette of the moon overhead. It was the night before the new moon, but he knew he couldn't wait the full cycle. The beast was gaining strength. Jet knew that wasn't a good sign. Something must be drawing it out. The thought gave him pause; he hadn't felt any influxes in power nearby.

Jet turned his eyes back to the deer, watching it find a spot to lay in the grass. He rolled his eyes. Creatures here were so stupid. It was nothing for him to spring from where he stood, catching the deer around the neck.

It snorted and bleated, struggling against his grip. He snapped its neck in an easy motion, using clawed fingers to rip into the animal's neck. Its heart was still faintly beating, and its crimson blood was dripping from where he had gouged it.

Jet drew a deep breath; the stench of the animal was making him feel sick. He didn't like drinking the blood of animals, but it was the only thing that calmed the entity that twisted against him, begging to be released. The deer's blood was hot and tangy against his tongue as he sucked at its puncture. It didn't take much to bind the spell, the whisper in his head falling silent.

He dropped the deer, pulling at the sleeve of his coat. Black runes were fading slowly beneath his skin, the only remnants of the curse he'd been bound by. He drew a slow breath as he turned his eyes skyward, feeling relieved.

He looked down at the deer's carcass, frowning. What a waste.

Jet turned away, running the back of his hand across his mouth. He scowled at the blood there. He started back toward the farmhouse, which was sitting peacefully on a hill in the distance. A soft crackle of leaves made him pause, his senses suddenly on high alert.

He stiffened, allowing his mind to seek out the source of the sound. He felt the slightest brush of an aura against his, making him clench his fists. Jet was still for a long moment, feeling it come slowly closer. He turned his head as it came close enough, his onyx eyes cutting through the darkness around him.

A woman stepped slowly from the trees, her grin baring fangs. "General," she said softly.

Jet scowled at the word. "Do not call me that," he snarled. Only a servant of Paraximus would waste time with his former designation.

She continued to grin hatefully, her cerulean eyes glittering in the dark. "That's your title, isn't it?" she asked tauntingly. She crossed her arms, seeming pleased with herself. "I didn't believe it to be true, that you would come here on Liana's behalf."

Jet bared his own fangs at her. "And I would still owe allegiance to the king who left me in her grasp?" he snapped. "Paraximus left me to rot with her."

She laughed then. "No need for hostility," she said, stepping toward him. "I was hoping that we could talk."

Jet eased slowly into a wider stance, feeling an attack would be imminent. "What is there to talk about?" He smirked lightly. "You bear my father's crest." His eyes shifted over the emblem pressed into the metal of the plate she wore across her chest. "You've clearly come here with the intention to kill me." He arched a brow at her. "Although, it is unclear how my father knew I was here."

The woman's grin slipped slightly. "Your father is a servant of the great Daya," she said proudly. "Daya has bestowed him with the ability to send whomever he wishes to this plane."

Jet tilted his head, pursing his lips slightly. "I'm not surprised," he said quietly. "He has been her slave for much longer than I can recall." He wondered what his father's price would be for the magic he now commanded.

The woman suddenly shifted, a weapon materializing in her hand. It was long, with a massive, curved blade. "I am Tanith, General," she said, letting the tip of the blade rest in the soil. "If you will join me, then I will relay this to Our King." Her cerulean eyes hardened. "Otherwise, I will slay you where you stand."

Jet smirked. "I can't decide which is more ignorant. That you would believe you could kill me or that I would return to that bastard."

Tanith scowled darkly. She said nothing as she leapt at him, swinging her scythe with ease.

Jet stepped back, unconcerned as it whistled through the air in front of him. "SLOW!" he barked. In a flash he leapt, pushing from the ground where he stood, claws aiming for her face.

Tanith barely dodged his razor talons, rolling away from him. She swung her scythe, watching as Jet leapt over it, landing easily on the bough of a large oak tree. "You are out of practice, aren't you, General?" she said derisively. "Where is the great warrior who slew a legion of Gandoran soldiers in a single motion!?"

Jet smiled. "That story has become even more embellished over the years!" He crouched on the bough. "It was a much smaller number!" He sprang at her again, ducking as she swung her scythe. He felt his claws drive into her flesh, her blood splashing across his face. He landed on the other side of her, his back to her.

Tanith fell to a knee, gasping. She pressed her hand against her side, looking over her shoulder at him. She growled as she watched him lick the blood from his fingers.

"I would have much preferred to have your blood than that of the foul creature I killed earlier . . ." His eyes were sparkling dangerously. "I think it's the magic that lends such a delicious taste to it."

Tanith moved painfully to her feet. The blood had seeped into her clothing, her magic knitting her wound together. "What kind of monster are you?" she asked through gritted teeth.

Jet smirked dangerously. "The kind not to be trifled with!" He flashed before her, catching her off guard. He drove his hand deep into her gut, delighting in the way she gasped, choking softly on her own blood. He intended to end her there, but the hate in her eyes never dimmed as she drew a dagger, driving it between his ribs.

Jet withdrew his hand from her gut, fury filling him. He stepped back as she dropped to her knees. "You will pay for that!" He ignored the pain as he yanked the dagger from his side.

Tanith staggered to her feet, swinging her scythe in desperation. She created enough space between them that she could leap away, into the boughs of the oak tree. "It won't be today, General." Her eyes were bright as she turned, fleeing into the night.

Jet thought to go after her, but he was still as he looked down at the wound to his side. It was bleeding profusely, making him clench his jaw. The fury was still coursing through him, but uncharacteristic pain stilled him. He growled softly as he bent, retrieving her dagger.

It dripped with his blood, but Jet could see a groove carved into the metal. He used his hands to break the handle from the end of the blade, a sickly sweet scent hitting his nose.

Wench.

She thought poison would incapacitate him?

Jet scoffed, letting the poison run to the ground. It seared the grass as it was absorbed into the dirt. He looked in the direction that Tanith had disappeared, feeling his gut twist with his rage. He would slay her, and any others that Paraximus had sent, without mercy.

Seth was standing on the porch, his arms crossed. His eyes widened as he saw Jet walking toward him, his clothing bloody, a dagger in his hand. "What the hell happened to you!?" he asked, anticipation clawing at him.

Jet walked slowly up the porch steps, his scowl dark. "What does this look like to you?" He held the blade out to Seth.

Seth took the dagger gingerly, turning it over in his hands. "Siccitan chalargentum," he whispered. He lifted it to his nose, catching a whiff of the poison. "Infinity flowers."

Jet drew a slow breath, easing to sit on the railing of the porch. "Paraximus sent a soldier, possibly more. They're here to kill me."

Seth's blue eyes widened. "That's impossible," he breathed. "The Limen is sealed!"

Jet sighed. "You are a fool," he said softly, his gaze narrowed as he looked across the porch. "My father, no doubt, has taken a blood oath to the goddess Daya." He could feel the wound to his side pulse painfully as his body mended itself. "He will not be stopped."

Seth shook his head. "If he has the power to send soldiers here, there's no telling what or who he'll send next." His brow furrowed with fear and uncertainty. "Do you think he knows about the Princess?"

Jet pursed his lips, lost in thought. "I don't know," he said softly. "The soldier that attacked me said she was sent to bring me back to him or to kill me." He looked at Seth. "There was no mention of Nyx."

Seth looked down at the blade in his hands. "You must keep your distance. They cannot know why you are here."

Jet nodded. This was probably the first thing he and Seth had agreed upon. He moved to his feet. "I will hunt her down, and any who came with her." He looked at Seth. "I'll keep them away from this place. If your identity is discovered, it won't be long before they come for you and Nyx."

Seth nodded. "Do what you must," he said softly. He looked back down at the dagger. He was lost in thought as Jet disappeared inside.

How could this have happened? What power did Paraximus possess that he could do such impossible things? Seth knew that Daya was a powerful force, but he'd never heard of a blood oath that allowed the bearer to gain her power. Fear crept through his chest. He had to protect Nyx, and he knew the only way to do it was to disappear from her life for a while, just like Jet said.

Seth frowned softly. He knew this meant he couldn't see Anna anymore. That fact cut into his heart. He'd grown quite fond of her. But to keep her safe, it was necessary. He turned and walked into the house just as Jet came down the hall from his room with his bag.

"I need to go with you," Seth said, his face determined.

Jet paused, looking Seth over slowly. "You aren't a warrior. Your strength is in healing. You would be in my way."

Seth's frown deepened as he looked at the dagger in his hands. "I can help you."

Jet shook his head, stepping toward Seth. "You would be of more assistance here," he said shortly. He took the dagger from Seth's hands. "Use your relationship with that little mortal girl to stay near Nyx. She needs you to watch over her."

Seth's frown gave way to a soft scowl. "I do not like this plan."

Jet smirked darkly. "You don't have to," he said. "You just have to do as I say."

Seth watched as Jet walked out the door, closing it softly. Everything about this plan felt wrong and left him with more uncertainty than hope. By the time Seth walked out to stop him, Jet was gone, disappearing into the trees around them. The unease Seth felt didn't lessen as he stood there, the night quiet.

$$\sim 10 \sim$$

Somewhere Near Lucky, Texas.

Monday, January 17, 2011.

TANITH WINCED AS SHE kneeled beside a winding river, the sun reflecting brightly across its surface. She looked up when Devyn appeared beside her. His arms were crossed as he looked down at her, a smug smirk on his face.

"I told you that was stupid," he said shortly.

Tanith plunged her hands into the water, splashing it across her face. "Shut up," she said softly. The water was murky, muddy in her hands, but it was better than nothing. Her clothing was stained with blood.

"Jet will kill you next time," Devyn said. "You cannot defeat him alone."

Tanith sat back on her heels. "He didn't seem any stronger than any other foe I've destroyed," she quipped.

Devyn's smirk widened. "You're an ass," he said. "The General has been in prison for the last century. Would you be at the top of your game if you were in his place?"

Tanith's eyes narrowed thoughtfully. "We don't have much time, then." She stood slowly. "We need to kill him while he's still out of practice."

Devyn nodded. Deep down, he knew that Jet would only get stronger. He recalled the General's methods, having gone to war with him before the Collapse. He was like a sponge, absorbing and learning another's fighting method as he went. In his prime, Jet would have an enemy figured out in two moves and dead in three.

Tanith's soft gasp pulled Devyn out of his thoughts. He saw her staring into the murky water, her eyes wide. She dropped to a knee as an image formed before them across the surface of the water.

"My King," she said, her hand over her heart.

Devyn was quick on her heels, bowing his head. "Highness."

Paraximus' image rippled with the waves across the river. "I see you've seen my son," he said darkly. His eyes were black, much like Jet's, his salt and pepper hair tied back from his face. An angry frown was on his face.

"He did not wish to come back to you, My King," Tanith said bitterly. "I will run him through the next time we meet."

Paraximus arched a brow. "You did not end him upon your first meeting?"

Tanith bowed her head, her eyes downcast. "I was unable to," she said softly.

"That's disheartening," Paraximus said, a dangerous edge to his voice. "You underestimate Jet."

Devyn glanced at Tanith, seeing distress across her face.

"I have no doubt he was weakened," Paraximus continued. "If you could not defeat him in that state, perhaps I chose wrong."

"No, My King," Tanith said quickly. "I am capable. But I was foolhardy, thinking I would go alone."

Paraximus looked to Devyn. "He will know Tanith's moves. He will not know yours."

Devyn nodded, a small grin pulling at his lips. "I have something for the General. He won't escape us."

Paraximus nodded. "Before you kill him, find out why he is there," he said slowly, pressing a finger to his chin thoughtfully. "Liana will have sent him on a mission of some sort. Discover what it is."

"Yes, My King," Tanith said.

"Where are Sophia and Lance?" Paraximus asked, his eyes shifting over them.

"We split to cover more ground," Devyn said. "We are to meet with them tomorrow with what we have learned."

Paraximus nodded again. "Good," he said. "Do not fail me."

Both Tanith and Devyn nodded. "Yes, Your Highness."

The water rippled again, Paraximus' image disappearing. Devyn glanced at Tanith, seeing how pale her face had gone. "We only have one more chance," he said slowly. "If we fail, he will send another to deal with us and Jet."

Tanith nodded, her haughty attitude gone. "We need a plan."

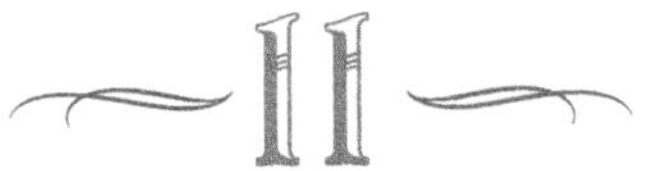

The Estrella Residence.
Monday, February 14, 2011.

Nyx sighed for the millionth time as she sat on the couch, flipping the channels on the TV. She ignored her best friend's texts, trying not to feel so miserable about herself. It was Valentine's Day, and she'd really hoped that Randy would have asked to take her to dinner or something. But instead, he'd been thick as ever during class today, only making small talk with her until it was time to leave. He'd even asked if she had plans, and she'd said no, hoping he'd take the hint.

He didn't.

The thought was more crushing as she sat there, trying to find something on that wasn't a rom-com or a show where the theme was Valentine's Day.

"Hey, sweetie," her aunt said, sitting beside her. She offered a smile. "What are you watching?"

Nyx sighed. "Nothing," she said shortly. "Nothing good on."

Dorothea looked over at her, seeing the way her brow was furrowed unhappily. "What's the matter?" she asked.

"It's stupid Valentine's Day," Nyx said through another sigh. "I thought Randy would ask me out tonight, but he didn't."

"Oh, that's too bad!" Dorothea said, putting her arm around Nyx's shoulders. "Maybe he wasn't thinking about it?"

Nyx shrugged. "Maybe," she said. "Anna won't stop texting me about how awesome her boyfriend is and the flowers he got her and blah blah." Nyx rolled her eyes.

Dorothea grinned. "Well, let's order a pizza," she said, standing and walking into the kitchen to find a phone book. "What do you want? The usual?"

Nyx turned and looked at her aunt, grinning. "Yeah, the usual."

Jet was beyond irritated as he pulled his car up to Seth's house. He was mildly surprised to see Seth's car in the driveway. He hadn't been here in several weeks, trying to track Tanith and her comrades. He'd made their hiding place one time, but they'd been difficult to follow since then. Jet had a feeling that one of them was using a glamor, but it was hard to know if he couldn't even determine who the others were.

He climbed slowly out of the car, feeling his body protest. He was actually tired, which was unusual for him. He walked slowly to the door, putting his key in the lock. He pushed the door open, surprised to see that the lights were off, candles lit around the living room.

"Seth?" Jet walked slowly through the door. He paused when he heard noises down the hall. "Hello?"

Seth suddenly appeared from his room, his brown curls disheveled. "Hey," he said quickly, trying to straighten his button-down shirt. "What are you doing here?"

Jet frowned at him. "Last I checked, I lived here, too," Jet quipped in Sarotian. "What's with all the candles?"

Seth smoothed his hand through his hair. "Anna's here," he said meekly. He inclined his head toward his room. "It's Valentine's Day."

Jet scowled at him. "Am I supposed to know what that means?"

Seth walked toward him, catching him around the shoulders and walking him to the door. "Listen, come back in a few hours, okay?"

Jet sighed. He'd been gone for just a few weeks, and Seth was behaving like this. And with a mortal, no less. "You're an idiot," Jet said as he walked down the steps. "And what about Nyx?"

Seth shrugged. "Nyx is fine," he said easily. "She's at home with Dorothea."

Jet narrowed his eyes at Seth. "Idiot." He turned and climbed back into his car, slamming the door. Seth was so stupid. While he'd been out, trying to kill the ones hunting him, Seth had been charming his new little girlfriend. It was pathetic.

Jet didn't look back as he pulled out of the driveway and onto the road. He guessed this was as good a time as any to check on Nyx. Since he wasn't allowed in his own house.

He drove down the highway, taking the curve that ended near her driveway. He parked his car at the end of the gravel road, out of the way of any passersby. He climbed out slowly, pulling his jacket around his shoulders. The wind was cold tonight as it blew through the trees, but Jet didn't mind. He climbed over an embankment and into the trees, winding his way toward Dorothea's house.

As he moved farther through the brush, the wind began to settle, blocked by the tall pines that surrounded their farm. Eventually, the pines gave way to an open field, which rolled down a hill. He could see the lights of the farmhouse as he paused. He drew a slow breath as he watched, peace settling over him.

"Well now, isn't this sweet."

Jet jumped, feeling his hands clench. He spun quickly, recognizing Tanith's voice. He growled softly as she appeared behind him.

"Who are you watching over, General?" she asked, her eyes darting past him to the farmhouse. "Must be someone important for you to have been on the hunt these last few weeks."

Jet was snarling at her, feeling bitter fury sweeping him. It was one thing for him to be chasing her, but for her to have snuck up on him so easily . . . He didn't like it at all. "I'm going to gut you!" he growled dangerously.

Tanith summoned her scythe. She didn't say anything as she swung at him, watching him dodge her attack easily. Every day since their last meeting, Jet had replayed her moves over and over in his head. He knew exactly what to expect as she swung her weapon, and he avoided her blows easily, ducking into her swing. He swung his fist, knocking her backwards. She hit the ground hard, gasping for the wind that was knocked from her lungs.

Jet advanced on her quickly with no intention to make her death easy or swift. He pulled the dagger she'd stabbed him with from a holster at his belt, twirling it easily. His gaze was deadly as he pinned her to the ground. "You're a fool," he growled, pressing his hand against her throat. "You shouldn't have come back."

Tanith gripped his wrist, a smirk pulling at her lips. "I didn't come alone."

Jet glanced up as hot magic sizzled the air. He leapt away from her, the sound of a whip cracking. Pain shot across his cheek, and he lifted a hand, feeling a single cut beneath his eye. He sighed in irritation as he looked up, seeing a blond-haired man drop to the ground.

He caught Tanith's hand, pulling her to her feet. "Hello, General," he said mockingly, flashing a grin.

"I hope you don't think that having another with you will save you," Jet said, feeling the cut on his cheek sealing shut.

"Actually, that's not my intention at all." Tanith swung her scythe. She looked to Devyn. "Go."

Jet watched as he turned and began down the hill, toward the farmhouse. Jet clenched the dagger tighter in his hands. Fear twisted in his chest. He couldn't let them get to Nyx. He sprang toward Devyn, but Tanith blocked him, swinging her massive blade. Jet avoided her blow and planted his foot against the flat side of her scythe, using the momentum of her swing to push himself away from her. She obviously didn't expect that, as she scowled darkly.

Jet smirked at her as he threw his dagger, watching it sink into her chest. She staggered back, pain furrowing her brow. She gasped, the blade having penetrated her heart. Jet stepped past her as she collapsed to the ground, her scythe clattering beside her.

"Idiot," Jet said, pausing as he stepped over her. "I'll be back to finish this." He turned away from her, springing down the hill. He was a blur as he ran after Devyn. He was much quicker than Devyn, managing to catch up to him. He leapt into the air, slamming his fist down where Devyn would have been, a seething crater appearing in the ground.

Devyn avoided his blow, surprise on his face as he rolled to his feet. "You are formidable," he said, wielding his lightning whip. "But it won't save you."

Jet rolled his eyes, the bones in his hand cracking and pulling themselves back into place. "Are all of you this annoying?" he asked. He waved his hands, silver magic sparking from his fingertips. Double-ended, hooked blades formed in his hands, glowing with the light of Jet's magic.

Devyn stepped back, using his searing whip to force Jet away. His eyes were trained on Jet's weapon of choice, known as the Geminaci. They were thick, steeply curved blades, with one protruding from either end of the handle. Only a very skilled swordsman could wield them without injury to themselves. Devyn knew this wouldn't be easy.

Sparks flew from where Devyn's whip struck Jet's blades. He didn't say anything, watching as Jet regained his footing, coming at him again. They traded blows, each swing of Devyn's whip forcing Jet farther from the farmhouse. Devyn knew he had the upper hand, and he swung the whip in a coil, catching Jet around the wrist. Jet paused as the whip wrapped around his arm, causing burning pain to shoot through him. He looked down, seeing the fiery energy eating into his skin. The stench of smoldering flesh was slowly filling his nose.

Devyn smirked as he pulled the whip, swinging Jet away from him. "Could this be the thing that ends you?" he taunted.

Jet landed in a crouch. The scorching pain wasn't doing anything other than making him angry. He released the silver blades, allowing them to dissolve. He caught the whip in his hands, giving it a hard pull, despite the way it cut painfully into the palms of his hands. Devyn lost his balance, being flung forward. Jet stepped toward him, knocking him to the ground. He pressed the lighting whip to Devyn's throat, watching as his skin began to blister and burn.

"You're a nuisance," he said softly. He pressed the whip harder, seeing it burn through Devyn's skin. It gave him pause. He hadn't seen someone die in a long time. Excitement rushed through him as he watched Devyn struggle against him, desperate to break free. Knowing he held Devyn's life in his hands made a heady feeling streak through Jet.

He intended to cut Devyn's head off, but a soft sound caught his attention. Distracted by his own thoughts, he didn't have time to react as the whistle of a blade filled the air, and pain shot through his body.

Jet looked down, his hands shaking as he saw Tanith's scythe blade protruding through his chest. Rage was filling him as he dealt a blow to Devyn, watching him fall still on the ground, unconscious, the golden whip vanishing with the loss of Devyn's energy. He moved slowly to his feet, gritting his teeth as he caught the scythe blade in his hands. The razor edges cut into his palms as he gripped it, pushing it through his chest.

He gasped painfully as it fell to the ground, his blood staining the green grass around him. He felt lightheaded suddenly, his body working in overdrive to repair itself. He turned to face Tanith, seeing her pressing her hand over her heart, still bleeding profusely.

"You're going to regret this," Jet said softly. His vision was becoming blurry, her scythe blade having been laced with a copious amount of poison.

Tanith forced a bloody smile. "I don't think I will." Jet missed the way her eyes widened as he bowed his head, the dark runes appearing across his body.

Jet smirked, feeling the whispers in his head suddenly. He could feel the beast twisting in his chest, begging to be released. He knew he was injured too badly to stop it, and with the way it demanded Tanith's blood, he didn't think he wanted to. His strength left him, and he sank down to a knee, feeling the world fading and a new strength filling him.

She will die.

The beast's voice was guttural, a gravelly growl that echoed through him.

Jet couldn't move as he gave in to the beast's clawing in his mind. He was suddenly a passenger in his own body, watching as the fiend moved to his feet. He was on Tanith in an instant, faster than she could track him, his hands driving into her chest.

Tanith's eyes were wide with fear. "What are you?" she breathed.

The beast snarled, contorting Jet's face into that of a demon. His razor fangs were bared, his eyes filling with bloodlust. "I am your death," the monster growled. His brute strength was immense as the beast snarled, ripping her in half.

Blood showered over Jet, and he sank to his knees, lapping at the crimson liquid that was pouring from her corpse. Long fangs dug into the meat that he pressed against his face, the smell of coppery blood pungent. Just as he'd said before, her blood was sweet ambrosia, fortified by the magic that had once coursed through her body. Jet could see the dark runes that covered his arms glowing as the fiend used his body to feast on Tanith's flesh. Eventually, the runes began to fade, and Jet collapsed, finding himself staring at the early morning sky.

He lifted his arms gingerly, feeling weak. It had been many years since the monster had taken control. He didn't like the way it felt. It used to bolster him on the battlefield, giving him a heady rush as he was bathed in the blood of his enemies, but now it left him deeply unsettled. He had no control over the beast when he was in that form, only blood being able to reset the runes that held the monster in check.

Jet rolled to his feet, looking across the field.

The farmhouse was dark in the distance, and Devyn was gone. Jet vaguely recalled seeing him running away in fear, but it felt more like something he'd imagined rather than something he'd actually seen. He looked down at the remains of Tanith's body, his lips curling in disgust. He needed to clean up this mess.

It didn't take him much time to dispose of what was left of her body, but it left him covered in blood and putrid ooze from her corpse. He knew he needed to get back. Seth would be pissed.

12

The Alvar Residence.

Tuesday, February 15, 2011.

"ARE YOU INSANE?!" Seth barked.

Jet pressed a hand against his eyes, feeling sick. He needed to let his body rest, but Seth hadn't stopped bitching since he'd walked in. "It wasn't my fault." He narrowed his eyes at Seth. "If you'd been doing your job, this wouldn't have happened."

Seth frowned then, hurt flashing across his face. "Did you take care of everything?" he asked, calming considerably.

"Of course," Jet said, exhaustion in his voice. "The only thing I can't do anything about is the fact that the other one got away."

Seth scoffed. "I doubt he'll be returning anytime soon," he said hotly. He felt his stomach turn as he recalled how Jet had looked this morning, covered in gore. He couldn't imagine the terror that Jet harbored that could reduce a body to a pulp like that. "Why didn't you tell me this could happen?"

Jet scowled at him. "I have control of it!" he snapped.

"You didn't have control this morning when you decimated that woman," Seth retorted.

Jet rolled his eyes. "She deserved it."

"But what about those who don't!?" Seth demanded. "What about Nyx? You were too close." He pressed a hand to his face then, obviously imagining what Jet would have done to her.

Jet shook his head. "She was never in danger." He didn't like the way his stomach curled in on itself. "I keep the blood curse satisfied." He looked away. "I lost control because my body was dying."

Seth drew a deep breath, sinking down into a chair. "You have to be more careful. We can't risk anyone knowing about this."

Jet pinned him with a weak glare. "No shit."

Seth pressed his hand against his face again, as if he had a migraine. "You should rest."

"Thanks, boss."

Jet rose to his feet, feeling relieved that he was finally being dismissed. He slunk to his room, falling face-first into his pillow. The sheets were cool against his body, which felt like it had been in a blender. He closed his eyes, falling into a dark sleep.

13

*The Abandoned Yand Farmhouse,
Outskirts of Lucky.*

Thursday, February 17, 2011.

EVYN DROPPED SLOWLY to the ground, glancing over his shoulder warily. It had been two days since he'd seen Tanith being devoured, but he couldn't shake the feeling that he was being watched. His senses were on high alert as he walked toward an abandoned farmhouse. He could feel two distinct auras moving inside.

He drew a slow breath as he walked up the steps. He just couldn't shake the image of whatever demon Jet had summoned. He closed his eyes briefly to clear his mind before stepping inside.

"Devyn, where have you been?" Sophia asked, her voice lilting from the living room.

Devyn stepped toward the entrance. The furniture was draped with sheets, litter and leaves covering the floor. No one had lived here in quite some time. Some of the windows upstairs had been broken, and birds had taken to nesting in the attic.

"I had to make sure I wasn't being followed," Devyn said, his voice trembling slightly.

Sophia rose slowly from the chair she was sitting in. Lance shifted at the window, turning to look at Devyn. "Where is Tanith?"

Devyn shook his head, his brow furrowing in distress. "There was an incident."

Sophia's hazel eyes narrowed. "She confronted Jet."

Devyn nodded. "We followed him to a place west of town," he said slowly. "She engaged him in battle and I left her to investigate." His eyes darkened. "Whatever he is protecting, it's there."

"Did you discover what it was?" Sophia asked, her lips pressing into a hard line.

"No," Devyn said, shaking his head. He brushed his blond hair from his face. "The General caught me. I would have been done for, if not for Tanith. She drove her weapon through his chest." Devyn frowned, confusion on his face. "Jet should have died."

Sophia's eyes widened then, as if she understood what had happened. She smirked then, chuckling softly. "You saw it, then."

Devyn looked at her, his face wary. "Saw what?"

Sophia stepped back to her chair, sinking into it. "Jet's *fax*."

"*Fax?*" Devyn asked softly.

"Yes," Sophia said, her smirk widening. "Our King used Daya's magic to trap Jet's *fax* and seal it away. It emerges when his life is threatened, as it clearly did when Tanith landed her killing blow."

"I still don't understand," Devyn said, scowling at her. "Why would Our King do that?"

"Jet was much more powerful that our lord," Sophia said, pulling the feather from her hair. "Rumors say that the castle walls shook on the day of Jet's birth, a sign of the magnitude of his power. To contain him, King Paraximus went to Daya, who showed him how to draw out Jet's *fax*, which in the language of old is literally the fire that burns inside us all, and seal it away, to be used only at Our King's will." She twirled the quill between her fingers absently. "When Tanith landed a fatal blow, the curse activated to save Jet's life. This makes him formidable and unstoppable."

"How do you know all of this?" Devyn asked, clenching his hands.

"You don't think King Paraximus would send us in unprepared, do you?" Sophia asked.

Devyn scowled darkly. "You knew he was capable of this, and you didn't warn us?" He stepped toward her, feeling an ache to drive his claws into her. "Tanith is dead because of you." A tingle of electricity shot through his fingertips.

Sophia looked up at him, her hazel eyes sparkling dangerously. "Tanith rushed to her death," she quipped darkly. "I warned her that Jet would not be destroyed so easily." She waved her quill, as if writing words.

Devyn stepped back, feeling the pull of her magic through the stale air in the house. He unclenched his fists and bowed his head. He didn't wish to fight her, knowing her magic was more powerful than his. "So then what is our next move?" he asked quietly.

Sophia looked to Lance, seeing him watching her carefully. He was her second-in-command, and he knew the situation as well as she did. She'd kept it from Devyn and Tanith in the hopes that they would do as they had done, and force Jet's transformation. She needed to know what she was truly against.

"We need to know what he is protecting," Lance said, his voice reverberating across the wooden floor. He glanced at Sophia. "Everyone has a weakness. Perhaps this is his."

Sophia nodded, looking back to Devyn. "Let him think we have gone into hiding," she said. "We will wait and watch, and when the time is right, we will destroy him."

Devyn nodded, but he didn't like the way her words sat in his chest. He didn't want to sit around until death came for them. Tanith's hadn't been pretty, and he knew theirs wouldn't be either.

14

The Estrella Residence.

Monday, March 28, 2011.

NYX PULLED HER SWEATER over her head, grabbing her bag and rushing down the stairs. She was running late today. "Bye, Aunt Dee!" she yelled as she ran out the door.

She didn't hear her aunt's reply, but it didn't bother her as she jumped into her white Mustang and fired it up. She winced as it chugged and grunted, as if it wouldn't start, before catching up to itself and revving. She patted the dash in relief.

"Good girl." She threw the car in reverse and hit the highway. She was so late for class.

As if her lateness wasn't bad enough, she couldn't find anywhere to park, and it was twenty minutes into class when she finally came sliding in. She opened the door to the classroom quietly, feeling all eyes on her as the professor paused.

"Thank you for joining us, Ms. Estrella," he said, his eyebrows and goatee pulling his face into a permanent frown. "But perhaps next time you should set your alarm earlier."

Nyx felt her cheeks flush a dark red. "Sorry!" she whispered, sliding into her seat beside Randy.

He looked over at her, grinning. "If I was you, I'd have skipped," he whispered softly. He picked up a piece of paper off his desk and handed it to her. "I was taking notes for you."

Nyx felt her face turn redder. "Thanks," she breathed. Her heart was racing, both from her mad dash to class and from the way Randy's smile made her heart flutter.

The class seemed to drag on forever, but finally the professor turned, his belly jiggling as he set down his whiteboard marker. "We'll pick up next time," he said gruffly.

Nyx began to gather her things, shoving her papers into her backpack.

"Hey, you wanna get coffee with me?" Randy asked.

Nyx smiled. "Yeah," she said brightly.

"Cool!" Randy said, returning her smile.

"Just a moment, Ms. Estrella . . ." the professor said suddenly. "May I have a word with you?"

Nyx glanced at Randy, who shrugged. "I'll meet you there."

Randy nodded, leaving her alone with the teacher.

Nyx swung her bag over her shoulder. "I'm really sorry I was late, Dr. Frank!" she said quickly.

Dr. Frank's eyes creased, a smile forming under his goatee. "That's not what I wanted to talk to you about," he said, his gruff demeanor disappearing. "I wanted to compliment you on your paper. It was a fantastic read."

"Oh!" Nyx said, surprise on her face. She smiled. "Thank you."

Dr. Frank nodded, still smiling. "Your ability to tell a story and to make correlations between facts is amazing." He turned and opened his briefcase. "I have something here that I thought you might be interested in."

Nyx watched as he pulled a flyer from his bag. She took it from him, seeing that it was for a workshop over the summer. "What is this?" she asked, looking at it.

"It's for the school paper," he said. "If they like your writing, you qualify for a chance to earn a scholarship and a position at the paper." He looked down at the flyer. "If you do well with the paper, Mark Johnson, the editor-in-chief, usually has contacts with the *Lucky Daily News*."

"Really!?" Nyx asked, feeling excitement sweep her.

Dr. Frank nodded. "You have a lot of potential, Ms. Estrella," he said, picking up his briefcase. He offered another smile. "I hope to see you go far."

Nyx was grinning as she walked with him from the room. Her eyes were taking in the flyer in her hands, pride swelling inside her. She'd never considered a job with the newspaper, but it was an exciting prospect.

She looked up as she stepped outside, into the bright sunshine. She started to pull her sunglasses from her bag, when her phone began to ring. She pulled it out, seeing it was Anna.

"Hey girl," she said.

"Hey!" Anna said, a smile clearly in her voice. "You're out of class, right?"

"Yeah!" Nyx said, glancing across the courtyard to the main building, where Randy was waiting. "Randy asked me to get coffee with him . . ."

"That's awesome!" Anna said happily. "You have to call me with details!"

Nyx giggled. "I will!" she promised.

"Oh, I wanted to know if you were busy tonight?" Anna said quickly.

"Uh, no, not really," Nyx said. "Why?"

"Seth wants us to go with them to dinner tonight for Jet's birthday. Thought you might wanna go to Deb's and get some food."

Nyx felt uncertainty sweep her. She still wasn't completely comfortable with the boys and she knew if she went that Anna would ditch her to hang on Seth all night. "I dunno . . ." she said slowly.

"Come on," Anna begged. "It'll be super fun!"

Nyx sighed. "Okay," she said. "What time?"

Anna squealed on the opposite end of the phone. "I'll text you."

Nyx frowned as she hung up the phone, Anna's text message dinging simultaneously. She didn't really want to see Seth, or Jet for that matter. But if it would make Anna happy, she supposed she could suck it up for one night. She pushed the thought from her mind as she walked to the main building to meet Randy.

Deb's Diner, Main Street.

Monday, March 28, 2011.

JET SCOWLED, FINDING THE rain annoying. The day had started off bright and nice, but rain clouds had rolled in, bringing with it a cold wind. Jet brushed wet strands of hair from his eyes, glancing up and down the street. He watched cars roll by, splashing the puddles that were forming along the curb. Annoyance flashed through him as he glanced over his shoulder at Seth, who was taking his sweet time digging things out of his car.

"What are you doing?" Jet demanded.

Seth stepped back from the car, closing the door. He offered a smile. "I brought Anna flowers," he said, holding up the bouquet of colorful daisies.

Jet shifted his eyes away, a disgusted sigh leaving his lips. He crossed his arms, stepping into the street. "I thought this was my party . . ." Jet mumbled. Seth was at his shoulder, his eyes fixed on the bright lights of the restaurant in front of them, obviously unaware of his grumbling.

"Are you sure they'll be here?" Jet asked as he stepped onto the curb.

Seth shrugged. "Anna said Nyx agreed to come. And this is the place they usually come to. So it seemed fitting for your party." He offered a grin.

As if on cue, a small white car pulled into a parking space. He glanced over at Seth, seeing a smirk pulling at his face, and he assumed it was Nyx's car. Clearly Seth was pleased.

"Come on," Seth said, leading the way inside. "Let's get a table."

Jet pressed his lips together tightly as he followed Seth to a booth. He slid into the side facing the door, his dark eyes able to see despite the glare of the lights on the glass.

Nyx was walking down the sidewalk, fiddling with an umbrella. She was frowning, hugging her jacket tighter. Jet watched as she stopped, digging through her purse for a moment. Jet expected her to come into the restaurant, but mild curiosity caught at him when she turned, patting down her clothes.

Her frown was more prominent as she kept digging, looking for something. Finally, she seemed to find it inside her bag. She looked uncomfortable as she turned, letting her gaze make its way inside the restaurant. Jet hadn't seen her in months, and the intensity in her eyes clawed at him.

Time seemed to stand perfectly still as she stared at him. Jet wondered what was flitting through her mind as her brow furrowed. It wasn't until she pressed her lips together and looked away that he was able to draw a breath. He frowned, his heart hammering in his chest. What had just happened? He'd never felt so pinned under anyone's gaze before.

Jet looked down at the table, rolling his shoulders slightly to try to relieve the tension in his body. Nothing had ever made him feel like this, filling him with a nervousness he couldn't place or stop. He crossed his arms tighter, glancing up when she entered the restaurant.

At first, she didn't seem like she wanted to come over to talk to them, but she made her way to their table. Her green eyes were conflicted as she forced a smile.

"Hey," she said, looking from him to Seth. She schooled her face into the perfect paradigm of surprise. "Am I early?" She looked nervous.

Seth smiled at her. "Hey Nyx," he said easily. "No, you're right on time. Anna is running late."

Nyx seemed to relax some. "Cool," she said, shifting awkwardly beside the table. "It's good to see you guys again." She looked at Jet. "I heard you were out of town, right?"

Jet could feel a scowl pulling at his face as he looked to Seth. He tried to stop it though, nodding his head. "Yes . . ." he said, looking down at the table. "I had things to attend to."

Nyx offered another smile. "Cool," she said meekly. Awkward silence was threatening to descend on them, but luckily Seth was there to save the day.

"Sit!" Seth said, motioning to the booth. "Get whatever you guys want. Dinner's on me."

Jet clenched his jaw to stop any ugly words from escaping him. The last thing he wanted was to sit here with them, acting like they were normal. There were more pressing things that needed to be discussed. They didn't have time to be celebrating his birthday like children.

Nyx glanced at Jet, uncertainty on her face. "All right." She looked at Seth's side of the table, a frown on her face. She knew Anna would want to sit beside her boyfriend. She started to set her purse on the seat.

Jet looked up at her, frowning lightly.

"Do you mind?" she asked quietly. She motioned to the fact that he was sitting in the middle of the booth.

Jet sighed, scooting over. He hated everything about this, including how close she was as she settled beside him. His eyes followed her motions as she tucked her purse onto the seat between them as if to build a barrier. She busied herself with anything other than looking at him. She brushed a strand of golden hair behind her ear, picking up her menu. She pressed her knuckle against her lips as she looked it over.

Jet let his eyes follow the curve of her face. She really was very beautiful, with long eyelashes that covered her deep green eyes. He hadn't really noticed at the bonfire, since his mind had been filled with thoughts of this new place and what he was sensing. After a moment, she drew a slow breath, her lips parting slightly.

Jet felt his stomach turning in knots, unable to tear his eyes from her. He felt the sudden urge to brush a strand of hair from her face when she shifted, her hair falling close to her eyes. She was lost in thought, brushing absently at the offending hairs.

"What about you, Jet?"

Jet turned his head, seeing Seth looking at him. "I'm sorry?" he said, hearing the curt edge to his own voice. Irritation was flooding him, but he couldn't tell if it was because of the trance Nyx had caught him in or the fact that Seth had interrupted him.

"What do you want to eat?"

Jet tried to keep down a scowl. "I don't know," he said dismissively. He looked down at the menu. "You know I despise this kind of food."

Nyx glanced at him, arching a brow. "What kind of food do you like then?"

Jet shrugged, still looking over the menu. "I prefer the food we have back home."

Seth's blue eyes narrowed and he forced a laugh with all his strength. "I know hamburgers aren't your thing, but you'll like these!"

Jet could feel the scowl slipping. "If you say so . . ." he clipped. "Just pick something for me."

Seth nodded. "Awesome!" he said, his voice chipper. "My favorite is the Double-Meat." He grinned at Nyx. "So delicious."

Nyx offered a genuine smile then. "It is really good." She looked down at her menu. "I like the original cheese-burger." Seth agreed that was a good one, too. Nyx turned her eyes to Jet as silence fell over them again. "So what kind of stuff do you like to do for fun?"

Jet stared at the table, mulling over his response. He knew what Seth had told him to say, but he also knew what he wanted to say. Finally, he forced a smirk. "I like to pursue personal interests," he said, letting his eyes shift down to Nyx again.

She glanced up at him, her cheeks turning bright red under his gaze. She thought that sounded weird, possibly highly suggestive. She wondered if they would ever have a conversation that didn't make her uncomfortable. She averted her eyes quickly, back to the menu. He took plea-sure from seeing her uncomfortable, thinking it was only fair for the way she made him feel.

"Hey everyone!"

Nyx looked up, a smile suddenly on her face. "Hey!" she said, relieved that her friend had finally joined them.

Anna was grinning as she slid to sit next to Seth, her eyes shifting around the table. "Did you order already?" she asked, looking to Seth.

Seth smiled gently, looping his arm around her. "Not yet." His smile widened. "We were waiting for you."

"Thanks, baby!" she said, leaning into him. She looked across to Jet and Nyx, clearly missing the tension that was sitting between them. "This is nice, right?" Anna giggled, looking up as the waitress came to their table to take their order. Once she was gone, Anna looked to Jet, leaning over the table excitedly. "So, how old are you today?"

Jet arched a brow, turning his eyes on Seth. "Uh, twenty-five," he said shortly, hating the lie. Today would actually be his 154th birthday.

Seth smirked. "So old," he said teasingly. He turned his eyes down to Anna as she gibbered about their ages. Apparently her birthday was coming up soon, and she had big plans.

The conversation was mostly lost on Jet as he snuck glances at Nyx. Her emerald eyes were bright as she laughed with the others. Something about the sound of her voice and the lilt to her giggles made Jet feel full of butterflies. He tried to fight the feeling down as the waitress brought them food and drinks. He wasn't one to indulge in food, since his body didn't require it, but the smell from the plates the waitress brought made his mouth water.

He felt the surprise on his face when she set a huge heap of meat and bread in front of him. What the hell was this mess? He'd never seen anything like it as he picked at the bread, lifting it to reveal colorful toppings. He was so engrossed with it that he didn't notice the way the others were watching him as they ate.

"What's the matter?" Seth asked. "Don't like what I ordered for you?"

Jet blinked, pushing the plate away slightly as he broke from his trance. "This looks disgusting."

Anna shared a glance with Nyx across the table, seeing her friend lifting her own burger to her mouth.

"It's actually really good," Nyx said, taking a huge bite. She offered a sloppy grin as she chewed.

Jet could feel his lip curling in disgust. Suddenly whatever attraction he'd felt to her was gone. She ate like a cow, chewing away at its cud.

"Just try it!" Seth said, pushing a forkful of something into his mouth.

"They don't have hamburgers where you're from?" Anna asked curiously.

Jet shook his head. "Not really." He eyed the burger for a moment before sighing shortly. "I'm not hungry." He leaned back in the booth.

Seth shrugged then, looking at Anna. "Suit yourself." He pulled Jet's plate toward him, eating Jet's fries.

Jet could feel his irritation giving way to bitterness. He didn't think he could stand much more of their conversation. He especially hated the way Seth could talk to anyone about anything. For a long while he had Anna and Nyx blabbering about nonsense, which had Jet nearly bored to tears, but then Seth shifted his focus to Nyx.

"So, Nyx, you like horses, right?" Seth said, folding his arms in front of his empty plates.

Nyx nodded as she chewed a French fry. "Yeah," she said. "We own a couple of horses."

Seth nodded, leaning forward slightly. "Do you ride them?"

"Oh yeah," Nyx said, smiling. "I ride every day."

Seth shifted his eyes to Jet then. Jet knew he was about to be put on the spot, and he clenched his jaw, trying not to shoot daggers at Seth. "Jet likes to ride, too," he said, his lips curling slightly.

Nyx turned to look at Jet then. "Really?" she asked, surprise on her face.

Jet looked down at the table, trying not to sigh.

"Oh yeah," Seth chimed before Jet could ruin his fun. "Jet's actually pretty good."

Nyx blinked, as if trying to imagine him on a horse. "Did you compete?"

Jet picked at the napkin in front of him. "You could say that," he said. "I used to train animals." Nostalgia suddenly hit him as he remembered the scent of leather. He didn't particularly like horses. Dragons were more his forte.

"Huh," Nyx said thoughtfully. "You should stop by sometime."

Jet glanced at her. He started to ask what the hell for, but she continued to speak.

"My aunt has a little filly that she hasn't been able to break." Nyx offered a smile. "Maybe you could give her some pointers."

Jet drew a slow breath, glancing at Seth. He hoped Seth knew how much he wanted to kill him. "Yeah, sure," he said shortly.

The conversation dragged on for a bit longer until the waitress took their plates and offered dessert.

"Actually," Seth said, looking to Jet. He grinned. "It's my cousin's birthday."

"Oh, I'll bring you the special!" the waitress said, winking at him.

"Thanks!" Seth said happily.

Jet narrowed his eyes, not sure what that meant. He looked up when the waitress neared again, setting a small cake on the table. Anna pulled candles from her bag, using a lighter to light them. Jet wanted to sink into the booth when they began to sing him a birthday song. Once it was over, Anna pointed to the cake.

"Blow out the candles and make a wish!"

Jet resisted the urge to roll his eyes, leaning forward and blowing. He watched as all the candles went out, and the group clapped softly. "Childish . . ." he muttered, looking at Seth.

"Well, it is your birthday," Seth said. He turned then, taking a box out of Anna's bag. "Is this it?"

Anna nodded, still grinning.

Seth looked at Jet, holding the box out to him. "We got you a gift." He drew a slow breath to stop Jet from interjecting. "I know we said no gifts, but you need this."

Jet took the box gingerly, turning it over. It was wrapped in brightly colored paper, bears wearing pointed hats on it. He glanced up at Seth, wishing Seth could hear his thoughts.

"Open it!" Seth encouraged.

Jet pulled slowly at the paper, revealing a plastic-wrapped box inside. He sighed shortly as he put the paper aside, a picture of a cellphone on the front of the box. "I thought I told you I didn't want this," he said, looking at Seth in annoyance.

Seth shrugged, grinning. "You know I never listen."

Jet nodded, looking down at the box. Maybe it wouldn't be so bad. "Well, thanks, I guess."

Seth was still grinning, talking about all the things the new phone could do. Apparently it was top of the line and had only been out a few months. Both Anna and Nyx expressed how jealous they were, while Seth produced the same phone from his pocket. Anna and Nyx gushed over how cool it was for a moment, while Seth cut pieces of cake for them.

Jet lifted his fork absently, pressing the sugary confection to his lips. Unlike the burger, the cake was actually good. He snuck glances at Nyx as she ate her cake, the frosting turning her lips blue.

Finally, the dinner was over, and Nyx looked to Anna. "I guess I need to go," she said softly. "Aunt Dee is expecting me back soon."

Anna frowned. "Are you sure?" she asked, pouting. "We're going dancing." She looked to Seth. "Right?"

Seth waved his hand. "Yeah, definitely." He was more concerned with the last bite of cake on his plate.

"I can't," Nyx said. "I have classes tomorrow." She picked up her bag and pulled it over her shoulder. "But we're still on for Thursday, right?"

"Yeah, for sure," Anna said. She jumped to her feet and hugged her friend. "I'll call you later."

Nyx nodded, turning to look to Jet. "Happy birthday," she said quietly, smiling at him.

"Th—thanks," Jet said, watching her bid goodbye to Seth and walk to the door. He wondered what the empty feeling that was settling in his chest was as he watched her go.

"Are you guys ready then?" Anna asked, leaning in to kiss Seth. "I have a curfew tonight."

Seth made a puppy face. "You do?" he asked in a pathetic voice. "What time?"

Jet wanted to gag.

Anna laughed, obviously finding it cute. "Two," she said. "So we should get going. I'll meet you guys there." She gathered her bag and the flowers Seth had brought for her, leaving as well.

Jet felt like he could finally relax once they were alone. He caught Seth's gaze.

"That went well," Seth smiled, his Sarotian words quiet.

Jet narrowed his eyes darkly. "I hate you." He stuck his fork into the rest of the cake on the table. "But I like cake."

Seth rolled his eyes. "I got her to come, didn't I?"

Jet shifted his eyes away, his thoughts tumbling. That didn't really mean anything. "That still doesn't solve the other problem."

Seth stood slowly, stretching. "In due time," he said. He angled his head. "Let's go." He grinned. "It's your night to celebrate." He paused. "How old are you actually?"

Jet rolled his eyes as he put the cover over the cake, bringing it with him. "Too old for this shit," he said shortly, following Seth to the car. He wondered if the cake came in any other flavors beside the white that he had in his hands. It occurred to him that life wasn't too bad here, if all he had to wonder about was cake.

Dirty Harry's was not as busy as it usually was on Thursday nights, but that suited Jet just fine. He sat down at a table on a lifted area where he could watch Seth and Anna twirl around the dance floor. He tried to drink a beer, but it tasted like sewer water. The alcohol here was pitiful. He'd have to drink everything at the bar in one go to even feel a buzz.

He set down the beer bottle, listening to it clatter on the table. Everything about this was annoying. The music was annoying, watching Seth and Anna make googly-eyes at each other was annoying, and being here in Lucky was annoying. A nagging thought in the back of his head was saying that he needed to be looking for Devyn, but another part of him knew that he wouldn't find anything right now.

He leaned over the table, twirling the bottle with his fingers. He couldn't remember the last time he'd had such a boring birthday. Well, if he didn't count the last 100 birthdays. Staring at a brick wall in a dark cell was pretty damn mind-numbing. He found his thoughts drifting.

A century seemed like a lifetime, but it also seemed like yesterday. The last time he'd celebrated a birthday, he'd been standing in the garden of his father's castle, watching a tall woman walk through the hedges. She'd grinned at him, waves of blue hair falling down her back. He'd always been enraptured by her, tranced by her bright smile, but more so by the way she'd cut down their enemies beside him. He'd wondered how so much vitriol and so much beauty could be contained in one hourglass figure.

His eyes followed Seth and Anna when they passed by. The place could have been on fire with people burning around them and they wouldn't have noticed. Seth's hand was resting along the small of her back, holding her close against him.

Jet knew what it felt like to be so in love with someone that the world didn't exist. He could remember the warmth of soft hands in his and could almost hear the soft pull of fabric as she had turned in her ball gown. Her sapphire eyes had cast a spell over him, promising him things that he never thought he could ever want. She wanted a life together and children, all the things normal people dreamed of. But he wouldn't have been able to give her any of those things, even if circumstances had been different.

The glass of the bottle shifted, groaning softly beneath the strain of his grip. Jet looked down, knowing that he could easily shatter it. He drew a slow breath as he released it.

He wasn't normal. He never would be normal again, not after the cruelties he experienced. His hand pressed over his heart. He couldn't be normal with the beast trapped inside him like it was. He'd been shown gentleness and kindness before, but that wasn't in him now. He'd tried to bury his true nature for her, and it only led to his untimely fall. His hands were stained with too much blood before he met her.

Jet blinked from his thoughts, trying to forget all of the other things about that life. He'd never be able to go back, and he doubted that he would ever see that woman again. His heart used to long for her, but now she was just a distant memory. And even if he could go back, did he want to? There was only vengeance now.

"Hi there."

Jet glanced up, seeing a woman standing in front of him. He frowned at her, watching her twirl a strand of red hair on her finger. There was a hunger in her eyes that he recognized.

"Can I sit with you?" she asked, flashing a grin.

Jet sighed. He didn't say anything, and she took that as an invitation to sit.

"I haven't seen you here before," she continued, her eyes shifting over him. She leaned forward, pressing her arms against her chest so that her cleavage was bared. "My name is Cassie."

Jet arched a brow at her brazenness. "Jet."

Cassie's smile widened. "You're a quiet one," she said, her eyes focused intently on his face. "You here alone?" She wasn't one to be deterred easily, clearly.

Jet nodded toward the dance floor. "I'm here with my . . . cousin." He felt like he could choke on that word. There was no universe in which he would wish to be related to Seth.

Cassie turned to look over her shoulder. Her grin was lascivious when she turned back. "The sex appeal must run in the family," she said teasingly.

Jet knew where this was going, and it made the annoyance seep deeper into him. He really didn't feel like fending off this girl's advances. "Just on my side." He lifted his beer again.

"You like to play hard to get, don't you?" Cassie asked, clearly ever more enticed by his aloofness.

Jet set the beer down, leaning his elbows on the table. The longer he looked at her, the more his mind was changing. What could it hurt? He had time to waste. "I don't think I am," he said, softening his voice and letting his eyes hold hers for a long moment.

"Huh . . ." she said, sitting back in her chair, a blush heating her cheeks. Jet noticed that her denim skirt was pulling up her thigh. She cleared her throat nervously. "So what are you doing here? You like to dance?"

"He brought me for my birthday." Jet shot a look at Seth. "But I don't really dance."

A sparkle came into her eyes. "Birthday, huh? Maybe your cousin did a good thing by bringing you here."

Jet smirked. "How do you mean?"

Cassie leaned forward, twirling her hair again. "I can make it the best birthday you've ever had," she said softly. She reached out, placing her hand over his.

Jet glanced at Seth one more time. He watched as Seth's eyes drank in Anna as she twirled away from him. Sudden bitterness gripped him. Anything was better than watching them. He turned his eyes back to Cassie. "Prove it."

— 16 —

Lucky Community College.
Monday, May 2, 2011.

"HOW DID YOU DO?"

Nyx looked up, seeing Randy standing beside the table. She brushed her hand over her face. She was exhausted, and she could feel it in her eyes. "I think I did okay," she said softly. They'd just finished their final for Dr. Frank's class.

Randy settled into a chair beside her. "What are you studying for?" he asked, looking over the textbook in front of her.

Nyx sighed, making a face. "Biology," she said with a grimace.

Randy grinned. "Maybe I can help you?" he offered. "I could quiz you or something."

Nyx smiled lightly at him. She closed the book. "Actually, I'm going to take a break," she said. "My eyes feel like they're about to fall out."

"Cool," Randy said. His blue eyes brightened. "Can I buy you some lunch?"

Nyx's smile grew slightly. "Yeah," she said quickly. "That would be great." She tucked her book into her backpack, following Randy to the campus sandwich shop. Fortunately, there was no line. Nyx was starving.

"I'll take a turkey club," Randy said to the cashier, looking at Nyx. "And whatever she wants."

"So many choices," Nyx said, looking over the menu. She couldn't decide, so she looked up at Randy. "Just make it two of those."

Randy was smiling at her as he handed the cashier some money. "These are my favorite," he said as they waited for their food. "My mom used to make these for me when I was little."

"She doesn't anymore?" Nyx asked, watching him brush his sandy hair from his face.

"Nah," he said grinning playfully. "She tells me I'm an adult and I need to make my own."

Nyx laughed softly. "That's unfortunate."

Randy nodded as they got their food and went back to their table.

They sat in silence for a moment, eating their sandwiches, before Nyx looked up at Randy. "So how do you think you did in Dr. Frank's class?" she asked.

Randy shrugged. "I don't think he really likes me," he said. "I'll be happy if I pass."

Nyx nodded. "Me too."

"Oh, come on," Randy said playfully. "You only have the highest grades in the class."

Nyx looked down at her sandwich, feeling embarrassed. "I just like to write."

"I noticed!" Randy said, his blue eyes sparkling with mirth. "You're a wizard with words!"

Nyx felt her face flush slightly. "It's not a big deal . . ."

Randy took another bite of his sandwich. "Okay, smarty-pants," he teased.

Nyx rolled her eyes. "You got any plans for the break?" she asked conversationally.

"Actually, I do," Randy said, excitement on his face. "I'm having a thing at Dirty Harry's on Friday night." He glanced down at his sandwich. "I thought maybe you'd want to come."

Nyx wiped her mouth with a napkin, feeling her heart skip a beat. "Yeah," she said quickly. "I'd love to."

Randy looked up at her, grinning. "Awesome," he said, relief in his voice. "I'm telling everyone to be there early. Ladies get in free before ten."

Nyx smiled brightly. "Yeah totally," she said happily. "I'll be there."

Randy nodded, taking another bite of his sandwich. They made small talk for a few more minutes before Randy stood, looking at his watch. "Got a math final," he said, pursing his lips in a playful pout.

Nyx nodded. "Well good luck!" she said. She waved to him as he turned and took off down the hall. She smiled softly as she pulled her book out again, flipping it open. She couldn't concentrate anymore, her mind consumed with Friday night. She couldn't wait.

17

The Brown Residence.

Friday, May 6, 2011.

THE SUMMER AIR WAS hot and sweet, filled with the scent of the orange trees that grew in the backyard of Anna's house. Nyx closed her eyes, enjoying the feeling of the afternoon sun on her skin. She tucked her feet under her as Anna pushed the porch swing slowly.

"These are my favorite days," Anna said quietly.

Nyx nodded. "Mine too," she said sleepily. They were silent for a moment before the sound of a car caught their attention. Nyx opened her eyes; a red Ford was pulling up the drive. "Is that Brad?"

Anna nodded. "Dad bought him that clunker." She shook her head. "Brad saw it on the corner down at Smith's and had to have it."

Nyx shook her head as a boy younger than Anna slid out of the truck, slamming the steel door hard. "Hey Brad!" Nyx said, waving.

Brad waved in return, jogging up the steps. He had brown hair and hazel eyes like Anna with a slight frame. He had on dirty jeans and a T-shirt. "What are you guys up to?" he asked.

"Just hanging out," Anna said, a slightly annoyed tone to her voice. "Thought you were going fishing or something?"

Brad nodded. "Forgot my sleeping bag."

Nyx smiled at him. "That's an important thing to forget." She glanced at Anna, feeling her friend's ire toward her brother.

Anna rolled her eyes as Brad ducked inside. "There wasn't supposed to be anyone here with me all weekend," she said, irritation in her voice. "It was just supposed to be us girls."

Nyx shrugged. "Seems like he's trying to be on his way," she said easily. She leaned back in the swing. "Where did your parents go again?"

Anna shrugged as well, sighing deeply. "Florida or something?" she said flippantly. "I can never keep track of them."

Nyx shook her head, grinning to herself. Anna's parents loved to go on cruises and it seemed like they were gone every couple of months on one. Eventually Brad came back, waving to them as he jumped into his truck and drove away. Once they were finally alone, Nyx looked to Anna.

"So what's up with you and Seth?" she asked.

Anna grinned slightly, shrugging. "Oh, you know."

Nyx shook her head, feeling confused. "No, I don't know," she said slowly. She watched her friend blush. "I'm not the one with the boyfriend."

"Everything is great!" Anna gushed. "He's perfect." She waved her hand. "Although, he has been kinda pissed at Jet lately."

"Really?" Nyx asked. That wasn't a surprise to her at all. She was under the impression that Seth was nice to Jet just because they were family.

"Yeah," Anna said. "He hasn't been coming home and Seth said he's been shirking his job and stuff."

Nyx frowned. "Really?" she said, surprised. "Why?"

Anna shrugged. "Seth thinks he's having some kind of quarter-life crisis or something." She frowned disapprovingly. "He said Jet goes home with a new girl every night and he's been over at that new club down the road."

Nyx rolled her eyes. "Why are men so stupid?" she asked.

Anna shrugged again. "I don't know," she said. "But I'm glad I got a good one."

Nyx smirked at her friend. "Lucky jerk."

Anna giggled. "Come on," she said, jumping to her feet and leading the way inside. "My mom made some frozen meals for us to eat before we head out."

Nyx followed her quickly, praying it was corn casserole. Anna's mom made the best corn casserole she'd ever tasted.

The night was hot as Nyx watched out the window of Anna's Mazda. Her heart was beating double-time as she sat there, listening to Anna sing the songs on the radio. She was so nervous to see Randy and she hoped she looked nice. She'd worn her favorite denim skirt and a red top with the new boots her aunt had bought for her. She felt slightly underdressed, especially since her red blouse dipped lower than she would have liked in the front, but Anna assured her it looked great.

Her blonde hair was down and loose, the night wind catching it as they finally arrived at Dirty Harry's and parked. Nyx tried to smooth her curls from her face, Anna at her elbow.

"I'm soooo excited!" Anna said, catching her arm. "I wonder what Randy's got planned for tonight!"

Nyx grinned and shrugged. "I don't know," she said softly as they waited in line. She handed her ID to the bouncer. "Hey Benny."

He looked up at her, nodding his chin in greeting. "Nyx." He handed her ID back and Nyx stepped inside.

The music was pulsing through the club, which was packed with people. Nyx glanced over at Anna, who led the way to the back of the room, where their normal table was. They both glanced up when a shadow loomed over them.

"Hey baby!" Anna said. She caught Seth around the neck, kissing him.

Nyx watched as he smiled down at her. She waved when he looked up, unable to hear his greeting over the music.

Seth caught Anna's hand, leading them to a table. "You girls want anything to drink?" he asked.

Nyx shook her head, watching as Anna told him what she wanted. Once Seth walked away, Nyx stood slowly, leaning over the table. "I'm going to look for Randy."

Anna nodded, taking out her lip gloss and busying herself with applying it.

Nyx pushed her way through the crowd around the bar, coming to the edge of the first dance floor. She leaned against the railing as she watched the dancers, wondering if Randy was among them. She was fairly certain she'd seen everyone go around at least once, when she recognized a tall, dark-haired figure leading a girl through the throng.

Nyx paused, watching an easy grin slide across Jet's face as he twirled his partner. He made it look simple and effortless, and she'd never seen him so relaxed before. She realized she was staring when he happened to glance up, their eyes meeting. Nyx quickly averted her gaze, feeling her cheeks turn red with embarrassment.

The song wound to an end and Nyx walked around the railing as the dancers began to trickle off the floor while new ones moved in to dance to the next song. Her eyes were still searching for Randy, and she was surprised when she felt someone behind her, a hand catching her around her waist.

"You look like you're waiting for someone."

Nyx looked up quickly, surprised to see Jet smirking down at her. "Uh, yeah," she said quickly, trying to step away from him. "Just looking for Randy."

"Do you dance?" Jet asked.

Nyx forced down a grimace. "Sometimes," she said slowly. There was a schmoozing air about him that Nyx didn't like.

Jet led her toward the floor without Nyx realizing her feet were moving. "Then go around with me."

Nyx drew a steadying breath as she let him take her hands, leading her in a two-step. His lead was easy to follow, and Nyx noticed that he had a rather smooth posture, much like a ballroom dancer. His step never wavered as he turned her around the floor.

"So how have you been?" Nyx asked, feeling her face turning red. She was super uncomfortable, especially since his eyes hadn't left her face.

"Fine," he said shortly. He pushed her away, spinning her in an expert move before pulling her back into his arms. "You?"

Nyx shrugged, feeling dizzy. "Can't complain, I guess." She turned her head, flinching as a couple who clearly couldn't dance came barreling toward them. She was surprised when Jet pushed her forward, making their escape feel effortless with his simple move. Nyx looked up at him, feeling impressed. "Where did you learn to dance like that?"

Jet smirked at her grin. "It was something we were taught in school," he said easily. "Dancing was a requirement."

"Oh," Nyx's eyes widened curiously. "So do you ballroom dance?"

Jet shrugged. "I do whatever," he said. His smirk widened. "Mostly just go with the flow."

Nyx could feel a smile pulling at her face. This was a person she didn't recognize. He seemed completely different from the guy she'd sat next to on his birthday back in March. She almost thought she might like him now that he was opening up. She let him twirl her again, catching his arm as he pulled her back to him.

"Anna said you've been out of town lately," Nyx said, watching his face. "Have you been back home?"

Jet shook his head, letting his eyes shift away as he steered her through the crowd. "No, just some places nearby." His brow furrowed slightly and Nyx thought she might have said the wrong thing.

"Where did you go then?" she asked timidly.

Jet's eyes shifted down to her, his lips pressed together. "Just away on business," he said shortly. "I had things to see to."

Nyx frowned slightly, feeling shut down. "Gotcha," she said. She glanced away, hating how awkward it felt.

Maybe he hadn't changed at all. "Well, seems like you're adjusting to life here in the States."

Jet nodded slightly. "It has its moments," he said. He spun her one last time as the song ended before leading her to the side.

Nyx wasn't sure if there was something he intended to say, because he lingered beside her for a moment, glancing at her. "Thanks for the dance," she said finally.

Jet nodded. He inclined his head then, his eyes softening slightly. "Can I buy you a drink?" he asked. He pushed his shaggy black hair from his face.

Nyx shook her head, feeling her cheeks heat with a blush. "Oh, no," she said quickly. "I don't drink, remember?"

Jet leaned against the railing. "That surprises me," he said airily. His demeanor had shifted suddenly, that schmoozing confidence about him again.

"Why?" she asked, feeling goaded. She didn't like the way he smirked, taunting her.

"Your friend drinks like a fish," he said, flashing a small grin. "I assumed you would, too."

Nyx narrowed her eyes at him. "We're friends, not clones," she said, feeling irritated. She crossed her arms. "Besides, you told me you didn't drink either."

Jet shrugged then, a pleased smirk coming to his face. "I assumed you weren't drinking at the bonfire because you were chasing that boy." He seemed surprised she would remember such a minute detail. "But tastes change." He let his eyes drift over her. "Mine have."

Nyx folded her arms more tightly, feeling violated. "You're gross!" she snapped. She turned away from him as he rolled his eyes.

"Nyx, wait," he said quickly, catching her elbow.

Nyx turned to face him, pulling her arm from his grasp. He didn't seem particularly bothered by her anger. "I was hoping you'd become normal," she said, aggravation in her voice. "But Anna was right about you."

Jet arched a brow, his eyes guarded. "And what did she say that was right about me?" he demanded.

Nyx scowled. "She said that you've been hooking up with a bunch of different girls," she said quickly. "No doubt you're some misogynistic asshole who thinks we're all the same!"

Jet crossed his arms. "I think it's super awesome that you know me based on hearsay from your friend," he said mockingly.

Nyx's scowl darkened. "Don't talk to me, you pig!" she snapped. She stormed away from him, pushing her way back to the table where she'd left Anna. She didn't like this at all.

The rest of the night was lame.

Nyx eventually found Randy, but he was snockered from drinking with his cousin, and he stumbled through every dance he asked her to join him in. Anna was glued to Seth's side and the Rogers twins were out of town with their parents, so they weren't even there to cheer her up. By the end of the night, Nyx had spent more time sitting at the table by herself than dancing like she'd wanted to. It especially irked her when she'd see Jet leading another oblivious girl around the floor.

Nyx thought the night couldn't get any worse when Jet appeared through the crowd, walking straight toward her. She scowled and leaned back in the booth when Jet slid across from her. "That seat is taken."

"Yeah, by my butt." Jet arched a brow at her, leaning back and resting his arm across the back of the seat.

Nyx rolled her eyes, looking away. She couldn't believe this.

"You should be out there dancing with that guy," Jet said. He was watching Randy, who was stumbling through another dance with a girl Nyx knew from class.

"Uh, yeah," Nyx said, feeling her face darken. "No thanks."

"I'd ask you to dance, but I'd hate for you to think I'm being misogynistic," Jet said. His eyes were daring her to challenge him with a comeback.

Nyx faced him, hating the smugness he was exuding. "I'd rather sit here the rest of the night by myself."

Jet smirked to himself and shook his head. "Look, can't we just agree to disagree?"

Nyx crossed her arms tightly. "I don't know," she said haughtily. "Seems like you're only asking me to dance because you ran out of new partners." She was really confused by him. What happened to the awkwardness, and where did this asshole come from?

Jet rolled his eyes. "Please." He smirked cockily. "I just got tired of having my toes stepped on." He looked over at her, his eyes appraising. "I like a girl who knows where her feet are."

Nyx frowned at him, feeling how hot her face was. She wasn't sure if it was a fluster or anger. "Sorry," she said shortly. "These feet aren't moving anymore tonight." She wondered if the culture shock had finally worn off for him. Maybe he had no redeeming qualities after all.

"Oh, come on," Jet said, offering a grin. He leaned forward. "You come here to dance, right? So dance with me."

Nyx glanced out across the floor. She wanted to retort that she'd rather dance with a broom handle, but she wasn't having fun anymore. It sucked to sit here and watch everyone else be happy. She looked back to Jet, sighing shortly. "Fine!" she snapped. "But only one dance."

Jet's smirk widened and he moved to his feet. He didn't say anything as he watched her begrudgingly slide from the booth and follow him to the floor. He offered a hand, which she took bitterly, letting him lead her on the floor.

Nyx let her hand rest against his bicep and turned her eyes away from his face. She tried to keep a frown on her face, but she couldn't maintain it as her spirits began to lift. She drew a calming breath when he spun her.

"It's about time you loosened up," Jet commented.

Nyx looked up at him, forcing a frown. "What does that mean?"

"Your movements are stiff when you're mad," he said, holding her gaze.

"Hn." Nyx turned her eyes away. "It's weird that you can tell that."

Jet shrugged. "It's not that weird."

Nyx looked at him. "Is that something you learned from your dance training?"

"Military," Jet said absently. He turned his eyes away from her face, his jaw tightening. What on Earth had possessed him to tell her that?

"Oh?" Nyx said curiously. "You were in the military?" She was surprised when Jet pushed her away in a spin, barely maintaining sync with the song.

"Was," he said shortly. "Not anymore."

"What branch?" Nyx probed. She stiffened when he turned his eyes on her, a scowl pulling at his face.

"It doesn't matter," he said brusquely. "It was a long time ago."

Nyx looked away, pressing her lips together tightly, anger welling inside her. "Sorry. Forgive me for trying to be personable."

Jet smirked then. "Forgiven."

Nyx sighed as she let him lead her around one more time before the song ended. She pulled her hands from his. "Thanks for the dance," she said, starting away from him.

"Where are you going?" Jet asked, stepping in front of her to stop her. The charm had returned to his face, as if he'd never been irritated with her at all. "You can't just ditch me."

Nyx crossed her arms. "I'm not dancing with you anymore," she clipped. "You can't be annoyed one second and fine the next." He had to be bipolar or something.

Jet sighed. "Would it help if I apologized?"

Nyx narrowed her eyes at him. "Would it be genuine?"

Jet offered a coy smirk.

"I'll take that as a no." Nyx sighed, looking away. She weighed her options. If she turned him down, he'd probably never leave her alone. "Fine."

Jet held out his hand once more.

Nyx drew a sharp breath as the song changed to an easy waltz beat, and Jet turned her to start her onto the dance floor. The momentum of the reverse forced her into Jet's chest, her hand bracing over his heart. Jet's hand was pressed against the small of her back and he threaded his fingers against hers. Nyx tried to draw an even breath as she realized how close his face was to hers.

His lead was gentle and smooth, and Nyx could feel a sweat forming on her brow. She couldn't bring her eyes to meet his, his scent engulfing her. She was flustered as he steered her away from an obnoxiously drunk couple, pressing her tighter against him. Every movement was confident and easy, and Nyx realized he was using dance to try to seduce her.

Her heart lurched at the thought, making her tense. How was that even possible?

"Something wrong?" Jet asked, his voice soft in her ear.

Nyx shook her head quickly. "No," she managed, her voice breaking slightly.

Jet smirked lightly. "Then why are you so nervous?"

Nyx made the mistake of looking up at him then. He was watching her with his dark eyes, his face so close to hers she could smell his breath. Up close he was beautiful, his gaze a trap from which she couldn't pull herself. Soft strands of dark hair were falling across his forehead, just tempting her fingers to touch them.

Nyx felt her stomach turning in knots. Was this how the other girls felt when they were tangled in his web? Nyx thought she would drown in his eyes, but then she was roughly jolted, someone colliding heavily into her back.

"Oh my God, sorry!"

Nyx glanced over her shoulder, drawing a ragged breath. A brunette was giggling with her friend, who she was trying to dance with in lieu of a boyfriend. They were awkwardly holding hands as they shuffled away.

"Are you okay?" Jet asked, drawing her gaze.

Nyx nodded quickly. "Yeah," she said. The song was thankfully ending, and she pulled away from him, running her sweating palms across her skirt. "I, uh, I gotta go."

Jet frowned as he drifted off the floor behind her. "Go where?" he asked.

Nyx shook her head, trying to reel in her thoughts. "I'm just tired," she quickly. "I gotta go home." She walked quickly toward the exit, feeling Jet trailing behind her.

"Hold on!" Jet said. "Didn't you come with your friend?"

Nyx winced, cursing under her breath. She turned and walked past him, twisting around him so that she didn't touch him. "Listen, just leave me alone, okay?"

"What did I do wrong?" Jet asked.

"I just need to go," Nyx said. Her eyes were scanning the crowd, looking for Anna. She caught sight of Seth's curly brown hair, and she pushed through the crowd toward him. She could see Anna standing beside him and she increased her pace. "Anna!"

Anna turned shakily, her brown eyes dull. "Hey!" she said, her smile too bright. Her voice was slurred slightly.

Nyx paused, catching her as Anna threw her arms around her.

"You know you're my best friend, right?" Anna breathed, the smell of alcohol on her breath.

Nyx forced a laugh. "Yes," she said. "And you're mine." She looked up at Seth, who shrugged. "Listen, I think we need to get you home."

Anna frowned. "Because I'm too drunk?"

Nyx nodded. Jet was right. Anna did drink like a fish.

"You should let Nyx drive you," Seth said, pressing his hand against her back.

Anna looked up at him. "Why can't I go with you?"

Seth smiled gently. "You and Nyx planned to spend the weekend together."

Anna nodded. "Okay."

Nyx felt relief streak through her as she caught Anna's arm.

"I'll see you later, baby!" Anna said, kissing Seth when he leaned down to her. A big, dopey smile was on her face as Nyx led her to the door. "Bye!"

Nyx rolled her eyes as they staggered to the front door. She didn't really pay attention to Anna's drunk ramblings as they made it to the car. Her brain was in a million different places as she strapped Anna in. She finagled Anna's keys from her and slid into the driver's seat to start the car.

"Can we play some music?" Anna asked, her head lolling against the headrest.

"Sure." Nyx absently switched on the radio. A pop song was playing, and Anna reached over to turn it up.

The music was white noise as Nyx got lost in her thoughts and the road. She couldn't believe what had happened. Had Jet really been trying to put the moves on her? Why? And why had she found herself falling under his spell?

He was rude and obnoxious and undeniably cute.

Nyx shook her head, trying to dislodge the thought. There was something seriously wrong with her if she thought anything about Jet was attractive. She tried to ignore the way her mind remembered the smell of his cologne. Once she got to Anna's house, she helped her friend inside and to lie on the couch. She eased herself into an armchair, watching as Anna fell asleep.

She couldn't have slept even if she hadn't been worried about Anna aspirating in her sleep. Her mind was too chaotic, roiling with her feelings. She sighed, relaxing in anticipation of a long few hours.

$$\sim 18 \sim$$

Lucky Community College.

Wednesday, June 1, 2011.

NYX SIGHED AS SHE plopped down into her car. She let her hands rest against the steering wheel, feeling exhausted and defeated. She stared across the parking lot at the building where the computer lab was. Inside she knew that a handful of lucky students were getting psyched up for their first assignment. It hurt to know that she wasn't one of them.

She'd submitted a paper and had really hoped she'd be a shoo-in, but the program could only take five, and she hadn't been one of those five. She drew a slow breath as she fought to keep her emotions in check. The disappointment was enough to make her want to cry. But that wouldn't do.

Nyx pulled herself together as she put the key in her car to start it. She jumped when a knock sounded on her passenger window. She looked up sharply. She was surprised to see the editor-in-chief waving at her. She rolled down her window. "What's up, Mr. Johnson?"

He smiled at her. He was older, with blond hair and brown eyes. "Sorry to startle you," he said quickly. "But I wanted to tell you I really liked your piece."

Nyx offered a smile. "Uh, thanks," she said slowly.

"I just wanted you to know that there is a class in the fall semester that I think you would really like," he said. "I think it would be great to help you and I'd love to see you submit a paper again for the winter break internship."

Nyx felt surprise on her face. "Really?" She grinned. "That would be awesome."

Mr. Johnson nodded. "We've got a new professor," he said. "Dr. Sophia Armand. She's supposed to be one of the best." He grinned mischievously. "She graduated from Harvard."

"Wow," Nyx said, impressed.

Mr. Johnson nodded. "She's got great references," he said. "So look into her class."

Nyx nodded. "Will do." She watched as Mr. Johnson stepped back and waved, turning to go back inside. The crushing feelings she'd felt before were lifting with the hope of her new lead. She wanted more than anything to get into Dr. Armand's class.

19

The Alvar Residence.

Friday, July 1, 2011.

JET DREW A SLOW BREATH as he ran his hand across his mouth. He released the dead animal in his hands, listening to it fall heavily to the ground. He looked around the woods, the summer night hot and still. Every time he came out here, he felt a crawling feeling, like he was being watched. He didn't like it. It didn't make him feel any better to know that there were still enemies out there, waiting for the right time to strike.

The night of the new moon was the hardest for him. He was at his most vulnerable, the *fax* swirling strongly inside him. The binding curse was at its weakest, and one misstep could mean death. Not death for him, but death for anyone around him. If he couldn't gain control of the *fax*, there was no telling when it would be subdued. Blood soaked the runes and solidified the curse, but animal blood wasn't strong. It didn't bind the way that blood of a person did, even an Inerse.

Jet stepped slowly away from the animal's body, letting his aura fan around him. He didn't detect anyone nearby, but that didn't ease the crawling feeling. He made his way slowly back to Seth's house. None of the distractions that this world had to offer could make his mind forget about the danger that loomed over them.

He felt unprepared and nervous as he thought about it now.

Nyx was just a child. She didn't have any control over herself or her behaviors, as was evident by the night that she had danced with him. He knew it wasn't fair, but he enjoyed toying with her; and she'd had no idea. She hadn't been able to resist.

They weren't ready, and at this pace, they never would be.

Jet sank to sit on the railing around the porch, looking up at the moonless sky. He didn't know if he could keep Nyx safe. He didn't know if he could keep her alive, or even himself. He didn't know what waited on the other side, but he knew it wouldn't be simple.

He closed his eyes, letting his thoughts drift back to a time when things were simple. The darkness was a comfort, reminding him of the blackness of the cell he'd sat in for so long. That wasn't simple. Not even remotely. He'd been constantly plagued by his failures and thoughts of revenge, forced to sit without any opportunity to appease his burning need.

The simplest time in his life had been when he knew his purpose. When he'd walked among his soldiers, knowing his enemies and how to destroy them. He'd known where his place was and he'd followed his orders to the letter, without any deviation. He'd never had to do much thinking for himself. That had been simple. Following orders was simple. And it had been fulfilling for a time.

Jet knew he couldn't go back to that now. He could never be a puppet ever again. He would rather die first and take as many of the bastards from his former life as possible with him.

The Abandoned Yand Residence.

The thirteenth day of summer,
905th year of the reign of King Paraximus.

Friday, July 1, 2011, Earth Time.

"H e's weak." Paraximus smoothed stray hairs from his eyes. "I have been watching him. His curse is poorly bound by the blood of animals."

Sophia nodded, watching King Paraximus in the mirror that hung in the hallway of the abandoned house. He looked terrible, with dark circles under his eyes and his skin ashen. "What would you have us do?"

"It is not time," Paraximus said slowly, drawing a haggard breath.

Sophia knew that catching Jet at a weak moment would be the only way to defeat him, but it wouldn't be easy to catch him. She knew that he was aware of their presence, despite the fact that he didn't know their faces, and he would not allow himself to wait too long to feed the binding curse.

"How much longer must we wait?" Sophia asked, an edge to her voice. She was tired of waiting. She wanted to kill him and go home.

Paraximus grinned slightly. "Patience, child," he said easily. "We must be patient." He glanced away. "There will be time." His eyes darkened. "You will feel his blood on your hands in due time."

Sophia pushed down a scowl. She didn't like that answer. She leaned back as she looked at her king. "I believe we have discovered his weakness."

Paraximus arched a brow. "You have found his target?"

Sophia grinned darkly. "A girl," she said slowly. "A golden-haired girl."

Paraximus' brow rose in surprise. "A girl, eh?" he asked darkly. "My son has always been weak when it comes to females."

Sophia smirked. That might be helpful.

"And what is special about this girl?" Paraximus demanded.

Sophia lifted a smooth print, turning it so he could see. "She bears a certain resemblance . . ."

Paraximus' dark eyes widened, his brow creasing with rage. "The lost Princess." His eyes turned back to Sophia. "She's been there this whole time?" Disbelief was in his voice.

Sophia nodded. "She's poorly guarded," she said softly, looking at the picture in her hand. "Jet is the only barrier between us and her."

"You will vet her for me," Paraximus said, his eyes darkening with desire. "If she is truly the offspring of Liana, she will be strong."

Sophia frowned. "You would bring her into your arsenal?"

"Don't tell me that you cannot weave your blood magic over her," Paraximus said, a challenge in his voice. "If she is powerful, then we could use her to destroy Liana."

Sophia smirked. It seemed particularly cruel to command the Princess to kill her own family.

"You must get to her," Paraximus said.

"I have a plan in motion, Highness," Sophia said, pleased. "I have arranged to become a teacher at the school she attends. I will observe her and when the time is right, I will bend her to your will."

Paraximus nodded. "If she cannot be controlled, you will destroy her."

Sophia bowed her head. "Yes, Your Highness."

"Do not fail me."

Paraximus yanked the door to the temple open hard, letting it slam against the wall with a bang. Mara was standing silently on the dais in front of Daya's statue, watching him blankly.

"Where is she?" Paraximus demanded, his voice booming around the room. "Where is Daya?"

Mara's lips pulled back to bare a snarl. "You will have some respect, King Paraximus," she said evenly. "Daya does not obey mortals, especially one whose life is bound to her."

"Why didn't she show me this?" Paraximus continued, rage creasing his face. "Why didn't she tell me the girl was alive?"

Mara glanced toward the statue. "You do not trust her plan, Idiot King," she said tauntingly. "If you fail, she will allow your enemies to claim you." She stepped down from the dais. "Now then, it is the night of Deimos."

Paraximus snarled at her. "Do not presume to lay your filthy hands on me!" he snapped. He stepped toward the dais, where a bowl was sitting on the floor, a knife inside it. Paraximus picked it up, drawing it slowly over the palm of his hand. He didn't wince as he squeezed, a stream of his blood falling into the water in the bowl.

The water rippled, turning black. A sudden, hot wind filled the temple, the scent of death in the air. Paraximus drew a slow breath, feeling strength fill him. He looked up, seeing Daya's stone eyes fixed on him.

"Prepare your warriors," Mara said, looking up at Daya. "Our Goddess will grant them her favor when it is time."

"You've been saying that for months," Paraximus growled. "When will it be time!?"

Mara's mouth quirked. "You will know, King Paraximus." She took a step closer. "But do not expect it to be handed to you. You will work for what you desire."

Paraximus scowled. When had he not struggled for what he wanted?

— 21 —

The Williams' Estate, Lucky, Texas.

Saturday, October 29, 2011.

THE NIGHT WAS BITTERLY COLD, especially for Texas weather. The wind whipped fiercely through the trees, threatening to topple the hairdo Nyx had begged her aunt to do for her. She drew a slow breath as she looked out the window at the massive house before her. It was lit brightly with lights around the trees and in the windows. It was the most beautiful thing Nyx had ever seen, and it made butterflies stir in her stomach.

"Here's your cover, sweetheart."

Nyx blinked, turning to take her silver wrap from her aunt. "Thanks Aunt Dee," she said, hoping she couldn't hear the nervousness in her voice. As far as her aunt knew, she was just coming to Randy's Halloween party with all of her friends. Nyx had left out the part about Randy finally asking her to come as his date. She hadn't wanted to jinx it.

Her aunt smiled slightly. "Call me when you're ready to come home."

Nyx nodded and opened the door, bracing against the cold. Her aunt stopped her before she stepped out, adjusting the gold tiara in her hair.

"There," she said.

Nyx smiled and took a deep breath, hefting the thick skirt of her gown from the front seat of her aunt's car, smoothing it the best she could. "How do I look?"

Her aunt's smile softened. "Wonderful," she said. "Just like a real princess."

Nyx returned her grin before closing the door and waving goodbye. Despite her nervousness, she couldn't wait to see the inside of the Williams' home. She walked slowly up the wide steps, seeing that a doorman greeted her.

"Good evening, miss," he said, opening the door for her and smiling brightly. He was wearing a black tuxedo and a black mask.

Nyx smiled at him. "Good evening." She lifted her hand, pressing nervously at the gold mask she'd picked out for the occasion. It felt strange and almost embarrassing to be wearing it in public.

"May I take your things, miss?" the doorman asked, motioning to a closet where he was hanging coats and purses.

"Uh, sure," Nyx said, handing him her cover and her little wristlet. "Thank you."

The doorman nodded with a smile. "Please have a good time."

The foyer of the mansion was brightly lit and warm, with cheesy Halloween skeletons and pumpkins decorating the way to the main room, where the sounds of a party emanated. A large staircase wound up to her right, the mahogany banister gleaming brightly. The steps were marble and smooth, with a straw scarecrow sitting on the bottom step. Nyx wondered what was on the second floor, but she pushed forward, seeing people milling in the hall in front of her. She knew she was a bit late, so she followed the noise.

Ahead was another open room, with large windows that overlooked the backyard, where a pool sparkled under floodlights. The patio and area around the pool was decorated with jack-o'-lanterns, which were flickering in the wind. She turned to her right when another hallway opened up, seeing the couple she was following heading into a huge ballroom. She gasped softly as she came closer, the sound of music becoming loud. The room was filled with people in poufy dresses and tuxedos.

Nyx grinned, watching the party. Everyone was wearing a mask, much like hers. She remembered thinking it was a really neat idea to have a masquerade ball. It seemed like so much fun. After a moment, she brushed a few looping curls that hung from her hairdo over her shoulder, scanning the room for Randy. She hoped she would recognize him in all the chaos.

Nyx was hopeful that after all this time Randy had finally taken her hints. This was the first time he'd invited her out as his date. She really hoped it wouldn't be the last.

The talk around town was that Randy Williams' parents got rich when they found oil on their property. Randy was born shortly after their windfall, so he didn't know anything different than the luxury he was accustomed to. He drove a fancy car and had expensive clothes and tastes. Nyx never thought he would really be interested in her, since he seemed to keep putting her off. She'd given up on him ever asking her out. So she was surprised when he asked her to come. Of course, it seemed like he invited all of the people they'd gone to high school and college with, so she might have come anyway, but it was thrilling to be here as his date.

A DJ was set up on the far end of the room. He turned down the lights and started a slow-dance song. Couples around her pushed to the dance floor, swaying gently in time to the music, but Nyx scanned the crowd.

"Nyx!"

She turned quickly, surprised by the voice calling her name. A grin slid across her face when she recognized her friend, despite the cat mask on her face. "Anna! I didn't know you were coming."

Anna hugged her, lifting her mask from her face. "Please, you think I'd miss out on this?" She laughed. "You look amazing, by the way."

Nyx glanced down at the golden dress her aunt had helped her pick out. It had been a lot of nothing at first, but her aunt was an amazing seamstress, and she'd made the dress more gorgeous than Nyx could have ever imagined. It had even been her aunt's idea to use some sort of adhesive to stick the mask to her face and draw large, golden designs around it. Nyx didn't feel like herself at all when she'd seen her reflection.

"Thanks." She looked at Anna's black dress. It was beautiful, too, with glittering tulle and sleek polyester waves. It accentuated Anna's pale features and dark brown hair. "You look amazing, too."

Anna grinned, catching her hand. "Have you seen Randy?"

Nyx shook her head. "I just got here," she said, letting Anna pull her down the hallway. "We were running late. Aunt Dee got carried away with the face paint."

Anna shook her head. "Naw, you look great." She grinned. "Sort of mysterious, even." She caught Nyx's hand. "He's been waiting for you. I saw him a bit ago when he asked where you were."

Nyx felt her heart catch as Anna led the way down the hallway back toward the foyer and into the massive dining room. The chairs had been removed from the room and a snack buffet and drinks had been set up on the table. Several people were manning the table, and Nyx assumed they were the hired help for the evening. Nyx wasn't sure how she missed this when she came in, as the room was full of people and chatter.

"Randy!"

Nyx felt her chest clench as Anna waved at him across the room. He smiled brightly when he saw them, excusing himself from the guests he was speaking to and walking toward them. Nyx could feel her face turning red. He looked so handsome in his prince outfit, his sandy-blond hair ruffled just enough to be fashionable. They had spoken about what they could wear so that they would match.

"Princess," he said teasingly, sweeping her a bow. "So glad you could make it." He leaned in to hug her. A grin pulled at his lips. "I've been waiting for you."

Nyx felt her face flush darker. "Well, I'm here," she said meekly.

"Do you ladies want something to drink?" he asked generously.

Anna shook her head. "Actually, I need to use the ladies' room." She glanced at Nyx. "I'll catch you two in a bit."

Nyx really wished her friend wouldn't leave, but Anna had a knack for disappearing and leaving her in uncomfortable situations.

Randy shrugged lightly as he watched her go before looking to Nyx. "Well, drink?"

Nyx nodded. "Sure," she said, hoping doing something would ease the embarrassment his presence brought her. She followed him to the table, watching as he handed her a glass of punch. She lifted it to her lips, taking a sip. A bitter aftertaste hit her, and she fought not to grimace. "What is this?"

"Sangria," Randy said. "Our chef made it for the party with the best wine we have." He seemed rather proud of this fact, missing the way Nyx grimaced slightly.

"Oh." She held the glass in her hand, wondering where she could ditch it. She didn't really want to drink here, especially not if her aunt was picking her up. Plus, the drink was very bitter and not at all something she enjoyed. She forced a smile. "Thank you."

Randy nodded obliviously, offering her his arm. "Would you like to dance with me?"

Nyx brightened. "Yes, definitely."

Randy was very pleased with her answer, escorting her from the dining room back to the ballroom. The DJ was playing country songs that were easy to dance to, and Randy took her hands, leading her effortlessly onto the floor in a two-step.

"So how is your paper coming?" he asked. "I'm pretty sure mine will be awful."

"Oh, you know," Nyx said absently, grinning as he turned her around the floor. "Boring." She was trying not to think about the term paper that would be due in their class on Monday. She was supposed to be arguing the merits of George Orwell's *Animal Farm*, but she had been struggling as well. "It's hard to talk about government run by pigs."

Randy shared her grin as he twirled her away and back into his arms. His eyes followed her movements, his handsome face softening. "Well, I'm glad you could put away your books for one night," he said.

Nyx felt her heart skip a beat at the way he was watching her. "Me too," she said, her face heating with a blush. She looked away from him, at the beautiful ballroom. "Your house is amazing."

Randy drew a quick breath, following her gaze. "I guess so," he said thoughtfully. He grinned when Nyx looked up at him dubiously. "I'm used to it, so I guess I don't see it the way everyone else does."

"Oh." Nyx kept her eyes trained away, watching the people around them. Her hands felt sweaty against the fabric of Randy's blazer. She wondered if he was as nervous as she was.

She was mildly grateful when the song ended and he escorted her from the dance floor. "Thanks," she said as he released her hand. She drew a deep breath, looking down as she smoothed her skirt. "So, there's something I wanted to ask you."

Randy leaned against the wall, an easy smile on his face. "Anything."

Nyx looked down, twirling the fabric of her dress nervously. "I was thinking that maybe you might like to—"

"Hey man!"

Nyx looked up, seeing a man appear beside Randy, lifting an ugly horse-faced mask as he clapped a hand on Randy's shoulder.

"Dude, Joe!" Randy said, grinning as he caught Joe's hand to shake it. "It's about time you got here."

Nyx recognized Randy's cousin, Joe. She watched as they exchanged words for a moment. She didn't particularly care for Joe. He was loud and crude and had a bit of a drinking problem.

"So Alan brought a bottle of SoCo!" Joe said excitedly. "We should do some shots."

Randy's eyes brightened, but then he looked at Nyx. "Do you mind?"

Nyx offered a smile. "I'll catch you in a bit." She didn't want to have him begging her for permission. That would be awkward. She felt the smile slip from her face as she watched him and Joe leave. She grimaced once they were gone from sight, disappointed. She knew it was his party and he had to play host, but he could have at least let her finish asking him to come dancing with her and her friends before he ran off.

"Hey, Nyx!"

She glanced over her shoulder, feeling her spirits lift immensely when she saw Abigail and Melanie Rogers. In true twin fashion, they were wearing the same dress and mask, in different colors. Nyx hugged them both, glad to see them. "I forgot you guys were coming."

"Yeah," Abby said, acting slightly bored. "Mom and Dad know Randy's parents from the country club, so here we are." She seemed less than happy about it. Melanie rolled her eyes beside her sister, making Nyx giggle. Abby was the more forward of the two, and Melanie was much more meek and thoughtful. They balanced each other out perfectly.

"How have you been?" Melanie asked happily. "We missed you on Thursday."

Nyx smiled apologetically. "Sorry," she said. "Aunt Dee wanted 'girl time.'" She rolled her eyes. Thursdays were normally their night to go to Dirty Harry's in town to dance.

"Ours has been into that, too," Abby said, rolling her eyes. "I think it's whatever Pastor Ryan said a few weeks back."

Nyx recalled the pastor's message about family and cherishing your loved ones. It had been after the death of a long-time member. She was pretty sure that was what pushed her aunt, too.

Melanie agreed. "Our mom made us go shopping with her," she said, disgust in her voice.

Nyx laughed. "I'm sure that was so fun." She knew how the Rogers girls' mother was; kind and generous, but always needed that new, expensive thing.

"Yeah, no," Abby said, her nose wrinkling. "Mom tries on everything she sees. We spent the whole day in the store."

Nyx grimaced. "That sucks."

"But at least we got to pick out our costumes," Melanie said, unfurling a fan. She waved it, her auburn curls wafting over her shoulder.

Abby grinned. "True."

"You guys look great!" Nyx said, watching them fan themselves and feign to be bored.

"You too!" Abby said. She closed her fan and reached to touch the paint on Nyx's face. "Did your aunt do this?"

Nyx nodded. "She added all the beading to my dress, too."

Melanie sighed. "Your aunt is so amazing."

Nyx grinned. "Only when she's not forcing me to hang out with her." They shared a laugh before walking down to the dining room.

Nyx got a glass of water while Abby and Melanie got themselves some sangria. They chatted a bit more, lingering in the foyer with a few other guests. Nyx let her eyes shift around the room, trying to catch Anna. She was beginning to wonder where Anna had slunk off to, when she suddenly appeared, holding the arm of a guy in a mask. She was beaming up at him, and he was smiling down at her gently.

Nyx rolled her eyes. Anna had been annoyingly happy since she'd been seeing Seth. It was kind of cute though that he was wearing a dog mask to go with her cat mask.

Anna caught sight of them as she walked with him, her face brightening excitedly. "Hey guys!" she said, dragging him behind her. "Look who's here!"

Seth lifted his mask, his blue eyes flitting between Abby and Melanie as Anna reintroduced them. Nyx didn't know why, but she always felt her breath catch when he looked at her. Even the first time they'd met at the bonfire, she'd been a bit star-struck.

"Hey, Seth, how's it going?" she said, lifting a hand in a small wave.

Seth's polite smile lifted some into a grin. "Good," he said, holding his hand out to her. "How are you, Nyx?" He arched a brow when she took his hand. "Or should I say princess?" He kissed the back of her hand in a teasing manner.

Nyx felt embarrassed as she stared at him. "I'm fine," Nyx said, smiling nervously. She pulled her hand back quickly. "Good to see you again." She couldn't keep her eyes off him as Anna drew his attention, telling him something that Nyx didn't pay attention to.

Seth was seriously what airbrushed people looked like in real life. He looked like he'd come straight from a magazine cover and into Randy's house, especially in the suit he was wearing. He had perfectly smooth, creamy skin and soft brown curls that fell perfectly across his forehead. But his eyes were crazy; they were an electric blue that seemed to look through her. He was gorgeous, and it was so unfair that Anna had managed to snag him. After a moment, he excused himself to bring Anna something to drink.

"He is a total babe," Abby said, watching him intently as he walked away.

"I know," Anna gushed, a goofy smile pulling at her face.

"Where did you find him again?" Abby asked. Her eyes hadn't left Seth's backside. She and her sister had been on vacation overseas for most of the summer, and this was only the second time they'd really seen Seth.

Melanie elbowed her sister then, giving her a dirty look. "Stop ogling Anna's man," she said, mock-threateningly.

"Oh no, ogle away," Anna laughed. "I do." She turned to look at Nyx. "We met him at Dirty Harry's one night. He's a great guy. Right Nyx?"

Nyx blinked, her eyes shifting from Seth to Anna. She smiled. "I think he's really nice," she said. "And you guys have been attached at the hip all summer." She rolled her eyes as she looked to the twins. "It's disgusting."

Anna's face lit up with happiness, even with Nyx's ribbing. Nyx knew it was because she was glad to have her best friend's seal of approval. Anna turned to the twins. "He's got a cousin, too."

Nyx felt as if she deflated, feeling her shoulders sag. Just thinking about him made her feel exhausted and irritated. She wanted to start cussing, but she stopped herself by taking a sip of her water. She hadn't seen Jet in a while, mostly because she'd been avoiding him. He'd approached her on several different occasions while they were out, but she always made sure to have a backup to dance with. She didn't ever want to be caught in his snare again.

"Oh, I need to see him," Abby said eagerly. "Point me in his direction."

Anna turned slightly, nodding over her shoulder discreetly.

The girls turned their eyes toward the door. Nyx wasn't sure why she didn't notice him sooner. She felt her face darken as he turned toward them, a redheaded girl with him.

"Well my night is officially ruined," she said softly, drawing the other girls' attention as she sipped at her water again.

"Why?" Melanie asked softly. "You know him?"

Nyx felt a scowl pull at her face. "Yeah," she said. "His name is Jet." She turned away, unwilling to look at him as he leaned in to whisper in his date's ear. "He's a super douche."

Abby, Melanie, and Anna shared a look. "He's rubbed Nyx the wrong way since they first met," Anna said, shrugging. "He pissed her off a few months ago." She smirked then. "Nyx has had it out for him since."

"What?" Melanie asked, her brows raising in surprise. "Where were we?"

Nyx sighed. "Be happy you've never met him," she said. "He's a total player and conceited."

"Well, douche or not, he's still fine," Abby said, watching him carefully.

"Yeah, but he's an ass," Nyx said, disgust curling her lip. "It's like his only joy in life is pissing me off when he sees me. And that sort of cancels out any hotness points."

"You know it's probably just because he secretly likes you," Melanie said, clearly trying to be reassuring.

Nyx rolled her eyes. "I doubt that. Every time I see him, he's got a new girl on his arm."

Her friends tittered and giggled as he came closer, but Nyx's face was stuck in a scowl. Just like Seth, Jet was perfection in real life in his party clothes. He had the nicest-looking, shaggy black hair she'd ever seen, and his onyx eyes were like Seth's: they could pin you in place. Only, something about the way he looked at her always felt predatory. Even now, he made her feel super uncomfortable by just being in the room.

"Hey girls," he said. His dark eyes shifted to Nyx's face, making her cross her arms tightly. He smoothed a strand of pitch-colored hair from his face, his eyes taking in the twins for the first time. "Who are your friends?"

Abby grinned then, clearing smitten with him. "I'm Abigail," she said flirtatiously. She inclined her head. "This is my sister Melanie." Melanie didn't say anything, her eyes wide as if she was intimidated by his presence.

Jet's easy smirk pulled at his face. He obviously was going to say something to charm Abby, but Anna cleared her throat, interrupting him.

"Seth is over there," Anna said unceremoniously, pointing over her shoulder. Her brown eyes shifted to the redhead on Jet's arm. "He went to get a drink for me, like a good date."

Nyx was secretly grateful for Anna's quick thinking. She didn't want to spend any more time than necessary in his presence. But she also wanted to laugh at the look on his face. Clearly he wasn't used to being shut down like that. She had to take another sip of her water to stop the grin pulling at her lips.

Jet arched a brow. He looked like he would have a retort for her, but instead he turned to the redhead with him. "Why don't you stay here and make some new friends?" he asked sweetly. "I'll bring something to drink."

Nyx rolled her eyes as his date giggled lightly, clearly tangled in his web of bullshit. She felt even more disgusted when they kissed, drawing it out a bit longer than necessary.

Once they were done sucking each other's face, Jet turned to them. He moved toward the dining room, stepping between Nyx and the rest of the group so that he was facing her. His dark eyes were focused on her, that smirk still on his face as he paused slightly. "Be nice," he said quietly.

Nyx gave him a death glare, but didn't say anything, a million ugly comments swirling through her head. He'd certainly loosened up in the time that he'd been living here with Seth, but how could he go from being a rude, mean jerk to being a flirty and irritating jerk? She always chalked it up to culture shock.

She turned her eyes to the redhead after he was gone. "What's your name?" she asked kindly. "I'm Nyx, and this is Anna, Seth's girlfriend. And you've met the twins."

The redhead narrowed her eyes at them, lifting her perfectly manicured nails to look at them. "Cara," she said shortly. She flipped her straight red locks over her shoulder, putting a hand to her hip and looking away.

"Where are you from, Cara?" Anna asked. Cara definitely wasn't from Lucky. She looked too posh to be from around here. Nyx wondered where Jet had found her.

Cara turned her eyes on them, clearly put-out. "Listen," she snapped, "just because I'm standing here doesn't mean we're going to be buddy-buddy, okay?" She had bright green eyes that she turned on Abby to pin her with a glare, her voice dripping with hatred. "And I don't appreciate you trying to talk to my man."

Abby made a disgusted noise, turning away. "Bitch," she mouthed.

Nyx agreed silently with her, looking to Anna and Melanie, who seemed equally disgusted. "Let's go dance," Nyx said finally, trying to ease the tension.

"Great idea," Melanie said blandly. She caught her sister's arm, dragging her away. Abby looked like she was torn about whether she should do unkind things to Cara or not.

"I'll wait here for Seth," Anna said, watching her friends go. "Meet you in there."

Nyx nodded, following the twins back to the ballroom. She hated leaving Anna with Jet's stupid date, but she definitely didn't want to stand around with them. She pushed the encounter from her mind as they walked into the ballroom.

The lights were turned down, a strobe flashing around the room. The DJ had finally stopped playing slow songs and he was jamming some awesome club beats. Nyx followed her friends into the crowd, lifting her hands and smiling as they swayed and bumped to the music. She liked being in the middle of the floor, immersed by the other people around her. She didn't think of anything else as she had fun with her friends.

They danced for a long time before the DJ came over the mic. He said something about playing a special song for all the lovebirds out there, and Nyx and her friends stepped off the floor. Abby and Melanie were talking, but it was too loud for Nyx to hear what they were saying. She let her eyes scan the floor, seeing Anna and Seth dancing together. Anna was smiling so sweetly at Seth, who was gazing into her face. Nyx felt her heart twist. She wanted something like that one day.

As if on cue, Randy appeared, catching her around the waist. His blue eyes were bright and his face looked flushed, probably from drinking with Joe. "Dance with me?" he asked, smiling.

Nyx nodded excitedly. She took his hand as he led her in an easy step. She tried to hold his gaze as he led her around the floor, but embarrassment made her face flush and she would look away. She noticed, though, that he was smiling down at her, and she was smiling, too.

She laughed when he turned her in a circle, her dress fanning around her. The song was winding down to an end, and Randy pulled her toward him, pressing her against him. Nyx let her hands rest against his chest, feeling her heart fluttering. Her eyes shifted to his lips, and she knew this was it. She leaned in, letting her eyes close slightly, anticipating the feel of his lips on hers, when a body suddenly collided with her, knocking her into Randy.

Startled, she whipped her head around, a scowl on her face. Anger filled her as she saw Jet twirling Cara away. He mouthed an apology, but it was clearly fake as Cara laughed, her eyes narrowed spitefully. Nyx knew it was intentional. Jet was too good a dancer for that to have been a mistake.

"Are you okay?" Randy asked.

Nyx nodded, barely hearing him over the music. Her nose had collided with his chin, making her eyes well from the stinging pain. She let him lead her in another dance as the track shifted to a new song, but the moment was ruined. All she could think about was what an ass Jet was. And why was he here, anyway? Had he even been invited?

Finally, the song ended. Randy once again was pulled away by Joe and his friends to drink, leaving Nyx standing with her friends. She wondered if she would ever get a chance to ask Randy to go on a real date.

She could feel sweat on her brow, and she dabbed it away lightly. She frowned as she saw gold paint on her fingers, and she excused herself to find the bathroom so she could check her makeup.

The downstairs bathroom was occupied, but the doorman directed her to the upstairs bathroom. She was almost to the stairs when she saw Jet and Cara come down the hallway. Cara let go of his hand to go into the dining room. Nyx had barely put her hand on the banister when she caught Jet's eyes.

The smirk she hated pulled at his face as he walked toward her.

"What do you want?" she asked bitterly.

Jet held up his hands. "Apologies, little princess," he said teasingly. "Why do you hate me so much?"

Nyx narrowed her eyes at him, his new nickname annoying to her. "Lots of reasons. Where should I start?"

Jet leaned against the banister. "I just don't understand why we can't be civil," he said innocently. He inclined his head, his onyx eyes watching her.

Nyx could feel her mouth pull in a scowl. "I didn't think you were capable of being civil," she snapped. "Since your head's so far up your ass and all."

Jet's smirk widened. It was almost as if he enjoyed this. "Well, you know how it is," he said dismissively. He started to turn away. "Catch you later." He winked at her. "Gotta find my date."

Nyx wanted to slap him. She had tried to give him the benefit of the doubt when they first met, but she wasn't going to tolerate him anymore. He was always a royal ass to her for no reason. She didn't understand what the allure was. How could he have so many girls hanging on him? She was starting to think she was the only one he treated this way.

"Whatever," Nyx said finally, turning away. "Just stay away from me."

Jet snorted an amused laugh. "Whatever you wish, little princess." He bowed mockingly to her before walking away.

Nyx started up the steps, shaking her head. If it wasn't for Randy, she would have left the moment Jet walked in the door.

Despite wanting to murder Jet, she was in awe as she climbed the marble stairs. The mahogany banister was thick and smooth under her hand. The rest of the house was just as elegant as the first floor, save for huge paintings that hung on the walls. Nyx couldn't believe that people actually lived here. It looked like something out of a movie or a museum. She found the bathroom easily, and took a few minutes to dab at her makeup. She glanced at the clock on the wall, realizing for the first time how late it was getting. She guessed she'd need to call her aunt soon.

As she left the bathroom, curiosity began to pick at her. She began to wonder what was behind the other doors, remembering Randy had once told her that his parents had a large library, and there was nothing she wouldn't give to see the Williams' home library. She walked to the first door, pushing it open slowly. She blinked against the darkness, realizing it was Randy's bedroom. She felt like she was intruding, but she couldn't stop looking.

She pushed the door open more and flipped on the light. The room was huge, with a four-poster bed on one side and a huge, flat-screen TV on the opposite wall. Red satin sheets and a comforter were across the bed and a game station controller sat on the bedside table next to an alarm clock and a picture of Randy and his parents. A computer desk sat by the window, cluttered with books and papers, and double doors led out to a balcony that overlooked the backyard so that she could see the pool house beyond the pool. She expected that she would see clothes and other belongings laid out, but, like the rest of the house, it was spotless, save for some small trophies and other knick-knacks from Randy's childhood.

"What are you doing snooping around?"

Nyx jumped, surprised when she saw Randy standing in the doorway. "I'm sorry!" she said quickly, feeling mortified. She didn't intend to stay long, much less get caught. "I was looking for the bathroom?" She hoped her lie didn't sound too feeble.

Randy grinned softly. "You missed it a couple of doors ago." He tried to lean on the doorframe, swaying slightly.

Nyx returned his grin, stepping toward him. "Well, maybe that's not entirely the truth," she said quietly. "I thought I might catch a glimpse into the life of Randy Williams."

Randy laughed then, stepping toward her. Nyx could tell he was drunk from his glassy gaze and the stink of alcohol. "Am I interesting to you?" he asked.

Nyx shrugged, feeling a blush heat her cheeks. "That remains to be seen."

Randy caught her gently around the waist, pulling her toward him. "I doubt that," he said softly, his eyes shifting over her face. "It seemed like you were about to kiss me before we were interrupted."

Nyx felt her face flush darker. "Is that so?" she managed. She hadn't forgotten at all, and she knew what was coming as he put his hand against her cheek, tilting her head back. Her heart caught in her chest when he leaned down, pressing his lips against hers. She didn't know what to do at first.

Her legs felt like mush, so she knew running wasn't an option. She closed her eyes, trying to absorb every moment of this. Despite being so nervous, kissing him was exhilarating. His breath was hot on her mouth, tasting of whiskey. When he pulled away Nyx realized his hands were low on her back, pulling her body against his. Her whole body was trembling and she sucked in a shaky breath.

"I thought we should finish what we started," Randy said. He brushed a strand of golden hair from her face, his eyes traveling across her face.

Nyx realized her hands were on his arms, gripping his blazer tightly. "What is that, exactly?" she whispered.

Randy didn't say anything, leaning down to kiss her again. "I've wanted you for a long time, Nyx."

Nyx felt her heart catch again at his words. She gasped when he used his grip around her middle to turn her, pushing her against the wall. His kisses were soft and gentle at first, but now they were desperate and forceful. She felt a sinking feeling filling her stomach, the moment going from sweet to unsettling. She tried to push him away.

"What are you doing?" she whispered, fear streaking through her.

"Don't fight it . . ." Randy said, kissing her neck. His hands were traveling to places Nyx did not want them to go. "I know you want me, too."

Nyx shook her head, still trying to struggle out of his grasp. "Randy," she managed, pushing him away. "I'm sorry, but—"

Randy pressed her harder against the wall. "You don't have to pretend with me." The smell of the alcohol was pungent as he breathed in her face.

Nyx felt sick as his fingers found the zipper on her dress, fumbling to pull it. She pushed harder against him. "Stop!" she said, shoving his arms away.

Randy caught her wrists, looking into her eyes, and Nyx felt her blood run cold. "I want this."

"Well, I don't." Nyx twisted in his grasp, feeling tears sting her eyes. "Randy, stop!" She was trying to be commanding, but her voice came out weak and scared. She turned her eyes to the door, hoping desperately someone would appear. When she saw the empty hallway, she closed her eyes, feeling her heart in her stomach. She knew she had to fight back.

She turned her face away when he tried to kiss her again, wishing she could sink into the ground. When Randy persisted, she managed to free her arm, slapping him hard across the face. "Get off me!"

She gasped painfully when Randy caught her chin roughly, shoving her head against the wall. "You're going to wish you hadn't done that," he said fiercely, practically growling at her.

"Please," Nyx begged, "I don't want this." She gasped when Randy suddenly caught her hair in his fist, yanking her head back.

"That's too bad." His eyes were cruel as he looked at her. "Because I do. And I always get what I want." He kept a hold on her as he reached for the door, pushing it shut.

Nyx braced herself for the worst. She drew a ragged breath, willing any power to come to her rescue. Her heart was racing in her chest, and she closed her eyes tightly.

"Hey, is this the—whoa."

Nyx gasped, surprised when Randy let go of her. She opened her eyes, blinking away tears. Jet was standing in the doorway. His dark eyes were narrowed as he took in the situation. A scowl started to creep across his face as he realized what he'd walked into.

"Fuck off, man!" Randy said, a scowl on his face. He stepped toward the door, pushing it. "Wrong door."

"Like hell it is," Jet said, pushing the door easily, making Randy stagger back. He stepped into the room, catching Nyx's hand. Nyx was surprised when he pulled her toward him, his eyes never leaving Randy. "Did this asshat hurt you?"

Nyx shook her head, drawing a ragged breath.

"You're going to regret this!" Randy said then, his eyes blazing angrily. He looked to Nyx. "You better not leave with him."

Jet scoffed, stepping in front of Nyx. "She can do whatever she wants, starting with getting the hell away from you," he said darkly. "You're lucky I don't break every bone in your body."

Randy stepped toward Jet suddenly, fury on his face. He swung his fist.

Nyx pressed her hands over her mouth when Jet stepped back, avoiding Randy's blow easily. In a simple move, he'd caught Randy's hand and spun him, pinning his arm to his back and slamming him into the wall. Jet twisted his arm harder, causing Randy to make a pained sound. Nyx was horrified when she realized that Randy was bleeding from his nose.

"Jet!" Nyx gasped. She reached for his arm, grabbing his blazer. "Stop! He's just drunk!"

Jet's eyes shifted to her, narrowed in irritation. He seemed like he wouldn't ease up at first, but then his posture loosened some. "I don't ever want to see you around her again, understand?" Jet hissed darkly, pressing Randy's face into the wall.

Randy was whimpering in pain. He couldn't speak, only nodded his head lightly. His blood was dripping down his chin, soaking into the white fabric of his costume.

Jet didn't say anything as he roughly released Randy, pushing him backwards so he tripped onto his bed. "You should sober up and do something about that nose," he said shortly, closing the door behind him as he stepped into the hallway. He turned to Nyx, his onyx eyes shaded, as if he would berate her. He put his hand on her back, leading her down the hall, away from the noise of the party. "Are you sure you're okay?"

Nyx nodded quickly. "I'm fine." Her mind was spinning. She could feel tears still pressing against her eyes. She couldn't believe what was happening. When did Randy become such a creep? She tried to blink from her stupor, looking at Jet. "What are you doing up here?"

Jet offered a smirk, one that left her feeling unsettled. "Looking for the bathroom."

Nyx didn't have words as she brushed at her face, drawing calming breaths. She knew if she let the tears start, they wouldn't stop. She could feel strands of her hair tickling her face, and she knew her up-do was ruined. The thought made her heart hurt.

"It's a good thing I happened by," Jet continued. He watched as she began to pull at the pins holding her hair in place. He noted the distant look in her emerald eyes as she let long, golden waves spiral around her face. He wanted to be snarky, but the hurt in her eyes kept him silent. "Do you need a ride home?"

Nyx let her eyes shift to him, shaking her head. "I just need to call my aunt." She could feel the tears pressing harder behind her eyes. She couldn't imagine the hurt her aunt would feel if she found out what almost happened. She couldn't stop the tears that started to roll.

He caught her hand. "Come on."

Nyx didn't know where he was taking her as he led her around the corner and toward a door. It looked like a closet, but Jet opened the door to reveal a small staircase that circumvented the foyer and any prying eyes. Soon, they were standing in the empty kitchen. Unfortunately, Nyx's surprise at Jet's knowledge of Randy's house was forgotten as a wave of sadness encompassed her. As soon as Nyx knew they were alone, she let the tears fall unchecked.

Jet surprised her when he reached for her, pulling her against his chest. "You didn't do anything wrong."

For several long minutes, all Nyx could do was cry. She knew it wasn't her fault, but it still hurt. She'd never thought Randy would be such a foul person or that he would try something like that. Not to mention, if Jet hadn't found them, he would have succeeded, and there was nothing she could have done to stop him. It was shocking and humiliating, especially since Jet had seen it. He knew what had happened, and that made her shame worse.

"I'm sorry," she whispered. She pushed away from him, trying to stem her tears. "You don't have to take care of me anymore." She looked up at him, mustering some bravery. "I'm fine."

"I'm pretty sure you're not fine," he said, crossing his arms. Anger began to crease his face. "Were you just going to stand there and let him do what he wanted?"

Nyx shook her head. "I—I don't know," she stammered. "I just . . . froze."

Jet was still scowling at her. "I'm pretty sure if it had been anyone else, you would have beat the shit out of them."

Nyx looked up at him, feeling angry suddenly that he was scolding her. "Why do you even care?" she snapped. "Who do you think you are?"

Jet leaned away. "I think I'm the guy who just saved your ass."

Nyx felt her brow furrow. It occurred to her that she was probably indebted to him now, and that left a sour taste in her mouth. "Well, I don't need you to stand here and babysit me," she said, trying to keep the angry edge to her voice. "You should find your date before she wanders away. She didn't look like she was smart enough not to drown in a puddle."

Jet's eyes narrowed slightly, something akin to humor flashing through them. "I'm not leaving you by yourself," he said sternly, shaking his head.

"Why?" Nyx demanded. "You're not my keeper." She started past him, toward the door to the kitchen. "Go bother your new girlfriend."

Jet caught her elbow, stopping her. "I don't care about her right now," he snapped. "I'm not letting you leave here alone. In fact, any sane person would accept a ride home."

Nyx yanked her arm away angrily, gritting her teeth. "Why? So you can boast about what a nice guy you are?" she snapped, turning on him. "Every moment we're in the same room together is unpleasant, and now you want to be a hero?" Her hands were shaking with anger. "And don't ever touch me again."

"That's what you should have said to the guy that tried to—"

"Shut up, Jet!" Nyx realized her reaction might have been a little much, but she didn't want to hear him finish that sentence. He didn't seem particularly fazed by her yelling, his eyes watching her, his lips pressed in a thin line. "I don't need reminders, okay?"

Jet crossed his arms, sighing shortly. "You're infuriating."

Nyx turned away. "Just like somebody else I know." She pushed open the kitchen door, seeing that she was standing in the dining room. It was mostly empty, save for the staff who were cleaning up the table. They didn't really pay any attention to her as she walked past them to the doorman.

"I need my wrap and my bag, please," she said.

The doorman was pleasant, nodding and smiling gently. He was completely unaware of what she'd just experienced, but she still felt like everyone knew. She felt dirty as she stood there, waiting for him to return with her things.

Once he came back, she pulled her wrap around her shoulders and opened her clutch, feeling a hint of relief. If she could talk to her aunt, she knew everything would be fine. She pulled her phone out and dialed her aunt's cell number. It rang a few times before going to voicemail.

"Hi Aunt Dee," she said, trying to sound cheerful. "It's me. I'm ready to come home now. Call me when you get this." She hung up, feeling overwhelmed. She just wanted to get the hell out of this house and never come back.

"Well?"

Nyx felt her body stiffen as she tucked the phone back into her clutch. "Well what?" she demanded. She didn't need to turn around to know Jet was hovering over her shoulder.

"Is she coming?"

Nyx turned to face him. "Of course she is!" she grumbled. She turned away from him. "I'm going to wait outside for her."

Jet followed her as they stepped out onto the terrace. The wind was still blowing steadily, making his breath fog in the night. He watched as Nyx sank down to sit on the steps, pulling her wrap tight around her shoulders. She slumped forward, her posture defeated. Jet debated for a long moment if he should just leave her here, but pity for her got the better of him. He stepped toward her, sitting silently beside her.

"I thought I told you to go away," Nyx said. Her eyes were distant, her brow furrowed. Jet couldn't tell if it was from the cold or the shitty situation.

"I can't just sit here?" he asked, his voice lacking the sarcastic tone he intended.

Nyx glanced at him, annoyance on her face. She didn't say anything for a long moment. "Fine," she said, sighing. "Just don't bother me."

Jet smirked. "Wouldn't dream of it."

Nyx shook her head as she pulled her wrap tighter, covering her nose and mouth. She tried not to think about everything as she stared across the driveway at the street beyond. She had no idea the night would go this way when her aunt dropped her off. She'd been so happy and excited, and now she just wanted to sink into the ground and disappear. She could feel tears pricking at her eyes again, and she reached up, feeling the mask on her face.

Annoyance flooded her suddenly, and she pulled it off, throwing it down on the ground. She didn't feel like a mysterious princess anymore. She just felt like a pathetic nobody. "Stupid," she whispered, pulling the tiara from her hair.

Jet shifted beside her, surprising her when he wrapped his coat around her shoulders. "You're not stupid."

Nyx shook her head, tears blurring the tiara in her hands. "I don't know why I didn't see it," she said. She drew a ragged breath as she sniffled and wiped the tears from her face. "I should have known . . ."

Jet moved closer to her, so that his shoulder was brushing hers. "You shouldn't beat yourself up over it," he said simply. "Some people are better at hiding their true nature than others."

Nyx glanced over at him, narrowing her eyes. "So then what are you hiding?" she quipped.

Jet smirked then. "I guess you'll just have to find out, won't you?"

Nyx scowled at him. She wanted to be mad at him, but she couldn't as she pulled his coat tighter around her shoulders to ward away the cold. She stared at the ground for a long time before she glanced over at him.

"I guess I should say thank you." She never thought those words would come out of her mouth, and they tasted bitter.

That smirk never left Jet's face. "Looks like that hurt a little bit."

Nyx looked away. "Yeah, my soul feels like its burning," she said dryly. She jumped when her phone suddenly began to ring in her purse. Relief was in her voice as she answered it.

Jet waited silently as she spoke to her aunt, watching her expectantly as she hung up.

"My aunt is around the corner," she said, moving to her feet.

Jet stood as well, taking his coat when she pulled it from her shoulders and offered it to him. He looked down the driveway when headlights came into view. "I guess this is goodnight then, little princess."

Nyx picked up her gold mask, looking over her shoulder at him. "I guess so," she said slowly. Her eyes narrowed as her aunt's car parked at the curb. "You should know one thing."

Jet arched a brow. "What's that?"

Nyx mirrored his aggravating smirk. "I still hate you." With that, she turned away without another word and climbed into the car.

Jet could feel his lips curling with humor. She was a handful, no doubt about that.

Lucky Community College.
Monday, October 31, 2011.

THE SUN FELT TOO BRIGHT as Nyx parked in front of the main building on campus. She'd spent all night working on her paper and she was exhausted. She just wanted to go to class, turn that bitch in, and never look back. Unfortunately, she knew she'd have to see Randy.

She felt nauseous at the thought. How could she ever look at him the same way again?

Slowly, she climbed out of her car, closing the door as she swung her backpack over her shoulder. She pressed her sunglasses farther up her nose, but they did little to stop the ache behind her eyes. She felt hungover as she crossed the parking lot, imagining a nice, big cup of coffee from the café. She could almost feel the steam tickling her nose and the smell the strong scent of coffee beans . . .

A honk made her jump and she looked at the car that she'd stepped in front of, her heart racing. She waved in apology to the driver, realizing she'd never seen the car before. It was a black Maserati coupe, and she couldn't help but stare as it went by. It was a beautiful car, but it became less beautiful as it was parked in a handicapped space and the driver slid out.

"You should watch where you're going," Jet called as he closed the door.

Nyx closed her eyes for a brief moment, pressing her hand to her forehead. Could her day possibly get any stupider?

"This is, like, the second time I've helped you out," Jet continued as he stepped onto the sidewalk beside her.

"What are you doing here?" Nyx asked, feeling her weariness get the best of her. She couldn't even pretend to be cordial. "And only an ass parks in the handicapped spaces."

Jet crossed his arms, his eyes hidden behind a pair of dark shades. "I think a 'thank you' would have been a more appropriate response."

"Thank you for what?" Nyx demanded. "Not running over me?" She rolled her eyes. "News flash, normal people don't run over other people."

Jet smirked. "I'm pretty sure we would both agree that I'm not normal."

Nyx sighed. "You got that right." She turned, shuffling toward the building. She knew Jet was hovering in her shadow, but she hoped if she ignored him he would go away. She did pretty well, all the way until she got to the counter of the café and ordered her drink, until he leaned over her shoulder.

"Make it two of those," Jet said.

Nyx turned slightly. "I'm not paying for you." She was slightly annoyed at how close he was standing to her, but the warmth of his body almost made her want to lean into him. She frowned as the thought flashed through her head. The lack of sleep was seriously messing up her brain.

"No . . . but I'm paying for you." Jet smirked, flashing a twenty dollar bill. He paid the cashier before generously dropping all of his change in the tip jar.

Nyx crossed her arms as she watched him pull his sunglasses from his face. She hadn't bothered to take hers off, but she hoped he could feel her glare behind them.

"Thank you is appropriate in this situation also," he said, standing beside her as they waited.

Nyx sighed in disgust. "I'll say thank you when you can prove that this isn't some bullshit ploy to get something from me."

"I would never do that!" Jet said, offering her another smirk.

Nyx could feel her nose wrinkling at the thought. "Sure you wouldn't."

Jet's smirk widened into barely a grin. He didn't say anything as the barista set their drinks on the counter. Before Nyx could snatch hers away, he caught them both, holding hers hostage. "What's the magic word?"

Nyx scowled. "Give me my coffee before I hurt you?"

Jet shrugged. "Close enough." He handed her a cup, watching as she cradled it in her hands, protecting it jealously. He followed her as she walked to a table and sank down in a chair. He took a moment to glance around the cafeteria, feeling the pull of an unfamiliar aura. After all these months, he knew he was finally closing in.

"So what do you want?" she asked, pushing her sunglasses into her hair. She looked up at him, her green eyes tired. "I'm sure you didn't come here to make small talk."

Jet sat across from her, leaning back in the chair. "You're right." He sighed as if he'd been busted. "I need to ask you something."

Nyx narrowed her eyes distrustfully. He looked like there was something genuine he wanted to say, but she knew better than to trust him. "What is it?"

"Well, it's kind of important," he hedged. He drummed his fingers on his cup, shifting his eyes across the café. A frown started to pull at his face, his eyes watching someone across the room. Nyx started to turn and see who he was staring at, when he suddenly looked back to her. "I don't know. Maybe I shouldn't."

Nyx frowned. It had to be important if he was having such a difficult time. She took a sip of her coffee, trying to think of a way to coax it out of him. "You can just ask," she said slowly.

Jet looked up at her. "You won't get mad at me?"

Nyx felt her frown deepen. "I promise I'll try not to."

Jet drew a slow breath. "Well, here goes." He met her gaze, giving her the most earnest expression he could muster. "Will you give me Abigail's number?"

Nyx took a moment to register his words, wishing she could bang her head on the table. She stood up slowly, summoning all her self-control. She wanted to launch her coffee at his face, but she knew that just wouldn't be appropriate. She couldn't waste good coffee like that. She had to set her cup down as his lips pulled in a smirk. She forced her voice to be calm when she spoke.

"You came all this way to ask me to give you Abigail's phone number?"

Jet leaned back in his chair, his eyes watching hers, ready for whatever she might do. "Well?" he prompted. "Will you?"

Nyx scowled darkly. "Go to hell!" she snapped. "I would never set my best friend up with one of the most disgusting, inappropriate people on the face of this whole planet."

"Oh come on." Jet was unfazed by the fury on her face. "You're overreacting."

Nyx dug her nails into the chair, trying to rein herself in. She really wanted to yell at him, but it wouldn't do to make a scene in the middle of the café. "You're a pig." She tilted her head, feeling brazen suddenly. "What happened? Your little redhead ditch you for something better?"

The laughter eased from Jet's face then, replaced by a sardonic smirk. "She didn't like seeing me with you."

Nyx felt surprise pull at her face. "Hm, imagine that." Cara's jealousy wasn't surprising, but the fact that Cara had been jealous of her was ridiculous. Nyx thought it was pretty obvious that she wanted to stab Jet with a dull pencil. It took a moment for the surprise to ebb enough that she could remember why she was disgusted with him.

"Still." She quickly picked up her coffee. "I will never let you feed your special brand of bullshit to any of my friends." She looked down at her watch. "Thanks for the coffee, but I gotta go."

Jet didn't move from the table. He lifted his cup to his lips, watching her. "See you later."

Nyx turned to look at him over her shoulder. "I hope not." She tried to forget about his presence as she walked across the courtyard to the building her class was in. She was mildly fuming as she walked in, feeling her feet slow and her heart catch painfully in her chest.

She was early, which wasn't unusual for her, so there were a few other students in the room, waiting for the professor. One of those few happened to be Randy, who was looking pointedly down at his desk. Nyx felt sick as she walked toward her seat, which was next to his. She wanted to move, but some little inkling of pride inside her stirred at the thought. He couldn't think he'd won and would force her to move. She didn't look at him as she walked to her seat and sat down gingerly.

The class felt like it dragged on when the professor finally showed. Nyx could feel every muscle in her body straining from how still she was sitting in her chair. When the professor asked for their papers and dismissed them, Nyx hung back. She wasn't surprised that Randy was the first to his feet, practically throwing his paper at the professor before dashing out the door. Once she was one of the last people left, Nyx got to her feet and took her paper to the professor's desk.

"Here you go, Dr. Armand." Nyx forced a smile as she handed the folder to her.

Dr. Armand smiled up at her. "Thank you, Nyx," she said kindly. Her brown hair was pulled back from her face in a bun and her glasses were tottering on the edge of her nose. "I look forward to reading this."

Nyx knew she should feel proud of her teacher's compliment, but she couldn't muster it right now. "Thanks."

Dr. Armand took off her glasses, her face becoming serious. "So, do you mind if I ask what was going on with you and Randy?"

Nyx grimaced, looking down. She hadn't realized that Dr. Armand paid that much attention. "We, uh, we had a disagreement," Nyx said, trying to think of the best way to word what she wanted to say. "We're not speaking anymore."

"Ah." Dr. Armand offered a sympathetic smile. "Well, if there is anything you need from me, you let me know, okay?" She straightened the stack of assignments. "I would hate for this to affect your class participation. I know you want to get accepted into Mr. Johnson's internship this winter."

Nyx forced her smile at the thought of missing out because of Randy. "I'm fine," she said quickly. "I'm focused on my grades."

Dr. Armand nodded. "Good," she said. She stood, tucking the folders into her bag. "See you on Wednesday."

Nyx didn't say anything as she followed her professor from the classroom, walking down the hallway the opposite way. She drew a calming breath as she walked to the parking lot. She was ready to go home and go back to bed, thankful that she only had one class on Mondays and Wednesdays. She pulled her sunglasses down onto her face, blinking against the bright sun. Her relief was gone as she neared her car.

Randy was leaning against the peeling bumper of her little white Mustang. His arms were crossed as he stared across the parking lot.

Nyx could feel her feet slowing. She debated whether she should turn around and go back inside, but she knew that wouldn't solve anything. Whatever Randy wanted to say, he would keep pestering her until he'd had a chance to talk to her. She drew a slow breath, pressing on toward her car. Once she was close, he looked up, straightening.

"What are you doing?" Nyx asked, trying to put on a brave face. "I don't want to talk to you."

Randy nodded, stepping away from her car. "I know," he said softly, his eyes downcast.

Nyx opened the trunk of her car, letting her backpack slide into it. She closed the lid a little harder than she intended, but she didn't really care. Maybe it would help get Randy to go away sooner. She turned slowly to look at him. "So then why are you here?"

"I just," he drew a slow breath, running a hand through his hair. "I guess I wanted to tell you I was sorry."

Nyx crossed her arms tightly. "Okay. I'll accept your apology." She watched as he met her gaze for the first time. "But that doesn't mean that I ever want to talk to you again."

Randy nodded mutely. "Just, don't tell anyone what happened, okay?"

Nyx felt her lip curl in disgust. "What?" she asked, thinking she'd misheard him.

"Please, Nyx," he begged, his eyes looking like they were filling with tears. "If word got out about this—"

"You want me to keep quiet about how you tried to rape me?" Nyx demanded.

Randy shrank back like she'd slapped him again.

Nyx shook her head, turning to her door. "I gotta go." She pulled the door open, gasping softly when Randy caught it before she could close it.

"How much money do you want?" he asked, his face serious. "Just name your price."

"You can't buy my silence," Nyx said. She pulled against him, scowling when he wouldn't release his grip on the door. "Get out of the way."

"No," Randy said. He leaned in closer to her, his eyes dark.

Nyx felt her heart leap into her throat. Fear clawed at her, but she tried to keep it in check. She felt her jaw clench, knowing she couldn't let him bully her. "Listen," she said, her voice a hard whisper. "I don't want to ever see you or speak to you again."

Randy leaned away a bit, surprised by the strength in her voice.

"I want to put your stupid behavior behind me and get on with my life," Nyx continued. "So move your ass out of the way and let me go home!"

Randy seemed like he would say something else, but then he relented, stepping back.

Nyx pulled the door shut quickly, hitting the lock button. She kept a death glare on him as she started her car and pulled out of the space quickly. She didn't look back as she burned rubber out of the parking lot. It wasn't until she was almost home that she took a deep breath, trying to calm the pounding of her heart.

23

Dirty Harry's, Main St.

Thursday, November 3, 2011.

THE SUN HAD SET several hours ago, and it was cold. The small buildings on Main Street funneled the wind straight down the road, blowing Nyx's hair back from her face. She pulled her jacket tighter, walking a bit faster. She could see the entrance to the bar at the end of the street and she didn't think she could get there fast enough. She struggled against the wind to pull the door open, sighing when she was finally inside the warmth of the building.

"ID please."

Nyx flashed a grin as she pulled her wallet out of her pocket. "Come on, Benny," she said teasingly. "I'm only here every week."

Benny returned her smile. "I know." He was a nice guy, very by the book as far as his job went, but was pretty short on words.

Nyx thanked him as she took her ID back and paid to get in. She tucked her wallet away as she stepped through

171

another set of doors into the bar. She could hear the music from the sidewalk, but it was blaring now that she was inside. Underneath the sound of the music was the roar of people laughing and talking. The bar was crowded tonight and she pressed through the crowd, toward the usual table they sat at. She waved as she broke through, seeing familiar faces.

"Hey girl!" Anna said, standing from the booth and hugging her. "We were wondering where you were."

Nyx returned her smile, sliding to sit next to her. "I had to park way down at the other end of the street." She smiled at Abby and Melanie across the table. "Where are the boys?"

"Seth is on his way," Anna said. She turned her eyes across the table to the twins. "And apparently they met two hotties over by the bar."

Abby nodded as she set down her drink. "Definitely hotties."

Melanie grinned. "Definitely."

Anna turned to look at Nyx. "Where's your man?"

Nyx looked down at the table, trying to keep her face neutral. "Uh, things weren't really working out with Randy." She hadn't told her friends about Halloween and didn't intend to. It was better that no one else knew.

"Is that why you left so quick the other night?" Melanie asked.

Nyx nodded. "He was drunk and just being stupid, and I was tired, so . . ." she shrugged.

"Well maybe our new friends have more cute friends," Abby said with a grin.

Nyx shook her head as she returned Abby's grin. "You're horrible."

They sat and giggled together for a while longer before Anna suddenly sat up straight, excitement on her face. Nyx turned to follow her gaze, seeing Seth's tall figure bobbing through the masses.

Nyx waved at him when he looked to their table, standing as he came closer. "Hey Seth."

Seth smiled kindly at her. "Hey." His smile grew as his eyes shifted to Anna, who was scurrying out of the booth into his arms.

Nyx looked away as they kissed. It was so cute she felt nauseated. She slid back into the booth, watching Abby pretend to gag. Melanie just laughed.

"So Seth," Abby said, drawing his gaze as he leaned back from Anna, "where's your cousin?"

Nyx wanted to facepalm.

Seth turned in the booth, putting his arm across the back and looking over his shoulder. "He was right behind me," he said dismissively.

"Maybe he got lost," Anna said, looking over at Nyx.

Nyx felt like she could kill her best friend. "Maybe he fell in a pit and died."

Seth looked down at Nyx, grinning. "He's not that bad."

Nyx narrowed her eyes at him.

"Well," Seth said, backpedaling suddenly, "he could stand to be a little less obnoxious."

As if on cue, Nyx turned her head, seeing Jet's tall form easing through the crowd of people. A scowl was pulling at his face until his eyes landed on them. It faded away in a smooth motion, making Nyx wonder if she'd imagined it.

"Jet, over here!" Abby lifted a hand, waving at him.

He walked toward their table, a smirk pulling at his lips. "Hi girls." His eyes shifted to Nyx, a taunt in them. "Got a spot for me?"

Abby giggled, pushing Melanie over to make room in the booth. "You can sit by me," she said, batting her eyelashes at him.

Jet smiled coolly, sitting beside her. He leaned back in the booth, draping his arm over the back of it. He lifted his chin at Nyx. "Where's your boyfriend?"

Nyx felt pure hatred shoot through her. "He's not coming," she said shortly. "And he's not my boyfriend."

"Oh, too bad," Jet said dismissively. He looked down at Abigail, who was practically drooling in his lap. "Can I buy you a drink?"

Abby nodded emphatically. "Just a beer."

To his credit, Jet looked at Melanie. "Mel?"

Nyx felt her nose wrinkle. Since when did he get to use pet names for her friends?

Melanie blushed darkly. "Sure," she said weakly.

Jet smiled then, a victorious sign.

Nyx turned to Seth and Anna. "You guys want a soda or something?" she asked.

Seth shook his head.

"Water for me," Anna said, leaning into Seth's chest. She whispered something to him that only he heard, which made him smile at her.

Nyx nodded shortly, sliding out of the booth, trailing after Jet. She waited until he turned the corner toward the bar, out of sight of her friends, before she grabbed him and pushed him toward the wall.

"Easy now." He threw his hands up. He was smirking still, letting Nyx know he already knew what she wanted. "What did I do this time?"

"You leave my friends alone!" Nyx snapped darkly.

Jet crossed his arms, exuding cockiness. "You don't control them."

Nyx could feel her hands clenching. "I'm warning you," she said, feeling her face turning red with her anger. "If you hurt Abigail, I'll kill you."

"Calm down, little princess," Jet said tauntingly. "I'm not going to do anything to your friend." He stepped closer to her, watching her face. "You know, if I didn't know any better, I'd say you were jealous."

Nyx felt her face flush suddenly. "Jealous of what?" she snapped. She suddenly was very aware of how close he was standing to her. "There is nothing about you to be jealous of." Her mind was suddenly swirling, making her feel dizzy and short of breath. "You're just a womanizing jackass."

Jet smirked again, unfazed by her insults. "Then why is your face so red?"

Nyx scowled at him. "I hate you." She turned away from him and marched toward the bar. She pressed her hands over her cheeks, feeling how red they were as she told the bartender what she wanted. She drew a slow breath as Jet appeared beside her.

He was still grinning smugly as he ordered drinks. Once they had what they wanted, he motioned for her to lead the way. "After you, little princess."

Nyx scowled darkly at him. "Stop calling me that!" she barked. "And don't ever call Melanie 'Mel' ever again." She started toward the table. "That's not her name."

Jet chuckled softly under his breath. "Whatever you say."

Once Nyx handed Anna's glass to her, she slid into the booth, sipping at her water. She couldn't look at Jet as he talked to Abby and Melanie. Abby was laughing in a profoundly fake way, and it made Nyx's hatred for Jet worsen.

"Hey, Nyx." Melanie's voice cut through her thoughts. She was smiling pleasantly. "Let's go dance."

Nyx felt her spirits lift immensely. "Okay." She slid from the booth, watching as Melanie told her sister where they were going. Both Abby and Jet had to slide out to let Melanie out, and Nyx flinched when Jet's arm brushed against hers.

His eyes shifted down to her, his face smug. Nyx hated that she didn't have any control of herself when he was near her. She thought she could escape him, but she watched as he put his arm around Abigail, obviously asking her if she wanted to dance as well. Fortunately, Melanie caught her arm and led her away into the crowd on the dance floor. As they settled into the beat Nyx could tell that Melanie wanted to ask her so many questions about what was going on between her and Jet, but the music was too loud for them to carry on a conversation.

Nyx tried not to think about it as she and Melanie swayed with the other people on the floor. She just wanted to have a good time and forget about Jet's nonsense. She was surprised, though, when Melanie suddenly caught her arm and pulled her in close enough to be heard over the music.

"Those are the guys we met earlier!" Melanie said, nodding her head.

Nyx turned to follow Melanie's gaze. Two men were standing on the edge of the dance floor, bottles in their hands. One of them caught Melanie's eyes and elbowed his friend, motioning to them. They were both quite handsome, just like Melanie and Abby had said. One was a bit shorter than the other with platinum-blond hair and blue eyes, while the other had brown hair and blue eyes. They were confident as they pressed through the crowd toward Nyx and Melanie.

"Hey," the blond said, leaning in to be heard. His eyes shifted to Nyx. "This your friend?"

Melanie nodded. "This is Nyx," she said, grinning brightly. "Nyx, this is Devyn. And that's his friend, Lance."

Nyx offered a feeble smile. She felt intimidated and uncertain as Devyn asked her to dance with him. She wasn't good at this sort of thing. She shot a look over her shoulder to Melanie as Devyn led her away, the song changing into a two-step. Her friend offered her a reassuring smile as Lance began to lead her in a dance as well. Nyx let her hands rest on Devyn's shoulders, feeling nerves twist in her chest.

"I haven't seen you here before," Devyn said suddenly, drawing her gaze.

Nyx offered a nervous smile. "Really?" she asked. "I come here with my friends all the time."

Devyn's lips quirked, baring a dazzling smile. "There's no way," he said teasingly. "I'm here every night. I definitely would have seen you." His eyes shifted over her face. "You're too pretty to miss."

Nyx felt her cheeks turn red at his compliment. She laughed softly. "Uh, thanks, I guess." She let Devyn twirl her, catching his hands as he pulled her back in. He was a good dancer. Nobody could compare to Jet, but Devyn was a close second.

"So do you live around here?" Devyn asked.

Nyx nodded. "Born and raised here."

Devyn's eyes were bright as he watched her face. "You don't seem quite like the country girl type," he said.

Nyx shrugged. "It's all I've ever known."

Devyn twirled her a final time as the song started to wind to an end. He was still holding her hands gently. "Can I buy you a drink?"

Nyx glanced over her shoulder, realizing that she was on the opposite side of the dance floor from Melanie. "I'm not thirsty," she said, looking back up at Devyn.

"Oh, come on," Devyn said, flashing his smile again. "You can at least let me get you a soda."

Nyx felt her stomach twisting. She was extremely uncomfortable, but she knew she could be overly suspicious sometimes. She held his gaze, feeling her suspicions and worries melting away. "Okay," she said finally. "But just a soda."

Devyn seemed pleased as he led the way to the bar and ordered drinks. "A beer for me," he told the bartender, "And whatever the lady wants."

Nyx dug her nails into the wood of the bar as she told the guy she just wanted a diet soda. She could feel Devyn's eyes on her. When she looked up at him, that pleased smirk hadn't left his face.

"We should go somewhere quieter," he said suddenly. "So we can talk."

Nyx balked at the idea, but she kept her face smooth. "I can't," she said quickly. "My friends are waiting for me."

Devyn paid the bartender and turned to face her. "I'm not trying to kidnap you," he said jokingly. "I just want to get to know you better."

Nyx felt her cheeks turn red. For a moment, she thought she was being silly. He was probably a super nice guy, and not to mention cute. She took a sip of her drink before nodding her head. "Okay."

Devyn grinned, catching her hand again. He led the way to the patio door, which opened onto the porch where guests could smoke. The patio was super crowded, but he managed to find a table near the corner of the building, giving them a bit of peace and quiet.

"This is much better." He sank into a wrought iron patio chair.

Nyx sat slowly across from him. "It's so loud in there."

Devyn nodded. "So do you go to school around here?"

Nyx nodded. "Over at the community college."

"What are you studying?" Devyn lifted his drink, taking a small sip.

"Still working on pre-reqs," she said, looking down at her cup. "I'm not sure what I want to do yet."

"Oh." Devyn leaned across the table, studying her face playfully. "You don't know what you want to do at all?"

Nyx shrugged, letting her eyes take in his features now that he was out of the dim light of the bar. She felt an easy smile pull at her face. "Maybe a writer or something," she said, feeling herself leaning toward him as well. "I like to tell stories."

Devyn's blue eyes seemed impossibly deep as his smile softened. "That's an awesome thing to want," he said, his voice softening. "You must be good with words."

Nyx felt her mind becoming foggy as she held his gaze. "Hm?" she breathed. She couldn't remember suddenly what they'd been talking about, feeling entranced. Her body felt warm and tingly, all the way down to her toes.

Devyn didn't break eye contact with her as he held his hand out. "You want to come with me."

Nyx nodded, missing the way he said it so succinctly, without a hint of question in his voice. She took his hand, feeling wobbly and rubbery as she stood with him. Her mind was entranced with him, and she couldn't turn her eyes away. She followed him without question from the patio and to the parking lot.

Jet turned Abigail in an expert move, shifting his eyes across the floor. He'd seen Melanie and Nyx bobbing and weaving through the throng during the last song, but now they were nowhere to be found. He had a bad feeling about this.

As the song ended, he pulled Abigail off the floor, leading her back to the booth. "I need a break," he said, offering her a smile. He watched as she batted her eyelashes.

"Okay." She was totally mesmerized by him, her body language reading excitement and desire.

Jet felt satisfaction at knowing it was so easy to charm these mortals, but he was distracted. "I'll be right back."

Abigail nodded, and Jet could feel her eyes on his back as he walked toward the bathrooms. Once he blended into the mass of people, he skirted around the bar, looking toward the dance floor. He walked toward it, hanging just on the edge. He didn't see Nyx anywhere, and he could no longer feel the hot press of her aura.

This was not good.

Jet caught Seth's eye as he and Anna went by, inclining his head. Seth pulled Anna from the floor on the far side, clearly making up some excuse to leave her. He then pushed his way through the crowd toward Jet.

"What is it?" he asked, his voice low as the Sarotian words rolled off his tongue.

"Where is Nyx?" Jet asked. Irritation was filling him.

Seth frowned, confusion on his face. "I thought you had an eye on her."

Jet gave Seth a glare. "If I had an eye on her, would I be asking you where the hell she was?"

Seth crossed his arms, drawing a slow breath. "We need to find her," he said shortly.

"No shit," Jet snapped.

"Do you think it's Sophia?" Seth asked.

Jet nodded, feeling his jaw clench. He'd first noticed her a few days ago, and was surprised when he realized that she was one of Nyx's teachers. He hadn't been able to decide what her plan was when he'd seen her Monday morning, hovering in the background. Clearly, Sophia had been watching her for weeks, and it was strange that she hadn't made her move yet. Nyx had no idea, which was how he preferred it. None of them were ready to expose their plans yet.

"Be ready." Jet turned away from Seth.

"Where are you going?" Seth called, a slight hitch in his English. It belied the uncertainty he was feeling.

"I'm going to find her," Jet said. "I have a feeling this won't turn out well."

With that he turned away from Seth, pushing his way quickly through the dance hall. He ran out to the parking lot, yanking the door of his car open. He knew where he might find Sophia, especially if she had lured Nyx away. He felt stupid suddenly. He shouldn't have been so quick to dismiss her.

The tires chirped as he pulled out of the parking lot.

He'd tried to lay low, like Nyx's stupid handmaid had requested, but it didn't look like that was going to work out anymore. Rage began to tickle inside him. If she'd just let him do things the way he wanted from the start, he wouldn't be doing this now. The handmaid was an idiot if she thought that Nyx was safe here.

Jet knew better than anyone that Paraximus could do whatever he wanted. He possessed the skill and power, and it was only a matter of time before he discovered where Nyx had been hidden all these years. She wasn't safe here, or anywhere anymore, now that she had a bounty on her head like this.

He took a turn sharply, feeling the tires of the car break from the pavement for a moment. He didn't have any time to waste.

Nyx was staring mutely out the window of Devyn's car as he pulled into the driveway of a house. It was a run-down, two-story farmhouse. She knew that she should have been scared, but she didn't feel anything as she sat there motionlessly. She could see a single light on inside the front room of the house, but it went out as Devyn stopped the car.

"Get out."

Nyx felt her body move without her consent. She stepped slowly from the car, staring at the house. She blinked slowly as Devyn crossed around toward her.

"Inside." His eyes shifted over her face. He smirked lightly as he followed her up the steps to the front door. Her mind was much more pliable than he'd anticipated, making his spell over her easy. He could have told her to do anything at this point, and she would have without hesitation.

He caught the door as they stepped inside the decrepit house. The scent of dust and mildew hit his nose as he closed the door behind them, turning the deadbolt. He looked up at Nyx, seeing her standing still like a statue, waiting for his next command.

"Over there." He pointed to the living room. "Sit."

Nyx moved wordlessly toward a couch, sinking slowly onto it. She felt like she was in a dream. Mild surprise filled her as she realized that a woman was sitting in a chair across from her. One leg was crossed over the other, her fingers pressed together before her face.

"Hello, Nyx."

Nyx stared blankly at her, realizing she knew this woman. "Dr. Armand." She could feel her thoughts tumbling through her head suddenly, but they felt muted and distant as Devyn sat next to her, draping his arm across the back of the couch behind her.

"Please, call me Sophia." Her normally gentle brown eyes were shimmering in the dark, a soft yellow glow emanating from them.

Nyx nodded mutely. Her mind was telling her that she should be scared, but that thought dissipated when Devyn pressed his hand against her back.

"She's strong," he said, looking over at Sophia. "But her mind is open and untrained." He glanced back at his captive. "I doubt she's ever even tapped into her power."

Sophia grinned, flashing a fanged smile. "That doesn't matter," she said easily. Her eyes were studying Nyx carefully. "Our orders were very specific."

Devyn frowned lightly as he looked to her. "Wouldn't it benefit our king to just kill her?"

Sophia's eyes narrowed as she looked at him. Her Sarotian words were clipped and angry. "It would benefit us more to have her," she snapped. "Even though she is untrained, she can be commanded."

Nyx drew a slow breath, turning her gaze from Sophia to the window over her shoulder. She knew that something was horribly wrong. She knew she should be terrified. Nothing about this situation made any kind of sense, but she couldn't make her body move. She couldn't summon enough energy to make herself feel afraid.

"Do you see?" Devyn demanded softly, watching Nyx's emerald gaze shift away. "She's fighting me."

Sophia paused as she watched Nyx's face. She tilted her head slightly, sitting forward in her chair. "Give me a moment with her," she said softly. "Your mind control is weak. My blood magic can bend even the strongest to my will."

Devyn nodded, moving to his feet, a scowl on his face. "I cannot sustain any control over her at a distance."

Sophia nodded, waving her hand as if he was bothering her. "It doesn't matter," she said. "Now leave us."

Devyn was silent as he stepped away.

Sophia listened until she heard the front door close behind him. Once she knew they were alone, she leaned back in her chair. "Nyx."

The girl's eyes shifted to her, wide and unfocused.

"Do you know where you are?" Sophia asked.

Nyx drew a slow breath. "No."

"But you know who I am?"

"Yes."

Sophia moved slowly to her feet. "I must say, I am surprised by your strength!" she said, stepping around the coffee table to sit slowly beside Nyx. "I felt your presence the moment you and Devyn arrived." She reached out her hand to lift one of Nyx's golden curls from her face. "You take after Liana."

Nyx's brow furrowed slightly. She felt like she was beginning to awaken, her thoughts racing. Who was Liana?

"You look confused," Sophia said, watching her face carefully. "Have you been so sheltered that you don't even know your own grandmother?"

Nyx turned her head slowly, her eyes blank as she looked at Sophia.

Sophia grinned slightly at her reaction. "Most people aren't able to break Devyn's grip." She used her fingers to lift Nyx's chin. "You are something special." She suddenly waved her hand, an elegant quill appearing in her fingers. "It's too bad that I have to break you."

Nyx drew a slow breath, feeling cold fear beginning to seep through her. Her body still felt paralyzed, but her mind was suddenly alive. She couldn't move as she watched Sophia reach for her hand.

"This is my favorite method," Sophia said slowly. "You see, this quill isn't just for writing." She lifted the feather, her eyes glinting with insane pleasure. "It does whatever I ask it to do."

Nyx felt her breath catch as the quill began to morph, growing into the long, sharp blade of a dagger. She couldn't believe what she was seeing. Was this even real?

"Nice, isn't it?" Sophia asked, her face pleased. "But it's not just a weapon. It can control people." She feigned sympathy. "I think you'd be a wonderful experiment for me. If I could control you, I could be more powerful than even King Paraximus. But I doubt you would be controlled for very long." Her eyes suddenly turned cruel. "But you shouldn't worry. I'm going to make sure you suffer long enough that you'll know what is happening to you. You will do my master's bidding and then, if you are lucky, I will grant you a swift death."

The fear that was flooding Nyx was making her heart pound painfully. She couldn't tear her eyes from the sharp steel that Sophia was wielding. Her mind was struggling to force her to move or scream or anything, but she was a prisoner in her own skin. She could feel tears pressing against her eyes. She didn't want to die.

Sophia lifted the dagger as Nyx struggled to force her body to move. The tears were escaping her eyes as she fought, feeling her arm suddenly move. She gasped as she realized the trance was breaking, and she threw herself forward, feeling the blade bite into her arm as she tumbled to the floor.

Pain coursed through her as Nyx turned onto her back, her body shaking weakly. She pressed her hand over a slash to her arm, her blood hot as it dripped across her fingers. Sophia was gazing at her, surprise on her face.

"Well," she said, moving to her feet. "This just proves my point, doesn't it?"

"S—stop," Nyx managed, trying to drag herself away from Sophia.

Sophia smirked. "I can't," she said simply. "I know you don't understand, but just trust that it's for the best."

Nyx lifted her arms as Sophia moved toward her. "Please," she whispered.

24

*The Abandoned Yand Farmhouse,
Outskirts of Lucky.*

Thursday, November 3, 2011.

JET MOVED SILENTLY through the trees that surrounded the farmhouse. He'd seen lights inside in the
previous weeks, but he'd assumed it was kids or vagrants.
He realized now that there was a strong shield around the
house, masking their auras.

He could see Devyn standing on the porch, leaning against the side of the house. He lifted a cigarette to
his lips, the flicker of a lighter brightening his face for a
moment. Jet felt his eyes narrow as he watched the small
man. He should have known that there would be more
with Devyn. He was a manipulator, able to bend energy
to his will, so it made sense that he would be needed. But
he clearly wasn't the leader.

Jet moved closer, feeling Nyx beyond the walls as he
passed through the cold magic of the shield. She was alive,
and panic was coloring her aura, making him feel tense

as he moved closer. He jogged silently toward the porch, vaulting over the railing. He watched as Devyn turned, surprise on his face.

"Hey!" Jet said easily, a deadly smirk on his face.

Devyn didn't move for a long moment, his blue eyes wide. "Wh-what are you doing here?" he demanded hotly in Sarotian. His face creased with a snarl. "You weren't supposed to find us here."

Jet's smirk widened. "I love it when you idiots underestimate me. Now I'm here to kill you." In a flash he was in front of Devyn, talons driving into Devyn's chest. He could feel Devyn's heart, warm and mushy, under his fingertips. It was beating quickly, fluttering like a bird in his chest.

Devyn was surprised, terror in his eyes as he stared at Jet.

"I would say sorry for not giving you a chance to defend yourself," Jet said, gripping the organ tightly. He watched as blood dripped from Devyn's lips, his breaths suddenly rasping as his lungs began to fill with fluid. "But I'm not. It would be a waste of my time and yours, and I can't have you alerting your comrades."

Devyn gasped as Jet wrenched his hand from his gut. Jet shoved him away, watching his body land heavily on the porch. He looked down at Devyn's heart in his hand, seeing it twitch slightly as he let it slip from his grasp. The sticky-sweet smell of it made his mouth water, but he sighed, reminding himself that this was no time to be distracted.

His dark eyes took in the crimson liquid dripping from his fingers as he swallowed thickly. He could feel his chest tighten, a whisper in his mind begging for a taste. He shook his head, dislodging the thought. It had been a week since he'd hunted, but the animal blood was a poor substitute compared to Devyn's. He flung the blood from his hand, turning to the door and twisting the door knob. There were things to be done.

Nyx's fear was suddenly tangible as he stepped into the house. The smell of blood other than Devyn's hit his nose, and he rounded the corner quickly. His eyes took in the scene before him and his body reacted before his mind had consciously processed what he was doing.

He caught Sophia's hand as she tried to plunge her dagger in Nyx's chest. She seemed mildly surprised as she looked up at him before suddenly twisting her wrist in a defensive maneuver. She swung the blade at him, leaping back.

"What are you doing here, Jet?" she demanded. Her eyes were taunting. "When did Liana let you out of her dungeons?"

Jet wanted to roll his eyes at her slight. Had everyone been living under a rock for the last year?

"Jet?" Nyx's voice was breathless.

Jet felt his jaw clench as he caught her when she staggered to her feet and into his arms. She felt cold to the touch, and her emerald eyes were confused and scared. Tears slid slowly down her face as she realized he was covered in blood.

"What's happening?" she breathed.

"You'll be okay." Jet looked back to Sophia.

"Aw, isn't this sweet?" Sophia said spitefully. "When did you become so soft, General?"

Jet scowled darkly, the title grating on his last nerve. "I'm going to gut you the way I did your pawn out there!" he growled in Sarotian. He felt Nyx's hands gripping his jacket tightly, knowing she didn't understand a word of what he was saying.

Sophia twirled her dagger, which morphed back into its true form. "We'll see." Her own Sarotian words were angry. She waved her quill, black ink beginning to ooze from the end of it.

"What is that?" Nyx gasped.

Jet pushed her behind him. "Stay back," he said darkly.

Sophia's eyes were glinting murderously as she waved her quill, as if she was writing. The ink began to grow and stretch, forming into a hulking creature. Claws and a muzzle began to emerge, glowing red eyes pinning Jet and Nyx.

Jet cursed softly in his native tongue as he watched the beast drop from the end of the quill like it was being birthed, falling to its feet. He turned to Nyx, pushing her toward the door. "Run!"

Nyx's legs were shaking as she stumbled toward the door and yanked it open. She gasped when she tripped, falling to her hands and knees. A scream tore from her throat as she realized she was staring down into Devyn's lifeless face.

"Let's go!" Jet barked, grabbing her quickly and hefting her to her feet. Behind him, the beast lunged for them, slamming into the wall with a crack. The porch shook beneath their feet as he pushed her toward the side of the house. The only good thing about newborns was that it took them a moment to find their footing.

Nyx vaulted over the railing, fear making every nerve in her body feel like it was on fire. She ran quickly toward the trees, hearing Jet on her heels. She gasped as the beast crashed around the porch behind them, the sound of wood splintering following them. Her lungs were burning and her legs were aching as she ran, stumbling through the underbrush. The only thing that kept her going was the sound of the monster as it tore through the trees behind them.

"We need to get to the river," Jet said, catching her arm as she tripped over a tree root. He took her hand, keeping her close.

Nyx was gasping for air. She turned to look over her shoulder as silence fell over them, missing the log that Jet had stepped over. She crashed heavily to the ground, crying out softly as pain shot through her.

"You are the clumsiest person I've ever had the misfortune of meeting!" Jet snapped, turning to haul her to her feet.

Nyx was crying softly, gasping in pain. "My leg!" she breathed, her eyes searching the trees for the creature.

Jet sighed in exasperation, turning and lifting her over his shoulder in a fireman's carry. Why had he agreed to this again?

Nyx held tightly to the back of his jacket as he jogged on. "What are you doing?" she demanded, her voice shaking. "Put me down!"

"You can be mad at me later!" Jet said, barely winded as he carried her. He felt Nyx jump suddenly, the sound of brush being tumbled through nearby.

She gripped his jacket tighter, struggling to get down. "It's here," she gasped, terror in her voice. "It found us!"

Jet turned his head, catching sight of it as it suddenly burst through the undergrowth. His eyes tracked the beast as it lunged for them. He leapt into the air easily, avoiding the beast's razor claws. He listened to Nyx scream, feeling her sliding over his shoulders. He sighed shortly as, in a simple maneuver, he swung her around and into his arms. He landed gently on the ground, ducking behind a tangle of trees before the monster regained its bearing.

Nyx pushed out of his arms, fear in her eyes. Jet moved quickly toward her, covering her mouth with his hand. "You have to be quiet!" he whispered.

Nyx used her hands to push his away from her face, drawing haggard breaths. "What are you?" she breathed.

"That's not important right now," Jet said softly, his eyes tracing over her face. "Stay here. I will come back for you when it's safe." He could feel her eyes on him as he stood, vanishing silently through the trees.

The scent of water was heavy on the air as Jet moved toward it. He knew the only way to defeat Sophia's monster was to douse it in water. He pushed through the trees, a steep drop leading to the river below. He turned slowly as he listened to the monster push through the brush behind him, a rank stench filling the air.

It smelled like dried gore and rotting flesh. As it shouldered its way through the trees, gobs of black ink stuck to the branches, killing them instantly. The ink dripped from its body, sloshing heavily to the ground. Its red eyes were boring into Jet as he stood there. Irritation flashed through him as it opened its maw, a choked growl leaving its mouth. It sounded like it was drowning in its own body.

Was this the best Sophia had? It didn't even seem completely formed.

If she thought her little blob would be enough to kill him, she was sorely mistaken. In his mind he was already deciding how he would make Sophia pay. She'd ruined everything with this little stunt. Not to mention, she'd just straight-up annoyed him.

The beast drew his attention again, lurching forward to dig poisonous fangs into him.

Jet braced himself, leaning into the monster's gooey embrace as it tackled him to the ground. When he tried to dig his own claws into the monster's body, his hands sank into the ink. The stench of it was heady and made him feel nauseous. He gritted his teeth as the beast sank its nasty teeth into his shoulder, feeling his collarbone splintering under the force.

"Bastard!" he growled, shoving the beast. His hands sunk further into it, keeping him trapped there. Pain coursed through him as the poison in the beast's bite began to flood his bloodstream, making his veins feel like they were filling with ice-cold fire. He knew he had to end this.

Jet used his weight to force the monster onto its side, allowing him to get his feet under him. With a fluid motion, he flung his arms, ignoring the searing pain in his chest. He realized he was falling with the beast, his hands still cemented into its chest, as it tumbled down the embankment into the muddy water below.

Nyx waited until deafening silence descended over her. She winced as she got to her feet, hobbling through the trees. She didn't know what was going on, and she didn't want to hang around and find out. Tears were clouding her vision, making it infinitely more torturous to find her way. Pain was shooting through her ankle and her leg. She didn't make it very far before a shadow formed in front of her.

Fear shot through her as she recognized Sophia's face.

"Where is your protector?" Sophia taunted, twirling her quill.

Nyx stepped back, knowing she couldn't escape this time. "What are you?" she demanded.

Sophia's lips quirked, baring her fangs again. "I'm an Auresi," she said softly. "And so are you."

Nyx frowned. "I don't know what that is!" she said, hearing her own voice shaking.

"We are magic users." Sophia stepped closer to her.

"What?" Nyx breathed. Sophia was crazy, obviously, but this was some next level kind of crazy.

"You are very strong." Sophia continued, her eyes shifting over Nyx. "But you haven't tapped the power of Aure yet. If you had, you could destroy me with nothing more than a whim."

Nyx shook her head. "I don't know what you're talking about," she said. She winced as she took a step back and pain shot through her.

"So much you don't know about yourself," Sophia said softly. She lifted her quill. "So much wasted potential." Her quill began to shift into the dagger once more. "But I will help you."

Nyx gasped as Sophia moved faster than she could track her, appearing before her. Sophia dealt a blow to Nyx's chest, sending her flying to the ground. Nyx coughed and sputtered for a breath, trying to wrap her mind around what she was experiencing. This couldn't be real. People couldn't move like that and do the things that Sophia did. Or the things that Jet did.

She forced her eyes open, watching Sophia twirl the dagger. Her eyes were murderous as she advanced, intending to drive her blade into Nyx and end this. Nyx drew a sharp breath when a shadow materialized behind Sophia. Her stomach turned when a sickening crunch filled the air and she realized a hand was protruding through Sophia's middle.

Sophia's eyes widened as she looked down, her blood staining her clothing. She couldn't move, feeling the power of her own poisonous ink working against her.

"Hurts like a BITCH, doesn't it!?"

Sophia forced a grin. Without a word, she spun, dislodging Jet's hand and driving her dagger into his flesh. She clearly thought she could get away, but Jet only smirked down at her.

Nyx felt faint as she watched Sophia withdraw her blade, intending to strike again. Before she could, Jet caught her by the neck, causing her to gasp for a breath, her fingers clawing at his.

"You've ruined all of my plans!" he said, watching Sophia's eyes grow wide. Tendrils of her ink were coursing beneath her skin as the poison consumed her body, winding up her neck as her heart raced. She tried to struggle against him, but her grip was weak as the light left her eyes. Jet slammed her roughly to the ground, his grip around her neck tightening. She choked and struggled, but her thrashing became pathetic. Soon she was still, the life gone from her eyes as Jet let go of her.

Nyx could feel her chest heaving as she fought for a breath. She watched as Jet moved to stand, turning his dark eyes on her. "You . . . killed her . . ." she managed, blinking quickly.

"It was us or her." Jet shook his hands in the air, flinging blood and ink from his fingertips.

Nyx shook her head, panic filling her. "What . . ." She looked up at him, taking in the blood and ink that covered his clothing and dripped from his hands. His hair was wet, strands of it hanging down into his eyes. "I don't . . ."

Jet offered her his hand. He watched her face pale as she looked at it. "We can't stay here," he said. "It's not safe."

Nyx drew a shuddering breath. "Not safe?" she whispered. "Nothing about this makes sense." Tears were filling her eyes again. She looked at Sophia's still form.

"How could I be safe with you?" Horror twisted her brow. "You're a murderer!"

Jet stepped toward her, ignoring the way she flinched away from him.

"Don't touch me!" she yelled, struggling against him.

Jet caught her wrists as she flailed, pulling her to her feet. "Don't you think if I intended to hurt you I would have?" he demanded. He watched her pause, her emerald eyes watery. "You have to trust me."

Nyx began to shake fiercely. She didn't say anything as she stared at him, fear in her very soul.

"Can you walk?" he asked.

Nyx shook her head slowly. She was in daze.

Jet was silent as he swept her into his arms. He half expected her to try to fight him, but she was strangely calm and silent as he walked through the trees. They emerged onto the gravel road that wound its way to the highway.

Nyx gripped his jacket tightly, looking over his shoulder. "Where are we going?" she breathed, still trembling against him.

"To see Seth."

Nyx felt her heart drop into her stomach. "Seth?" How was Seth involved in all this?

Jet sighed shortly, exasperated. "Seth can answer all your questions," he said brusquely.

Nyx was silent as Jet carried her to his car, which he'd parked at the end of the road. He made sure she was safely inside and closed the door before walking around. He mumbled something about getting his seats messed up as he slid into the driver's seat. Nyx gripped the door handle tightly, feeling her stomach drop as Jet pulled onto the road. If she could have run away, she would have thrown the door open and bailed. Even as dull pain shot through her leg, she still considered it.

Nyx couldn't make sense of what was happening. She didn't believe in magic, but she knew what she'd seen. She looked down, feeling pain once again in her arm. The sleeve of her jacket was torn and bloodied from where Sophia had cut her. She shuddered at the thought, feeling sick. If magic wasn't real, then what the hell were these people?

"Sophia, she . . ." Nyx drew a shuddering breath, looking at Jet. "She made her feather turn into a knife." Confusion made her fear worse. "And she made that monster. She said she wasn't human."

Jet nodded as he took a curve too fast for Nyx's liking. "That's true," he said quietly. His face was set in a deep frown.

"She said that I'm not human," Nyx said hesitantly.

Jet's eyes shifted to her then, his expression unreadable.

"She said I haven't tapped the power of the . . . 'Or-rey'"? she whispered, watching his face. "What does that mean?"

Jet clenched his jaw. "The power of Aure," Jet said, correcting her. "Aure is the source of Auresi magic." He bit his tongue suddenly, shaking his head. He knew she wouldn't understand what he was talking about anyway. "Look, Seth can explain it better than I can." Inside his head he was kicking himself. How could they expect her to trust them after all this?

"Why?" Nyx suddenly demanded. "Why can't you tell me what the hell is going on?"

Jet shook his head. "I just can't."

Nyx leaned back in her seat, feeling betrayal suddenly sitting heavy in her chest, on top of her fear. "I always knew you were an asshole." She was gazing out the window, once again weighing her options for making an escape.

Jet glanced over at her, a smirk pulling at his face. "I just saved you. Can't be that much of an asshole."

A field stretched beyond the window as Nyx tried to sort her thoughts. "What was that . . . thing?" she asked, disgust wrinkling her face. She glanced over at him, seeing the goo that was still coating his clothing.

Jet's smirk faded. "Golem," he said shortly. "Made from ink."

Nyx drew a slow breath, trying to remember if she'd ever read about what a golem supposedly was in her literature class. "How did you get rid of it?"

Jet's brow quirked. "Golems are funny creatures," he said softly. "They disintegrate in water."

"That's why you needed to find the river," Nyx whispered, understanding in her voice.

Jet nodded mutely, glancing at her. Maybe she would take their news better than he thought. She was being surprisingly calm, but he knew that could change in an instant.

He turned onto a road that wound up a hill to a house. It was small, but it was brightly lit, sitting alone on the hill. Jet pulled the car up to the garage and shut it off. "Seth will explain everything." He hoped he sounded reassuring because he didn't believe in what he was saying to her.

Nyx frowned after him as he slid out of the car. She took a moment to gather her thoughts before she pushed open the door. Her ankle twinged as she stepped out of the car, deterring her once again from making a run for it. Jet was waiting for her by the door as she limped up the porch. He opened it slowly, holding it for her.

Nyx was surprised by their house when she stepped inside. She'd half-expected it to be like a frat house when she'd thought about it before, but after what happened, she thought she might see some weird crap like frogs in jars and potions being boiled. Instead, the living room was furnished with a couch and chairs, a glass table in between. A big-screen TV was on the wall, a football game playing. The house was brightly lit and spotless. Down the hall Nyx could see bedrooms, which appeared to be clean as well.

"Stay here."

Nyx winced as she sank onto the couch, watching as he disappeared down the hallway and into a room. She could hear voices, presumably him and Seth talking, and then Seth came out of the room, Jet in tow. She felt her heart skip a beat at the way they were both watching her, their eyes concerned.

"Are you hurt?" Seth asked, walking over to her. His eyes found the cut to her arm. "Let me see this."

Nyx flinched as he sat beside her, trying to push down her fear. She drew a sharp breath when he pressed his fingers against her arm as he looked at her injury. "I'm okay," she whispered. "It doesn't really hurt anymore."

Seth was frowning. "It's deep," he said slowly. He looked up at Jet, clearly unhappy.

Nyx frowned at him when he said something unintelligible to Jet. Jet looked exasperated. She turned to look at Seth when he looked back to her. "What is going on!" she demanded. She looked between them. "That sounds like the same language that Sophia spoke."

Seth drew a slow breath. "That's because it is." He reached out, wrapping his hands around her arm.

Nyx jumped, wincing in pain. "Hey, what—" Her eyes widened as soft, bright sparks jumped from Seth's hands to her arm. She could feel warmth seeping through her where he touched her, taking away the pain.

After a moment, Seth released her. He watched her carefully as she examined her arm, shock on her face. Through the hole in her jacket there was nothing but pink skin, any sign of a cut gone.

"How did you . . ." She looked up at him. Fear crossed her face. "What are you?"

"We aren't from here," Seth said gently. "We aren't like humans. We can touch the power of Aure and Aucer, which gives us abilities to heal. " He held her gaze, watching emotions flicker across her face. "We were sent here."

Nyx shook her head, confusion clouding her mind. "Why?"

"To keep you safe."

Nyx drew a shaking breath, seeing the earnest look on his face. "Me?" she whispered. "But why?"

"You . . . you aren't human, either," Seth said softly. "You are special, and far more powerful than the rest of us."

Nyx shook her head suddenly. "No," she said quickly. "That's not possible." She looked up at Jet, seeing his arms crossed and a scowl on his face. "I was born here. And I don't have magic or whatever."

Seth shook his head. "That's not true. You weren't born here. You were born in a place called Gexalatia, in a city called Regius Carmen. It's where your parents are from."

Nyx shook her head harder, feeling tears filling her eyes. "No," she said, her voice breaking. "Aunt Dee said . . ." Her eyes suddenly widened. "Aunt Dee?" Was she one of them too?

"She isn't from here either," Seth said. "But she's not like you." He looked up at Jet. "Or like us. She's a true human, an Inerse."

Anger suddenly creased Nyx's face, covering her confusion. "You're lying!" she said, her voice dark. She moved to her feet, her ankle no longer hurting. "You're both lying!" She was trembling as tears slipped down her face. "This is some kind of trick!"

Seth stood slowly, shaking his head. "No, Nyx," he said, his brow furrowing. "We would never lie to you."

Nyx shook her head, backing away from him. "If what you're saying is true, then my whole life has been a lie!" She couldn't believe that. She wouldn't. There had to be a simpler explanation, even if it was more sinister.

Jet turned to Seth then, saying something softly. His eyes were dark and irritated.

"Don't talk about me in your made-up language!" Nyx barked. She felt crazy. This couldn't be happening. It was further infuriating when Jet sighed, rolling his eyes.

Seth stepped toward her, reaching a hand to her. "If you'd calm down, I can explain everything—"

Nyx pulled away. "There's nothing to explain," she whispered, fear on her face. "You're both liars!" She turned her eyes on Jet, gritting her teeth. "And murderers."

Seth looked pained for a moment. "Then I don't have much of a choice, do I?" he asked softly in Sarotian.

Jet shook his head mutely. He knew this plan wouldn't work. He hadn't expected her to have this big of a meltdown, but he knew she wouldn't believe them.

Nyx felt fear seize her as she watched their exchange. When he stepped toward her quickly, catching her wrist, she twisted and struggled against him, swinging her fists. "Let me go!"

Seth ignored her, pressing his hands against her cheeks. He mumbled soft words that Nyx didn't understand, holding her gaze.

Nyx suddenly felt exhausted, as if she hadn't slept in days. She tried to fight against him, but her body was losing the will to fight. His words were like a lullaby, filling her with warmth and comfort. Her eyes drifted closed, her knees buckling suddenly.

Seth caught her, laying her gently on the couch and kneeling beside her. "I shouldn't have done that . . ." He looked over his shoulder at Jet.

Jet shrugged. "It was necessary," he said dismissively. He obviously didn't care about the repercussions of this, but that didn't surprise Seth in the least.

Seth looked back down at Nyx. "I don't know how long it will hold," he said. "Her magic is much stronger than mine." He stood slowly. "We have to be careful not to trigger a resurgence of memories."

Jet didn't seem particularly bothered. "There's not much time left anyway. A few more weeks and she'll have to know."

Seth nodded, clearly unhappy. "What about Sophia?"

"Dead."

"You're certain?" Seth asked, turning his gaze on Jet.

Jet nodded, brushing his pitch-colored hair from his face. It was stiff, the ink drying in it. "Of course I am," he said, a hint of indignation in his voice. He turned away from Seth and Nyx, shrugging off his jacket. "I need to shower."

Seth drew a slow breath as he turned to look down at Nyx. He could only hope his memory block would hold.

25

The Estrella Residence.

Saturday, November 5, 2011.

Nyx opened her eyes slowly, feeling a headache pounding behind her eyes. She hadn't felt well since the day before. Her mind felt foggy and her thoughts were slow. It was unsettling. She had woken yesterday with a splitting headache, unable to remember what had happened the night before. She'd asked her aunt how she'd gotten home, since she'd driven her car to Dirty Harry's and it wasn't in the driveway. Her aunt had made that face she made when she was disappointed.

"A nice young man with black hair brought you home," her aunt had said. "You were clearly very drunk."

Even now, as Nyx looked out her bedroom window, she had a feeling that wasn't right. She didn't remember drinking anything, and that made it seem worse. She'd cried a lot yesterday, thinking maybe she'd been roofied or something. But that didn't make sense, either, because she'd been with her friends and then Jet had brought her home. Or, something like that, anyway.

It took her a long time to get out of bed, even though she knew it was getting late in the day. She had chores and animals to feed, but she felt terrible. She had to force herself to put on her dirty jeans and T-shirt, wishing that she could just go back to bed instead. When she stepped into the hall, the light from the window felt too bright, making her head feel cloudier. Going down the stairs was painful, making her brain feel like it was being jarred inside her skull.

Nyx could hear her aunt in the kitchen, making breakfast. The smell of eggs and bacon made her feel nauseous as she sank down into a chair.

"Hey Sweetie," her aunt said, looking over her shoulder. She frowned when she saw Nyx's pale face. "Are you sick?"

Nyx let her head fall into her hands. "I don't know," she said slowly. "I feel terrible."

Dorothea crossed to her, wiping her hands on a dish rag before pressing them against her face. "You don't feel like you have a fever."

Nyx groaned. "Maybe I'm getting the flu."

Dorothea frowned more deeply. "Why don't you try eating some breakfast?" She set a plate in front of Nyx, watching as she picked up a piece of bacon and nibbled on the end.

Nyx could feel her face screwing up as her stomach turned. "I'm not really hungry," she said, pushing the plate away.

Dorothea crossed to the sink and took a glass out of the cabinet, filling it with water. "Here," she said, handing Nyx the glass. "Why don't you go back to bed?" She offered a smile. "I'll take care of the chores. You rest."

Nyx nodded, taking the glass. She groaned pitifully as she moved to her feet and shuffled into the living room. She was pretty sure the sun was mocking her, as it felt brighter every time she walked past a window. She made her way back up the stairs and shed her clothes as she pulled the curtains and closed her door.

She lifted the water to her lips, feeling terribly thirsty as she sat on the end of the bed. She downed the water quickly before falling back onto the mattress. She pulled the blankets up to her chin, feeling the fog consuming her. She'd never felt so out of sorts before, and she didn't like it. She hoped a nap would help it pass.

Soft jingling pulled Nyx out of her sleep. She turned over in her bed, trying to ignore it, realizing that it was her phone. It didn't stop, continuing to ring for a long time. She was disoriented as she reached for it on her nightstand, seeing it was Anna's number.

"Hello?"

"Hey," Anna said, surprised and uncertain. "What's wrong with you? Are you sick?"

Nyx sighed, pressing her face in her pillow. "I don't know," she mumbled. "I feel like crap."

Anna laughed. "Drink too much the other night?" she asked teasingly.

Nyx frowned, lifting her head from her pillow. "I didn't drink anything," she said, irritation in her voice. "I don't even like alcohol."

"Well, that's not what Seth told me," Anna said. "He said you were wasted, and Jet had to drive you home."

Nyx sighed. She couldn't believe that everyone kept saying that. It almost made her feel crazy. She knew she hadn't been drinking. So why did everyone claim that she had been?

"Well, so I guess this means you don't want to go to the movies tonight," Anna said, changing the subject.

Nyx groaned softly. "Oh crap," she said, turning on her side. She'd totally forgotten about going with Anna to see a movie. "Yeah, I can't. I feel terrible." She offered a forced laugh. "Besides, I don't think Aunt Dee will let me out of the house again."

Anna chuckled. "Since you're a drunky and all?" she asked teasingly.

"Yeah," Nyx said, a bad feeling sitting in her chest. "Just take Seth this time."

Anna sighed. "All right," she said. "But we're doing a two-fer next week."

Nyx smiled softly. "Yeah, sure."

Anna told her to feel better and then hung up the phone. Nyx let it slide from her fingers, hearing it plunk onto her rug. She hated this. She knew she wasn't crazy, but why couldn't she remember what happened on Thursday?

She opened her eyes, staring at the ceiling as she lay there. The sun was going down outside the window, leaving the room in murky, late-afternoon shadow. She pressed her hands against her eyes, trying to remember exactly what she did on Thursday. She remembered getting ready to go out and fussing with her eye makeup. She'd wanted to try different shades, but she couldn't find the palette she'd just bought.

Then, she knew she got in her car and talked to Anna on the phone, agreeing to meet at their regular table. She remembered stopping for a cow that was crossing the highway. All these little things were so specific, but she couldn't remember anything particular from around the time she arrived at Dirty Harry's. She kept getting glimpses of images and feelings of things that happened, but nothing that was detailed or that stuck.

The coiling feeling in the pit of her stomach was worse. Once again, the thought that she'd been drugged assaulted her . . . but she couldn't imagine who would have done that to her. She knew Seth would have been with Anna, and Jet was flirting with Abigail, but then, where had she been?

Nyx gritted her teeth, rolling over to pick up her phone. She was just about to send Melanie a text message, when the phone suddenly dinged in her hand. She snorted softly, seeing a message from Melanie. "Speak of the devil."

M: *So how'd it go with Devyn the other night?*

Nyx felt her brow crease with confusion. *Devyn?*

M: *Yeah, that cute blond guy?*

Nyx wracked her brain. She didn't remember a blond guy. She let the phone rest against her chin as she tried to remember what his face even looked like. She realized she was biting her lip hard as she texted Melanie back. *I don't remember him.*

M: *Lol. Anna said you got pretty drunk, but I didn't think you were THAT drunk.*

Nyx felt her lip curl in disgust at the smiling emoji in Melanie's text. *I swear I wasn't drunk!*

M: *Are you sure? I saw you at the bar with Devyn before you guys disappeared.*

Nyx's heart twisted. Had this Devyn guy done something to her? She felt sick again. She put her phone on the nightstand, pressing her hands over her face. She needed to remember.

Irritation and disgust filled her as she realized the only person who would really know what happened was Jet. Since he'd been the one to bring her home and all. She grabbed her phone, finding his number in her contacts. She never thought she'd have to use it, since she never wanted to have a conversation with him in the first place. Sure, he'd been kind on Halloween, but Nyx felt like that was a one-off. She felt herself shrivel inside as she typed up a message.

WTF happened Thursday? Everyone says I was drunk . . . And you brought me home . . . ?

She debated whether she should send the message or not, feeling foolish. She felt like an ass needing his help, but she felt worse not knowing. She hit send, her heart in her throat. She didn't have to wait long for a reply.

J: *Yeah. And yeah.*

Nyx scowled at the phone. That was far from helpful. *Melanie said I was with a guy.*

J: *Yep. He was buying you drinks.*

Nyx could imagine him sitting at home, thinking of the most infuriating way to answer her questions. It didn't help her aggravation when she pictured him giggling and rubbing his hands together maniacally as he did so.

You are being sooo not helpful right now.

Jet sent back a shrugging emoji. *Idk what you want from me.*

Nyx scoffed at the phone, setting it roughly on the nightstand. She pulled the blankets over her head, trying to will herself to fall asleep. She wanted this day to be over and the last few days to be very distant memories.

26

Lucky Community College.
Monday, November 7, 2011.

NYX STRAINED TO SEE beyond her windshield as she pulled into the parking lot. The weather was crap, rain pounding down on the roof of her car. She managed to find a parking spot, but it sucked, way out in the back of the lot. She sighed in irritation as she realized she didn't even have an umbrella in her car. Her only saving grace was the fact that she'd put on a hoodie before leaving the house.

She got out, feeling the rain soaking her as she walked to her trunk and grabbed her backpack. She sighed, deciding being in a hurry was a waste of time, since she'd be soaked by the time she got to the door anyway. She didn't know why she'd woken up in such a bad mood this morning, but it'd caused her to be late. It made her mood worse when she walked past the coffee stand, dripping wet, knowing she was late to her class.

The scent of the coffee was amazing and tantalizing, but she knew she didn't have time, and that made the frown on her face deepen. She felt like she would bite off anyone's head who pissed her off, including Randy. She was ready for a fight as she walked in the door to the classroom, a snarky remark on her lips if Dr. Armand said anything.

Nyx paused as she entered the room, confused suddenly. An older woman was standing in front of the class, speaking about something. She stopped when Nyx came in, perching a hand on her rather large hip.

"Hello," she said, not smiling as her eyes looked over Nyx in displeasure. "Please have a seat. I was just telling everyone that Dr. Armand won't be returning."

Nyx felt confusion swamp her. "Oh," she said, walking to her chair and sliding into it. Her pants made a wet, slick sound across the plastic of the seat. She happened to glance at Randy, who was staring at her like she was crazy. She wanted to have an angry retort for him, but she stuck with shooting him a death glare until he turned his eyes away.

"So, anyway," the woman said, "I'm Patty LaGrange and I'll be your substitute until the end of the semester." She turned and waddled to the desk, where she had a stack of papers. "Fortunately, Dr. Armand graded your papers before she was called away." She set the stack on the table at the front of the room. "Just come grab your paper and we'll pick up next class with *Paradise Lost.*"

Nyx arched a brow as she looked around the room. She'd walked all this way in the rain just for this? She sighed shortly as she got to her feet. She had to wait in line to get her paper. She was satisfied that she'd gotten a B on it. She didn't bother to read Dr. Armand's notes at the back like she usually did, instead just throwing it into her bag and walking to the coffee stand. At least she could still get her fix.

She could feel her mood improving as she got to the counter. "Venti mocha blend." She shoved her money at the cashier.

"Oh, sorry," the guy said. His eyes were half-closed like he'd smoked a bowl before he'd come to work. "Machine is down."

Nyx let her hand drop to the counter. "So, you don't have any coffee?"

The guy shook his head, readjusting his hat.

"But, coffee is, like, all that you sell," Nyx said, frustration lacing her voice.

The guy shrugged. "We're out today."

"Then why are you even open?" Nyx snapped, turning away and shoving her money roughly into her pocket. She felt like she wanted to either cry or break something as she walked to the door. She pulled her hood over her head and crossed the parking lot back to her car. Could this day possibly get any stupider?

The Abandoned Yand Property.
Monday, November 7, 2011.

THE RAIN WAS POURING DOWN, making the ground slick and muddy. Even with the blanket of leaves over the topsoil, Jet still slipped through the mud as he followed Seth through the trees. He blew drops of water from the ends of his hair.

"Are you sure this is the place?" Seth asked, turning to look around.

Jet nodded. "I'm positive." He looked around the area, seeing the trees where he'd hidden Nyx. He walked toward it, frowning. "This is where I left Sophia's body."

"There couldn't possibly be another place?" Seth asked. Jet understood the nature of his questioning, but it was still irritating.

"I think I'd recognize where I was standing when I realized we were royally fucked," Jet snapped angrily. "I left her here and brought Nyx straight to you."

Seth was scowling softly as he stood next to Jet, his brown curls wet and dripping. They both were soaked, and now they both were pissed off. "You think someone found her?"

Jet shook his head, looking over his shoulder. "No one comes out here," he said matter-of-factly. "That's why Sophia was hiding here."

Seth sighed as he brushed water from his face. "Coyotes?"

"There would be evidence of animals," Jet said, feeling his nails digging into his arms, which were crossed tightly. Irritation was seeping through him again.

"There couldn't have been another with her?" Seth asked carefully.

Jet shook his head. "There was only one other here with her and Nyx." They had just dealt with Devyn's body, which was still where Jet had left it. It didn't make sense that Sophia would disappear but Devyn didn't.

Seth looked at him and Jet knew exactly what he was about to say.

"I know," Jet snapped, sighing in disgust. "She obviously wasn't dead."

Seth sighed again, turning around and walking toward the car. "We've got to find her," he said.

Jet was close on his heels, pushing wet branches from his face. "Not necessarily," he said. "She'll come for Nyx."

Seth paused, turning to look at Jet, incredulousness on his face. "Would you seriously put her in danger like that?" he demanded.

Jet arched a brow, unconcerned. "We would kill Sophia before she got to Nyx."

Seth scoffed, his face angry. "That's twisted, even for you," he said sharply. "And it's blatant disregard for Nyx's life."

Jet lifted his hands. "Sorry," he deadpanned. "Sheesh."
He pushed past Seth. "You got a better plan?"

Seth was silent for a long moment as he followed Jet
back to the road. He took his keys from his pocket, looking
over the roof of the car. "We'll have to wait for the rain to
stop." He opened his door.

Jet slid in, curious to hear where Seth was going with
this obviously stupid plan. He shut the door, using his
hands to rustle the water from his hair. Rain drops flung
across the dash and the windshield, giving Jet a particular
kind of enjoyment. He watched the way Seth frowned at
him as he started the car. Petty revenge for Seth acting
like he knew better.

"We'll have to track her," Seth said.

Jet turned to look at him, arching a brow. "Do you
know how hard it was for me to find her in the first place?"
he asked, annoyed. "She won't make it easy a second time.
Not now that she knows I'm here."

Seth put the car in drive and pulled onto the highway.
"That's just the risk we'll have to take," he said. "We can't
put Nyx's life in danger." His brow knit together. "And we
can't put a strain on the memory block. If it comes undone
without the proper technique, it could harm her."

Jet rested his arm on the window, looking at the fields
and numerous cows that rolled by. "Well, we're already
screwed," he said shortly. "What else could possibly go
wrong?"

Seth was silent as he drove down the highway.

Jet knew there was no other way to lure Sophia out, and
he knew that Seth was thinking about that. Sophia wouldn't
be caught, especially not now that the rain had washed away
any trace of her. She would appear on her own terms when
she had recovered, and she would be out for blood.

"We need to tell her," Jet said quietly.

Seth shook his head, pressing his lips together tightly. "Absolutely not," he said shortly. "Those weren't our instructions."

"To hell with your instructions," Jet snapped. "Liana isn't here. How could she know what's best for anyone when she's not even living this shit right now?" Anger coursed through him. He wouldn't be controlled by whatever she thought was the right thing. "She sent me to make sure Nyx gets back to Gexalatia. And now it's time for us to do things my way."

"I'm not okay with that," Seth said emphatically. "Our Queen has her reasons. I have no reason to doubt her judgment."

"That's because you're just a slobbering lap dog for her," Jet growled. The car felt too small suddenly. His onyx eyes were pinning Seth with a deadly glare. "If she asked you to jump, you'd ask how high."

Seth surprised Jet when he slammed on the breaks, the car sliding across the wet road to a stop. His blue eyes were blazing as he looked at Jet. "Let's get one thing straight," Seth snapped. "I trust her judgment. I wasn't asked to come here to watch over Nyx because I just happened to be standing around when she needed someone. She chose me."

Jet arched a brow. He'd never seen Seth get mad before.

"I was hand-picked by Her Majesty," Seth continued. His gaze was suddenly scornful. "I knew working with you would be difficult, but I never imagined that I would loathe anyone the way I've come to loathe you."

Jet scoffed. He could feel bitter anger twisting inside him, making him want to hurt Seth. But he knew that wouldn't do. He said nothing as he opened the car door and stepped out, lightning flashing across the sky. He slammed the door shut a little harder than necessary, seeing the car rocking at the force.

Seth was out in an instant, a scowl on his face. "Where are you going?" he demanded.

Jet smirked darkly at him. "I'll do things my own way," he said shortly. He turned away then, ignoring Seth as he called his name.

The rain picked up, wind causing it to come down in thick, sideways sheets. Jet's mind was made up as he stepped into the trees along the roadside. He was going to do whatever it took to lure out Sophia, and Seth would just have to live with it. He couldn't protect Nyx forever and he couldn't expect her to survive in her ignorance. She would have to know, or she would never make it to Liana alive. Too many people were trying to kill her.

As far as Jet was concerned, Seth, Liana and the hand-maid were wrong. He could do a lot to keep Nyx alive, but no one could expect him to stand against all of the obstacles that they would face by himself. He needed her to be self-sufficient enough that she could carry on if something happened to him. A year would have been plenty of time for him to train her, but neither Seth nor Dorothea would see it his way, and now it was too late. The opening of the Limen was too close for him to even teach her how to properly defend herself.

Collectively, they were all making the worst decisions on Nyx's behalf, and not even giving her the opportunity to choose what she wanted. He knew it shouldn't matter to him, since his own freedom depended solely on returning her to Liana, but it didn't seem right. Nyx would most likely die, and she would never know why.

And that didn't sit well with him. He wouldn't die for Liana's cause willingly, and he didn't expect Nyx to either.

The Alvar Residence.

Wednesday, November 16, 2011.

IT WAS LATE.

The roads were dark as Seth turned down them. He was still smiling softly as he thought about his evening with Anna and Nyx. They'd gone to Deb's Diner to have dinner together and then went to a movie. Anna had stuck to his side the whole time, and Nyx had made gagging noises the whole time. He wouldn't trade that for anything. He was glad that his spell had seemed to hold and that the confusion she'd struggled with had dissipated as she believed Jet's lie.

He'd felt terrible, knowing he'd been the cause of her bad mood. But he knew it was necessary, like Jet had said. He just hated the thought of what it would do to her when they had to tell her the truth and the spell came undone.

The headlights of his car were bright as he turned down the driveway that led to his house. He wasn't expecting anyone to be there, and he slowed as he saw the reflection of taillights. He clenched his jaw as he realized it was Jet's car. He slowed to a stop and climbed out, walking slowly up the porch.

Seth looked at the clock as he came inside and shut the front door behind him, switching on a table lamp to dispel the darkness. He hadn't seen Jet in a week, and he didn't know where Jet had been. They hadn't spoken since the argument the week prior.

Seth set his keys slowly on the table, hearing the sound of the shower running. He settled on the couch, waiting for the water to shut off. Once it did, he listened for the door to open.

Steam filled the house, making the air humid. Seth turned and looked over the back of the couch. Jet paused in the hallway, using a towel to dry his hair as he turned to look at Seth. He lifted his chin in greeting, his onyx eyes bright.

"Sup," he said nonchalantly.

Seth felt irritation fill him. "Where the hell have you been?"

Jet arched a brow, swinging a T-shirt over his shoulder. "What, are you my mother now?" he asked sarcastically.

Seth scowled. "You can't just run out on your duty," he snapped. "You've left Nyx unprotected."

Jet smirked darkly. "Actually," he said, walking toward Seth. "I haven't." His bare feet were silent on the hardwood, only the swish of his sweatpants filling the silence.

Seth's scowl melted into a frown. Jet seemed too pleased with himself.

"I've been looking for Sophia," Jet said. "There are rumors of a string of deaths in Shreveport."

"That could be anything," Seth quipped. "It's a significantly populated area."

"You would think that," Jet said, nodding his head. "Except for the part where all the victims were found drained of blood."

Seth's blue eyes narrowed. "Why would Sophia need blood?"

"Her golem," Jet said as if it was the most obvious thing in the world. "She uses blood ink."

Seth turned to look toward the door, lost in thought. "So does this mean you've found her?" he asked absently. He felt foolish suddenly. He should have trusted Jet's instincts.

Jet pulled his T-shirt over his head. "I know she's not working alone," he said. "There was another that crossed with her. I haven't been able to track him or find Sophia yet."

"But she knows you're looking," Seth said, frowning deeper. "Either she's stupid or she's luring you."

Jet shrugged. "It doesn't matter," he said. "When I find her, I'll make sure she's definitely dead."

Seth didn't like this at all. "What could she possibly be planning?"

"I don't know, but I know it's going to be a real pain in the ass," Jet said shortly. "Ten deaths in as many days means she's got something big in the works."

Seth looked up at him. "Do you think she will come back here?"

Jet smirked again. "I'm pretty sure she never left."

Seth winced at the thought. He felt extremely foolish. While he was sitting around, twiddling his thumbs and entertaining Anna and Nyx, Sophia could have been watching them. "What do we do?"

"We wait," Jet said confidently. "I'll stay near Nyx. Sophia will come for her."

Seth couldn't stomach the thought of putting her in harm's way knowingly, but what other choice was there? He nodded mutely, drawing a slow breath. His thoughts were tumultuous for a moment before he looked back to Jet. "Have you taken care of yourself?"

Jet scowled darkly suddenly. "I told you I'm fine," he snapped. "I don't need you to remind me. Why do we have to have this conversation every month?"

"We'll have more than Sophia to worry about if you don't feed," Seth said quietly. That was something he didn't want to experience, let alone think about.

Jet turned away, walking around the couch. "I have time. Still eight days until the cycle ends."

Seth knew he was pissed. He listened to Jet slam the door to his bedroom like a temperamental teenager. He wasn't surprised when Jet reemerged a moment later, clad in jeans and boots and a black T-shirt. He was pulling a jacket over his shoulders as he walked to the front door.

"Don't stay out too late now," Seth said patronizingly.

Jet shot him a glare over his shoulder. "Screw you."

Seth rolled his eyes as Jet disappeared, the engine of his car roaring to life and fading as Jet pulled out of the driveway. At least that was one thing he could count on about Jet. He never did anything willingly or without a fight.

The Estrella Residence.
Thursday, November 17, 2011.

YX USED A THICK curling iron to wrangle her naturally curly blonde hair. She winced as she brushed her knuckle against the iron, pressing it against her tongue to cool the minor burn. She glanced at the clock, feeling rushed. She was late meeting Anna and the others at Dirty Harry's. She'd already missed dinner with them since her car wouldn't start. She'd spent almost an hour tinkering with it before begging her aunt to let her take the truck. By that time she was covered in grease and needed to shower again.

Finally she was done and she unplugged the iron. She grabbed the new jacket her aunt had bought for her last week. She'd lost her black leather jacket somehow, probably during her drunken escapade, and her aunt had been really cool about it. It was surprising to Nyx, but she didn't think anything of it. She ran down the stairs and pulled on her boots by the front door.

"Aunt Dee, I'm going!" she called, grabbing the truck keys.

"All right, Sweetheart," her aunt called from the kitchen. "Love you."

"Love you too," Nyx said, yanking the door open and rushing out to the truck.

She pulled herself up into the seat, starting the big diesel. It rumbled to life, whistling as Nyx threw it into reverse and pulled out of the driveway. Her heart was beating quickly as she drove down the road, trying to remind herself that she would get there when she got there. She felt so rushed and irritated that she had missed dinner.

It was so strange that her car didn't start when she went out to leave. It had been fine just that morning when she'd gone down to the grocery store for her aunt. It was weird. But the car was also almost ten years old, and her aunt had bought it used for her. So there was no telling how much longer it had before it crapped out on her.

Jingling suddenly filled the cab of the truck, the passenger seat vibrating.

Nyx looked down, rummaging through her bag to find her cell phone. She was mildly annoyed when she saw Jet's number on the screen. He was probably there already, and Abigail was probably hanging all over him. It was disgusting to think about. And not because she gave a crap about Jet. She didn't want her friend to get hurt by him.

"Hello?" Her voice was irritated.

"Hey," he said, ignoring her tone. "Where are you?"

"I'm on my way," she said shortly. She glanced at the clock as she reached to adjust the heater. "Why are you calling me?"

"Eh, Anna was pestering Seth, so," Nyx could pretty much hear him shrug, "doing him a favor."

"Well I'll be there soon," she said, sighing deeply. She looked up as rain drops began to hit the windshield. She looked around the steering column, her irritation worse as she realized she didn't know how to turn on the wipers. "Damn it."

"What's wrong?" Jet asked.

"I don't know how to use this," Nyx said angrily. "My car wouldn't start, so I'm in Aunt Dee's truck."

"Hn." Jet fell silent.

Nyx found the right lever, but only after turning the headlights off and on and hitting the blinker, of course. She only felt mildly better. "So, let me let you go," she said, realizing he was still waiting quietly. "I'll be there soon."

Jet drew a slow breath on the other end, as if he meant to say something, but he blew it out, as if he thought better. "All right," he said distractedly. "Just be careful."

Nyx arched a brow at the phone. "Be careful?" she asked. "That's a strange sentiment, coming from you."

"Yeah, don't get used to it," Jet quipped. "Bye."

Nyx laughed to herself as she hung up, dropping her phone back into her bag. She wondered what all that was really about.

She was still lost in thought as she took a turn, switching to her bright headlights. Country roads were the worst sometimes, super dark at night and even worse when it was raining. The last thing she wanted was to hit a deer or pig or, heaven forbid, a cow. She was slowing down as she came around the curve, seeing a car approaching.

She switched off her brights, but the car coming toward her didn't. She scowled, thinking it was super rude. The car passed without incident, but it took Nyx a moment for her eyes to adjust.

Her heart lurched hard suddenly as a figure appeared in her headlights. She reactively slammed on the brakes, but the truck was heavier than her car, and unable to stop quickly enough. Nyx did the only thing she could think of, swerving around what appeared to be a person in the road.

The truck started to hydroplane, her tires losing grip of the wet pavement. She closed her eyes, the world a blur as the truck spun, going off the road.

Confusion was thick in her mind as she blinked, feeling sharp pain shoot across her head. The truck had come to rest in a ditch, tires still spinning. Nyx took her foot off the brake and put the truck in park, pressing a hand to the side of her head. Her fingers were warm with blood from where she'd hit it against the window.

She groaned as she looked around, trying to decide what to do. Aunt Dee was going to kill her. She'd told Nyx on numerous occasions never to do what she'd just done, even for an animal. But then, had there really been a person in the road?

Her heart skipped a beat as she fought to unbuckle herself, seeing that her bag had been thrown from the seat, its contents spilled in the floorboard. Her phone was nowhere in sight, and she pushed at the door, feeling it was wedged shut. Concern filled her. Who the hell was out in the middle of the road in the dark?

Nyx leaned over the arm rest, feeling pain shoot through her head as she tried to reach for her bag to find her cell phone. She glanced up, fear catching her as she realized there was someone standing outside the passenger door. A startled scream caught in her throat as the door was yanked open, a dark-haired man reaching for her.

"Hey, get off me!" she yelled as he caught her, hauling her easily from the truck. Her fear was worsened as she realized that she vaguely recognized him, but she couldn't place his face.

"Hello Nyx, darling."

Nyx stumbled to keep her footing as she looked up the ditch. Confusion was thick in her already muddled thoughts. "Dr. Armand?" she breathed. Her heart caught painfully in her chest suddenly.

"It's Sophia, remember?" Sophia was standing on the road, rain dripping from the ends of her brown hair. Her eyes were bright, shimmering a deep crimson, filled with anger and bloodlust. Tendrils of black wound across her skin, making her appearance even more demon-like.

"What happened to you?" Nyx whispered.

Sophia grinned, baring a row of sharp teeth. "You don't remember, do you?" she asked, her voice cruel. "Jet must have had Liana's servant erase your mind."

Nyx frowned, not understanding what she meant. She felt cold from both fear and the rain that was soaking them.

"It's no matter," Sophia said, her glowing gaze shifting to the man behind Nyx. "Bring her."

Nyx felt his hands wrap strongly around her arms. She struggled against him. "No!" she gasped. "Let go of me!"

The man glanced up at Sophia, who nodded almost imperceptivity. He surprised Nyx when he swung his hand at her, striking her across the face and knocking her to the ground.

Her head swam painfully from both his blow and her injury. She felt nauseous and dizzy, unable to push herself up out of the wet grass. She couldn't resist him when he lifted her from the ground and draped her over his shoulder.

30

Dirty Harry's.

Friday, November 18, 2011.

JET LOOKED DOWN AT THE phone in his hands. The clock had just rolled over to midnight. He'd been trying to entertain himself and keep his brain busy by flirting with Abigail, but he couldn't anymore. He'd stepped outside onto the patio, trying Nyx's cell again. He knew something was wrong when it went to voicemail for the third time. He sighed shortly as he tucked the phone away and walked back inside.

Seth was standing at the bar, ordering a drink. He looked over to Jet, his brow furrowed. "Well?"

Jet shook his head. "Still no answer." He sighed, brushing his hair from his face. "This can't be good."

Seth's blue eyes darkened with worry. "I'll tell Anna we have to go."

Jet shook his head again. "No," he said quickly. "The last thing we need is the attention. Tell her Nyx is having car troubles and I've gone to get her."

Seth clearly didn't like the idea of lying to his girlfriend, but he nodded. "Okay," he said. "Let me know as soon as you find her."

Jet nodded.

He turned and left the dance hall quickly, dodging the rain as he jumped into his car. He sighed shortly as he hit the highway.

Why did this always have to happen? He hadn't been able to have a decent night out in weeks. He guessed it was karma for trying to hit on Nyx's friends. The thought made him roll his eyes.

The road was slick as the rain poured down. He was getting tired of the stupid weather, too. His windshield wipers were on as fast as they could go, but it didn't help much since he was driving too fast anyway.

Jet felt his heart sink as he turned a bend, seeing headlights on the side of the road. He hit the brakes quickly, pulling over. He recognized Dorothea's truck as he jumped out of his car.

"Nyx!" He jogged to the truck, hearing the engine still running. He yanked open the passenger door. "Nyx?"

The cab was empty, and it made the feeling in his chest worse. His breath caught as he looked across to the driver's side window, seeing a small smear of blood on the glass. He cursed to himself in his native tongue, turning the truck off and tucking the keys into his pocket.

He climbed to the road, looking down it, feeling his heart twisting with rage. He would find Sophia, and he would gut her. He wouldn't make her death easy or swift if she'd done anything to hurt Nyx.

— 31 —

The Lucky Factory.

Friday, November 18, 2011.

NYX BLINKED, TRYING TO ease the pain in her head. She was sitting on a cement floor, her hands bound behind her back. Faint sunlight was trying to push through the dirty windows of the factory. Nyx could still hear rain falling outside, thunder booming and shaking the building. The factory air was cold, making her tremble.

She watched as the dark-haired man stood silently nearby, his eyes trained on Sophia. She was leaning over what appeared to be a tub of some kind, filled with crimson liquid. She was speaking in a language Nyx didn't understand.

Nyx gasped when the air began to shift inside the building, turning ever colder. Her eyes were wide as she watched Sophia wave a mottled hand, a feather quill forming. Her head pulsed behind her eyes, making her pain worse, but filling her with a sense of déjà vu.

"You don't remember yet," Sophia said, turning her crimson gaze on Nyx, "but you will." She grinned her demon smile, making Nyx's heart skip a beat.

Nyx pulled against the ropes that bound her, fighting the tears that were filling her eyes. She didn't want to become part of whatever sick thing Sophia was doing. She drew a ragged breath when Sophia turned toward her, the end of her quill dripping with blood.

Sophia said something to the man beside her that sounded like a command.

"No!" Nyx gasped as he lifted her from the floor and shoved her to her knees at Sophia's feet.

Sophia was still grinning as she looked down at Nyx. "I was just going to kill you, but now I think it's time to have some fun." She motioned to the man.

Nyx flinched as he drew a knife. Her head swam with her fear as she expected him to drive it into her flesh. She drew a ragged breath when he cut her hands loose, catching her right wrist in a painful grip. Nyx tried to struggle against him as he held her hand out to Sophia, but his grip was like iron, keeping her still.

Sophia reached out a hand, her fingers deathly cold as she used them to uncurl Nyx's fist. "Don't worry, darling," she said, venom in her voice. "It won't hurt long."

Nyx couldn't look away as Sophia used her quill to pierce the end of her finger. Her eyes widened as the drop of blood that beaded on her skin was sucked into the quill, causing it to ignite with golden sparks. The feather began to turn gold, and Sophia's grin grew more evil.

"You're mine now, Princess," she said coldly.

Nyx drew a slow breath, feeling searing pain beginning in the end of her finger. She gritted her teeth as it began to seep through her hand and down her arm, increasingly painful as it went. The man had released her, and she fell forward, bracing her hands on the cement floor. Her breaths were quick and labored as the burning pain began to fill her whole body.

Sophia's grin never wavered as a scream tore from Nyx's throat. She was pleased as she watched her writhe on the floor for a long moment.

The man turned to look at her, his eyes mildly concerned. "Are you sure this won't kill her?" he asked in Sarotian.

Sophia turned her eyes on him, seeing him flinch slightly. "She's too strong," she growled. "And even if it does, so what?"

The man turned his eyes back to Nyx, watching as she became still. "Now what?"

Sophia lifted her quill, using a writing motion. "To your feet," she whispered, using her native tongue to lace power into her words.

Nyx's eyes opened slowly, the emerald green fading from her gaze, replaced with a vacant blackness. She moved slowly to stand, staring silently at the ground.

Sophia could feel a sudden power beginning to seep from Nyx's body, pulsing against her. Surprise filled her. She had known the Princess would be a force to be reckoned with, but this was something entirely different. She waved her quill again, writing Sarotian words into Nyx's mind.

Kill him.

Nyx turned her head then, her eyes staring blankly at the man beside Sophia.

His face instantly pulled into a scowl and he slid into a defensive stance. "What did you command her?" he demanded, his voice angry.

Sophia grinned darkly. "Just testing her, my dear Lance," she growled. "It's nothing personal."

Nyx took a step forward, blinking to stand before him. White-hot magic was pooling in her fingers, dripping to the floor like molten gold. She swung her fist at Lance. He barely had time to dodge her burning attack, feeling the liquid magic searing into his skin as droplets hit him. He flash-stepped away from her, grimacing against the power that was eating away at him like acid.

"Call her off!" he demanded.

Sophia didn't move, her eyes taking in the raw strength Nyx was exhibiting. "She's beautiful." Her crimson eyes were wide with awe.

Lance scowled more deeply, leaping away as Nyx moved toward him again. Her movements were easy and fluid, her eyes unfocused as she followed Sophia's orders. Lance knew it was useless, but the will to live was too strong for him to just let her obliterate him.

He waved a hand, forming a solid steel katana in his fist. He swung the blade at Nyx, watching as she easily side-stepped his strike. His blade whistled as it cut through the air, missing her every time he swung his arms. He noticed that her eyes were focused on the sword, and he grinned.

"That's right, girl," he said, leaping at her. He looked up as she leapt into the air, avoiding the crushing blow he dealt to the floor and landing easily on a beam high above him. He waved his hand, an energy shield forming around him. "You're afraid. And you should be."

Sophia scowled at his insult. She started to give Nyx another command, but she stilled her hand when Nyx tilted her head. She pushed off the beam with lightning speed, the floor shaking as she caught Lance, slamming him into the concrete. Her hands were pressed against his chest, a bright light causing Sophia to lift her hands to shade her eyes.

The air rippled and shimmered around them as Nyx drew her strength, releasing it with a window-shattering boom. The light flashed and disappeared as quickly as it had come, the air feeling hot suddenly.

Sophia blinked, taking in the scene.

Nyx was standing slowly, Lance's body completely vaporized. The floor was seared from the heat and magic, shards of glass sparkling as they fell to the floor. Nyx was still as she waited for Sophia's next command.

Sophia felt a trill of excitement shoot through her. Lance's shield had been completely decimated by Nyx's touch. She walked slowly toward Nyx, grinning. "You truly are something else," she said as she stood next to Nyx. "The most powerful that Our King could find have been defeated by you as if they were nothing."

Nyx turned slowly to face her, her eyes still black and empty.

Sophia reached out to smooth Nyx's hair from her face, drawing her hand back in surprise at the heat that was still rolling off Nyx's skin. "I have a task for you," she said, pleased. She motioned to the tub, where her blood concoction was beginning to bubble, clearly under the influence of the surge of power Nyx created.

Nyx stepped slowly toward it, causing the concoction to roil fiercely, as if something was alive beneath the surface, aching to escape.

"Bring my creation to life," Sophia whispered, leaning close to Nyx's ear. "And take it with you to destroy Jet."

The rain wasn't letting up. If anything, it was getting worse as Jet drove down a curve in the road. His hands were tight around the steering wheel. Where was Nyx? Where could Sophia have possibly taken her?

A sudden spark of something caught Jet's eye, and he slowed the car, pulling over to the side of the road. Despite the heavy rain, he stepped out, feeling something immensely powerful just beyond the trees. Anticipation crawled down his spine as he stepped through the tree line. His eyes scanned the darkness, a powerful aura pulsing against him. It was hot and almost inviting, something familiar about it tickling his senses.

Jet turned his head suddenly when the spark he'd seen from earlier caught his attention again. His heart twisted in his chest as anticipation filled him. He knew he wasn't alone. Bright light began to fill the darkness then, and Jet's feet stilled as a figure stepped from the trees.

"Nyx?"

She was standing just inside a clearing, perfectly still as the rain dripped from her face and the ends of her hair. The glow was emanating from her body, surrounding her with golden light.

"What are you doing?" Jet asked, stepping toward her. The anticipation was worse as he moved forward.

Nyx still didn't move, and Jet could feel his chest tighten. Was this an illusion? Was he being lured into a trap?

Still, he pressed forward, coming within arm's reach of her. Her clothing was soaked, and her eyes were downcast, her lips parted slightly as she drew a slow breath.

"You're kinda freaking me out," Jet said slowly. He reached out a hand to touch her. "Nyx?"

She suddenly reacted then, catching his wrist in a painful grip. She was impossibly strong as she held him in place, her lifeless eyes shifting to his face.

Jet gritted his teeth. What had Sophia done to her? He braced when she suddenly flung him away from her, as if he weighed nothing.

"What the hell?" Jet breathed. He realized he was staring up at the sky, lying flat on his back. He was disoriented for a long moment, turning his eyes back to her. "Nyx, snap out of it!"

Nyx turned to face him then, squaring her shoulders toward him. She waved her hands, two gold swords forming.

Jet moved to a knee. This was new.

Jet's breath stuck in his throat as he stared at her, realizing that he'd seen those curved scimitars before. He didn't know what he was up against as his eyes drifted over the small girl before him.

A sudden memory faded across his mind, making him scowl darkly. "You're reading my memories," he said. Even from his distance he could see the Priorae symbols that formed on Nyx's swords, symbols she couldn't have possibly known. How was this possible? Was this Nyx's power, or was this Sophia's?

Nyx tilted her head then, her eyes still void of emotion.

Jet rose to his feet, forming his Geminaci swords in his hands. He wasn't sure how this fight would turn out, but he was more afraid of what would happen to Nyx. Her magic was extremely strong, just like he'd always guessed, but that didn't mean that she would be a match for the *fax* if it came down to it.

"I don't want to fight you," he said, lifting his blades in a defensive stance. "But I will if I have to."

Nyx's lips suddenly lifted in a taunting smile. "You will die."

Jet's eyes widened at the Sarotian words that flowed from her lips. Nyx couldn't speak Sarotian, or sword fight, for that matter. He didn't have time to dwell on that, though, when she suddenly leapt for him, swinging the golden scimitars in a practiced manner.

Jet parried her blows, ducking under her swings and weaving away from her. She landed with her back to him, but that didn't slow her down as she spun, murder in her eyes. In a swift maneuver, she dissolved one of her swords, sending a searing blast of gold light at him. Jet jumped out of the way, feeling the heat from her attack burning as it went past him. A tree behind him took the brunt, exploding with a shower of gold sparks.

Despite missing, Nyx still didn't slow as she swung her remaining sword at him. Jet lifted his weapons, using them to catch Nyx's blade in his own. She strained to break free as Jet held her still.

"Come back to me, Nyx," he said through gritted teeth. "This isn't you."

Nyx scowled deeply, fighting to wrench the scimitar from his grip. Hatred was on her face as she looked up at him. She didn't say anything, surprising him when she suddenly let the sword dissolve from her fingers, leaping away from him.

"If you want the Princess back, you must come find her."

Jet scowled darkly. "Sophia!" He realized that the words coming out of Nyx's mouth were not her own. "Release her!"

Nyx shook her head, smirking then. She turned, vanishing quickly into the trees.

Jet drew a haggard breath as he stood there, staring after her into the darkness. This wasn't good at all.

32

The Estrella Residence.

Saturday, November 19, 2011.

GUILT WAS SITTING heavily in Seth's gut as he watched Dorothea sink down onto her couch.

"I shouldn't have let her go out," Dorothea said, using a tissue to wipe her eyes. Pain furrowed her brow as her tears began anew.

"Don't worry, Dorothea," Seth said, kneeling before her. His blue eyes searched her face. "We will find her."

Buzzing filled the silence and Seth pulled his phone from his pocket, answering it quickly.

"We have a problem," Jet said, his voice angry on the other end.

Seth frowned. "A bigger problem than Nyx being missing?" he asked sarcastically.

Jet growled into the receiver. "There was an influx of Auresi magic," he said shortly. "Stronger than I've ever felt before. I'm sure you can guess what that means."

Seth felt his face turn pale. "That is a problem," he whispered.

Jet grunted humorlessly. "I've tracked it to the abandoned factory. You should probably get your ass down here." His voice quieted, an uncharacteristic edge to it. "I don't know if I can do this alone."

Seth stood quickly, looking at Dorothea. "Stay here," he said darkly. He walked out the door quickly, climbing into his car. "Are you there already?"

"Yeah." Jet grew silent for a moment. "Shit."

Seth knew that wasn't good.

"I've gotta go," Jet said, fury in his voice. "Sophia is here."

Seth felt his heart drop as Jet hung up the phone. He gunned the car as he pulled onto the highway. He had a feeling everything was about to go to hell.

Jet threw his phone into the passenger seat, stepping slowly from the car. He watched Sophia as she sauntered toward him, the feather of her quill sticking out of the tangled braid in her hair. He drew a slow breath as he stared at her grotesque new form.

"You seem surprised, General," Sophia said, baring her gnarly teeth.

Jet arched a brow. "You were already ugly inside," he said slowly. "Now your appearance suits you."

Sophia paused, perching a hand on her hip. "Very funny," she said patronizingly. "But I'm sure you're wondering how I survived."

Jet crossed his arms, shrugging lightly. "Actually, I wasn't," he said. "You're going to die soon, and that's all

I care about." He let his eyes shift around, searching for any sign of Nyx.

Sophia smirked. "We'll see about that," she said flippantly. "But you should know that I found a way to control my own body."

Jet's eyes narrowed. What did that mean? Was that how she was controlling Nyx?

"It's what prevented me from dying," she continued, her smirk growing.

"So?" Jet demanded.

Sophia shrugged, pulling her quill from her hair. "I just thought you should know." She waved the quill then, writing Sarotian symbols in the air.

Jet could feel the magic she was painting with, and he gritted his teeth. "Can you not summon a golem this time?" he asked scornfully. "It took days for the stench of ink to come out of my hair."

Sophia's crimson eyes darkened as she finished weaving her spell. "My golem will be the least of your worries."

Jet turned his head, feeling a spike of hot magic filling the air. He was stringing together curses in his head as he spun, seeing Nyx standing behind him. Surprise clawed at him as he stared at her, the air around her shimmering with the heat of her magic. It was different, seeing her in the coming daylight. She was immensely powerful, growing stronger with every passing moment, and he wondered how in the hell he missed her. He felt his chest tighten at simply being so close to her, the *fax* whispering in his head.

"Nyx?" He watched as her eyes shifted to his, dark and void of life. He felt his heart twist. "What has she done to you?"

"The same magic that keeps me alive is what binds her to me," Sophia said from behind him.

Jet gritted his teeth, feeling fury fill him. He turned quickly, flashing toward her. His talons dug into the ground as Sophia leapt away easily. "She's not your damn toy!"

Jet's rage was only tempered when he felt Nyx shift behind him. He barely managed to dodge the searing flame of her attack as she came at him, releasing a burst of power into the ground where he'd been standing.

"Nyx, you have to stop this!" he yelled as he landed a few feet from her. He noticed that her movements were zombie-like, yet fluid as she turned and moved toward him again.

He stepped back, avoiding another of her blows, noticing that her eyes never met his. He knew what he might have to do to stop her, but he really didn't want to. He avoided another searing blow, catching the back of her jacket as she reached for him. He pinned her roughly to the ground, feeling his heart twist as he pressed her face into the dirt.

"Get yourself together," he ground out. "Don't let that bitch control you!"

Nyx turned her head then, bracing her hands against the ground. She was still for a moment, and Jet thought he might have a chance to bring her back, but then she reached behind her, catching his arm.

Jet was surprised when she pushed herself up and yanked him down with surprising force, pinning him to the ground with her knee against his chest. He could feel the heat of her aura burning against his skin, the voice in his head becoming louder suddenly. Nyx pressed a hand against his chest, summoning searing magic.

Jet grimaced as pain began to course through his chest where she was touching him. He tried to push her off of him, but she was strong, keeping him pinned as she forced more of her energy to pulse through his body. He gasped painfully, the *fax* twisting harder inside him. If he didn't get away from her soon, he knew the *fax* would kill her.

"I expected more from you, General," Sophia said, stepping closer. Her eyes were wild with delight. "But I will be happy to see you die."

Jet caught Nyx's hand as she suddenly moved as if to drive her fingers into his chest. "You don't want to do this," he managed, searching her face for any sign of the girl he knew was in there. "You're not a murderer."

Nyx's brows rose slightly.

Jet felt hope spark inside him. "That's right," he said, his arms shaking lightly. "If you kill me, you'll become everything you hate."

Nyx's brow furrowed then, uncertainty stilling her. Her eyes were still empty, but Jet knew he was reaching her.

"You have to fight her, Nyx," he whispered through gritted teeth. "Don't let her do this to you."

Sophia suddenly stepped closer, a snarl on her face. "Kill him," she commanded in Sarotian. "He's trying to get into your head. Just finish him."

Jet's eyes never left Nyx's. "I'm not in your head," he said, feeling her relax slightly. "I would never do to you what she's doing." He was surprised when Nyx blinked slowly, the fire in his body lessening. "You only have one choice." His eyes shifted to Sophia. "You have to kill her and break her spell over you."

Nyx was still for a moment, but then she turned her head slowly, a hint of green streaking through her eyes as she blinked again. She rose slowly off of Jet, facing Sophia.

Sophia wielded her quill, writing frantically in the air. "Obey me!"

Jet moved quickly to his feet. He started toward Sophia, when a roar suddenly split the air. He stilled, turning as the old building behind them shattered, a hulking, oozing golem staggering from the mess. "Are you kidding me?"

The golem was ten times the size of the first one, lurching and dripping all over the ground. The ink was burning into the soil, noxious fumes filling the air. Sophia laughed as the monster swayed toward them.

"Isn't it beautiful?" she asked, her voice crazed. She turned her eyes on Jet. "I couldn't have made this magnificent beast without her."

Jet scowled darkly. "She didn't know what she was doing," he growled. He moved toward Sophia, readying his claws. "You're going to pay."

The golem was much quicker than Jet expected, suddenly leaping at him. He barely managed to avoid the beast's massive, dripping paw as it defended Sophia. She was still cackling behind her creation.

"If I can't have her, then you both will die!"

Nyx was still and unmoving, staring blankly at the beast as it moved toward her.

Jet rolled to his feet, sprinting toward her. "Nyx, get out of the way!"

Her eyes flickered to the golem as it reared back, intending to deal a fatal blow. She didn't seem fazed as she lifted a hand, liquid gold once again dripping from her fingers. Jet's feet stilled as the golem swung at her, her hand stopping it dead in its tracks. The air reverberated with the blow, a rumbling screech leaving the golem's throat.

"Holy shit," Jet breathed. How had she done that? He'd never seen anyone stop a golem with a single touch. He was further surprised when she twisted her hand, causing the beast to howl in pain and rage.

Its arm twisted unnaturally to the side, baring its chest. With a smooth motion, Nyx struck with her opposite hand, a blast of white magic tearing a hole through the monster's chest. She released it, letting it collapse in a soggy puddle to the ground. Golden sparks jumped across the monster's body, devouring it.

"No!" Sophia gasped, rage pulling her face into a grotesque snarl.

Jet turned to face her, seeing her lift her quill, forming it into a pure spike of energy. Fury filled him as he realized her target was Nyx, and he leapt at her, catching her around her throat. He slammed her into the ground, a hand on either side of her head. He smirked darkly.

"Stay dead this time."

He gave a smooth twist, feeling her head separate from her body. Her hands fell limply at her side. Her quill shimmered, devolving into its normal shape, falling noiselessly to the ground. Jet turned, stepping on it with his boot, feeling it splinter. Inky blood oozed from the quill. With the spell broken, Sophia's body began to liquefy, the ink that kept her alive staining the ground.

Relief filled Jet for a moment as he turned away from what was left of her carcass, looking at Nyx. She was standing very still, her eyes unfocused as her magic continued to destroy the golem. Jet stepped toward her, feeling defensive.

"Nyx?"

She turned her head slowly at the sound of his voice, blinking languidly.

"You're safe now," he said gently, stepping closer. He froze when she turned toward him, prepared for whatever would happen next. Anticipation filled him at the thought of having to fight her, but he drew a sharp breath when her eyes suddenly rolled back, her knees buckling.

He jumped toward her, catching her into his arms as she fainted. He held her against his chest, kneeling slowly on the ground. "You're safe," he whispered, brushing her golden hair from her face as he laid her on the ground. "You're okay."

The sound of tires on gravel met his ears and he looked up, frowning as the car slid to a stop and Seth jumped out. His blue eyes took in the scene, landing on Nyx.

"What the hell happened?" Seth demanded as he jogged toward them.

Jet pinned him with a glare. "Why am I not surprised that you'd show up after the fight is over?"

Seth kneeled beside him, pressing his hands to Nyx's face. "Is she hurt?"

"She fainted," Jet said softly. He looked up at Seth.

"From what?" Seth demanded.

Jet smirked. "It's a long story."

33

The Alvar Residence.

Saturday, November 19, 2011.

JET LIFTED NYX'S LIMP form from the front seat of Seth's car, carrying her slowly up the front steps. Seth was ahead of him, turning on lights and walking quickly to the kitchen to find sugar and water. Jet eased her down onto the couch, sitting on the floor beside her. He drew a slow breath, pressing a hand against his chest, feeling taxed.

A frown was pulling at his lips. It was a good thing he'd heeded Seth's warning about needing to feed. If he hadn't, he knew it would have been impossible to resist the call of the voice in his head. Being so close to something as pure as Nyx's magic had made the entity inside him writhe in pain. He blinked from his thoughts when Seth came into the room, a soda in his hand.

"Help me sit her up," Seth said shortly.

Jet caught one of her arms, pulling her into a sitting position. He listened to her groan softly.

"Drink," Seth said, pressing the can to her lips. "It'll help you regain your strength."

Nyx took a sip around a slow breath. As soon as the sugary substance met her tongue, she lifted her hands, trying to guzzle the whole can.

"Slowly," Seth said, pulling it away. He watched as she sagged against Jet when he settled beside her on the couch. Seth pressed a hand against her cheek. "Can you hear me?"

Nyx nodded slightly, her eyes still closed.

"Can you open your eyes?"

Nyx blinked slowly, her gaze unfocused. The blackness of Sophia's control had faded away, leaving her eyes a deep emerald green.

"Do you know where you are?" Seth asked.

Nyx's eyes shifted over his face as she nodded.

Seth nodded, his eyes roving over her, searching for any sign of injury. "Just rest," he said then.

Nyx sighed, leaning against Jet's shoulder and closing her eyes. It didn't take long for her to fall into a deep slumber.

Seth sat back on his heels, drawing a slow breath. "I don't know what to expect," he said softly. "She might remember, and she might not."

Jet nodded. "You should have been there," he said, arching a brow as humor flitted across his face. "It was the craziest thing I've ever seen."

Seth was clearly unhappy. "This isn't the way things were supposed to go."

Jet rolled his eyes. "I already told you that we couldn't do things the way the handmaid wants to," he said. "Too many things get out of control so fast." He shook his head, looking down at her. "If she hadn't been under Sophia's control, she would have died."

Seth moved to his feet, lowering himself in a chair. His eyes were pensive as he watched Nyx sleep. "I've never heard of what you described," he said after a moment. "Of magic so strong it runs like water."

Jet shrugged the best he could without waking Nyx. "You don't have to believe me," he said. "But I know what I saw."

Seth pursed his lips. "Not even Liana can wield magic in that way."

Jet nodded, looking down at Nyx. "I've read stories of the ancient Priorae, but . . ." He shook his head, his thoughts chaotic. As far as he knew, there was no one who could do the things he'd just seen Nyx do. Of course, a lot could have changed in a century, but he didn't think it was likely.

"The Priorae haven't existed for thousands of years," Seth said shortly.

Jet's eyes were still fixed on Nyx's face. "You know everything is a cycle," he said. "The magic always flows in equal parts, and if one side becomes unbalanced, the other will right it."

"And you think there has been a loss of balance?"

Jet looked up at Seth, seeing the dubious look on his face. "Look, I can't see the future or whatever," he said, scowling at Seth. "I just know what I saw."

Seth drew a slow breath. "I believe you." He turned his blue eyes on Nyx. "We should let her sleep."

Jet nodded, carefully maneuvering her so that she was lying on the couch.

"I'm going to see Dorothea," Seth said, standing and grabbing his keys. "You should rest as well." His eyes shifted over Jet, reserved. "No doubt being near her like that was difficult for you."

Jet had to fight down a bitter scowl. "I'm fine," he said quickly. But it wouldn't hurt to take a breather.

Seth nodded, disappearing out the door.

Jet watched Nyx sleep for a long moment, his eyes taking in the curve of her face. Her eyelashes touched the top of her cheeks, her golden hair fanned about her. He had to admit, if only to himself, he was impressed. He never thought she would amount to anything, but she'd surprised him today, even if she didn't know it. There was hope for her yet.

He smirked lightly to himself as he turned away and walked down the hall to his room. She would probably be pissed if she knew he was standing there watching her.

It was dark when the soft scent of her aunt's perfume woke Nyx. She blinked slowly, her mind swimming in confusion. She stared at the ceiling, realizing it wasn't one she recognized. Her eyes shifted around the unfamiliar living room, her heart skipping a beat. She tried to sit up, seeing her aunt asleep in a chair across from her.

Soreness shot through her arms and back. "Aunt Dee?" she whispered. "Aunt Dee, wake up."

Her aunt blinked, her eyes opening slowly. She turned on a table lamp as she got out of the chair. "How are you feeling?" she asked, concern furrowing her brow as she sat beside Nyx on the couch.

Nyx winced slightly. "Sore," she said, looking around. "Where are we?"

"Seth's house," Dorothea said, smoothing Nyx's hair from her face. "You were in an accident."

Nyx frowned at her. "Why didn't we go to the hospital?" she whispered.

Dorothea's brow furrowed. "There wasn't any need to," she said gently. "We knew you were okay."

Nyx shook her head, further confused. "How long have I been here?"

"It's been two days," Dorothea said softly.

Nyx pushed herself up, away from her aunt. "I've been passed out for two days and you didn't think I needed to go to the hospital?" she asked, her voice on the edge of incredulous. A flash of a memory shot through her mind, making her press her hand to her head. "What happened to me?" She winced as she recalled Dr. Armand's twisted face.

"You were taken by a woman," Dorothea said slowly. "She did things to your mind."

Nyx pressed her hands harder against her face. "Dr. Armand?" she breathed. A stinging pain coursed behind her eyes. "She wanted to hurt me."

"Be still," Dorothea said, catching Nyx's arm. "You aren't ready yet."

Nyx pushed her hands away, feeling like her brain was going to explode. Her memories were suddenly pulsing against the inside of her skull as if someone had turned on a faucet. "Her face," she breathed. "Oh God, her face." Sophia's crimson eyes were seared into her mind's eye, as well as the black tendrils that stained her skin and her jagged teeth.

"I have to get out of here—" She blinked her eyes quickly, moving to her feet, feeling out of breath. She couldn't make sense of the things her mind was supplying her with. She was on the edge of hyperventilating as she staggered toward the door.

"Please, Nyx, you can't leave." Dorothea stood, her voice filled with hurt. "You're confused."

Nyx's legs felt weak as she crossed to the front door. Her hand was on the door knob when it twisted under her fingers. She stepped back in surprise as the door opened and Jet's dark eyes found hers.

"Where are you going?" he asked, blocking the doorway.

Nyx stepped back, drawing a ragged breath. "I need to get out of this house," she said. "I need fresh air." She tried to push past him, her knees buckling without her consent.

Jet's arms were around her, steadying her. "You need to sit down," he said. "You shouldn't be moving around."

Nyx gripped the sleeves of his jacket tightly. A flash of memory made her flinch like she'd been hit, Jet's face filling her thoughts, blood on his hands. Nyx pressed her hands against her face, shaking her head. "Why am I seeing these things?" she gasped.

Jet looked over her head at Dorothea, who was wiping silent tears from her eyes. He drew a slow breath, looking back to Nyx. "We need to talk."

Nyx didn't like the way he said that as he helped her to a chair. She looked up when Seth came out of a door, his eyes surprised.

"How are you feeling?" he asked as he came into the room.

Nyx gripped the arms of the chair tightly, feeling as if she would crumble at any moment. "Confused," she said stonily, looking between the three of them. She watched as Jet inclined his head at Seth, who seemed to understand his message.

Seth settled on the couch next to Dorothea, who was sniffling and wiping her eyes. Jet hovered on the edge of the room, his arms crossed tightly. Nyx clenched her jaw, looking between them. She knew she wouldn't like what they had to say.

"Well, I guess I should start," Dorothea said, her voice wavering. She brushed a strand of brown hair from her eyes. "Nyx, I've been keeping a secret from you for a long time." She looked down at her hands in her lap. "I know it was wrong, but you were in danger, and it was the only way to keep you safe."

Nyx could feel her lips curling in disgust as hurt shot through her. She was afraid to hear the rest of what her aunt had to say.

"You were born in a place called Gexalatia," Dorothea continued. She looked up at Jet, hatred filling her gaze. "For many years it has been plagued with war. Your parents were casualties of this war."

A sharp breath stung Nyx's throat as tears filled her eyes. "You said they were killed in an accident," she breathed, feeling betrayal like a lump in her throat.

Dorothea looked down at her hands, shaking her head. "I'm sorry," she said, her voice choked. "I brought you here to keep you alive." She looked up at Nyx. "I was doing what we thought was best for you."

"We who?" Nyx asked, anger beginning to steel her.

"Myself and Liana," Dorothea said softly. "Your grandmother. She asked me to bring you here and to raise you as my own."

Nyx looked down at her hands, realizing she was trembling. "I have a grandmother?" she whispered. She looked up then, suspicion mingling in the hurt in her eyes. "As your own?"

Dorothea nodded quickly, more tears filling her eyes. "I was only a handmaid in your mother's attendants," she said, sobbing softly. "I helped care for you. This is why I was chosen to bring you here."

Nyx sat back in her chair, the wind sucked from her body. "Handmaid? I don't understand . . ."

Dorothea shook her head as she wiped at her eyes. "In Gexalatia, there is a country called Ymber. Your grandmother is the Queen Mother of Ymber. And you are a Princess of Ymber. I am only a servant."

Nyx clenched her fists tightly. She didn't know if she wanted to scream at Dorothea or if she wanted to just stand and walk from the room. She drew a slow breath, trying to calm the rage that was flitting through her. "What does this have to do with Dr. Armand?" she asked, swallowing hard, her mouth suddenly dry. She looked at Jet when he shifted.

"She was from Ymber as well," he said matter-of-factly. "She was a dissenter, sent here by the King of Siccita, Ymber's rival country. Her mission was to kill you."

"Why?" Nyx asked, pressing a hand to her head. Everything was happening too fast. "Why do I have memories of things . . . things I can't understand . . ."

Seth stood then. "I placed a memory block on you," he said, stepping toward her. "I can remove it, but you must allow us to explain to you what you've seen."

Nyx felt cold with fear suddenly. "A memory block?" she asked.

Seth nodded. He closed the distance between them, pressing his hands against her face. Her eyes grew wide with fear as Seth whispered soft Sarotian words. A heavy warmth settled over her suddenly, making her feel tired and weighed down. Then, as soon as the feeling came, it lifted, making her feel dowsed in ice water. She shuddered as pain shot through her, vivid flashes of moments running through her mind like river rapids.

Seth stepped back as she gasped painfully, doubling over in her chair. She coughed and gasped for a breath, gagging against the onslaught of memories. As the initial wave washed over her, she drew a hard breath, sobbing softly. Seth looked at Dorothea, seeing that her brow was twisted with sadness.

For a long moment, all Nyx could do was sob. She remembered Sophia trying to kill her, standing over her with a dagger, and Jet driving his hand through her guts. She remembered the terror she'd felt when she thought she would die in the factory, and the numbness she'd felt as Sophia used her controlling spell to force her to do her bidding. She drew a shuddering breath as she remembered standing over Jet, prepared to kill him, his words being the only thing that stopped her.

Nyx struggled to regain her composure, wiping at her face. She looked up at Dorothea, feeling bitterness fill her. "Why did she want me dead?" she asked finally. She ignored the way Dorothea's face fell.

"You are the princess," Dorothea said. "Your return would ensure the survival of the Estrella line. She and others like her would do whatever it takes to keep you from going home and becoming who you're supposed to be."

Nyx sat straight in her chair, pressing her back against it. "Who am I supposed to be? A princess?" She could feel her fears giving way once again to anger. "And what makes anyone think that I want to go to this place?" she asked bitterly. "This is my home, here in Lucky."

"It was always the plan," Dorothea said weakly. "You don't belong here. You belong in Ymber, in Regius Carmen, with your family."

"And what is my family?" Nyx demanded. "A bunch of freaks?" She lifted her hands. "Why was I able to do the things I did?" She looked at Jet. "Why did I stop the golem?"

"You're an Auresi," Jet said evenly. "The blood that runs through your veins allows you to tap into the power of the creator, Aure."

Nyx frowned in confusion. "What?"

"That's where your power comes from," Jet continued, ignoring the look on her face. "The reverse of the coin are Acerbi, who draw power from Aucer."

"I don't have any idea what that means," Nyx said bitterly.

Jet shrugged. "It's not really important right now," he said. "You just have to believe what we're telling you."

Nyx shook her head, the anger burning through her. She was beginning to feel foolish. "So, if any of this is actually true, why haven't any of you told me?" she demanded. "Why wouldn't I be allowed to make my own choice?" She looked down at her hands, remembering the burn of the magic or whatever it was as it filled her. "Why didn't you tell me what I really am?"

Dorothea shook her head, tears streaking down her face. "I'm sorry, Nyx," she said. "I only did what I thought was right."

Nyx gritted her teeth, moving to her feet. "I can't be here right now," she said, still shaking from the onslaught of emotions coursing through her. She held Dorothea's gaze. "I can't look at you right now."

Dorothea looked like she'd been kicked as she bowed her head. Nyx walked to the door and yanked it open, slamming it behind her. Dorothea looked helpless as she turned to Seth. "What can I do?" she asked, crying softly.

"Leave her alone," Jet said, looking toward the door. "She needs to process what she's been told."

Seth put his arm around Dorothea's shoulder to comfort her. "Someone needs to keep an eye on her."

Jet sighed shortly. "I'll do it," he said, walking to the door. He opened it, blinking against the cold wind that blew into his face. He turned his head, seeing Nyx sitting on the swing on the far end of the porch. He leaned against a column, watching her stare across the field that surrounded the house.

"What do you want?" she asked darkly.

Jet drew a slow breath as he turned to look across the driveway. "I'm just here to make sure you don't do something stupid."

Nyx turned her head then, pinning him with a glare. "You're the last person I want watching me." Her eyes shifted over him suspiciously. "And who are you, anyway?" She looked away. "You're obviously not from Europe."

Jet tried to force down a smirk. "Clearly," he said in agreement.

Nyx pressed a hand over her face. "It makes sense why you were so weird back then," she whispered. Suddenly all his stupid idiosyncrasies made sense. She felt a strange mixture of rage and sadness sweep her again as she looked at him. "You can't make me leave." Her gaze was vehement. "I'm an adult, and I don't want to leave."

Jet arched a brow at her, turning his back against the column. "You're getting ahead of yourself," he said. "You don't even know how truly wrong you are for this world."

"What the hell does that mean?" Nyx snapped.

"You aren't meant for this world any more than fish are meant for the sky," Jet said easily. His eyes were pensive as he stared at the porch. "Some of the things I've seen would make this life feel like it's standing still."

Nyx was frowning at him. "I don't know what any of that means."

Jet looked at her, mischief in his eyes. "Let me show you what you can be," he said. "Then decide if you want to return to Gexalatia." He smirked. "Once you get a taste for it, you can never go back."

Nyx turned away, feeling her chest tighten. Did she want that? She stared at her hands, which were clenched on her knees. She could remember the way it felt as whatever she'd tapped into coursed through her body. It had filled her with a strength and peace she'd never felt before, and thinking about it now made her want to feel it again. Even when the golem had come barreling down on her, she'd never felt any fear. There had just been the very singular knowledge that she would be okay and that no harm would come to her.

"How can you be so sure?" she whispered.

Jet turned to face her. "I know you better than you think," he said.

Nyx scowled, looking up at him. "Big words for the person who I hate most in this world. Seems like I know you better than you think, too." She'd known he was an ass, and now he was proving to her that he was a liar. There had to be irony in there somewhere.

Jet smirked. "Just give me a chance," he said. "You won't be sorry."

Nyx looked down again, apprehension coiling inside her. How could she possibly make a decision like this? She wasn't even sure that any of this was real. What if this was all a dream, a side-effect of the accident she'd been involved in? She remembered running off the road. What if all of this was just fevered imaginings?

Jet straightened. "Think about it."

Nyx glanced at him as he turned and walked back into the house. Her heart was as heavy as the silence that fell over her. She didn't know who to trust or what to believe anymore.

— 34 —

The Estrella Residence.

Monday, November 21, 2011.

Nyx was sitting on her bed, staring at the wall. She could smell her aunt cooking breakfast, but she wasn't hungry. Guilt was eating at her as she thought about all the chores that were going undone that morning. She hadn't left her room or even bothered to get dressed. She'd just been sitting on her bed for nearly an hour. She hadn't slept at all since Saturday night, unable to reconcile the things that she was experiencing with what she had thought was reality.

A knock sounded at her door. "Sweetheart?"

Nyx crossed her arms tightly. The last person she wanted to talk to was her aunt. She didn't say anything, feeling miserable.

"Nyx? Can I please come in?"

Nyx drew a slow breath. She didn't have anything to say to Dorothea. She let the silence continue to linger, hoping her aunt would take the hint.

"I get it," her aunt said beyond the door, "you're trying to punish me. I don't fault you for that. But you have to know that I love you. Nothing about that has changed."

Guilt shot through her suddenly. She knew that what she was doing wasn't fair. But she couldn't just forget about all the hurt she felt.

"I'll be downstairs if you need me," Dorothea said finally. "I'd really like to talk to you when you're ready."

Nyx turned away, drawing a ragged breath. She wondered if she should just let her aunt talk to her. Actually, that woman wasn't her aunt. She was some stranger who had taken her from her real family, if what she said was true. The thought made her heart ache. Dorothea had raised her. How could she not be her family? Why was everything so difficult now?

A soft sound made Nyx jump, and she turned toward her window. The sound came again, and Nyx realized something was hitting her window. She crawled across her bed and stepped onto the floor, pulling the blinds open. She looked down into the yard, surprised to see Jet standing there, smirking lightly. Nyx scowled when he tossed another rock at the window.

She undid the lock and yanked the window open, leaning out of it. "What do you want?" she asked bitterly.

Jet tilted his head. "We've got things to do, remember?"

Nyx narrowed her eyes at him. "I don't feel good today."

Jet crossed his arms. "Pouting up there isn't going to make you feel better. Just come down here."

Nyx drew a slow breath. It was a nice day out. The sun was out and the sky was perfectly clear, even though the air was chilly. She looked back down at him, feeling stubbornness get the best of her. "No." She pushed the window shut and pulled the blinds.

She didn't want to see anyone today. She climbed back into her bed and pulled the covers up to her chin. She didn't want to be outside or ever leave her room again. She was mad at all of them, and she would punish them by being mad at them. She knew it was childish.

Another sound on the window made her turn her head. She scowled, flipping the covers back roughly and jumping to her feet. She yanked the blinds open, intending to give Jet a piece of her mind, when she realized he wasn't standing in the yard like before. She frowned as she opened the window slowly. Where the heck did he go?

"Hey."

Nyx looked up, surprised to see him sitting on the roof over the window. His knee was drawn up toward his chest while his other leg swung easily over the edge. The same taunting smirk was on his face.

"How did you get up there so fast?" Nyx asked, watching him warily.

Jet leaned forward, wrapping his fingers around the edge of the roof. "It's not hard," he said simply. "I'm not going to leave you alone until you come out of your tower."

Nyx scowled at him. "I told you I don't feel good. So go away." She started to close the window again, but she froze when Jet suddenly dropped from where he was sitting, his boots landing on the window sill.

Nyx stepped back as he crouched there for a moment before stepping into the room. Her heart was racing as she watched him. She didn't understand how he could have done that.

"Why is it so dark in here?" Jet asked nonchalantly as he looked around. "Is that what you do when you're brooding? Turn off all the lights?" He didn't like to sit in the dark if he could avoid it.

Nyx crossed her arms tightly. "I'm not brooding," she snapped. "I'm angry."

Jet shrugged, sitting slowly on the end of her bed. "Same thing."

"Get out of my room," Nyx said tensely.

Jet looked at her, his dark eyes unconcerned. "You told me you would try to see things my way," he said easily. "This doesn't feel like trying."

Nyx dug her fingers into her arms. "I don't want to try today."

"Then when?" Jet asked, still watching her. "We don't have a lot of time."

Nyx frowned. "What do you mean?" she asked, feeling her chest clench. She didn't want to think about being forced to leave her home and her friends.

Jet glanced down at the watch on his wrist. "One month from today the Limen will open and you need to be ready."

Nyx clenched her hands harder. "I don't understand," she whispered, feeling afraid suddenly. "There's been a countdown this whole time?"

Jet nodded. "We only have twenty-four hours to cross," he said shortly. "We can't miss our window."

Nyx shook her head. "I don't want to go," she said quickly. "You can't make me leave."

Jet looked at her, annoyance in his eyes. "We've talked about this," he said. "You don't belong here. You belong in Gexalatia, in Ymber, with people who understand you."

Nyx looked down, tears in her eyes. "I've never been any different than my friends here," she said. "Why do I have to learn to be different now?"

"You've always been different," Jet said, standing slowly. "Even though you weren't aware of it, you were weaving small spells over the people around you. You've been influencing the humans that you surround yourself with from the very beginning."

Nyx's brow furrowed. "Are you saying I'm not capable of having friends?" she demanded. "That I'm not likable?"

Jet shook his head, a humored sound escaping him. "The first night I met you, you were charming that boy," he said. "He never liked you, you made him think he did."

Hurt was on Nyx's face as she looked away. "That's not true," she said stiffly. She wiped rogue tears away.

"It is true," Jet said, feeling sorry for her suddenly. "If you would let me train you, you will feel what the rest of us feel. We can sense your magic, your aura. You are strong, but you're untrained." He sighed shortly as he looked at her. "At best you could maybe accidently keep yourself alive, at worst you wouldn't know what to do and you'd die."

Nyx looked up at him. "Die?" she breathed.

Jet nodded. "The Crown has many enemies," he said, his lips quirking. "Why else would you have been brought here?"

"I've never done anything to anybody," Nyx said, her voice shaking. "I don't understand any of this."

Jet held out a hand to her. "Come with me. I will help you understand."

Nyx stared at his hand for a long moment. She remembered when he'd offered it to her before, when he was covered in blood and ink. She looked up at him. "I have to get dressed."

Jet smirked, letting his eyes shift over her. "Wear something comfortable."

Nyx drew a slow breath as she pulled on her boots and laced them around her ankles. Anticipation was coiling in her chest. She didn't know what to expect as she stood slowly. She used an elastic band to tie her hair back and opened her window.

Jet had climbed out the window to give her some privacy, and he was perched on the edge of the roof like he'd been before. He looked down at her when she poked her head out. "Took you long enough."

Nyx scowled at him. "Shut up," she said. She looked around, wondering how in the heck she was supposed to get up there with him. "I hope you don't expect me to come up there with you."

"Why?" Jet asked. "Are you afraid?"

Nyx's scowl deepened. "No," she said shortly. "I just don't want to go up there."

He smirked. "Give me your hand, little princess." He held out his hand to her once again.

Nyx looked down at the ground, feeling a sense of vertigo. She hated heights. She looked up at him, seeing him waiting patiently. "How do I know I can trust you?" she asked warily.

Jet shrugged. "You either do or you don't," he said. "There's no in-between." He watched her face. "So which is it?"

Nyx braced her hands on the window sill, looking down once more. She swallowed thickly as she looked back up at him, putting her foot on the sill and moving shakily to stand. She looked up, feeling his hand wrap firmly around hers.

He was grinning victoriously as he pulled her up next to him. "That wasn't so bad, was it?"

Nyx knelt slowly beside him, feeling as if every movement might send her toppling off the roof. "I hate heights," she breathed as she eased to sit. Her eyes never left the ground.

Jet rested his arm across his knees, leaning to look at her. "If you keep looking down, you'll miss what's right in front of you."

Nyx drew a ragged breath, lifting her eyes from the two-story drop. She paused as she realized that the view was spectacular. She could see the rolling fields around their house, surrounded by the trees in the distance. Horses were grazing peacefully, too far away to be heard as they snorted and whipped their tails. The sky was a perfect shade of blue, and the sun was warm up here.

"A princess should never look down," Jet said quietly beside her. "Her eyes should always be looking at what is ahead, and not what is at her feet."

Nyx glanced over at him. "Thanks, Confucius."

Jet rolled his eyes. "It's the truth," he said, stretching his legs out in front of him. "You can't see where you want to go if you're always looking at where you've been."

"So how do I decide where I want to go now?" she asked, glancing down at the ground again. "Seems like I only have one option."

Jet shook his head. "You never have just one option." He leaned forward. "You can choose to fall," he glanced over his shoulder at her, his onyx eyes sparkling mischievously, "or you can decide to jump."

Nyx drew a sharp breath as he stood in a fluid motion, stepping over the edge. She leaned forward quickly, expecting to see him lying on the ground. Instead, he landed easily in a crouch, standing slowly to look at her. Her head swam as she realized how far he'd jumped.

"Your turn," he called.

Nyx shook her head. "No way!" she yelled, her voice shaking. "I can't do that. I'll break my damn neck!"

Jet shook his head. "You can do it," he said easily. He crossed his arms. "I thought you trusted me."

"I don't trust you that much!" Nyx yelled, feeling sick and irritated. How was she going to get down? There was no way she could clamber back into her window.

"It's all or nothing," Jet said, an annoyed edge to his voice. He needed her to believe him and in him. How could he teach her if she didn't trust him? "Don't worry. I'll catch you."

Nyx stared down at him incredulously. "You'll catch me?" she demanded.

Jet clenched his jaw. He was losing his patience with her. "Don't make me come back up there and throw you off."

Nyx's face paled at the thought and she leaned back. She drew a steeling breath. She'd seen Jet outmaneuver a golem. He'd done that crazy jumping business. She knew that she should believe him, but she couldn't stop imagining her face crashing into the ground. "Okay," she breathed. "I can do this."

Jet arched a brow as he watched her move shakily to stand. She gasped when her feet slid slightly, falling so that her hands could grasp at something. Unfortunately, there was nothing to grab onto. She seemed to catch herself, though, and she straightened slowly.

"Now what?" she asked, her voice hitching slightly.

"Just jump," Jet said.

"How do I know you'll catch me?" she asked, her eyes worried.

"You either trust me or you don't," Jet reiterated. He watched her as she shook her head, clearly having an internal dialogue. He wanted to roll his eyes when she sat on the edge of the roof, dangling her feet over. Things would be so much easier if she'd just hurry up.

"I can do this," Nyx breathed. "I can do this." She met Jet's gaze, seeing that he looked bored. "You could at least act like you're ready."

"I am ready," he said easily. He uncrossed his arms. "Now come on. There are other things to do."

Nyx scowled at him, drawing a slow breath. "If I die, you can't have any of my stuff."

Jet smirked and shook his head.

Nyx braced her hands. "Here I come," she said weakly. She closed her eyes, knowing she'd just have to do it. She'd just have to go and not think about it.

Her heart leapt into her throat as she pushed off the side. She drew a sharp breath, unable to do anything as she felt herself falling. She was jolted when she felt Jet arms come around her.

"Was that really so hard?" he asked.

Nyx blinked, her pulse pounding. She was breathless and speechless for a moment before she pushed out of his arms. She didn't say anything as she took several shaking steps away from him. She'd never been so happy to be on solid ground.

"Now we can get to the fun part," Jet said behind her.

Nyx turned to look at him over her shoulder. "It better not be any more of that," she said quietly, still trying to catch her breath.

Jet shook his head, that smirk still pulling at his face. "I'll try to tone it down," he said dismissively. He turned, indicating that she should follow.

Nyx's knees were wobbly for a long moment as she trudged after him. The cold breeze helped to clear her mind as they walked past the barn and into the pasture. She could see the horses in the distance as they lifted their heads, watching them carefully. Bolt, the black stallion, threw his head up, trumpeting a call to her. Nyx grinned, whistling low to him.

Bolt, the fatty he was, came trotting over with the expectation of finding food. He seemed like he would come straight to her, but he drew up short, stilling as his ears fixed on Jet. Nyx watched as he lifted his head, clearly in fight or flight mode.

"Bolt?" she called. "Come here buddy."

Bolt snorted hard through his nostrils, still fixed on Jet.

Jet narrowed his eyes at the horse. Prey animals always recognized danger when it was close by, and this horse was no different. It was wary of him, and it made him want to chase it away.

"What's gotten into you?" Nyx asked, taking a step toward him.

"Don't," Jet said, catching her arm.

At his motion, Bolt spun around, kicking out as he took off in a gallop across the field. He rounded up his herd and shepherded them to the other end of the pasture.

Nyx looked up at him, confusion on her face. "He's never acted like that before," she said.

Jet let go of her. "Animals are sensitive to our auras," he said, glancing after the horse. "The animals here don't really understand what they feel."

Nyx frowned. "What's this aura you keep talking about?"

"It's an energy field that surrounds all of us," he said, walking away from her. "It's the magic that we share with our creators and our life force."

Nyx trailed after him. "Life force?"

Jet nodded. "If it's ever stolen from you, you will die," he said, glancing at her.

Nyx sighed shortly. "Apparently there are a lot of things that I can die from," she said quietly.

Jet smirked at her. "There are a lot of things that will kill an Inerse, too," he said. "But you have your strength on your side. It will help you survive things that would kill Inerse."

"In-er-say?" Nyx asked, the word feeling foreign in her mouth. "What's that again?"

"Humans," Jet said. "Like your friends." He looked over at her. "Like your handmaid."

Nyx frowned at him. "You mean Aunt Dee."

Jet nodded, pausing. He could see the conflict and the irritation in her eyes.

"Why do you keep calling her my handmaid?" she asked. "She's my aunt."

"She's not your aunt," Jet said shortly. "She's a servant."

Nyx scowled at him. "You're heartless," she said bitterly. "She raised me."

Jet shrugged. "It doesn't matter to me," he said quickly. "Call me heartless if you want, but your life is more important than hers."

Hurt flashed across her face. "How can you say that?" she breathed.

Jet turned to face her. "Because it's true!" he snapped. "You are royalty. She isn't."

Nyx shook her head, turning away from him. This was unbelievable. Just when Jet acted like he had some redeeming qualities, he started behaving like this again. She took a moment to reel in her feelings. "Where are we going?"

"Up there," Jet said, nodding toward the pond in the distance.

Nyx walked past him toward the pond. A large oak tree was leaning over the water, lending shade over the water. In the summertime it was one of her favorite places to sit and have some time alone. She walked to it, feeling a sense of belonging as she sank down onto a large root that protruded from the ground. She didn't look at Jet as he crouched beside her.

"What are we doing here?" she asked, drawing a slow breath. The shade made the air feel colder.

"I'm going to tell you how to access your magic," Jet said.

Nyx turned to look at him, frowning. "Access it?"

Jet nodded. "Children are taught at very young ages to tap into their power." He turned his eyes from the pond to her. "You weren't. You've never had a direct connection to the Creators." He looked back at the sparkling water. "It's in there, something innate that everyone can feel, but that's all it is for you right now. Feelings and emotions. You need to get control of those feelings and emotions and understand where they come from." Jet looked at her. "You can't let your emotions control you. That's how things spiral out of control."

Nyx watched him, feeling her brain racing with thoughts. "What do you mean, creators?" She looked down. "Do you mean like what you said about Randy?"

Jet nodded. "You let your own feelings influence you." He eased to sit in the grass. "So we're going to start small."

Nyx frowned at him in confusion. She watched as he lifted a hand, gasping when a ball of light sparked from his hand. "Holy crap," she breathed. She leaned in closer. "How are you doing that?"

Jet smirked. "Magic."

Nyx narrowed her eyes at him. "Seriously."

"Hold out your hand," he said.

Nyx reached out slowly. She watched as Jet moved his hand toward hers, the orb flickering like a flame. "What is this?" she asked.

"It's called an augarlux," Jet said. He caught her hand with his free one, turning the orb over into the palm of her hand. He watched as she jumped.

The orb was cold against her skin, but she felt a rush of heat through her fingers as it drew on her strength to stay lit. She blinked in surprise when it began to turn from white to a soft gold. "Am I doing this?" she whispered.

Jet nodded silently. He reached his hand out, letting it rest against the top of the orb. It began to swirl, turning black against his touch. The black began to swirl against the gold. Jet could feel the heat of her power through the augarlux.

"Why is mine gold and yours is black?" Nyx asked.

"I can change mine to whatever color I want," Jet said, looking at her over the top of their hands. "What you see is just the raw power that you can channel." He could make the augarlux turn white or red or whatever, but the black was what pulsed through him. It was his raw aura when it touched hers, being purified by her strength.

"So how do I make my own?" Nyx asked.

Jet took the augarlux from her hand, waving it away. "You have to touch what we call the Power of Aure."

Nyx frowned. "What's that?"

Jet drew a slow breath. Explaining years of history was going to be extremely tedious. He needed to dumb it down for her. "We were created in the image of the gods, Aure and Aucer," he said slowly. "Aure is the light and order, while Aucer is the darkness and chaos. Auresi are the children of Aure and Acerbi are the children of Aucer."

Nyx was staring at him, clearly confused.

"Does that make sense?" Jet asked.

Nyx nodded slowly. "I can follow," she said slowly. "But what does that have to do with me?"

"You're Auresi," Jet said simply. "You are a child of Aure, and you carry his light inside you."

Nyx frowned, swallowing thickly. She still didn't really understand what that meant. "So, how do I use the power?"

"You've got to tap into it," Jet said.

"And how do I do that?

Jet sighed. This was going to be irritating. He turned to face her, crossing his legs, trying to think of how to explain it to her. How could he explain something to her he'd been doing his whole life?

"Give me your hands," he said, holding his out.

Nyx looked down at him as if she wouldn't, but then she gingerly put her palms against his.

"Close your eyes. Think of your favorite things." Jet wrapped his fingers around hers. "Imagine a perfect day. How it looks, how it smells."

Nyx drew a slow breath as she closed her eyes. She didn't know what she was supposed to be doing, but she conjured the image of a summer day, sitting under the tree, listening to Bolt splash in the pond. "Now what?" she asked quietly.

"Stop talking," Jet said, wanting to roll his eyes. "Just think about how you feel."

Nyx frowned, but kept her eyes closed. The chilly breeze had been pressing against her skin, but as she thought about her favorite summer days, the feeling of something warm, like a blanket falling around her shoulders, filled her. The sudden scent of a hot, summer wind filled her nose, and she drew a deep breath, drawing the scent deep into her lungs.

She loved summer, and peace flooded her, easing the worry that had been clawing at her heart. She was in a field, with lush, green grass surrounding her. She could hear the swish of a horse tail and the munching of grass. She was laying on her back, staring at the sky, which was blue and bright. The wind was blowing around her, pulling strands of her golden hair into her face.

Movement caught her eye, and she turned her head, surprised to see huge, white feathers beside her. She drew a slow breath as she realized it was a massive wing, and she turned onto her side. It hid the creature the wing belonged to, but Nyx wasn't afraid as she reached for it. She gasped softly when something like fire shot through her finger tips as they brushed the soft feathers. A sudden fluttering filled the air, along with bright, blinding light. The dream seemed to end abruptly, making Nyx draw a sharp breath as she felt the cold wind blowing around her again. She felt invigorated suddenly, as if she'd had a hot bath and a good meal, but her mind was swirling with a strange feeling she couldn't place.

"Open your eyes." Jet's voice suddenly sounded too close, as if his lips were beside her ear, and her eyes flew open.

The sun felt too bright suddenly, and she blinked rapidly, trying to get her eyes to adjust. Nyx realized that she felt funny, and different. Things felt too close and too sharp as she looked around. The noises of birds and insects felt loud, and Jet's eyes were sparkling too brightly in the daylight.

"What's happening?" Nyx breathed. Her heart was racing.

A small smirk pulled at Jet's lips. "I can't imagine how it feels," he said. His voice was too loud, even though he was speaking softly. His eyes were searching her face. "Things must be too sharp suddenly."

Nyx blinked, feeling as if she'd been watching her life through a tube television and she'd just now gotten high definition. She felt out of sorts, almost as if she was high. "Is this the magic?" she whispered, her voice shaking slightly as she looked around.

From where she sat, she could see each individual wave that rolled across the pond with the breeze. She could see the details of the blades of grass around her, and the minute grooves in the tree trunk beside her. A movement caught her eyes, and she realized it was a tiny insect, something she would have never noticed unless it was right in front of her.

"Yes."

Nyx shifted her eyes back to Jet, feeling instantly something different about him. He suddenly seemed dark, as if he was a void. He hadn't moved, but another sense was shifting into overdrive as she looked at him, telling her brain that he was dangerous. It made her heart race suddenly, and she drew a sharp breath. She could recall one time, very faintly, the feeling of tasting purple, and it was like that, so nonsensical and disjointed, but it made sense to something inside her. He felt cold to her suddenly, even though his hands on hers had been warm.

His eyes were watching her intently, catching every emotion that was playing across her face. "You can sense my aura," he said, answering the confused and startled look on her face.

"Is that what this is?" she whispered.

Jet nodded. "You'll be able to feel it around others as well," he said. "You can read a person's feelings from their auras; their happiness and sadness. Even fear."

"And humans?" Nyx asked, feeling the distinct urge to pull her hands from his and move as far away from him as possible. "Inerse. Do they have auras?"

"No," Jet said. "They have a life force, which you can sense with training, but nothing like an aura."

Nyx nodded mutely, the disturbed feeling never leaving her. She looked down at her hands, seeing his were hovering just over hers. She thought it was odd that he wasn't touching her like he had been, but something streaked through her, telling her that she didn't want to be touched by him. Like he was something to be avoided at all costs.

"Now that you feel the magic, summoning the augarlux is simple," he said suddenly, drawing her attention. "Whatever you can imagine, you can summon. Just be careful. Some things draw a lot of energy, and that's dangerous."

Nyx nodded, looking up at him, feeling her skin crawl. She shivered, despite no longer feeling cold. "Will I get used to this?" she asked, her eyes guarded as she looked at him.

Jet nodded, shifting his gaze to her hands. He wasn't sure if he should be offended. He could tell that she was suddenly repulsed by him. It had nothing to do with the dark magic that flowed through him, and everything to do with the *fax* that curled in his chest. Her magic was powerful, and more pure than any he'd ever felt, and he could imagine how he suddenly looked through her eyes. Whatever he was, it was unnatural, and it was stark against everything inside her, he was certain. To him, she felt like she was made of white light, and she was hot and burning.

Her aura was bright, pushing hard against the darkness he harbored. Until she learned to control it, he knew she was a walking beacon.

He looked down, pulling his hands back from hers. Even with inches in between them, her magic scorched against his. White magic and black magic were natural enemies, but he'd also heard them compared to a yin and yang. They were two sides of a coin, each one balancing the other. But her magic was much stronger than anything he'd witnessed.

"So how do I make the augarlux?" Her voice was soft and uncertain. Her eyes were fixed on their hands.

Jet lifted a hand. "The simplest way to explain it is for you to imagine it," he said, turning his hand over. It was simple for him to summon the swirling light, but it was natural for him.

Nyx frowned, pushing down the new feelings inside her. She did the same as he had, holding out her hand. Despite concentrating, she didn't see or feel anything happening. "Aren't there supposed to be magic words?" she whispered, staring hard at her hand.

Jet suppressed a smirk. "Are we circus magicians now?" he asked, a condescending edge to his voice.

Nyx narrowed her eyes at him, feeling irritation flare inside her. "Clearly you were born with augarluxes in both hands," she said angrily.

A snide retort was on Jet's lips, when suddenly a bright light lit the space between them. It was huge and blinding for a long moment, and he lifted a hand quickly to block the light.

"I'm doing it!" Nyx suddenly gasped.

Jet scowled, lowering his hand. Just as she said, there was a swirling augarlux hovering just over her hand, but it was bright like a burning sun. "Do you mind?" he snapped. "That thing is bright as hell."

Nyx's eyes were wide and surprised. She stared at it mutely. It was bright, but that's how she'd imagined it. She'd imagined what the sun would look like if she were to hold it in her hand and wished for that. She shook her head, amazed as she gazed at it. Despite the brightness, it didn't hurt her eyes like she thought it would.

"This is so cool," she breathed. She waved her hand slowly, watching as it followed her wherever she went. "How do I make it solid like yours?"

Jet's scowl didn't ease. The magic pulsing off the thing was obnoxious, sending scorching ripples that pushed against him in an obnoxious way. "You need to get it under control first," he said bitterly. "Something like this is completely impractical. This would get us killed for certain."

Nyx frowned, looking over at him. At the look on his face, she felt the excitement leave her. "Well it didn't come with a dimmer switch," she snapped.

"Send it away," Jet said, forcing the irritation on his face away. "Start over." She would never learn if she didn't practice.

Nyx's frown deepened. "How do I do that?" she breathed. Her eyes shifted back to the augarlux. She tried to focus on it, thinking about what she wanted it to do. She was surprised when it dimmed and flickered, but didn't fade away.

"Hand motions help," Jet said shortly. "Like this."

Nyx looked over, watching as he summoned a light and then he waved his hand, sending it away with a short motion.

"Imagine you're putting out a fire or turning off a light," he said.

Nyx pursed her lips, turning back to the bright ball in her hands. "Go out," she whispered, waving her hand. She gasped in surprise when the augarlux suddenly flew away from her, as if she'd thrown it, landing in the grass. It made a heavy sound, like it was made of thick glass.

"Well then," she said. She glanced over at Jet. "Now what?"

Jet sighed heavily. "Call it back to you," he said shortly.

"How do I do that?" she asked, staring at it. It was swirling brightly, tendrils of bright gold arcing through it.

"Trial and error," Jet said, looking over at it. She needed to come up with her own solutions, since clearly whatever he suggested didn't work for her.

Nyx scowled at him, realizing he wouldn't help her anymore. She gathered her thoughts together as she looked back at the ball. She furrowed her brow at it, as if it was a wayward child. "Look here, augarlux," she whispered. "It's time to turn off."

Its sudden disappearance was disorienting.

"Well," Nyx whispered, seeing a sunspot in her eyes. She blinked to try to clear it. "That's one way to do it, right?"

Jet grunted mutely, looking at her. "That was stupid."

Nyx fought down a grin. She could hear the mild sur-prise in his voice. She closed her eyes for a brief moment, feeling his presence beside her like a blast of cold, dark air. It was weird and disorienting.

"Summon it again," he said, drawing her gaze. "But not so bright." His dark eyes were difficult to read as he watched her.

Nyx drew a slow breath, holding out her hand. She tried to picture the augarlux like a candle, with soft light. She was surprised when the magic began to form slowly, twisting and turning into a soft, warm ball of light. It was dim, and much easier on the eyes than the first had been. Nyx felt excitement fill her, a grin sliding across her face.

"It's working," she breathed.

"Now send it away again," Jet said quietly. He watched her face, feeling his guts twist and somersault at the smile on her face. He'd never noticed the dimple in her cheek when she smiled before.

Nyx frowned lightly, staring at the light. If imagining a candle had summoned it, then maybe extinguishing it would be the same. Slowly, she brought the ball toward her, blowing softly on it. Her heart leapt in surprise when it blew out, much like a candle flame.

"Did you see that?" she asked suddenly, excitement in her voice.

Jet sighed shortly, trying to keep his face smooth. Her happiness was refreshing, but also slightly annoying. "Only a child would enjoy playing with an augarlux."

Nyx looked at him, still grinning. "Then I'll admit that I'm a child," she said. Her happiness was infectious.

"Just practice," Jet said suddenly. "If you can master this, then I can teach you something else."

Nyx felt surprise streak through her. "How much more is there to learn?" she asked.

Jet smirked at her. "Oh, this is just the beginning," he said, laying back in the grass. "Now get busy."

Nyx frowned at him, but turned her eyes back to her hand. She wondered what else she was capable of.

It was late into the afternoon when Nyx finally decided to go into the house. She'd been sitting with Jet, practicing her augarlux, while he told her about the Creators. It was a lot of lore to take in, and Nyx wondered how much of it was true. She believed in God, but that was before she knew she was an Auresi. Did that mean that there was more than one god?

She didn't want to think about it too hard as she walked up the porch. The paint on the railing that had once been so white now looked faded and patchy in places with her sharper eyesight. As she put her hand on the door knob, it felt cold and she could smell the brass that it was made of. She pushed open the door slowly, taking a deep breath. She could smell a hint of floor cleaner and the burned remains of bacon grease, just beneath the faint scent of this morning's breakfast. The house was quiet as she stepped inside, but her ears picked up the faintest creaks from the house shifting. All of the lights were off and sunlight was pouring in through the open window curtains. It still felt too bright and Nyx felt like she could have seen better in the dark.

Nyx let the door close quietly behind her as she looked around. She didn't want to, but she knew she needed to make peace with her aunt. "Aunt Dee?" She stepped farther inside. "Aunt Dee?"

"In here."

Nyx heard her voice come from in the kitchen, and she walked slowly toward the doorway. She could see her aunt sitting at the kitchen table, reading a book in the sunlight that was streaming through the window beside her. Dorothea put down the book and a cup of tea, her eyes tired as she looked up at Nyx.

"I guess you were doing some training?" she asked tentatively.

Nyx nodded. "Jet is teaching me," she said shortly. She crossed her arms as she stood there, unable to meet her aunt's gaze. She could smell the hint of the black tea that her aunt loved to drink.

"Good," Dorothea said pleasantly. "I'm glad."

Nyx frowned at her. "Are you?" she asked, an edge to her voice. "Are you glad that I'm learning the truth?"

Dorothea looked down at the table. "I am glad," she said softly. "It's a heavy burden to keep the truth from your child."

Nyx clenched her hands. "I'm not your child," she snapped.

Dorothea looked pained. "You may not be my blood, but you are my child," she said. "I raised you. And I love you."

Nyx looked away. "I just can't understand," she said softly. "Why would you want to keep my whole life from me?"

Dorothea stood slowly. "I didn't," she said quickly. She stepped toward Nyx, watching as she looked up at her distrustfully. "I wanted you to have a normal life." Her eyes were welling with tears. "I wanted you to belong here. Not to keep you ostracized."

Nyx shook her head, feeling hurt and compassion for her aunt. "But you couldn't have told me?"

Dorothea reached for her hand, catching it in hers. "I never knew when or if we would be able to go home," she said. She brushed Nyx's hair from her face. "Why would I burden you with that when there was never any certainty?"

Nyx felt her face soften. "Why did we have to leave?"

Dorothea drew a deep breath. "It's a long story," she said softly. "We should sit."

Nyx sat down at the table, watching Dorothea slide into her chair. She let her new eyes drift over Dorothea's face, seeing small imperfections in her face. Wrinkles were forming at the corners of her eyes and her mouth, making her suddenly look much older than Nyx remembered.

"There has always been a rift between our home country of Ymber and our neighbor, Siccita," Dorothea said softly. "For as long as I can remember." She smiled gently. "I was only twenty years old when I brought you here."

Nyx looked down at the table. Her aunt wasn't much older than she was now. She couldn't imagine the burden it was to raise a baby alone at that age.

"Being Inerse, I was born into the middle of a war that had been raging for centuries," Dorothea said. "Auresi and Acerbi are ancient beings." She looked up at Nyx fondly. "Your grandmother, Liana, is well over five centuries old."

Nyx frowned. "How is that possible?" she breathed.

Dorothea shrugged. "It's the gift of the Creators," she said easily. "It is a blessing, one that Inerse are not fortunate enough to be a part of." She let her fingers drift across the cover of her book. "But because of that, Liana and Paraximus, the King of Siccita, have been at war for a long time."

"Why?" Nyx asked.

"They were married once," Dorothea said. "They had some kind of falling out. Your father came with Liana, his mother, to Ymber and he met your mother there." She smiled as she looked up at Nyx. "They were very happy."

Nyx's brow furrowed. "What really happened to them, Aunt Dee?" she asked softly. "How did they really die?"

Dorothea looked down at the table, drawing a deep breath. "Well, Sweetheart," she said slowly, her voice troubled, "they were murdered."

Nyx felt like she'd been stabbed in the chest. "Murdered?" she whispered.

Dorothea nodded. "An assassin managed to infiltrate Regius Carmen," she said. "Your parents were killed trying to keep you safe, while I fled with you." Tears began to fill her eyes. "Your mother handed you to me and made me promise that I would take you far away and care for you and never bring you back there unless you could be safe."

Nyx felt like she wanted to cry, too, as she watched Dorothea. "Then why do I have to go back?" she asked. "Jet said that there will be people who want to kill me. That doesn't sound safe to me."

Dorothea wiped at her face. "It's not," she said through a ragged sigh. "But it's necessary." She offered a weak smile. "Liana isn't getting any younger. She needs you to come home and learn from her so that you can take your rightful place when she is gone."

Nyx looked down at the table. "So you think that this is the right thing for me to do?" she asked softly. "To go home, wherever that is?"

Dorothea reached across the table and caught her hand. Nyx looked up at her slowly, uncertainty in her eyes. "I know it is," Dorothea said softly. "We all have a purpose, and this is yours."

Nyx looked down again, trying to fight down the fear and uncertainty that was filling her. She pressed her free hand over her aunt's, feeling the warmth of her skin. "I'm sorry I was mad at you."

Dorothea offered a smile. She moved to her feet and walked around, wrapping her arms tightly around Nyx. Nyx drew a hitching breath as she breathed in Dorothea's perfume, her natural scent filling her nose just beneath it. She wrapped her arms tightly around Dorothea's middle.

"I'm sorry, too," Dorothea said, kissing the top of her head. "I only want what's best for you."

Nyx nodded. "I know."

35

The Brown Residence.

Wednesday, December 7, 2011.

NYX HAULED HERSELF OUT of Anna's car slowly, her entire body aching. Her training with Jet was horrible, always ending up with her getting her ass kicked and lying on the ground. He was trying to teach her some "simple" self-defense maneuvers, but they were never as easy as he said. She was coming to realize she wasn't a fighter. If she had to choose fight or flight, her first option would be to run away as fast as she could.

"Dude, what's up with you?" Anna asked as she walked around the car.

Nyx sighed. "This new workout I've been doing," she said. "I feel like I've been hit by a bus."

Anna laughed, the scent of cigarette smoke still clinging to her skin. To Nyx she smelled like she'd rolled around in an ashtray, even though Anna's smoking had never bothered her before. She hadn't decided if her heightened senses were a good thing or not.

Nyx followed her into the house, setting her overnight bag down on the couch. Anna's parents were gone again on another vacation. Apparently they wouldn't be back until the week before Christmas. She could hear Brad upstairs in his room, even though he was being fairly quiet. She felt a pang of sadness fill her as she sat down slowly on the couch.

There wasn't much time now before the Limen opened. Jet had explained to her that they had a short window of time to cross before it was closed for another year. Nyx didn't want to think about leaving her friends, but as the days flew by, she knew that the reality wouldn't be staved off any longer. She wanted to spend as much time with Anna as possible, especially since they wouldn't see each other anymore. Jet told her that Seth would handle Anna's questions, but it was stupid that she couldn't just tell her friend herself.

She had to fight down her thoughts, feeling tears press against her eyes. She drew a slow breath when Anna came back with a soda in her hands, which she handed to her.

"So you brought your stuff for tonight, right?" Anna asked.

"Duh," Nyx said, forcing a grin as she looked at her friend.

"Cool." Anna took a sip of her drink. "So what's up with you and Jet? Thought you couldn't stand the guy, but seems like you two are pretty buddy-buddy these days."

Nyx looked down quickly. "Nothing's up with us," she said quickly, hearing the lie in her own voice. She wanted to say that he was turning out to be a nice guy, but that was a lie. He still had his head up his butt, no matter how she tried to spin it. "He's just a good dancer."

"Yeah, okay," Anna said, grinning devilishly. "But you know what they say about good dancers."

Nyx glanced over at her. "What?" she asked. She had the distinct feeling that she wouldn't like what Anna was about to say.

Anna leaned toward her, lowering her voice. "If you two dance well together, you'll do other things well together, too."

Nyx felt her face flush. She shoved her friend playfully, surprising herself at how hard she actually pushed Anna. "You are such a pervert!"

Anna laughed as she fell over on the couch. "Whatever," she said. "Don't lie and say you hadn't thought about it."

Nyx drew a shaking breath as she sipped her drink. It would be impossible not to think about it now.

The night was cold as Nyx slid painfully into Anna's car. She couldn't believe how sore her body was. Jet told her that her magic would help her heal, so she wondered how she would feel if he hadn't been teaching her how to use it. Nyx turned to look at Anna as she shut her door.

"I can't believe it's so cold," she said, starting the car. She rubbed her arms quickly.

Nyx frowned as she realized that the cold wasn't really bothering her like it normally would have. She hated the cold. But she didn't really notice it now.

"So what are you doing for Christmas?" Anna asked, looking over at her.

Nyx shrugged, feeling guilt plaguing her. "I don't know yet," she said softly. "Aunt Dee has been talking about taking a trip." She didn't like the lie, but it was the closest she could come to the truth.

"Oh," Anna said excitedly, "where to?"

Nyx shrugged. "Not sure yet."

Anna laughed lightly. "You aunt doesn't seem like a last minute planner."

Nyx shrugged. "What about you guys?"

"Probably same old stuff," Anna said. "But I'm going to ask Seth to come."

Nyx grinned. "To meet your mom and dad finally?"

Anna nodded. "You know, this feels like a thing," she said wistfully. "Like, I can picture us getting married and stuff."

Nyx looked down, feeling her stomach coil. "That's really awesome," she said softly, feeling sick. The realization of all the things she would miss out on hit her.

She would never see her best friend get married or have babies or even be there for her when things were hard. So many life events that she'd never even realized she wanted to be a part of she would miss. It wasn't fair.

Nyx could feel tears threatening to well in her eyes again. She'd thought she wanted to spend all the time she could with Anna, but now she was feeling like maybe it would be best if she didn't. She needed to start distancing herself, so the pain would be less when she left. She let silence linger between them as they pulled down Main Street and parked.

Nyx knew Anna could tell something was wrong. She kept shooting her looks, her brown eyes concerned. As they neared the door to Dirty Harry's, Anna caught her hand.

"Did I say something wrong?" Anna asked.

Nyx turned to face her friend. "No," she said quickly. She wanted to offer her friend an excuse for her behavior, but nothing would make sense. "Everything is fine." She forced a smile. "Really."

Anna frowned, but nodded. "Okay," she said uncertainly. "You would tell me if it wasn't, right?"

Nyx nodded. "Totally," she said, waving her hand to try to clear the air. She just wanted to go inside and try to put all of these feelings aside for a while.

Anna nodded, turning and leading the way inside.

Once they had paid their way to get in, Nyx followed Anna to the back to their usual table. She looked up, seeing Seth and Jet already sitting there. Melanie was sitting across from them, laughing at something Seth was telling her.

"Hey guys," Anna said as they came close enough.

Seth's eyes lit up as he stood to kiss her.

Nyx looked to Jet, seeing him leaning back in the booth, his arm across the back. She looked to Melanie. "Where's Abigail?"

Melanie shrugged. "Some guy asked her to dance," she said in explanation.

Nyx shook her head. Abigail had flirted with Jet for a little while, but Nyx guessed that Jet had made it clear nothing would ever happen. She'd given up on him after a couple of weeks and obviously hadn't thought twice about it.

Nyx slid to sit beside Melanie, avoiding looking at Jet. She felt like they had a dirty secret to hide from everyone else. Well, everyone except Seth. She didn't like the way it made her insides twist with guilt. She sat quietly, taking in her friends as they chatted. Abigail soon joined them, gushing about the guy she'd been dancing with.

Sadness streaked through Nyx. She would miss this. She glanced up at Jet, seeing him watching her silently. She had a feeling he knew her thoughts when she looked down at the table.

"Hey, let's go dance," Melanie said.

Abigail grinned and slid out while Melanie pushed Nyx out of the booth. Their favorite song was playing through the speakers. The twins didn't notice how down she was as they bopped their way to the dance floor and pushed into the middle of the fray.

It was a Wednesday night, so the dance hall was not as crowded as on Thursdays and Fridays, but there was a pretty good-sized crowd on the dance floor. It was easy to find the beat as Melanie and Abigail swayed beside her. Their smiles were infectious, and Nyx felt her misery lifting slightly as she danced with them. The pulsing beat changed to a country song that couples were two-stepping to and Nyx followed the twins off the floor.

A guy came up and caught Abigail's hand, pulling her back onto the floor. Nyx saw Anna and Seth going around as well, and she looked up in time to see Jet walking toward her. He held out his hand to her.

"Dance with me?" he asked.

Nyx looked at Melanie, who waved her to go on.

"I'll find my friend," Melanie said. "He'll dance with me."

Nyx nodded, taking Jet's hand. She tried to forget about everyone around them as she let Jet twirl her around the floor.

"What's up with you?" Jet asked as he pulled her back to him from a spin. "You're just going through the motions."

Nyx drew a slow breath as she looked up at him. "I just don't know if I can do this," she said. "I hate lying to everyone, and they won't know what happened to me when I'm gone."

Jet frowned lightly. "Don't worry about that," he said. "Seth will take care of it."

Nyx looked away. That wasn't the point. "I'm going to be alone," she said quietly. She wondered if he heard her over the sound of the music.

Jet spun her away and pulled her back, bringing her in closer than she was before. "You'll have me," he said, close enough that Nyx could feel his breath on her ear.

Nyx felt her cheeks blush lightly. "I don't know if that's a good thing," she said.

Jet smirked at her, leading her in a different step as the song changed to a slower beat. He could feel her shoulders loosen as he led her. Her face eased some, the worry that was furrowing her brow disappearing. The anticipation that tinged her aura eased away, being replaced with happiness as he twirled her.

Nyx was content to let him lead her around for several songs, feeling the soreness easing from her muscles. "We haven't been dancing in a long time," she said breathlessly as Jet caught her in his arms.

Jet shook his head, his onyx gaze watching her carefully. "We were here two weeks ago," he reminded her curtly.

Nyx's grin never wavered, despite his tone. "That's a long time for me," she said. She felt dizzy as he spun her several times before catching her free hand and pulling her to him again. She realized she was sweating lightly as the song ended. "I need a break."

Jet nodded, releasing her hands and following her as she stepped off the floor. "I'll bring you a drink," he said, watching as she nodded, sliding into their booth. He walked to the bar, ordering her a glass of water.

Everyone else was still out on the floor, so Nyx was alone as she sat there. She glanced up, noticing a man leaning against the bar, watching her. He was older, probably in his forties, and he looked drunk, his shirt stained and wrinkled. Nyx felt her heart drop into her stomach as he pushed off the bar and started toward her.

Jet frowned when he felt the change in Nyx's aura. He turned around, seeing the man was standing at the table, talking to her. He didn't feel anything untoward about the guy, but he didn't like it.

His insides twisted in that weird, uncomfortable way again, this time filling him with a bitterness he hadn't expected. It was the same way he had felt before, when they'd been sitting under the tree, and it was a feeling he hadn't felt in some time. He could feel a scowl pulling at his lips as he approached, hearing the man ask Nyx to dance. From the way he slurred slightly, Jet could tell he'd had too much to drink.

Nyx glanced up, catching his gaze, discomfort on her face. Jet could tell she wanted to decline as he reached the table, setting her water down in front of her.

"Oh-ho," the man said suddenly, looking up at Jet. "There's the lucky mister taking you home tonight, huh?"

Nyx felt her face flush red suddenly. She bit her lip, looking up at Jet.

"Damn straight," Jet said. "So beat it, old man."

Nyx felt her eyes widen as the man grumbled about Jet being an asshole, shuffling drunkenly away to find another victim. Her face was still beet red as Jet slid to sit next to her. "Uh, thanks," she said quickly, sliding her water toward her. The plastic cup was cold in her hands, and she pressed her hands to her face, trying to force her furious blush to go away.

Jet didn't say anything as he watched the man shuffle to another table full of girls at least half his age. "Pathetic," he said. He looked over at her, seeing her eyes were fixed on the table.

Nyx drew a breath, taking a sip of her water. "It happens, I guess," she said uneasily. Her heart was racing as she tried to avoid looking at him. She was surprised at how easily he had handled the situation, and her fluster began to return as she thought about the man's insinuations. She couldn't believe the audacity of some people, and she couldn't get over how effortless it had been for Jet to tell the guy to get lost.

Her thoughts suddenly shifted back to that night, so long ago, when he'd made her feel this way the first time. Anna's words suddenly echoed in her mind. She felt her face flush more at the thought, and she took another sip of her water, wanting to crawl under the table and disappear. The silence was suddenly very uncomfortable as they sat there. Nyx was hoping for a distraction to help her clear away her thoughts. She was surprised when a slow song began to play and Jet reached down to take her hand.

"Come on," he said, seeing her emerald eyes were wide and her cheeks were still flushed. "I'll teach you another type of dance."

Nyx bit her lip hard, feeling her mind supplying her with things she didn't want anyone to know she was thinking.

It was a dance that Jet was very familiar with and something that had been a favorite in the courts. Lately, his thoughts had been consumed with his homeland, namely what things would be like once they returned. He knew it could never be the way it was before his capture, and thinking about it made his stomach twist in knots. But one thing he knew was dancing. Unfortunately, it was a difficult step, but he guessed that was what he enjoyed about it. There had been few who could keep up with him.

Nyx felt her heart skip a beat, pounding wildly in her chest as she slid out of the booth behind him, letting him lead her to the floor. He caught her hand in his, placing her free hand on his arm. His movements were gentle and flowing as he began to lead her in a dance she'd never seen before. It was awkward at first, as she learned the steps, but then it became easy as she relaxed, letting Jet steer her around the floor. She glanced up at him after a moment, seeing his eyes were surprised.

"You're doing well," he said, a lilt to his voice that betrayed his surprise. He could remember others trying hard to impress him by learning the steps, but this dance required a finesse that few could master.

"It's not hard," Nyx said, feeling her cheeks darken at his compliment.

Jet arched a brow. "This is a difficult step for most," he said easily. He felt that weird, uncomfortable twist in his chest again. There had only been one woman who could match him, both in this dance and in other things. But, somehow, remembering her felt like nothing as he twirled the little blonde girl in his arms.

Nyx met his gaze. "Really?" Her breath caught at the way his eyes were searching her face.

"It is a very difficult dance," Jet continued, lost in his thoughts. "I've only seen it done well between two who know each other intimately."

Nyx felt her face flush again, and she stumbled slightly. What was he insinuating? She looked down at her feet, wishing she could melt into the floor. Why was he having this effect on her tonight?

"Eyes on me," he commanded softly. "If you will trust me, I will lead you."

Her face flushed more as she looked up at him. She couldn't speak as she held his gaze, letting him lead her effortlessly. The song was winding to a gentle end, and he spun her away for a final time. When she twisted back to him, reaching for his arm, he caught her hand, halting her movements as the song faded away. Nyx drew a sharp breath as she stared at him for a long moment, her heart beating double-time. Her eyes widened when he reached up, her fingers still tangled in his, to brush strands of hair from her eyes.

Nyx realized her legs had turned to rubber. She didn't know if she had the ability to speak or move as she gazed into his face, feeling her cheeks turning steadily redder. Her mind was racing as she realized that this was one of those moments that she had always dreamed about. It was like a scene from a movie, and she licked her lips lightly, her brain telling her she should kiss him.

She held tighter to his hands, leaning in toward him.

Surprise flashed across his face, and he suddenly stepped away from her, dropping her hands like they were hot potatoes. The hurt that suddenly cascaded through her was crushing as the DJ's voice was loud through the speakers, effectively muting anything either of them could have said. Nyx couldn't look at him as she walked quickly off the floor, feeling a constricting tightness around her heart. She was so embarrassed and confused. Had she read the situation wrong?

"Nyx."

She gritted her teeth, crossing her arms as the sound of her name caressed her ears. Something about it made her want to cover her ears, but she refrained. She didn't know how to feel as she spun to face him.

Jet's onyx eyes were soft suddenly as he looked at her. He seemed as if he was struggling to find words as he drew a breath. "I'm sorry," he said suddenly.

Nyx felt confusion begin to mingle with the hurt as she looked at him. She wasn't quite sure what he was apologizing for, but it was strange and uncomfortable. She'd never heard him say he was sorry for anything.

"It's fine," she said quickly, hoping he would just let this go. She forced a smile, feigning tiredness. "I think I need a break."

Jet nodded, following her silently back toward the booth. His thoughts were racing as he trailed behind her. He didn't know what had come over him. He'd felt as if he was falling as he stood there, looking into her emerald gaze. He didn't know what had possessed him as he'd held her hands in his, feeling drawn to her in a way he'd never felt before. Everything about that moment was disconcerting, and he suddenly wanted to be rid of her as much as he was sure she wanted to be rid of him.

The others had returned to the table and Nyx melted into the booth between Abigail and Melanie, engrossing herself in their conversation. She did her best to avoid Jet the rest of the night, until Anna said she was ready to go home. It was uncomfortable as Nyx slid out of the booth while Seth and Anna walked toward the door. She hoped Jet would leave her alone, but she was almost to the door when he stopped her.

"Nyx," he called. He didn't have any words as she paused, turning to look at him. His guilt was worse when he realized hurt and confusion was flooding her aura. He could feel some sort of desperation seeping through him as they stared at each other.

When Nyx finally found her voice, it was soft. "What's up?" she asked quietly. Her heart was pounding in her chest, making her feel lightheaded. She just wanted to escape from this place to try to sort out her thoughts.

Jet frowned, feeling his guts twisting painfully. He realized he didn't have any words as he stared at her, watching her frown at him. "See you tomorrow?" he asked lamely.

Nyx looked down, shaking her head lightly. "I need a break tomorrow," she said. "A rest day or something."

Jet nodded mutely. He didn't say anything else as he watched her turn and walk out the door. He didn't follow her, knowing that's what she wanted. He couldn't explain the sudden barrage of feelings as he stared hard after her. What in the hell was wrong with him?

The solstice was almost here. He didn't have time for this. There was no time for this weakness that was creeping into him. He needed to protect her, and he couldn't do that if his head was in other places. He drew a short breath, telling himself he was being stupid. He was just uncertain about what would happen when they reached Gexalatia. That's all this was.

36

The Estrella Residence.

Tuesday, December 13, 2011.

NYX GRUNTED AS SHE FELL to the ground, looking up at Jet as he towered over her, his arms crossed and his dark eyes shadowed against the overhead sun.

She scowled.

She was getting really tired of having her butt kicked all the time. It was making Jet a really cocky jerk, and it was making it difficult to continue training with him. It was especially irritating because he seemed to only be acting like this because of the other night at Dirty Harry's.

She sighed as she fell back in the grass, realizing that they'd fought a lot longer than normal, and that they'd managed to cover a lot more distance than normal. Her body was sore as she lay flat on the ground, hearing Jet grumbling.

Her strength was incredible in human standards, but when he showed her what he expected her to be able to do, she realized she had a long way to go. Since then, her days consisted of endlessly practicing with Jet and listening to him boss her around, and every now and then stopping to take a break to eat and sleep.

He hadn't spoken to her about what happened the other night, and he was being curt and more rude than usual. Everything she did was wrong. She needed someone to talk to, but her aunt and Seth had told her that it would put Anna in danger to involve her. That thought always helped her to keep her mouth shut, especially after a hard day of being beat up by Jet.

"You can't possibly be worn out yet," Jet said, standing over her, frowning as he gazed down at her. His voice cut through her thoughts, becoming increasingly obnoxious the more she heard it.

Nyx scowled as she glared at him. "Just because you can go for three days without breaking a sweat doesn't mean everyone else can," she snapped, her voice soft with her lack of energy. "I just spent the better half of the day chasing you halfway to the moon." She sat up, growling. "So shut up!" No matter how hard she tried, she could not seem to stop being angry with him.

Jet crossed his arms, his dark eyes narrowed, but he remained silent, apparently picking his words carefully, stopping the snooty retort that he knew Nyx was expecting as he watched her fall back in the grass.

"Look," he said, clearly battling his temper, "We've been out here training for a month now, and you're nowhere near ready. You need to start taking this seriously."

Nyx sat up quickly, feeling dizzy as she did so, whether it was from her sudden blinding rage or weariness, she couldn't tell. "What the hell do you think I'm doing?" she demanded, her emerald gaze furious. "I can't get any more serious than this. Jeez!"

She yelled in frustration, turning away from him and struggling to her feet, muttering profanities as she went. She stumbled slightly as she took a few steps, feeling dizzy again. "You've been so goddamn pissy lately! Why don't you just take some time and sort through whatever the hell it is that's going through your thick skull, and call me when you're done!"

She stormed into the trees, following the path of destruction she'd managed to carve since they got started that morning.

Jet's dark eyes were narrowed furiously as he watched her walk away. Once she was out of sight, he turned to the nearest tree, slamming his fist into it, the pain welcome as blood ran down his arm from his split knuckles. He glared down at his hand, thinking that the tree had fared far worse, as it had splintered as if it'd been hit by lightning.

He sighed as he slumped against the stump that was left, letting his eyes drift back to where Nyx had vanished into the brush. He hadn't meant to be so harsh on her, but his thoughts were always a confused jumble around her. He was trying to focus on the task at hand and forget about what happened last week. It didn't matter because once the Limen opened his mind could only be focused on one thing, and that was keeping her dumb ass alive.

It was irritating that she was so weak still, and he often wondered if he was pushing her too hard. But the thought was fleeting as he remembered that he had a deadline to make, and they were quickly running out of time. They couldn't stay hidden forever, especially not with the amount of power she was learning to release, and the thought was putting him on edge more and more every day. He expected Paraximus to send others, just like he'd done with Sophia, and he knew that wouldn't be an easy battle.

Jet growled softly as he cursed to himself, knowing that he needed to sit her down and really talk to her. He couldn't keep pushing her like this and expect her to hold up under all the pressure unless she really wanted to, which he expected she did, as she had sworn to do the best she could when they began.

He glanced at his knuckles a final time, seeing that they'd healed, just as he expected, and he wiped the blood away quickly, before pushing himself off the stump and leaping into the trees after Nyx. He could feel her angry aura nearby, and it didn't take him any time at all to find her, sitting on a fallen tree about a half mile away, muttering angrily to herself as bitter tears slipped down her cheeks.

He paused as he neared, kneeling in the bend of the tree he was in, taking a moment to watch her. He could hear her going on about what an ass she thought he was, and he rolled his eyes at her childish comments. After letting her rant for a moment more, he dropped from the tree, landing easily with a soft thud.

He instantly noticed the shift in her aura as she let it fan out around her, something she was becoming good at, letting it brush against his. He watched her shoulders hunch over more as she crossed her arms, clearly pouting. Rolling his eyes again, he stood slowly, walking toward her.

"Go away!" she snapped.

Jet sighed, gritting his teeth as he ignored her, sitting beside her on the tree. He could tell this was going to be yet another test of patience for him as he watched her turn slightly so that her back was to him. He tried his best not to sigh out of frustration as he took a moment to gather his thoughts, ignoring her again when she demanded that he leave her alone.

"I'm not going to leave you alone," he said evenly when she repeated herself for the third time. "We need to talk."

Nyx turned quickly at this, leaning forward to let a hand rest on the log between them, her deep green eyes blazing. "Damn right!" she snapped. "Why the hell are you always so angry?" Her voice was demanding. "I understand that we've got a lot to do, and in not a lot of time, but do you have to act like you've got a stick rammed up your ass all the time?"

Jet felt his eyes widen at her colorful choice of words, and for a moment, he had to fight the urge to laugh incredulously at her. He narrowed his eyes at her, wishing right at that moment that he could just drop-kick her back to where he found her. When he realized that his temper was about to make things difficult, he closed his eyes, pinching the bridge of his nose and drawing a shallow breath. He felt as if he was murdering any pride he had left with his next words.

"I'm sorry," he ground out, his face contorted with anger as he opened his eyes again.

"You should be!" she accused.

Jet felt his jaw clench tightly as he fought the urge to yell at her. He could not believe what he'd been reduced to. The once-General for the most powerful being in all of Gexalatia was sitting here, with the Queen Mother's heir, fighting with her as if they were small children. It was laughable, the whole damn predicament, and for a moment, Jet felt his loathing for Nyx outweigh his loathing for Paraximus. But that was until he drew another breath, steadying his frayed nerves, applauding himself for not trying to tear her throat out right there. He realized that she was royalty and whatever, but gods above help him, he was about to snap.

"Dammit, Nyx," he said softly, trying to control his temper, "I'm trying to be patient with you, but I've just about had all I can take." His dark eyes flashed. "Any more of this, and it'll be a miracle that I don't just tear you into a million freakin' pieces." He watched the intensity of her glare waver a bit as she realized he was completely serious, although, to her credit, her eyes never strayed from his.

"So why don't you already?" she asked, her voice less demanding than before. "Just go ahead and put both of us out of our misery." Her emerald eyes flashed just as deadly as his with her challenge.

Jet felt his anger dissipating slowly at her astounding courage, and he sighed after a moment, feeling the tension leave his shoulders as he did so.

"That's not what I'm here to do," he said softly, shooting her a glare, "as much as I'd like to." He cracked his knuckles, taking a moment to gather his thoughts before he spoke again. "I feel like we need to come to some sort of agreement. I know I'm being hard on you, but we don't have much time before the portal opens again." The last part came out as a furious hiss.

Nyx swallowed hard as she realized that they were getting down to the nitty-gritty, and things were getting nasty quickly, as their tempers began to run high with the increasing urgency.

"If you're so antsy to get back to Gexalatia, why did you wait so long to tell me?" she asked, her voice still holding an edge, even though she forced it to soften a bit as she realized what a fine line she was walking with Jet already. She didn't think he'd actually follow through on any of his threats, but right now she didn't want to push her luck.

Jet's eyes snapped to her, dark and wolfish, and it made her shiver. She hated it when he got this way. "You weren't ready," he said.

"And I'm ready now?" she quipped.

Jet shrugged as he looked away. "I don't know if you would have ever been truly ready," he said. Because of how Dorothea had raised her, Nyx could have gone on living this life if he'd never come to get her.

Nyx looked down at her hands, feeling her chest constricting. Now that she wasn't so angry with him, her thoughts were shifting back to the other night. It made her want to facepalm, but she resisted, drawing a short breath. "Jet?"

"Hn?" He looked over at her.

"About the other night . . ." She couldn't hold his gaze, feeling her face turning red.

Jet moved to his feet quickly, surprising her. "I don't want to talk about that," he said shortly.

Nyx frowned at him. "Why?" she asked, feeling hurt filling her.

"We need to keep training," Jet said. "We don't have time for nonsense."

Nyx felt her heart drop into her feet. She tried to push down the feeling, looking down at her feet. "Right," she said softly.

"Let's take a break and pick it up afterwards," Jet said, turning away from her.

Nyx nodded. "Okay," she said softly. She felt small as she sat there, long after he'd started back toward the farmhouse. She didn't know why she felt this way.

Celo Cavus, Siccita.

*The eighty-eighth day of fall, the 905th year
of the reign of King Paraximus Lamia.*

December 18, 2011, Earth Time.

THE SOUND OF BOOTS on marble was soft. A sword shifted in a scabbard at a man's side as he walked. The walls of the palace around him rose up into arched ceilings, gothic-style edging making the castle feel dark. Statues of beasts rose out of the ground around him, but he paid them no heed as he walked swiftly to a set of large doors. A servant pushed them open as he neared.

Inside, King Paraximus sat in a high-backed throne, his dark eyes watching as girls danced before him. Musicians were playing deep bass drums, and the girls were clacking finger chimes as they swayed to the beat. Around the room, courtiers were gathered, watching the display. If Darwren was to understand it, the dancers were a gift from a neighboring country as an offering of peace.

He bypassed the dancers, noticing that he didn't draw any attention, save for that of the man sitting on the throne. He kneeled on the steps of the dais, seeing the King beckon him to come forth.

"What news do you bring me, Darwren?" he asked darkly. His pitch-colored eyes narrowed, strands of salt-and-pepper hair falling around his face.

"It is the *Marianya*," Darwren said softly. "She and the *Madelief* have gone down, My King."

Paraximus turned his head, looking at Darwren, his night-eyes steadily darkening as a scowl came to his face. The *Marianya* was one of his biggest war ships. He'd sent it to the Bay of Antiquus at Daya's behest. The *Madelief* was only a merchant ship, but they both were carrying precious cargo, namely dragons to be sold in the northern country. Rage flitted through him at the thought that Daya was not honoring her side of the agreement.

"I see." Paraximus' words were soft, but the fury was plain on his face. His knuckles were white as his hand tightened around the goblet. With a pop, it caved to the pressure, blood-red wine suddenly running across the floor.

Paraximus stood when a servant scurried toward him, wiping the mess up and offering a new goblet. He said nothing as he looked to Darwren, who was cowering before him.

Darwren felt fear course through him, but he continued. "It appears to have been attacked in the night by dragon riders."

"Dragon riders," Paraximus murmured, his thoughts churning behind his eyes. A deadly grin suddenly slid across his face. "This is an act of war, committed on our ship by the Northern Kingdom."

Darwren looked down at the floor. He felt doubt ease across his conscience. The Queen Mother did not employ dragon riders. If anything, it was the pesky Pangere they'd been dealing with, but his King was looking for any reason to declare war on Ymber. "It appears so, Your Highness."

"Prepare my forces, Darwren," Paraximus said, lifting a goblet slowly. His ebony eyes shifted back to the dancers. "We must respond in kind." Perhaps Daya knew what game she was playing after all.

Darwren bowed, preparing to stand, when Paraximus suddenly stopped him.

"What word is there of Aterro, Darwren?" he asked softly, his voice dark. He kept his eyes trained on the girls before him.

Darwren felt the fear twist inside him once more as he rested his knees on the floor. "He is prepared, as you requested," he said slowly.

"Bring him to me, Darwren," he said. "It is time to send him on his way."

Darwren kept his head bowed. "Yes, My King," he said quietly.

"Your allegiance honors my brother," Paraximus said. "Your father."

Darwren looked up, surprised. "My King?"

"Prepare your forces to march to the Wall," Paraximus continued. "You will bring me the Atturon girls."

"Yes, My Lord," Darwren said, bowing low.

With that Paraximus was gone from the throne room.

Anticipation and uncertainty were swirling in Darwren. He knew he couldn't fail. His life depended on doing as he was commanded.

38

The Estrella Residence.

Tuesday, December 20, 2011.

NYX FELT SICK AS SHE muddled her way through her morning chores. She tried to put on a face for Aunt Dee, but she realized she was failing miserably when her aunt sat down on the couch beside her, offering her a mug of warm tea. It was well into the afternoon now, and Nyx hadn't been able to make her body do anything other than sit here miserably, staring at the lights on the Christmas tree. They seemed too cheerful.

"What's wrong?" Dorothea asked gently, pushing strands of blonde hair from Nyx's face.

Nyx looked down at the tea in her hands. She didn't even know where to start. What was she more upset about? The fact that she'd tried to kiss Jet and he'd rejected her? Or the fact that this was it, that tomorrow she would never see this place or her friends again? She felt tears well in her eyes at the thought.

"Oh, Sweetie," her aunt whispered, pulling her tightly to her. "Everything will be okay." She brushed the tears from Nyx's face. "You'll see."

Nyx looked at her aunt, nodding her head as she drew a ragged breath. "I hope you're right, Aunt Dee," she said softly. She liked that her aunt didn't always need answers to know what the right thing to say was. She didn't know if she could have spoken about it, even if she had wanted to. She looked up at the clock that hung on the wall, seeing the time. "I have to meet Anna."

Dorothea nodded, watching as Nyx rose to her feet and collected her jacket and her purse. "I'll see you tonight," she said softly. "We'll need to pack what you want to take with you."

Nyx nodded. "I'll try not to stay out late," she said. She walked to her, hugging her tightly. "I love you, Aunt Dee."

Dorothea returned her hug. "I love you, too," she said softly. Her heart suddenly felt heavy as she watched Nyx leave.

She felt sorry for Nyx, but she knew this was for the best. Tomorrow was the solstice, and this was the only time Nyx would have left to see Anna. Dorothea didn't know how Nyx would be in the morning, and she sank down onto the couch, looking down at the mug on the table. Her chest felt tight as a lump began to form, making tears mist her eyes. Everything was about to change, for both of them.

Nyx turned her radio down as she reached the mall. The loud music had helped to keep her thoughts from running away with her, but she still had to wipe away rogue tears

that she couldn't stop. She knew it wouldn't do to be crying when she saw her friend.

She made her way into the mall, a smile coming to
her face when she saw Anna sitting on a bench. When she
caught sight of Nyx, she jumped up, walking to her and
hugging her.

"Hey," she said, smiling brightly. "I've got so much
shopping to do!"

Nyx returned her smile, feeling sad suddenly, despite
fighting her feelings. "Maybe we should get started then,"
she said quietly.

"Let's go eat some dinner first," Anna said, wrapping
her arm in Nyx's and leading her to the food court. "I need
energy to fight this crowd." The mall was packed with
last-minute shoppers.

Once they had shouldered their way to the food court
and were seated at a table, Anna shoved a vegetable into
her mouth, looking at Nyx. "So how are things with Jet?"
she asked brightly. "Things seemed kinda weird a couple
of weeks ago."

Nyx looked down at her plate, feeling her heart twist.
"Uh, yeah," she said softly. "It's fine." She felt her face
turn red. "I might have tried to kiss him, and now things
are super weird."

Anna's eyes widened. "You tried to kiss him," she said
slowly. "And he turned you down?"

"Well, yeah, kinda," Nyx said quietly. She could feel
her face turning red with embarrassment. She pushed at the
rice on her plate, her spicy chicken suddenly looking gross.

Concern was in Anna's eyes. "What happened?"

Nyx winced. She didn't want to get into details. "We
were dancing and the moment just felt right, you know?"
she said quietly, feeling small suddenly. "But he didn't

feel the same way obviously." She set her fork down. "But I guess it's okay." A ragged sigh escaped her lips. "He's an ass anyway."

Pity was on Anna's face. "I didn't even know you had feelings for him," she said quickly. "Do you love him?"

Nyx shook her head slowly. "I don't know, Anna," she said. "I don't know how I feel."

"Well, obviously you have feelings for him," Anna said easily. "Otherwise you wouldn't be so upset right now." She waved her fork. "Besides, you guys are always together when we go out. If that's not love, I don't know what is." She offered a grin.

"It's not like it matters," Nyx said again. "I'm going on vacation with Aunt Dee, and he's going back home." She wished so badly that she could tell Anna that she was going with him. She hated lying.

"So you should tell him how you feel," Anna said quickly. "Convince him to stay."

Nyx pushed her plate away, looking up at her friend. "I don't know if it's worth it," she said. She forced a smile. "There's no guarantee I'll be able to stand him for very long."

Anna shrugged, returning her smile. "Well that sucks," she said softly. Her plate was mostly empty. "Let's walk around. We'll forget about it for a while."

Nyx nodded quickly. "Let's go." She wanted to enjoy this time as much as she could.

It was like old times as Nyx and Anna walked around the mall, filling Nyx with nostalgia. They were in and out of every store, trying on all the clothes they could find and picking out Christmas gifts. Nyx was especially happy with the gift she'd found for her aunt. It was a cute little cook that matched the wallpaper in their kitchen. She knew her aunt would love it. They stayed until the stores began to close. Once they were finally ushered out of the mall, it was beginning to get late.

"Look at all the stuff we got," Anna said, holding up her myriad of bags. Unlike Nyx, she had both parents and Brad to buy for. And Seth, of course.

"We did good," Nyx said, looking down at her small crop. All she had was her aunt's gift and a small box for Jet. She didn't know why she bought it. She wasn't sure she would even give it to him. She also had a small thing for Anna that she wanted Seth to give her when they were gone. The thought made her heart hurt.

"You need to call Jet," Anna said, misreading her face. She suddenly grinned. "You should try to see him tonight."

Nyx fought down a grimace. She didn't want to see him until tomorrow. It was already bad enough that she had been training with him every day. The cringe was strong when he was around. "I don't know," she said.

Anna shook her head. "You never know until you try," she said. Nyx looked up, realizing she'd followed Anna to her car. She watched as Anna popped the trunk, putting her bags into it. When she was done, she turned back to Nyx. "Call me and let me know how it goes."

Nyx nodded, feeling her chest constrict and her stomach turn. "Sure," she said. She felt the tension worsen when Anna suddenly pulled her into a strong hug. She could feel tears pressing against her eyes. She would never get the chance to call Anna. This was the last time she'd see her best friend.

"Everything will be fine," Anna said, releasing Nyx. "You'll see."

Nyx nodded. She hoped Anna was right as she bid her goodbye and walked to her car, which she'd parked nearby.

She pulled her cell phone from her pocket, feeling her heart plummet as she thought about sending Anna a message telling her how much she appreciated her friendship and loved her. She slid slowly into the front of her car, turning the engine on.

Her heart was twisting as she stared at the phone for a long time. Why couldn't Anna know what was going on? It's not like it would hurt anything. And Anna would have Seth, so maybe Nyx could talk to her through Seth. She tried not to cry as she put the car in drive.

Jet scowled as he looked at Seth, who was standing on the edge of the trees.

"I don't know how he came through without me noticing," Seth said, his voice troubled. "I've been scouting the Limen all week."

Jet's scowled deepened. "It doesn't matter now," he said darkly. "We need to find him." He realized he was being curt with Seth, but he hadn't been in a good mood for a couple of weeks. Even now, thinking about it made him feel angrier. He was ready for this charade to be over, and he was aching to kill someone.

Seth nodded, vanishing in an instant into the trees around them.

Jet turned and walked to his car, sliding into it. His thoughts were consumed with the task at hand. He knew where Aterro would be headed, and he knew he had to cut him off. He couldn't allow anyone to reach the Princess, and he threw the car into drive. His eyes were scanning the trees as he sped down the road. He knew Aterro and anyone with him would be difficult to detect, using the power of the solstice to cover their presences.

Jet was coming around the curve toward Nyx's house when movement suddenly caught his eye. His heart leapt into his throat for a moment, and he hit the gas, seeing a figure moving in the trees. He gripped the steering wheel tighter as he caught up to the figure.

Satisfaction filled him as he realized it was his prey. He gunned the car, watching as the figure darted into the road. He didn't slow as he slammed into a heavy body, the windshield shattering as the body rolled over the top of the car. The squeal of tires filled the night as Jet slammed on the brakes, swinging the car around to shine his headlights on a man lying in road.

Slowly, he stepped out of the car. He listened as the man coughed and sputtered.

"Bastard," the man coughed, his Sarotian of a southern dialect.

"Where is he, Shan?" Jet asked suddenly, crossing his arms as he stood over the man. Jet knew he was an Acerbi, as he was, and in a few minutes his body would begin to heal itself.

"Screw you, Jet," Shan gasped, writhing on the ground. His blood was turning the concrete black in the darkness.

"Wrong answer," Jet growled suddenly, feeling the irritation in his chest shifting into something stronger. The scent of Shan's blood was heady as Jet stepped toward him, hefting the large man from the ground. He smirked darkly at the way Shan groaned in pain. "I'm really not in the mood tonight."

Shan's sharp cry was pleasant to Jet's ears as he twisted Shan's arm, feeling bones snap under the force. "You're too late," Shan gasped suddenly around the pain.

Jet growled suddenly, baring fangs. His tolerance for shit was gone. "I won't ask you again," Jet said fiercely, using his foot to press against the shattered bones in Shan's back, using his grip on Shan's arm as leverage. He wouldn't make this quick or easy.

Shan collapsed to the ground, gasping as he pressed his forehead to the cold pavement. Jet could imagine that the pain was horrendous, and it sent a thrill of excitement through him. He hadn't shed anyone's blood in a long time. Torturing this imbecile was a pleasant change from the bullshit he'd been put through recently.

"He will already have her before you can save her," Shan growled. He grunted a short laugh, despite the pain. "We all know Liana has made you soft, General."

Jet snarled at him. The fury that caught at him was sudden and momentarily made him lose his cool. Without thought, he slammed his foot into Shan's head, watching as his brains spurted across the street. He drew a slow breath to compose himself as he stepped back from Shan's body.

"No one calls me that."

Jet turned away from the bloody mess on the roadway, walking to his car. He revved the engine, spinning the car into the right direction. He had to get to Nyx before the rest did.

Nyx was miserable as she pulled her car into her driveway. For a long time, she sat in the vehicle, listening to music, crying softly. She hated that everything had happened this way, and she knew it was over. Her tears were steady as she pulled the box from her passenger seat. It was plain, brown cardboard with the store's logo. Nyx still didn't know why she couldn't just tell Anna.

She sniffled, stemming her tears as she opened the box, pulling a gold bracelet from the pillow inside. The links were decorated with a twisting design, and it had seemed like the perfect gift. Anna could always wear it and never forget about her.

The thought made Nyx feel heartsick as she got out of her car and pulled out her key to unlock the front door. She refocused her attention as she stepped inside, surprised that the house was dark and that the air was stale and hot. A funky odor made her cover her nose.

"Aunt Dee?" she called. She wrinkled her nose, wondering what the heck her aunt had cooked that smelled so terrible.

Nyx closed the door behind her, dropping her bag on the couch. She shrugged out of her jacket and laid it across the back of the couch as she pressed the switch on the table lamp, watching it glow softly as she glanced around for the source of the smell.

"Aunt Dee, I'm home." She was surprised by the silence that greeted her. The hairs on her neck stood on end suddenly, but she tried to ignore the feeling.

Her eyes flitted to the kitchen, which was dark as well, and she walked toward it, checking her watch. It was late, after midnight, but the door to her aunt's room was open and her aunt was not inside. Nyx paused in the doorway of the kitchen, frowning as she noticed that the small light that stayed on all the time was out, leaving the kitchen coated in a murky darkness.

"Aunt Dee?"

Nyx stepped slowly into the room, surprised when her boot slipped slightly across the linoleum floor. Quickly, she grasped the doorframe, fumbling for the light as she grumbled to herself about remembering to remind her aunt to pay more attention when she mopped the floors. Her aunt liked to do it later in the evenings, when she knew they wouldn't be in and out of the kitchen. Nyx blinked when she finally found the switch and bright light flooded the room.

For a moment, she was frozen as her eyes adjusted to the light and finally registered what she was seeing. The puddle she had slipped in was a dark crimson, and she bent slowly, frowning as she studied it. She didn't understand what she was staring at, at first, but then she glanced up at the wall, seeing that the same liquid was oozing slowly down the walls.

She gasped as she realized that the apple-printed wallpaper was covered in it, and she stood slowly, feeling dread and terror sliding down her spine like icy fingers. She slowly let her eyes rove around the room, the terror increasing with every second, until finally they landed on a pale hand.

Nyx screamed, trying desperately to back-pedal from the room. She didn't even register the pain as she slipped again, slamming into the floor. All she could see was crimson everywhere; the walls, the floor, splattered across the drapes and the window and littering the kitchen table. She couldn't breathe as she moved to her feet, feeling tears in her eyes as she realized the foul smell she had vaguely noticed was the stench of blood. She felt her stomach turn as her mind took a moment to process what she had seen.

"Aunt Dee?" she choked, leaning against the doorframe as she peered into the kitchen.

She didn't know why she did it, but maybe a small part of her was hoping that Dorothea would answer her. She instantly felt the sickness overwhelm her as her eyes landed upon her aunt's hand, which lay on the cold white tiles, unmoving and colorless. Nyx had to turn away as she retched on the floor, thankful that the table hid her aunt's body from view. She didn't want to know what she looked like, but the pallid color of her skin and the amount of blood was enough to tell her that her aunt was gone.

Nyx felt as if she was moving in slow motion as she collapsed to the floor, using her arms to support herself. She couldn't see past the tears in her eyes, and she couldn't stop the small sobs that were choking her. Her mind was racing, and panic was starting so set in. Who could have done this? And why? Why her aunt?

She realized she was trembling violently. She drew a ragged breath, sniffling loudly as the panic continued to assail her.

What if the attacker was still in the house? She needed to call Jet.

Nyx felt as if she was moving too slowly as she managed to push herself up, using the wall behind her as support, and she stumbled to the phone that lay on top of the piano, which was pushed up against the stairwell. She tried to tell herself to calm down as she reached for the receiver. She picked it up quickly and somehow managed to dial, even though her hands were shaking so badly she had to try several times.

When she finally got it, she pressed the phone to her ear, feeling her heart drop to her feet when she realized there was no dial tone. Desperately, she tried hanging up and redialing, only to realize that it was useless. She felt terror grip her as she dropped the phone on the floor, turning and running to the front door. All she could think about was getting to her car and driving herself as far away from here as possible.

If the attacker was still here, she didn't want to be his next victim.

Her hand was poised over the brass knob when suddenly the lights went out, encompassing her in inky darkness. She felt every muscle in her body tense as she froze, feeling her heart beating a hundred miles a second. Her mind went blank for a moment, all of Jet's training suddenly leaving her.

The air was too hot and stale suddenly as she drew quick, ragged breaths, trying to calm herself as she backed away from the door, glancing around in fright. She couldn't see anything, and she stifled a scream when she backed into the table, the lamp smashing loudly as it hit the hardwood floor. What was going on?

Her hands were trembling terribly as she lifted them to press them to her face. Quickly, she ran to the door. Unthinkingly, she yanked it open, and another scream tore from her throat.

"I've been waiting for you."

Crimson eyes glittered in the darkness, and a tall figure stepped toward her.

Nyx backed away quickly, feeling her thoughts run dry. Her heart was thrumming wildly in her chest, and all she could do was stare at the dark stranger. She knew he was there to kill her. More tears filled her eyes.

Her brain was frozen as her back collided with the wall. This was it. She could feel helplessness and hopelessness making her feel weak as he advanced on her, a beam of light from the floodlight outside falling across his face. She gasped, her eyes widening as she pressed her back tightly up against the wall. There was something unearthly and devilish and inexplicably beautiful about his face, but his aura was dark as it pressed against hers, filling her with dread.

He was grinning as he cornered her, his glittering eyes flashing in a way that made her tremble. She noticed instantly that his smile was tipped with two razor fangs, and she winced when he reached out, wrapping his hand firmly around her neck, the tips of his nails sharp as they dug into her skin. She gasped desperately, both for air and out of fear, when he easily lifted her off the floor, much in the manner that a child would lift a doll.

"I must say, Princess," he said darkly, his grin fading to an amused scowl, "I'm surprised you haven't put up more of a fight."

Nyx flailed helplessly in his grasp, clawing at his hand as she fought to draw a breath. She knew it was useless, but she struggled anyway, the drive to live more intense than the thought of just giving up. Her vision was becoming blurry and the lightheadedness that was setting in was making her feel sick.

Her assailant took a moment to study her as he held her before him. Nonchalantly, he brushed a strand of silver hair from his eyes, before dropping her on the floor. Nyx could feel his eyes on her as she writhed and gasped for a moment, pain shooting through her neck and shoulders, her lungs screaming for air. He remained unmoved as she coughed and choked, the lightheaded feeling subsiding slowly and her vision returning. Once she could see, she opened her eyes and looked up at him.

"Why are you doing this?" she asked, her voice a raw whisper. She could hear the pleading note to her voice, and she watched as he grinned.

He chuckled softly as he crouched to speak to her. "It's nothing personal," he said quietly. "I've been given orders." Nyx flinched when he reached out slowly, dragging his nails across her cheek. They were cold like steel, and she could feel the razor edges digging into her skin. "Your guardian was too easy." A disappointed look crossed his face. "I had hoped that you would put up more of a fight and make this interesting, but . . ." He shook his head, his silver hair wisping around him.

Nyx gasped when he grinned malevolently again, and she watched as he raised his hand.

His nails glinted softly in the pale light, and her eyes widened as fear gripped her heart painfully when they grew longer and sharper. She thought to struggle, to fight or run, but when she tried to move, she couldn't make her body obey. She felt despair overcome her, and she saw different faces suddenly flash before her eyes; the faces of her friends, Jet and Anna, and her aunt's face. She felt sorrow suddenly form in her chest at the thought of her aunt. It wouldn't be long before they saw each other again.

"Goodbye, Princess."

Nyx closed her eyes tightly, preparing to feel what she knew would be excruciating pain. It seemed like an eternity passed. The pain never came. Slowly, she opened her eyes, gasping at the sight that greeted her.

So silently that he could have just materialized there, Jet stood over her. His voice was quiet with a sharp edge to it. "Nice try, Aterro." It took her a moment to realize that the first man had somehow flashed across the room, blood trickling from a gash on his cheek, just shy of his eye.

"Jet," he snarled, baring his fangs. His eyes began to glow a dangerous crimson, this time a deeper shade from when they had been shimmering with bloodlust. "How dare you interfere."

Nyx scrambled back across the floor, away from Jet, pressing her back to the wall. Her heart was racing wildly in her chest. Relief and fear were mingling in her chest as she stared at Jet's back.

Jet crossed his arms, an amused grunt leaving his lips. "Sorry about that," he said easily. "But I can't just let you waltz in here and kill her."

The one called Aterro smirked darkly. "It's been awhile, has it not, cousin?"

Nyx couldn't see Jet's face, but she watched as his hands clenched, and she felt confusion swamp her. They were cousins? She pulled herself farther away from him, her fears renewed, a small, gasping sob escaping her.

"Not long enough," Jet said quietly, his voice a dark whisper. He turned slightly, glancing over his shoulder at her. His onyx eyes were glittering furiously as he looked her over. "It's a good thing you didn't hurt her." At the sight of her fright, he felt pity for her before he remembered how she'd spoken to him when they'd seen each other last. Satisfaction filled him at the thought that she was getting what she deserved. Now she could finally understand what he'd been warning her about.

His eyes shifted to Aterro when he laughed darkly. "Why?" Aterro demanded. His eyes were patronizing. "Would your mistress have been upset to find her in pieces?"

Nyx jumped when a growl tore from Jet's throat, and he lunged at Aterro. The movement was so swift she missed it, seeing Jet only when he was on the other side of the room. Her eyes widened, and she clamped a hand over her mouth to stop a startled scream when a sickening, crunching sound echoed through the room.

She realized Jet's hand was buried up to his wrist in Aterro's gut. Aterro's back was to the wall, and he seemed momentarily surprised.

"Do that one more time," Jet snarled darkly. He watched as Aterro winced, but grinned.

"My, my, cousin," he managed, his voice strained, "quite the temper still, I see."

Jet growled at Aterro, digging his hand deeper into his flesh. "Tell me why I shouldn't rip you apart right now," he said, his voice surprisingly calm, but with an angry edge.

Aterro's grin grew slightly. "You can try," he said darkly, his voice soft. He suddenly shifted, swinging his arm at Jet's face. Their movements were blurs as they struggled for a moment, Jet slamming Aterro into the floor.

Nyx jumped when Aterro winced, Jet's hand smashing into his chest, the sound of his blood gushing from the wound and bones breaking making her feel sick again. "Answer my question," Jet said, his tone never changing. She was surprised when Aterro grimaced, his blood oozing across the floor and staining his clothing.

"Go to hell, Jet," he said quietly, his crimson eyes narrowed dangerously as he glared at his cousin.

Nyx flinched, pressing her back into the wall as Jet suddenly caught Aterro by the wrist. He twisted Aterro's hand violently, ripping it from his body. She couldn't bear to look when she saw the blood dripping from what had once been Aterro's hand.

Jet grinned as he looked at it. "You're not answering my question," he said darkly, dropping the appendage to the floor. "And you have several more things I can break off if you won't talk."

Nyx could feel vomit in her throat, and she turned her head, pressing her hands to the floor as it forced its way from her stomach. Tears were streaming down her cheeks as she tried to understand what was happening. This was not the Jet she knew. He was some terrifying monster now, parading around with Jet's face.

She jumped when another sickening crack filled the air, and she glanced up in fright, feeling faint as she pressed her back to the wall. She gasped when she saw that it looked like Aterro had lunged for Jet, and missed, slamming his remaining fist into the hardwood floor. How the hell was he still standing after what Jet had done to him?

"I'm going to tear off your head and bring it to Our King," Aterro growled, clearly furious. Blood was turning his clothing dark and pooling from the stub that was his arm, but he ignored it as he straightened, his eyes never leaving Jet, who had leapt away from him to stand near her again.

Nyx glanced up at Jet, trembling as she realized that, again, he had moved too quickly for her to track him. A small sob left her lips when he turned to her. "Are you injured?" His voice was soft, but his eyes were narrowed angrily, and blood was still dripping from his fingers.

Nyx couldn't find the words to form as she stared at his hands, tears slipping flagrantly down her cheeks. It wasn't until his lip curled slightly in a snarl that she was able to make her body cooperate, and she shook her head.

"Good," he snapped. He angled his head toward the door. "Get out." He turned back toward Aterro. "I'll take care of this."

Nyx didn't waste a second as she forced herself to her feet. Her legs felt like rubber as she stumbled across the floor, but she didn't look back as sounds of a violent fight suddenly erupted.

Unthinking, she ran as fast as she could from the house, feeling sheer terror forcing her to keep going. She didn't even think about her car, instead taking off on foot down the road, since she wouldn't have been able to find the keys anyway. Her nearest neighbor was not for almost two miles, and she didn't know how far she had gotten before weariness caught up with her, causing her to trip and stumble, bringing her crashing down into the tall grass. The adrenaline that had enabled her with the strength to run as far as she had suddenly left her.

Tears were still streaming from her eyes, and she sank to her knees, her brain reeling and her heart racing in her chest. She couldn't make sense of what had just happened, and she bowed her head, praying that it was just a nightmare and that she had been asleep this whole time. Feeling terrified and frustrated, she covered her face with her hands, sobbing quietly.

"Wake up," she whispered desperately. "Wake up, wake up, wake up, wake up!" She dug her hands into her hair, feeling desperation and anger grip her. "Wake up, dammit!"

All she could do was sit there for a moment, breathing deeply, letting the cold night air help to clear her head. Once she realized that she wasn't dreaming, she felt more tears crowd her eyes as she tried to erase the images in her head. She couldn't make the sight of all that blood and her aunt go away, or the thought of Aterro's bloody hand.

She felt a small sob wrack her as her heart twisted painfully, and she wrapped her arms around her chest, trying to block out the horrifying memory of Jet's face as he'd grinned, delighted in Aterro's pain. She choked on the sobs, feeling her stomach turn, purging itself again into the grass. She was so consumed in her grief that she jumped when headlights suddenly lit up the road.

Frightened, Nyx turned quickly, unable to make herself move fast enough as she gained her feet before tripping and collapsing heavily to the ground again. She felt fear engulf her when she realized the vehicle was slowing down, and she forced herself to move, afraid that the man from her house was still after her. It took her a moment to regain her feet, and as soon as she did, the car had already stopped and the driver was already climbing out. She felt more tears filling her eyes as she saw that it was Jet, and she started to back away.

"Jet," she gasped, her voice a choked whisper. She watched as he advanced on her, seeing his hands were no longer bloody as they were caught in the beams. In fact, there was no sign that what she'd seen had actually happened. "No, please . . ." Hopelessness swept her as he walked toward her, and she knew she didn't have the strength to fight him off when he reached for her arm.

"Get in the car."

Nyx shook her head slowly, unable to see anymore. "No," she whispered, hysterical. "I can't do this." Her knees were trembling and she felt as if she would collapse. "I can't." She gasped when he roughly caught her arm in his hand, making her look at him. His face was blurred by her tears.

"Nyx, listen to me." Brief pity flashed through him as she blinked the tears from her eyes, holding his gaze. Her whole body was shaking fiercely as she struggled against his iron grip. "You aren't safe here. Get in the car."

Nyx didn't know how to feel as she stared at him. There were too many questions, and not enough answers. Her brain couldn't process them all. She was trembling violently as she stared at him. How did she know that he would protect her and wouldn't turn on her? She'd seen him dismember a man with his bare hands.

She gasped sharply, her fear tangible when he suddenly pulled her into his arms, holding her tightly to his chest. "You have to trust me," he whispered. "I'll keep you safe."

Nyx dissolved into more tears as her thoughts shifted to her aunt. No one had been there to keep her safe. But Jet had come for her. He had stopped Aterro. Right?

She was still trembling as she let him lead her back to the road, where the car was. He opened the passenger door for her, and silently she slipped inside. She watched with frightened eyes as he closed the door and walked around to the other side, her heart racing as her stomach twisted, making her feel sick again.

She drew long breaths, trying to calm herself, but she still jumped when he opened the door and slid in silently. "Why?" she breathed, her voice trembling. She sniffled and wiped at her face as he put the car in gear, his eyes trained on the road.

"Why what?" he said softly.

"Why Aunt Dee?" she asked, her tears leaving her eyes sore and her body feeling cold. She watched him, noticing that his hands were clenched tightly around the steering wheel. "Why did she have to die?" Her voice was a tiny whisper.

Jet was silent as they sped dangerously around the curves in the road, and she fastened her seat belt. She felt desperation rising in her the longer he remained silent. Why wouldn't he answer her? Was she so important that her aunt had to die?

"My aunt is dead!" she gasped suddenly, feeling tears in her eyes again. She tried to draw a breath, feeling as if she couldn't take in enough air. "Is she dead because of me?"

Jet shifted his eyes out the window, his brow furrowing lightly. "I'm sorry, Nyx," he said quietly. "But her life doesn't matter as much as yours. We've talked about this."

"Why weren't you there?" she yelled, unable to stop herself. Jet didn't look at her for a long moment. "Answer me!"

Fear and fury were filling her as he continued to drive, and she lashed out in anger. She lunged at him across the cab, grabbing the steering wheel. The car tipped and spun, lurching wildly before Jet could bring it to a stop. Once they were still, he threw it in park, his eyes furious as he caught her wrists tightly. It was only the sudden pain on her face and fear in her eyes that kept him from hurting her.

"My duty is to you!" he snarled suddenly. She could see his fangs behind his lips suddenly. "Your aunt wasn't important. Her death is just a product of war, and you have to accept that." He could feel the bitterness from the last few days catching up to him. "She isn't the first, and she won't be the last."

Nyx shrank back against the door, holding her arms tightly to her body as he released her. This wasn't the Jet that she thought she knew. This was someone dark and scary and deadly, some demon that she never knew even existed. "I just—" she breathed, finally finding her voice.

"You're a princess," Jet snapped darkly. "Aterro was sent to kill you because you're the next in line for the throne. You're a priority over anyone else."

Nyx gasped softly. She blinked more tears from her eyes. "I don't want this," she whispered.

"You don't have a choice," Jet said roughly. He was annoyed as he forced himself to be calm. He knew he shouldn't be taking his feelings out on her, but he had a hard time compartmentalizing. The only reason he'd shown up to save her was because that was his job. And because he hated Aterro.

Nyx was dazed as she turned her eyes away. "But I . . . I didn't . . ." She shook her head slowly.

Jet sighed heavily. "You can go home and be safe, or you can die for nothing."

Nyx shook her head, her hands still trembling. "And you'll make sure I get there?"

Jet turned his dark eyes away from her. "Liana sent me here to protect you," he said quietly. "My task was to come here and watch you and keep you safe. You have my word that I'll fight until my last breath to get you home."

Nyx's eyes were wide as she looked up at him. She couldn't catch her breath suddenly as she turned away from him. She pressed her hands to her face as she looked out the window, trying to pull herself together.

Jet watched her for a long moment. He knew she was struggling to be okay, but there wasn't any time for that now, and part of him didn't care. He put the car in drive, easing back to highway speed. He needed to get her to the Limen. It would be open soon. They didn't have any time to waste.

The silence stretched between them for a long time before Nyx felt like she had the courage to look at him. She turned to glance at him, before her eyes shifted back to the road. He hadn't moved or said a word, and it made her heart flutter nervously in fear.

Nyx felt her chest constrict tightly, and it made her want to cry again. She couldn't stop the thoughts that were suddenly coursing through her. "You . . . you're not going to," she choked on the words, terrified to hear the answer, "kill me . . . are you?" She watched as his eyes shifted to her, an unreadable expression in them at first.

"I gave you my word that I would keep you safe," he said in that quiet manner that unsettled her.

She looked away, feeling her fear growing. "Right," she managed, wringing her hands tightly. She couldn't look at him as she brushed at a rogue tear. She drew a ragged breath as she tried to keep the heartache at bay. There was no going back now.

The Limen, Somewhere Near Lucky, Texas.
Wednesday, December 21, 2011.

THE CLOCK SAID IT WAS 2:00 a.m. when Nyx's distressed brain finally told her that she needed to sleep. Jet had been driving for a long time now, so long that she had lost track of time. The silence was making her drowsy as the road noise turned into a soft lullaby, and she leaned her head against the glass, letting her eyes drift closed. Maybe if she closed her eyes, when she woke again, this would all be over. Maybe when she opened her eyes again, things would be normal. It wasn't long before she was lost to vague sleep.

Hazy scenes began to flash through her mind's eye, but none that were lasting enough for her to remember. She was falling farther and farther into the darkness, almost to the point of no return, when suddenly a bloody corpse flashed through her mind. Nyx jerked awake quickly, a strangled cry leaving her lips as she glanced around wildly, expecting to see her bloodied kitchen. She was almost relieved when she realized that it had just been a dream.

"She wouldn't have wanted you to remember her that way."

She glanced over at Jet, seeing that his eyes were trained on the road and his face was void of emotion. How had he known that?

"The handmaid—" He caught himself. "Er, Dorothea. She never wanted this for you."

Nyx shook her head, feeling sadness course through her. Then why did things have to happen like this? Hadn't there been any other way?

She looked over at Jet. How was it that just hours ago she'd been upset because she was leaving with him? And now, here he was, some monster that she'd never even realized. She remembered the way he'd looked as he stood over Aterro, her heart racing with panic. She shivered. Just because Jet knew her didn't mean that she knew anything at all about him.

She watched as he glanced down as he reached for the console and opened it, producing a rectangular-shaped object. She watched warily as he offered it to her, feeling her insides twisting into nervous knots.

"What's this?" Nyx asked, trying not to wrinkle her nose as she took it.

"Chocolate."

She turned it over in her hands, surprised when, as they drove under a street lamp, the brand was briefly illuminated. For a moment, she felt strangely comforted. It was her favorite kind. She stole a glance at him, feeling her heart twist. Was the Jet she knew still in there somewhere?

"Uh, thanks," she whispered.

She stared at the chocolate bar for a long time, feeling her thoughts fading, leaving only aching numbness in its place. Unthinkingly, she began to unwrap the chocolate, glancing out the window as the lights of a gas station came into view. She was surprised when Jet pulled into the parking lot.

"What are we doing?" she asked quietly, feeling slightly unnerved. Thoughts of escape suddenly flooded her.

"Getting gas," he said, as if it was the most natural thing in the world.

Nyx watched as he slid out the driver's side door, and she followed his lead, stepping out into the cool night air. She watched him carefully as he pulled a credit card from the inside of his jacket and swiped it before he began to fill the car. His dark eyes shifted to her across the top of the car.

"You should wait inside."

"I just need to stretch my legs," she muttered, closing the passenger door and stepping back a moment to look at his car. She realized suddenly that the hood of the car that she loved so much was severely dented, and she noticed for the first time the broken glass across the windshield. From the inside, it hadn't looked so bad. The chrome grill was bent and jagged, and she realized there was something smeared across it. She pressed her hand to it, feeling it was wet and sticky.

She gasped and jumped back quickly when she realized what it was. Blood. Tears suddenly crowded her eyes as she looked over at Jet, seeing him watching her carefully. "Who does this belong to?" she whispered, lifting her palm. Her eyes were startled when he moved toward her.

"No one you knew," he said darkly, his voice soft. He frowned when she flinched away from him when he reached for her hand.

There was a strange light in his onyx gaze that unnerved her: something predatory and distinctly dangerous that she couldn't place. She could feel a cold chill creeping up her spine as he stared at her like that for a moment, like he was warring with himself, before he looked away. He said nothing as he ducked inside the car and produced a white handkerchief, which he tossed at her.

She caught it, using it to wipe at her palm. When she looked up at him, she saw that Jet had taken the opportunity to slink away from her back to the pump where he assumed his air of nonchalant disinterest.

For a moment, she was frozen as she stared at him. How could he act like killing people was something so easy? Like spilling their blood was nothing for him. The chill crept across her spine again, and she shuddered, turning away.

"Where are you going?"

Nyx resisted the urge to wince at the edge to his voice. "Bathroom," she muttered distractedly, before vanishing into the gas station.

She tried to keep her cool as long as she was in view of the windows, and her hands started to tremble as she felt his eyes following her. She could see a short hallway in front of her, and she breathed a sigh of relief when she stepped into it, knowing it sheltered her from his all-seeing gaze. Once she was inside the bathroom, she closed the door and locked it, walking to the sink. Her heart was pounding quickly in her chest and her breathing was quick and ragged. She glanced at her reflection and noticed how pale her face looked, and she could see that her reflection was trembling. She turned on the water, scrubbing desperately at the blood that was staining her skin. Once it was gone, she turned away from the mirror and leaned against the sink, trying to tell herself to calm down. She could feel her chest tighten with worry.

What was she going to do?

She was terrified. Despite what Jet said about not killing her, there was no guarantee. He'd killed his own cousin, for crying out loud. She could have been nothing to him. Nothing more than a job.

She knew there was something not right about him: something that just freaked the hell out of her. She could feel her hands trembling as she threaded her fingers together to try to stop the shakes. She knew that she had to get away from him. She had to find a way to escape and get help. She didn't know where she could go, since they were out in the middle of nowhere, but maybe if she could call Anna she could be rescued. She couldn't go with him to Gexalatia. That felt like a death sentence.

She felt a stab of hope pierce her, and she straightened from where she was leaning on the counter, glancing around quickly. But how? There were no windows, and the vent was entirely too small.

She closed her eyes, sighing tensely. Maybe she could slip out through the back.

Slowly, she unlocked the door and pushed it open, glancing down the hall. She was still sheltered from Jet's view, and she pressed herself against the wall as she tried to stay in a position where she knew he couldn't see her. Her heart was pumping furiously as she slipped into the back room of the station and glanced around. She felt it lurch when she saw the door that led outside to the back of the station, and she ran toward it, wincing when, as she twisted the knob, it creaked loudly.

She felt only slightly relieved when she opened it and stepped into the cool night air, glancing around and seeing no one. She knew she wasn't home free yet, and she wouldn't be until she was safe far away from here, but she felt her heart soar at the sight of the field that stretched out behind the building. She didn't think twice as she dashed from the building and into the tall grass. She could barely feel the sting of the tall grass as it whipped across her face and arms, but fear that Jet would find her kept her running on. Even when she stepped in a dip and stumbled, her ankle protesting, she kept running.

She couldn't go back, no matter what he said. She couldn't let the people on the other side kill her.

She wasn't sure how long she ran, but when she finally stopped, the building was a small sight in the distance, and her lungs were screaming for air. She had never been very athletic, but she thought that was the longest sprint she had ever managed. Her legs felt like rubber, and she collapsed to her knees, clutching the front of her T-shirt as she tried to catch her breath. The fear from earlier was beginning to subside, but she knew that Jet would figure out what she'd done soon, and when he did, she would need to be far away. She struggled to push herself up, focused on where she would go and what she would do, so much so that she screamed when she realized she wasn't alone.

"I thought I warned you against this," Jet said, his arms crossed as his tall frame was silhouetted by the moon. His dark eyes sparkled dangerously, and Nyx noticed that he had shed his jacket. His arms were tensed tightly, and his hands were clenched in fists.

She backed away as she stared at him, feeling her heart screaming in terror as it slammed against her ribcage. Adrenaline was coursing through her again, but this time it was because she knew he was going to hurt her and that she would be running for her life.

Unthinkingly, she turned and tried to run, her brain in flight mode. She knew she couldn't hope to match his strength, and so she did all she could do, but it wasn't enough. It was too easy for Jet to flash in front of her, blocking her escape.

"I'm not here to kill you," he said darkly, even though his eyes flashed angrily. "Stop resisting." His teeth were clenched tightly, as if he was trying to control himself, and Nyx gasped when he reached for her and caught her arm tightly. She could feel his nails digging into her flesh, and she winced, afraid he would do to her what he did to Aterro if she struggled.

"Why are you doing this?" she asked, trying to resist the enormous strength of his pull as he tried to drag her back. Tears were flooding her eyes again.

"I'm only here to deliver you," he said darkly. She could tell that he had calmed considerably, as if he was exasperated.

"Why do I have to go?" she asked, a slightly demanding edge to her voice. She was not someone's property. She shrank back a bit when his eyes shifted to her. "What happened to the Jet I know?"

"It was a ruse," he said quietly, anger in his eyes. The words felt good suddenly as he realized that he didn't have to let her play with his head anymore. He didn't have to pretend anymore. "I'm not who you think I am."

Nyx didn't move as he stared at her. "Why didn't you just tell me?" she asked, her heart aching. Why had he played this game with her for a year? He'd done all he could to make her like him. Hell, she'd tried to kiss him. But now, he couldn't seem bothered by her opinion or what she wanted.

His gaze was dark and unreadable. If she hadn't made him feel like shit the other night, maybe he'd be able to muster the energy to be more kind to her. But he never wanted to be that person again. He didn't know why he let her catch him off guard like that to begin with. He didn't have feelings. He only followed orders.

"Come on," he said, tugging her after him as he ignored her question. "We don't have time for this." She was helpless as he practically lifted her off her feet and dragged her along, much in the manner that she didn't weigh anything.

Silence surrounded them as Jet drove. He didn't look at her, his eyes on the road, his thoughts elsewhere. Nyx didn't think she wanted to know what he was thinking as she sat in silence. She kept her eyes turned away from him, exhaustion catching up to her after a while. She could feel herself trying to nod off, but each time she jolted awake.

"You should try to rest."

Nyx jumped at the sound of his voice, drawing a quick breath as she looked over at him. She didn't want to talk to him, and she swallowed thickly when he didn't look at her, resuming his stony silence. She winced when a pang of hunger shot through her. She hadn't eaten anything since he'd given her the chocolate, and that hadn't been very appetizing. She still had it tucked into the pocket of her jacket, which Jet had rescued from her house and thrown into the back of his car.

"Where are we going?" she whispered finally.

Jet glanced at her. Something in his dark eyes told her that he wasn't in a talking mood. "We're not far," he said quietly.

Nyx grimaced, turning to look out the window. Her stomach twisted again, an emptiness filling her. "I'm hungry," she said softly, keeping her face turned away from him.

He sighed suddenly. "I have nothing to give you," he said, looking over at her. The irritation was heavy in his voice. He could see her reflection in the glass of the window.

"What's going to happen to me?" she whispered suddenly. Her voice was soft and afraid.

Through the reflection he could see a tear slip down her cheek. "Nothing," he said shortly. "You'll get to where you need to go."

Nyx looked over at him, using the sleeves of her jacket to wipe her face. "Are you sure?"

Jet shook his head in aggravation. "Let me worry about it," he said curtly.

Nyx held her middle as her stomach gurgled again. "I should have listened to you," she whispered.

Jet arched a brow, sliding her a glance. "Yes," he said simply. "But we're past that now."

Nyx didn't feel good as she turned to look back out the window, seeing the sun was finally beginning to crest over the horizon. It didn't appear to her that they were headed anywhere as stretches of wooded land began to flash before her eyes. She felt her heart catch in her throat when he began to slow the car. He pulled it off the road, a thin opening through the trees suddenly appearing.

"Where are we?" Nyx whispered, feeling her heart suddenly racing.

A bad feeling overcame her as he pulled the car through the trees, a clearing coming into view. Her heart skipped a beat when another man suddenly was visible, waiting for them. As soon as he stopped the car, she threw the door open. Her breath caught in her chest as she walked toward him.

"Princess," he said, casting his blue eyes down and sweeping her a bow. Brown curls fell across his forehead.

"Seth," she whispered. She ran to him, throwing her arms around his middle. "Seth, Aunt Dee . . ." She gasped softly, tears running down her face again.

Seth lifted his eyes, looking over her shoulder at Jet as he put his arms around her. "I will take care of everything," he said softly. "I am only here to see you off."

Nyx looked from him to Jet. "You're not coming?" she asked, feeling her heart racing. This had to be some cruel trick. How could Seth just let her go alone with Jet? She'd known Seth wasn't coming with them, but hearing it made her heart seize with fear.

Seth angled a look at Jet, disapproval on his face. His voice was soft as he spoke to Jet in that language that Nyx didn't understand. She felt her jaw clench at the way Jet rolled his eyes.

"Hello?" she barked suddenly. "I'm right here!" She crossed her arms, anger seeping through her. "Don't talk about me like I'm not standing here."

Jet shot her a dark look. Seth surprised her when he suddenly bowed his head. "Apologies, Your Grace," he said gently.

Nyx frowned at him. "Don't call me that," she said bitterly. "I'm just Nyx, like I've always been."

Seth's brow furrowed. "I must stay here," he said gently. "It is my duty. We've talked about this." His blue eyes were pinning Jet with a bitter look.

Jet sighed shortly as he walked back to the car, opening the trunk. He hefted a black bag out, slinging it over his shoulder. "Stop looking at me that way," he commanded as he walked to Seth, dropping the car keys into his open hand.

Seth's lips pursed. "What did you do to the car?" he demanded, seeing the dents and broken glass.

Jet arched a brow at him. "Shan got in my way."

Seth looked like he wanted to roll his eyes, caught somewhere between being appalled and annoyed. "Unbelievable."

Jet smirked then. "I know you'll take care of it," he said. "Let's go."

Nyx spared a glance at Seth, who nodded for her to follow after Jet, annoyance on his face. They were silent as he led the way into the trees. Brambles and thin branches pulled at her clothes, and she hissed when a thick stem of brambles tore into her jacket. She'd never been one for the woods, and this felt like nonsense. Fear overcame her again as she stared at Jet's back.

She glanced over her shoulder at Seth, seeing his blue eyes were trained on her. "Why are you doing this, Seth?" she asked quietly. "I don't want to go."

Seth's face softened. "This is what you were meant to do, Milady," he said gently. He hadn't realized that it might feel like a punishment to her. "You'll be safer in Regius Carmen than you will be here."

Nyx frowned. "But I don't want to leave," she said, pausing to look at him. "Please don't make me leave."

"When Dorothea came here with you, it was always her intention to return you," Seth said easily. "Now is that time."

Nyx felt her heart ache at the mention of her aunt, and she clutched her middle tightly. Her heart ached painfully, and a rumble of hunger shifted through her. She sighed shortly, wishing this would get better and that the pain would go away.

"Here."

Nyx glanced over her shoulder, surprised when Seth offered her a packet of toaster tarts. She frowned as she looked up at him.

"Anna gave them to me when I left this morning," Seth said gently in explanation. "You need them for your journey."

Nyx took them, feeling tears fill her eyes at the thought of her friend. "Will you let her know . . ." She couldn't finish, unsure of what she was asking as she shook her head.

"Of course," Seth said gently.

"There's a gift for her," Nyx said, feeling fat tears slide down her cheek. One landed with a splat on the wrapper.

"I'll make sure she gets it," Seth said as Nyx looked up at him. Was Seth like Jet? Only pretending to care about Anna to get close to her? The thought made her heart ache fiercely. Anna deserved better than that.

"Do you love her?" Nyx whispered suddenly. She looked hard into Seth's face. "Or was she just a convenient way to get to me?" Her emerald eyes were borderline angry as she watched him.

Surprise was written across his blue eyes. He didn't seem to know what to say for a moment, and he glanced away. "I do love her," he said softly. There was an edge to his voice, despite the way he tried to cover it. He didn't want to be rude to her, but it was insulting to him that she would think so lowly of him. "In all the time I've been here, she is the only one I care about." He offered a small smile. "If it wasn't for you, I would have never found her."

Nyx wiped at her face with the sleeves of her jacket, forcing the anger away as a small smile pulled at her face. "I'm glad," she breathed. She glanced up at Jet, feeling bitter. "At least you didn't pretend to be something you're not." She looked back at Seth suddenly. "How long have you been here?"

Seth offered a small grin. "That's a story for another time."

Nyx frowned at his response, jumping when Jet's voice suddenly echoed through the trees.

"If you ladies are done gossiping," he said roughly, "I'd like to get there this year."

Nyx sniffled, feeling Seth's hand on her shoulder. "Keep your panties on," Seth mumbled. Nyx felt a small smile pull at her lips as she let Seth steer her in the right direction.

It felt like forever before they finally broke through the trees, the edge of a ravine dropping dangerously before them. Nyx stepped to the side, looking down as Jet and Seth stood on either side of her.

"You realize you're wasting your time, don't you?" Jet suddenly demanded, looking over her at Seth. "Your human girl will just get old and die."

Nyx turned her eyes to him. She didn't know what possessed her, but she stepped toward him, shoving him roughly. What the hell was his problem? He hadn't had a nice thing to say in longer than she could remember. "Don't talk about Anna like that!" she yelled suddenly. "Just because you don't have a heart doesn't mean regular people don't." Tears were suddenly in her eyes again. She was so angry, her hands were shaking. She felt sharp hurt fill her as she wished that he would have left her for Aterro. It would have been better than this hell.

"Princess," Seth said, catching her shoulders. "It's all right."

Nyx looked up at him. The calm in his face took her by surprise, and she felt the fight leave her suddenly.

"Cold and unfeeling is Jet's way," he said, his blue eyes hard as he looked at Jet.

Nyx drew a ragged breath, trying to calm herself. She tried not to think about the way Jet had made her feel weeks ago, and how he'd been trampling on her since then.

She didn't think he was cold and unfeeling. She thought he was heartless and spiteful.

"This is ridiculous," Jet said, turning his dark eyes to the bottom of the ravine. He shot Seth a dirty look. "You know I'm right."

"It doesn't matter," Seth said calmly. He looked to Nyx. "We have other things to focus on."

Jet nodded abruptly, all business. "I'll check it out."

Nyx gasped when he suddenly leapt from the edge. She fell to the ground, staring down into the ravine. She pressed her hands over her mouth to stop a startled cry when Jet landed easily in a crouch. She shook her head, disbelief filling her. Sure, he'd jumped off the roof of her house, but nothing like this before. How far could he fall without injury?

"How did he do that?" she breathed.

Seth knelt beside her, his blue eyes narrowed. Jet was such a show-off. "With more training, you can do that, too," Seth said.

Nyx turned to look at him, her stomach knotting. Jet had said that to her. "I'm not sure I'm cut out for this," she whispered.

"You're capable of more than you think," Seth said, watching her face. "You are Auresi, blessed by Aure." His blue eyes were serious. "Your magic is more pure than anyone we've ever seen before. You can do whatever you believe you can do."

Nyx wrinkled her nose. "Are you sure?" she breathed.

Seth nodded. His thoughts were swirling as he watched Jet walk through the ravine. "I will miss you," Seth said then, a smile sliding across his face. He waved his hand suddenly, something like sparks jumping from his motion.

Nyx gasped as the sparks glittered, forming into a single white rose. She knew she shouldn't have been surprised. "How . . . ?"

Seth's smile widened as he handed it to her. "You will learn in time," he said gently. He watched as she took the rose, turning it over in her hands. "In Gexalatia, white roses are given as parting gifts, much as they are here."

Nyx looked up at him. "Parting gifts?" she asked, her brow furrowing.

Seth nodded his head. "But I'll see you soon." He winked at her suddenly. "Time passes much differently for us."

Nyx didn't understand what that meant as she watched him stand. She caught his hand when he offered it to her, pulling her to her feet. She felt her face flush when he suddenly caught her into his arms.

"Here we go," he said.

Nyx felt her breath catch as he leapt from the side of the ravine suddenly. Her heart was in her throat as they fell. She held tightly to his neck, fear making her feel nauseous. She gasped when he touched down lightly, setting her easily to her feet. She felt lightheaded as she turned away from him, pressing her hands to her knees. It was a long moment before the sick, dizzy feeling left her.

"My apologies, Princess," Seth said as she straightened.

Nyx waved her hand, unable to find words for a moment. She narrowed her eyes at him when she saw the barest hint of a smile pulling at his lips. "That was dirty, Seth," she said finally, bitterness in her voice.

"Maybe I should have warned you," he said, the humor still on his face.

Nyx nodded. "Yeah, maybe," she said. She turned her eyes in the direction Jet had gone, feeling her breath suddenly catch in her throat.

A wall rose up before them, stark and firm in the ravine. It had to have been at least two stories tall, surrounded by dense foliage. Vines and brambles twisted their way up the side of the wall, creating a green waterfall around it. It was covered everywhere, save for in the middle, where a portion of it was bare. As they came closer, a sudden wind picked up, blowing Nyx's golden hair around her face. A scent suddenly hit her nose, making her stomach flip. Somehow it was familiar, but it was lost in a distant memory that Nyx couldn't seem to summon.

She swallowed thickly as she walked toward Jet, seeing him waiting for them, his dark eyes irritated.

"What is this?" she breathed as she reached him.

"Limen," Jet said shortly. He turned his head, his dark eyes seeing beyond the wall. "This will take us to Gexalatia."

Nyx realized her heart was racing, and fear filled her. She turned to look at Seth, feeling panic clawing at her. "Please don't make me go," she whispered.

Pity flashed across Seth's face. "There is nothing here for you," he said softly. He stepped toward her. "Besides," a small smile creased his face, "Gexalatian winters are beautiful."

"When can I come back?" Nyx gasped, feeling tears in her eyes.

"Maybe never," Jet suddenly said. He was watching her passively. "You have a job to do."

Nyx's eyes were wide as she looked up at Seth. "I can never return?" she breathed. She shook her head as tears began to slide down her cheeks.

Seth caught her tightly in his arms. "Everything will be okay," he said softly. He looked up at Jet as she cried softly. His own stomach was twisting in knots at the thought of sending her with Jet. Once she left Earth, they were on their own.

Jet was watching her, bitterness in his eyes. He didn't notice the way Seth arched a brow at his reaction. He hated the way that she took comfort from Seth, her tears slowing as he held her at arm's length.

"There isn't much time, Princess," Seth said. He smoothed her hair from her face. "You must let Jet take you."

Nyx looked up at him. She didn't want to go, but she knew there was no choice. She stepped away from him, brushing the front of her T-shirt and trying to pull herself together. She turned, feeling her heart sink at the way Jet was watching her, his dark eyes narrowed.

"Oh, before you go," Seth said, drawing her attention. "Anything other than gold and silver, you must leave it here."

Nyx frowned at him. "Why?" she asked.

"The Limen won't allow metals to cross," Jet said suddenly. "Only gold and silver."

Nyx patted down her clothes. "I don't have anything," she said finally, looking up at Seth.

He nodded, his eyes shifting over her carefully. "Is there anything you would entrust to me, Your Grace?" Seth asked softly.

Nyx drew a ragged breath, feeling her thoughts swirling painfully. "Just . . . my home, and . . ."

Seth nodded, understanding filling his eyes. "I'll take care of everything," he said quietly. "Now go." He looked to Jet. "You don't have much time."

Jet nodded, watching as Nyx walked toward him. Nervousness was on her face as she stared at the wall, avoiding his gaze. "How does this work?" she whispered.

Jet smirked lightly. "It's a portal," he said. "Just step through."

Nyx swallowed thickly, walking toward the wall. She gasped softly when, as she reached out her hand, the portal shifted, sending ripples through the wall. It was cold and slick to the touch, and it made her pull her hand back. Fright tugged at her as she stared at it. She wasn't sure if she could do this. And what waited on the other side for her? She gasped in surprise when Jet caught her hand.

He didn't look at her as he drew a slow breath. "Follow me."

Nyx drew a sharp breath as he took a step forward, disappearing into the ripples. She suddenly realized she was being pulled along behind him, and she held her breath as she went headfirst into the portal.

For a moment, all she could see around her was darkness. She realized she was being gently pushed along, as if she was being moved by a current, something pulsing her toward a light that was steadily becoming brighter. She felt her heart leap painfully with fear as the current pushed her roughly forward. She broke through the light, falling to her knees, gasping for air, her body trembling. Beads of sweat were rolling down her face as she realized she'd been holding her breath, and she looked up when she saw she still had Jet's hand wrapped tightly in hers.

He was calm as he stood beside her, pulling her gently to her feet. "That wasn't so bad, was it?" he asked.

Nyx didn't know how to feel as she stood on shaking knees. She looked around, gasping softly. Two large and very bright moons hung in the dark of the sky, surrounded by a myriad of stars. The moonlight bathed the earth below in enough light that she could almost see as clearly as if it were day. Her amazement suddenly gave way to fear as silence and heaviness began to settle over her.

Dead, pale earth covered the distance around them. Dull, gray mounds rose into the air in short intervals, and a chill shook her. The air was cold, as if there should have been snow, but there was none on the ground. All around them, stark, gray mountains rose up sharply, making the place feel secluded and lonely. Large, fanged beasts were carved into the rock faces. They looked as if, at any moment, they would pull free of the rock and maul them. There was no foliage anywhere, not even on the sides of the mountains that were facing the mounds.

"Where are we?" she whispered.

Jet's face was set in a frown. "This is where the Prioraes are laid to rest," he said quietly. "Or something like that."

Nyx looked at him. She didn't understand what he meant, the word sounding foreign when he said it. She watched as he sighed shortly.

"These are burial grounds," he clarified. "Ancient tombs."

Nyx felt her heart lurch painfully. "Why would someone put a portal in a graveyard?" she whispered.

Jet turned away from her, lifting his bag across his shoulders. "It's said that the Prioraes were some sort of gods," he said easily. "That the magic from the Limen is from their presence. Commoners call this place forbidden and have legends that the dead sometimes rise from the mounds."

Nyx drew a ragged breath, staying close to him as he began to walk away. The mounds were deathly silent, not even the wind making any sound as it tossed strands of her hair around her face. It made the creeping feeling worse.

"Do you believe that?" she asked quietly.

Jet shrugged. "It doesn't matter to me," he said curtly. "The magic serves its purpose. And I doubt the old bones in this dirt want to walk again."

Nyx frowned at his back. He wasn't as angry as he'd been a moment ago, and she had to wonder at that. She watched as he led her into the mountains.

"Where are we going?" she asked.

Jet glanced at her over his shoulder. The annoyance returned to his face. "If there is anyone waiting for us, they'll be here in the mountains."

40

The Manor of Sorona, Ymber.

The first day of Winter, the 851st year of the reign of Queen Liana Estrella.

ELLIE COULDN'T SEE.

The smoke was so thick it blinded her, stinging her eyes and choking her. She dropped to her hands and knees, trying to crawl under it. She could feel terrified tears flooding her eyes, making it even more impossible to see. Outside, the sounds of battle could be heard, along with panicked screaming. She still hadn't gained enough sense to know what was going on. All she could piece together was that she had been peacefully asleep, and then all hell had broken loose.

She crawled toward the nearest doorway, peering cautiously into the hall. She listened, hearing the sound of voices and the heavy fall of footsteps. Feeling her heart leap in fright, she crawled quickly down the hallway, trying to make it to the next room. The sound of footsteps seemed to become louder and faster. She was almost there, when she suddenly felt a hand grab her.

She screamed, but it was silenced by another hand on her mouth.

"Shut up, Ellie!"

She turned to face her attacker. "Raphael!" she gasped, grabbing onto his tunic. "What's happening? Where is my sister?"

"We're being attacked," he said. She watched as he glanced around, pulling her behind him into a nearby room.

"Ellie!"

Ellie glanced around, seeing her twin sister reach for her. "Bailey," she gasped, pulling her into her arms. She could feel her terror rising as she looked to Raphael. "Where is our father?"

Raphael said nothing, instead turning to heave a bookcase out of the way. Ellie was surprised to see him uncover a door. "We don't have time for that," he said, turning to look at them. His sea-green eyes were desperate. "It is King Paraximus' army. We have to go."

Ellie felt her heart stop in her chest. She had heard the rumors that he was trying to invade Ymber, but she never thought that the Queen Mother's army would fail, or that he would make it past Paries' Wall. The only entrance was through the Custos Obduro, which was hundreds of miles from Sorona.

Ellie felt frozen with shock and fear. Bailey was gripping her arm tightly.

"Come on," Raphael said, ushering them into the darkness. "We must go now."

Ellie couldn't think as she followed him through the dark, winding tunnel. This couldn't be happening. Before she knew it, a blast of cold air hit her face, and she found herself running after Raphael across the courtyard. She glanced around, feeling sick at the sight of her father's castle burning. Her brain couldn't comprehend all that she was seeing, and she felt confused and nauseous.

"Don't look," Bailey gasped, holding tightly to Ellie's hands. "Just run."

Ellie felt her body lock up as she watched servants run screaming from the house, and the smell of burning flesh hit her nose. Hulking beasts were dragging people to the ground, tearing their limbs from their bodies, their hair-covered bodies shimmering wetly with blood in the light of the flames. Beyond the manor, the small town was on fire as well, the chaos palpable even from where Ellie stood. She couldn't look anywhere but at the carnage. She didn't feel Bailey's hand slip from hers as she stopped dead in her tracks, unable to do more than stare at the people she once knew as they were murdered and burned alive.

A sudden sickness knotted her stomach, and she turned away, vomiting. She felt faint and sick, and she fell to her knees in the snow, tears in her eyes. She closed her eyes, wrapping her arms tightly around her stomach, trying to hold herself together. This had to be a bad dream. Was it possible it was a vision?

"Ellie! Come on!"

Ellie barely registered the sound of Raphael's voice. This wasn't happening. It couldn't be real.

"Ellie!" Bailey gasped, helping Raphael jerk her sister roughly to her feet. "They're coming!"

Ellie shook from her stupor for a moment, the sounds of voices reaching her ears. Glancing over her shoulder, she felt her legs turn into mush. A group of the horrible beasts was running toward them, their eyes flashing malevolently in the darkness.

"Raphael!" Bailey screamed. Panic was on her face as Raphael drew a sword, preparing to fight.

A shadow suddenly fell over them, landing with a crash. When Bailey looked up she saw her father's dragon, Bartuk, standing over them, snarling viciously at the enclosing soldiers. Relief filled her momentarily as Bartuk lunged for one, catching his body in his massive jaws. Bartuk was trained for war, and he was a large, magnificent beast, taught to devour the enemies of his master.

"Get on!" Raphael commanded, climbing onto his scaly shoulders and pulling her and Ellie on after him. Once they were safely aboard, Bartuk flapped his massive wings, lifting them high into the air. The howling of the beasts could be heard below, but it faded as the cold air hit their faces. Bailey looked to her sister, seeing her blue eyes were wide and frightened. She caught her in her arms, pulling her against her chest. At the contact, Ellie dissolved into tears, sobbing hard against Bailey's shoulder.

"Is she okay?" Raphael's voice was gentle as he held on behind them.

Bailey shook her head, her pale blonde hair fluttering around her face. "I don't know if any of us are." She held her sister tighter, fighting through her own tears.

I hope you enjoyed this book. Would you do me a favor?

Like all authors, I rely on online reviews to encourage future sales. Your opinion is invaluable. Would you take a few moments now to share your assessment of my book on Amazon or any other book review website you prefer? Your opinion will help the book marketplace become more transparent and useful to all.

Thank you very much!

About the Author

E. Paige Burks, budding author of *The Heart of the Guardian*, is a graduate from Texas A&M University with a degree in Agricultural Communication and Journalism.

Her book, *Return to Royalty*, won the 2016 Author U Draft to Dream Award in the Young Adult category and has been nominated for USA Best Book Awards and International Book Awards.

When she is not writing fantasy and love stories, she enjoys Mexican food, singing out loud, cuddling with her cats, and taking long naps.

E. Paige Burks lives in Houston, Texas with her husband, four dogs, three cats, three horses, and a single bird named Ricki.

A special preview of

Return to Gexalatia

BOOK TWO

of

A Gexalatian Tale Series

Sorona, Ymber.

*The second day of winter, the 851st year of the
reign of Queen Liana Estrella.*

Thursday, December 22, 2011.

IT WAS THE BRISK WINTER WIND on her face that
brought Ellie back to herself. She groaned softly, feeling
disoriented. She felt even more confused as she looked up,
seeing herself surrounded by snow-laden forest.

"Hey." Bailey was sitting beside her, sharing a blanket
with her. Her blue eyes were concerned as she looked at
her twin. "How do you feel?"

Ellie shook her head, feeling a headache pulsing behind
her eyes. "What time is it?" she whispered, pressing her
hands to her face. "Where are we?"

"It's morning."

Ellie's gaze snapped to the side, and she saw Raphael
standing across the clearing from them. "Morning?" she
whispered. She looked around, seeing smoke billowing in

the distance. Confusion was heavy in her mind suddenly. "What's going on?"

Raphael walked toward her and Bailey. "Sorona was attacked last night," he said carefully. "Do you remember?"

Ellie felt her breath catch in her throat. Of course she remembered. She'd seen it with her own eyes, but she'd hoped it was just a vision. "It was real?" she whispered. She felt her stomach twist painfully.

Bailey caught her hand. "Yes," she said gently. "This was not a vision."

Tears flooded Ellie's eyes as she stared at her sister. "And Father . . ." Her voice was barely a breath.

Bailey shook her head. "Raphael searched for him," she whispered. Tears filled her eyes as well, but she fought through them. She needed to be strong. "He's gone."

Ellie felt Bailey's words hit her hard, making her gasp softly. For a moment she couldn't speak and could barely draw a breath. She felt like she'd been struck in the gut. The wind left her body and she felt limp and helpless and numb. She felt unwarranted tears falling down her face. To think that her family could just vanish in the blink of an eye, and by the hands of an enemy . . . The grief that assailed her was almost overwhelming. She held tightly to Bailey when she pulled her into her arms.

Raphael knelt beside them, feeling pity streak through him as he caught Bailey's gaze. "I scavenged what I could," he said softly. "There was nothing left. They burned the manor and the fields and pillaged everything. Everything has been destroyed." He sighed.

"They were looking for us," Bailey whispered, her blue eyes holding Raphael's gaze. She watched Ellie shake her head, trying to regain her composure.

"Why us?" Ellie breathed, tears rolling down her cheeks. She looked from her sister to Raphael. Her voice was hard and ragged when she spoke again. "Why?"

Raphael shook his head. "It could be coincidence," he said through a tense sigh. "Perhaps they came through the bay and are pushing through to Custos Obduro."

"It's more than that," Bailey said softly. "They want us." She held Raphael's gaze. "I'm certain of it. King Paraximus wants us to tap the Visus so that he can finally defeat the Queen Mother."

"How do you know this?" Raphael asked, watching her face carefully.

Bailey looked down, holding her sister tightly. Tears flooded her eyes. "I dreamed it." Guilt was on her face. "But I couldn't have known it was real."

Raphael shifted his eyes away. "It doesn't matter," he said, rising to his feet. "We can't stay here anymore." Bailey and Ellie hadn't had any training with the Visus. They couldn't have known dreams from visions otherwise.

Bailey nodded, sniffling and pulling herself together. She knew that it wouldn't do any good to stay. She paused when Ellie didn't follow, seeing her sister wrap her arms around her middle. "Ellie?" she whispered.

Ellie shook her head, her tears falling quickly. "No," she breathed, feeling a sob welling inside her. "We can't go! We can't just leave our home like this."

"We have to, Ellie," Raphael said, his voice stern. "It's dangerous here."

Ellie shook her head, sobbing quietly. She felt Raphael put his hands on her shoulders, and she shook her head, fighting him. "We can't go without Father!"

Raphael sighed then, pulling her into his arms. "Ellie," he whispered, holding her tightly, "I'm sorry. He would want you and Bailey to leave and stay safe."

Bailey turned away as she watched her sister cry. She had to fight her own tears, feeling her heart breaking over and over again. To think that their father was gone . . . it was impossible.

She'd never really considered it before, but her father had been almost immortal to her. He had always been there for her and Ellie. He had been her rock and her foundation and the only man that she had ever loved with all of her heart, unconditionally and eternally. And deep down, she knew it was that way for both of them. She would never be able to heal from this, but she'd always been the stronger of the two of them. She was the first born, and it was her duty to protect Ellie.

Bailey looked down at her sister. "We have to go to Regius Carmen," she said finally, seeing Raphael look at her. "Father often spoke of the Queen Mother. She will help us. We will go to her."

Raphael nodded. "Yes," he said slowly. "That's what he would want." He looked down at Ellie. "Get ready while I prepare the dragons."

Ellie blinked slowly, her eyelashes wet against the top of her cheeks. She shifted her eyes to gaze at Raphael and Bailey. They were working meticulously about the clearing, building a large pyre. As she gazed at them she wondered if they felt the way she did. She knew her sister probably did, but Bailey had always been so strong. So had Raphael.

Ellie watched as he brushed strands of dark brown hair from his face. She knew she should be helping. She shouldn't be laying here, not when they were still in danger. She moved slowly to her feet, feeling their eyes shift to her.

"What can I do?" she asked meekly. She clutched her blanket tighter, the air filling with a chill.

"We're almost done," Raphael said, letting his hands rest on his narrow hips. He looked down at the wood he and Bailey had gathered. "This will draw the Sagiers away."

Ellie frowned. "Sagiers?"

Raphael nodded. "The beasts we saw during the attack. They'll be coming after us."

Ellie shook her head. "How do you know that?" she asked.

"Our father saw this," he said softly, sighing as he looked at Bailey. "He warned me about it." He glanced up at Ellie, seeing her staring at him.

"What do you mean, he *saw* this?" Bailey asked cautiously.

Raphael shrugged. "Despite misgivings, our father could touch the Visus as well," he said, gazing into the trees. It was beginning to get dark. "He was shown a vision. He knew Paraximus would come for him."

Ellie felt anger fill her briefly. Her father's sight was very weak and hard to predict. "If he knew then why didn't he do something!" she demanded. She stepped toward Raphael, fury filling her. "If you knew, why did you hide this from us!"

Raphael's eyes flitted to her in surprise. "I was instructed not to do anything," he said, his voice stern. "Father was afraid if I knew too much that it would alter his vision." He turned his face away. "All I know is what he taught me and what he prepared me for."

Ellie felt bitterness grappling with her good sense. She wanted to punch him. "And what did he prepare you for?" she asked, her voice shaking.

Raphael crossed his arms, squaring his shoulders to equal her fury. "To protect you and Bailey, whatever the cost," he said evenly. "You have a duty to fulfill. Our father knew this."

Ellie looked away from him, her eyes meeting Bailey's. The bitterness made her heart ache and her stomach twist in knots. "Don't pretend like you care," she snapped angrily. "He wasn't even your real father."

Bailey drew a sharp breath, stepping toward her sister. "Ellie!" she breathed angrily.

"No," Raphael said, raising his hand to still her. "She's right." He turned his eyes back to Ellie. "I may not be blood, but I'm all you have left."

Ellie narrowed her eyes at him, bristling. "How do we know we can trust you?" she whispered.

"Ellie, stop!" Bailey stepped toward Ellie quickly. "What is wrong with you?" Her blue eyes were blazing as she stared at her twin. "Raphael is our brother!"

Ellie's face softened, tears springing to her eyes. "He didn't tell us," she whispered, her voice shaking.

"He was right not to," Bailey said, scolding her sister. "You know how fickle the Visus is. If Raphael had said anything, things would be different." She caught Ellie's shoulders when her tears fell faster. "We might not be alive now, if not for Raphael."

Ellie shook her head, dissolving into tears. She held tightly to Bailey when she pulled her into her arms. "I just don't want this to be real," Ellie breathed, drawing hiccupping breaths.

Bailey held her tighter. "I know," she whispered. She turned her eyes to look at Raphael. "None of us do. But we all know what we have to do."

Raphael let his eyes shift to the ground. Silence fell around them, save for Ellie's soft sniffles. He didn't know what he was supposed to do, but at least he was trying.

After a moment, Ellie pulled away from her sister. "Did they take it?" she whispered, wiping at her face. Her voice was defeated.

Raphael frowned at her. "Take what?" he asked.

"The book," Bailey said, looking from Ellie to Raphael. Her voice was soft. "Father had a book that contained our history."

"No." Raphael shook his head. "It wasn't there."

Ellie frowned at him. "How do you know?" she asked.

"There's no time for it now," he said, his eyes turning toward the setting sun. "All I can say is that your father knew that you and Bailey would need to escape." He glanced up at her. "And he has prepared me to find a way."

Ellie wasn't sure what he meant, but she watched as he and Bailey moved to action, strapping what little they had to Bartuk and his mate, Ellena. By the time they were finished, darkness had fallen over them completely. It made Ellie nervous, but Bailey caught her hand.

"It'll be okay," she whispered.

"We need to get going," Raphael said as he tightened the last strap. Ellie watched as he pulled something from Ellena's back, before turning to her and Bailey. "Father left this for you."

Bailey tilted her head as he handed her the bundle. It was heavy in her hands, and she unwrapped it to find a leather scabbard. "What is this?" she asked, gripping an ivory handle. As she drew it confusion swamped her. "Father left us a sword?" She turned it over in her hands, feeling as if she'd seen it before.

Raphael watched her deep blue eyes rove over it, drinking in the smooth silver blade. "He said you would know how to use it when the time was right," he said gently.

Ellie stared at it as well, wondering what that meant. She and Bailey had never had any formal training. After a moment, Bailey tucked it back into the leather sheath, tying it to her belt. She looked up at Raphael. "I guess we're ready, then," she said.

Raphael nodded. He boosted her and Ellie onto Bartuk, before turning to light the bonfire he had created. "We don't have a lot of time," he said, running back to Ellena as the fire began to spread quickly. "Remember, fly low."

Bailey nodded, staring at the fire as it began to rage suddenly.

Ellie was surprised by how fast it caught, and she was even further surprised when odd noises suddenly filled the surrounding trees. It sounded almost like the howl of wild dogs, and Ellie felt frightened when movement flashed in the trees around them and she held tightly to Bailey.

"Bailey, fly!" Raphael commanded.

Bailey kicked at Bartuk, listening to him growl a warning rumble and bare his teeth. He snapped as a hairy body suddenly leapt at them, barely dodging Bartuk's razor fangs, before the dragon launched into the air. The sound of his leathery wings catching the wind was deafening, and Ellie forced her lungs to draw a breath and her heart to slow. She glanced over her shoulder, seeing Raphael leaning in close to Ellena's neck. She felt her heart stutter when surprise and fear suddenly crossed his face.

A hard body suddenly slammed into her, knocking her from the dragon's back.

"Bailey!"

Her scream was lost as Ellie felt herself falling. She knew impact was eminent with the treetops, and she was surprised when she never reached them. It took a moment for her to realize that someone had caught her. She opened her eyes, gasping when she looked up into two glittering red eyes.

"Sorry, girl," the soldier purred, carrying her close to his chest. His armor was cold, and a Siccitan crest was stark across his chest. "But we can't just let you escape like that."

Ellie felt his muscular arms tighten around her, and she twisted in his grip. "No," she gasped, struggling against him. "Let me go!"

She listened to him chuckle softly. "Struggle all you want," he said, unceremoniously tossing her over his shoulder. "You won't get away from me."

Ellie kicked her legs and flailed helplessly, feeling frightened and unsure. She didn't know what to do, and she searched the sky for Raphael. "Raphael!" she yelled, her voice cracking with her fear. "Bailey!" She listened to the soldier chuckle again, and he leapt from the treetop, the force of his landing knocking the breath from her chest.

"Don't bother," he growled. "They can't hear you." Once they were on the ground, he dropped her into the snow, standing over her. "Or at least, they won't be able to once my Sagiers are through with them."

Ellie grimaced as she righted herself, and she scrambled backwards, away from him. "What do you want from me?" she whispered, her voice shaking. She watched as he came a few steps closer.

"Oh don't worry," he purred, kneeling to be on her level. "We aren't going to kill you." He grinned a fangy grin, flexing his muscles through his black uniform. "You're too valuable right now for that."

Ellie swallowed thickly, feeling tears flooding her eyes. "And my sister?" she asked, afraid to know the answer, but even more afraid not to ask the question.

The soldier's grin grew, maliciousness shining in his eyes. "We only need one of you." He laughed when Ellie gasped, and he watched as she covered her mouth with her hands, fighting back her tears. "She's too stubborn to be of use to us."

Ellie shook her head, bowing it. "No," she breathed, feeling a sharp stabbing pain in her chest. Fear filled her. "Please don't kill her." She gasped, a small sob escaping her as she wept. Too many emotions were flooding through her for her to grasp a coherent one. She couldn't think, and she was numb and helpless when he suddenly grabbed her arm and pulled her to her feet. She couldn't even protest as his iron claws dug into her soft flesh.

"Let's go," he commanded harshly.

Ellie couldn't resist him, and instead followed obediently. What more was there for her to do? She felt hopelessness flood her again with renewed strength.

Raphael gasped, swinging Ellena around as he watched Ellie fall. The Sagiers were nothing but dark streaks as they dashed in and out of the trees. He felt desperation flood him as she vanished from sight. He cursed to himself.

"Ellie!" he called, knowing he wouldn't receive a response. "Ellie! Where are you!"

He let Ellena land in a treetop, and she snarled, whipping her head to the side. Raphael was surprised when she roared suddenly, and a dark streak swept in front of her nose. Furiously, she swiped at it with a massive claw, a dull thud resounding as she caught a Sagier. Raphael heard the Sagier squeal as Ellena bit into his body and swallowed him. Dumbfounded, he stared at her, listening to her rumble happily.

"Uh, good girl, Ellena," he said, patting her shoulder meekly. He watched as she turned her head to gaze at him with a single golden eye. He reminded himself not to get on her bad side. Drawing a breath, he pulled at the reins, turning her to gaze across the sky. "Come on, we have to find Ellie."

The sound of a deeper roar caught their attention, and Ellena swung around quickly at her mate's call. In the distance, Bartuk was struggling with several Sagiers as they leapt around him, the flashes of his silver scales catching the moonlight. Bailey was holding desperately to his back, swinging her sword. As Ellena rushed to his side, Bartuk swung his massive tale around, managing to take out two Sagiers at once, protecting Bailey from their attack. Raphael drew his own sword from where it was tethered to Ellena's back. Once they reached Bartuk's side, Raphael swung from Ellena's back, managing to catch a Sagier. He grunted as their bodies collided, and he rammed his blade into the Sagier's heart as they both slammed into the tree.

The Sagier growled, a pained whine escaping his muzzle as his eyes flashed in the darkness.

Raphael shoved the blade of his sword into the tree, pinning him there. "Where is she?" he demanded, scowling at the creature. He watched as the Sagier bared long fangs, blood beginning to drip from his lips.

"Gone," he growled, his breathing shallow. His voice was unnatural and guttural, just like the rest of his wolfish form.

Raphael's blade was protected by an enchantment which Lord Willem Atturon had placed on it. He could tell that it was working as the Sagier grimaced, a sight that few were lucky enough to witness. Feeling empowered, he twisted the blade slightly, watching the Sagier's glittering gaze widen, before narrowing viciously.

"Tell me how to find her," Raphael growled.

The Sagier bared his long fangs again. "You won't find girl." He snarled, opening his gaping jaws to snap at Raphael. "You die!"

Suddenly enraged, Raphael drew his blade, watching as the Sagier gasped and doubled over. His iron claws dug into the tree limb, cracking under the force. "I'll give you one last chance," he offered, holding the edge of his blade over the creature's neck.

The Sagier pulled its lips back in what was supposed to be a grin. "You kill me," he growled. "I tell nothing."

Raphael stared at him for a moment. The Sagier's blood was dripping across the splintered wood, staining it crimson. His breathing was labored and he was drawing haggard breaths. His tongue was lolling from his lips like a dog, but his eyes were blazing with a fury that no animal could muster. It was disgusting, watching this abomination live.

Without another word, Raphael swung his blade, easily decapitating the beast. He didn't bother to watch his body fall from the tree as he turned his eyes skyward, whistling. Bailey appeared with the dragons, her eyes wide as she gazed at him.

"Did you find her?" Bailey asked. Her voice was shaking as she watched Raphael pull himself onto Ellena's back.

"No," he said shortly. "But Bartuk can scent her out."

Bailey swallowed thickly, trying to keep tears at bay. She leaned down, watching Bartuk turn his eyes on her. "Find Ellie," she told the dragon. Bartuk's golden eyes seemed to hold understanding in them, and without delay, Bartuk lowered his head, scenting for her, before springing away.

Ellie stumbled over a tree root, whimpering as she fell to her knees. Tears began to fall anew, and she gasped as the soldier grabbed her arm and pulled her up again.

"Let's go," he said harshly, pushing her forward. "Enough of your games."

Ellie felt her tears coming faster. She didn't know what was going to become of her. She pulled her arm out of his grasp, trying to warm herself against the cold wind that was beginning to blow. Ellie shivered, feeling the wind blowing right through her. She wasn't sure how long they'd been walking, but it seemed like the soldier was waiting for something. After a few more minutes, he stopped her, allowing her to sit and take a break.

"Don't move," he said darkly as he pushed her to the ground. His eyes were angry as they glowed softly in the moonlight. "If you're not here when I come back, I will find you and cut off your legs." He grinned maliciously. "We only need part of you."

Ellie swallowed thickly, watching as he sprang into the tree above them and vanished. Once he was gone, she doubled over, sobbing softly for a moment. She couldn't believe this was happening.

What had she done to deserve this?

She felt her sobs begin to diminish after a moment. Despite her fear, she was finally beginning to run out of energy and tears. She used the back of her sleeve to dry her face, sniffling pathetically. After a few moments, she looked up into the tree, wondering to where her captor had vanished. He'd been gone for much longer than she expected.

The thought of escape flitted across her mind briefly, but she pushed it away. There was no way she could hope to out-run or out-maneuver Paraximus' soldier. He was too fast and would be able to follow her scent too easily. Heaving a heavy sigh, she prepared herself to wait for his return. She was starting to wonder how much longer she would have to wait, when suddenly noises came from above.

It was faint at first, before it began to get louder and turned into the sound of fighting. The clash of blades could be heard, and Ellie jumped to her feet. She heard yelling, and then suddenly a crash as something came falling through the branches. She screamed as whatever it was landed with a crash, and she backed away, staring. After a moment, she realized it was two bodies, and she watched as one began to move.

"Ellie?"

She gasped and ran forward, watching Raphael rise to his feet, pulling his sword from the dead soldier's body. The snow was stained red from the soldier's blood.

"Raphael!" She threw her arms around him, feeling him grunt as if he was in pain. "Are you and Bailey okay?" she asked, stepping back to look at him.

He nodded, sheathing his sword. "Let's get out of here," he said. He whistled, and Ellie watched as Bartuk and Ellena swooped down from the treetops. Bailey was sitting safely astride Bartuk's back, and she held out her hand to pull Ellie on behind her.

Coracinus Mountains, Ymber.

The second day of winter, the 851st year of the reign of Queen Liana Estrella.

Thursday, December 22, 2011.

NYX FROWNED, FOLLOWING JET. She didn't know how she was supposed to feel as they wound their way through a trail. They'd been walking since before sundown. Jet made her rest while the sun was at its highest, but he said they needed to move at night. It was safer, and he said it would be less taxing on her body. She wasn't so sure about that.

The moons had lent enough light to the burial grounds, but here the mountain faces cast long shadows, leaving them in a thick, murky darkness. Every nerve ending in her body felt like it was tingling, anticipating a fall into some abyss she couldn't see or a bite from some monster she couldn't fathom. Her heightened senses and eyesight were a help, but she knew it wasn't good enough. She wasn't suited to this super-darkness, and she tripped, crashing heavily to the ground.

She gasped as sharp stones dug into her hands. Despair caught at her for a moment. She was in a strange land with someone who, she assumed, didn't care what happened to her; and now she was in pain, scrapes stinging on her hands and her knees.

Nyx was surprised when she looked up, seeing Jet's dark eyes sparkling as he stood by her, a hand reaching down to her. Her heart caught in her chest as she realized a soft light was hovering just over his shoulder. She recognized the augarlux.

"Are you sure that's safe?" she breathed as she caught his hand, allowing him to help her.

"Doesn't seem like we have a choice," Jet said.

Nyx frowned at him. "Why?" She watched as the light swirled in a small mass beside him, shifting as he turned away from her.

Jet sighed. "Don't you ever stop asking questions?" he asked, the irritation heavy in his voice. "You couldn't see, so I summoned it for you."

Nyx realized she was trembling. "Thanks," she whispered. "I could have done it myself."

Jet suddenly stopped, rounding on her. "Let's just get this out of the way," he said sharply. "You're to do nothing unless I tell you to." There was an anger in his voice that Nyx couldn't place. "I'm suited to this place and everything in it." His voice echoed quietly off the walls around them, making the darkness feel pressing and sucking. "If you wish to survive, you'll do as I say."

Nyx wrapped her arms tightly around her middle, the feeling to flee heavy in her mind. She wasn't sure what she'd done to anger him so much, but he'd been like this since they crossed. She was beginning to wonder if it was her, or if there was something he wasn't telling her.

"You'll have to trust me."

Nyx's heart was racing as Jet stood in front of her, his dark eyes watching her. "What is it you're not telling me?" she breathed.

Jet's eyes narrowed at her, as if he was irritated that she could read him. "Nothing I haven't already said," he snapped. "Every moment we spend here in the open brings us closer to being found."

Nyx was pretty certain she didn't want to know who he was talking about. She felt small and alone as he turned away from her, pressing forward. She followed closely behind him, clinging to the light of the augarlux.

Nyx wasn't sure how long she'd been following Jet through the darkness of the mountains. She could feel weariness pulling at her eyelids, and she could feel her feet dragging against the stone beneath her. She wiped at her face, wishing she could draw on reserve energy, but she didn't have any left. The thin air and the stress of getting to this point were finally dragging her down.

She felt the toe of her boot catch an uneven spot, and she stumbled forward, barely catching herself. Her palms and knees were still stinging from her earlier encounter with the ground. "I need to rest," she whispered meekly. She looked up at Jet, seeing that he paused a few feet away from her. He was clearly unhappy.

"We can't stop here," he said slowly, as if trying to force his voice to be calm.

Nyx bowed her head. "I'm exhausted," she breathed. She didn't even have the strength to fight with him. She hadn't slept in too long, afraid to close her eyes for fear of what she would see.

Jet scowled darkly, walking toward her. "There are caves ahead," he said shortly. He caught her hand, pulling her up.

Nyx gasped in surprise when he swept her feet from under her, holding her close to his chest. She was tense as he carried her effortlessly. "Is all your energy an Acerbi thing, too?" she asked.

Jet shook his head, his eyes turned ahead. "It's training."

"Oh, right," Nyx breathed. "Military." She let her head rest against his shoulder, the fatigue heavy in her bones. "I wish I could be more helpful." Her voice was small.

Jet frowned. "Me, too."

Just as he promised, they reached a series of caves. He carried her inside, setting her down carefully. He waved the augarlux to the floor, dimming it as he dropped his bag beside it. "Rest," he commanded, watching as Nyx eased to the floor. "I'll keep watch."

Nyx drew a ragged breath as she watched him stand in the entrance, the augarlux throwing light on his back. She felt tired and sick, and she reached into her pocket, feeling the toaster tarts Seth had given her. She pulled the package from her pocket, feeling her stomach turn.

Her heart hurt. She missed Seth and Anna and Dorothea. She wished she could go back and stop all this from happening, but knowing it was done sent a sharp pang of hurt through her. Pitifully, she opened the toaster tarts, breaking off a chunk and putting it in her mouth. Silent tears slid down her face as she savored the taste.

They were strawberry. Her favorite.

Despite feeling consuming sadness, she was desperately hungry, and she finished off the pastries, tucking the plastic wrapper back into her pocket. She wiped at her face as she let her head rest against the wall, trying to sleep. She was worthless without any energy.

She didn't know how much time passed as she dozed lightly. She could feel the bad memories fading as her mind succumbed to a much-needed sleep. She didn't dream of anything, and the darkness was welcome. She could have stayed like that forever, but Jet didn't let her enjoy it long.

"Wake up," he said quietly.

Nyx lifted her head, seeing that he was kneeling before her, his hand on her shoulder. "What time is it?" she asked groggily.

"We have to go," Jet said, glancing over his shoulder in a distracted way. "We're being followed."

Nyx felt his words hit her like a bolt of lightning, and she was on her feet in an instant. "By who?" she breathed.

Jet shook his head, waving his hand to call the augarlux to him. "We need complete darkness," he said softly. He wrapped his hand around the augarlux, effectively extinguishing it.

"But I can't see," Nyx breathed. She was terrified as she stood in the dark.

"I can," Jet said, catching her wrist gently. He swept her into his arms, carrying her from the cave.

Nyx gasped when a blast of air suddenly hit her face, and she realized they were moving. And very fast at that. She buried her head into Jet's shoulder, trying not to think about what was happening. She drew a sharp breath when Jet suddenly stopped. He lowered her to her feet gently.

"Summon a soft light," he said.

Nyx did as he said, mustering a pathetic augarlux. Jet caught it in his hand, infusing it with his energy to brighten it some and then pressing it back into hers. It was cold to the touch, blackness pressing against the gold inside. "If you need me, use this to call me." He pointed, his dark eyes glinting in the faint light. "Follow the trail to the forest."

Nyx felt her heart lurch as she realized he was leaving her. "But, I don't know how," she breathed, feeling panic assailing her. "I don't know where I'm going."

Jet's eyes narrowed in the faint light. "You'll be fine," he said sharply. He reached into his bag, pulling three long knives from it. They were tucked safely in leather sheathes. "Take this." He handed her one.

Nyx shook her head as she took it, her hands shaking. "I thought you couldn't bring—"

"It's special," Jet said bitterly. "Try to remember your training." He pulled the bag over his head, dropping it unceremoniously around her shoulders. "Now shut up and go."

"But where are you—"

Jet turned to look at her, his dark eyes dangerous. "I'm going to do what I do best," he said, his voice clipped. "I don't need an audience."

Nyx drew a sharp breath. Her heart skipped a beat as she realized he was going to kill the ones following them. She was mute as she nodded her head. She didn't want to see anyone else die.

"Wait for me at the forest," Jet said. He turned away from her. "If I haven't come by sunrise, then follow the trail to the nearest town. There is a map and some supplies in the bag." He drew a slow breath, unable to look at her. "Someone will find you and make sure you get to Liana."

Nyx felt tears in her eyes as he suddenly vanished, leaving her alone. Her heart was racing with fear as she stared around the canyon. She was desperately afraid as she turned, pushing on down the trail. Her hands were shaking as she lifted the augarlux over her head, lighting the way.

Jet drew a slow breath, forcing himself to be calm. Being free of Nyx suddenly made him feel like a weight had been lifted from his shoulders. He wasn't good at separating things, and all he'd been able to think about was how miserable he felt every time he looked at her. He couldn't tell if it was from the weeks before, or if it was because of everything he'd just put her through. He tried not to think about it as he took a moment to clear his head. It wouldn't do to be distracted.

He lifted one of the two weapons he'd taken, pulling the scabbard back to reveal a long-bladed dagger. He lifted it, running his finger across the blade. He felt satisfied when a red line appeared on his skin, blood beading from it as the wound sealed itself, the magic pulsing through him, healing the cut quickly. They were chalargentum blades, made for times like these, the silver-steel able to repel magic and kill monsters.

He shifted his attention from the blade, sliding it into the scabbard at his side. He could feel the others in the distance, their life force distinct against the blackness of the canyon. He knew they could probably feel him, too, but only because he was allowing it. He knew he was much stronger than they were, and this would be an easy fight.

Slowly, he crept through the darkness, coming to a bend in the trail. He stilled, holding his breath as voices could be heard.

"Our commander hasn't returned," one whispered in Sarotian.

"That doesn't matter," another snapped. "The message has been sent."

Jet frowned, feeling his heart skip a beat. What message were they talking about?

"Enough chatter," a third said, clearly the leader. "The General and the girl are here. This is where we'll take them."

Jet narrowed his eyes, feeling bitterness well inside him suddenly. He hated that term, and he clenched his jaw, feeling them come closer. He waited until the first man rounded the bend. It was easy enough for him to catch the man off guard, swinging his head painfully into the rock around them.

The man slumped to the ground as a second drew a sword, swinging it at Jet. Jet dodged it easily, blocking the second man's arm as he dealt a swift blow to his chest. The second man fell back, gasping for air, his sternum crushed under the force. Jet didn't toy with the third man, slinging a blade at him. It struck home, sinking into the man's eye, rendering him useless as he collapsed to the ground.

Jet walked toward him, yanking the dagger from the dead man's flesh. This had been too easy. He turned his onyx eyes on the second man, seeing him gasping as he pressed his back against the stone walls around them. Jet had spared him because of the badge on his sleeve. He'd noticed it immediately.

Fear was in the man's eyes as he watched Jet walk toward him. Despite the darkness, he could see the silver of the dagger gleaming with his comrade's blood. He couldn't find words as Jet walked toward him, kneeling slowly.

"Who is your captain?" Jet asked softly. His eyes shifted to the badge. "Second Lieutenant."

The soldier shook his head. "I won't tell you," he said angrily. Pain was etched across his face as he drew a hard breath.

Jet smirked lightly. "That's interesting," he said slowly. "I believe I'm still your superior."

The soldier scowled at him. "You are a traitor," he snapped bitterly. "A deserter. I don't have to answer to the likes of you."

Jet scowled at him. He couldn't stop the anger that welled in him suddenly. In an easy motion, he dug the dagger into the soldier's leg. He watched, unfazed, as the man cried out softly, his breaths ragged. "Shall we try that again?"

The soldier turned his face away. Pain furrowed his brow, but he shook his head. "I'll never talk," he gasped.

Jet nodded slowly. "I suppose it doesn't matter," he said slowly. He yanked the dagger from the man's flesh, listening to him whimper. His body wasn't healing. Jet realized then that the man was Inerse, with a spell cast over him to hide the ugly scent of his skin, as were the others. A sick feeling suddenly caught at him. In a swift motion, he was on his feet, his hand wrapped around the man's neck.

"Who else is with you?" he demanded, baring fangs at the man.

The soldier shook his head, weak laughter leaving his lips. "It's too late," he breathed. His hands were wrapped tightly around Jet's wrist. "Your princess will be dead soon."

Jet gritted his teeth, fury seeping into him. "She's not my princess." He slammed the soldier roughly into the stone wall, driving his dagger into the man's heart.

He stepped back from the dying man as he coughed and sputtered, wiping the blade on the man's clothes.

He was stupid for having thought this would be easy.

Nyx lifted the augarlux, watching as light cascaded around her. The canyon was eerily silent, just like the burial grounds had been. It didn't make her nervousness ease as she pressed forward. She didn't have any idea of what time it was, or what the forest would look like when she reached it. She thought to take out the map, but she knew she had to keep moving. She didn't think it would be much farther.

The sudden shifting of rocks made her jump, and she spun around, using the light to illuminate the path behind her. Fear filled her as she realized she was alone, and she turned away, letting her hand rest on the sheath at her side. Her hands were shaking as she struggled through the canyon, a hill suddenly cresting in front of her. The path going up was rocky, and she felt the ground shifting beneath her boots as she scrambled to the top. She felt her breath catch as she reached the top of the hill.

Before her, an expanse of forest reached for miles. Just as Seth had told her, it was beautiful, covered in glistening white snow that was tangled in the tops of the trees. She pulled at her jacket, a cold breeze pushing into the canyon. Her heart was racing suddenly as she stared at the landscape. Gexalatia didn't look anything like she had imagined. Large, winding tree boughs arched around, making the forest look like a gnarled mass of monster limbs. Treetops reached for the sky around the limbs, a fine sheet of white powder coating everything.

Once again, she saw the moons glittering brightly in the night sky, the light of countless diamond stars filling the void of the night. This put anything in the Texas sky to shame.

Nyx looked down, seeing that the pathway down to the forest was steep. She held tightly to the strap of her bag, trying to make her way down. She gasped when she lost her footing, skidding and sliding down the rocky trail. She landed in the snow-covered grass hard, feeling the wind knocked from her for a moment. She rolled onto her back, coughing as she tried to catch her breath. Once she felt less like she'd been hit in the gut, she rolled onto her stomach.

A gasp left her lips as she looked down, seeing stems of grass poking through the snow. She sat up quickly, feeling startled. The grass was a deep cerulean in the white light of the augarlux, which had slipped from her fingers and rolled across the snow. Nyx stood quickly, taking a step back. She'd never seen grass so blue and beautiful.

She turned her attention away from it, pulling the bag Jet had given her from around her shoulders. It was heavy as she let it fall to the ground, kneeling beside it. She pulled it open, digging through it. Just as he said, it was filled with a blanket and a leather flask and some other things. Under the blanket, she found a paper folded neatly, and she pulled it out. She frowned when she saw more knives glistening in the bottom of the bag. She sighed as she realized that's why the bag was so heavy.

Carefully, she unfolded the paper, seeing that it was indeed a map. She smoothed it across the snow, so that the light from the augarlux was casting over it. She frowned, seeing that words were written on it in a language she couldn't make out. She guessed it was the language Jet and the others spoke, and she felt a scowl pull at her face.

She couldn't read maps. And she definitely couldn't read a map that she'd never even seen before. She fell back in the snow-covered grass, sighing deeply, trying to push the fear that was rising inside her away. Jet had told her to follow the path into the forest. He had told her to wait for him until sunrise, and it wasn't sunrise yet.

Her stomach twisted painfully with anticipation as she turned her eyes back toward the canyon. She hadn't heard any noises, and she didn't know what Jet was up against. What if he didn't come for her?

Nyx shook her head, forcing the thought away. She would handle those things when she got to them. She drew a ragged breath as she folded the map back together, laying it carefully inside the bag. She slung it over her shoulders, bending to scoop the augarlux into her hands. She figured the safest place was away from the main trail, and she turned, seeing the darkness of the trees had become illuminated by a soft light. Flowers were opening inside the tree line, where the snow couldn't touch them, emitting a gentle light as they unfurled their petals.

Slowly, Nyx walked closer, bending to look at the flowers. She drew a sharp breath, seeing how large and beautiful they were. As she came within arm's reach, the glow suddenly brightened, as if the flowers knew she was there. Amazed, she reached out her hand, wanting to pluck one. She drew a sharp breath when the flower suddenly zipped closed, turning dark. Nyx frowned at it, turning her head when all the flowers around her suddenly dimmed, curling around themselves. She thought maybe she'd been the cause, but then the sound of footsteps came softly behind her.

She straightened and turned, thinking it was Jet. Relief was filling her, but it was too soon as she saw bright blue eyes glowing down at her. A woman formed against the light of the augarlux, a vicious grin on her face. Her eyes were smug as she spoke coldly to Nyx in an unfamiliar language.

Nyx clutched the augarlux painfully in her hands, her heart racing. "I—I'm sorry," she managed. "I don't understand—"

Faster than Nyx could react, the woman was on her, cold hands wrapped tightly around her neck. Nyx gasped a strangled cry, fighting desperately to draw a breath. The augarlux fell from her fingers as she dug her nails into the woman's wrists, trying to break her iron grip. Nyx couldn't tear her eyes away from the woman's face as she coughed and gagged. She was desperate as she tried to think, feeling her knees buckle, a fog pressing against her mind. The woman's weight was heavy as she held Nyx down, a malicious grin sliding across her face.

The blade.

The thought hit Nyx suddenly, and she reached for it, her fingers fumbling for it against the blackness that was threatening to consume her. Nyx heard her attacker gasp when she swung the knife, releasing her suddenly. Nyx coughed and choked as she writhed on the ground, turning to see the woman standing over her. She was dressed in a black leather uniform, a coat of arms emblazoned into the leather over her left shoulder. Thin sheets of armor covered her chest and other strategic places.

Nyx realized she'd gotten lucky with the dagger, managing to drive it between pieces of armor.

The woman had dark blue eyes which were glittering like cat's eyes, and she was too small to have been so strong.

She began to speak, her words sounding angry as her eyes blazed, the wind tossing waves of navy hair across her shoulder. She yanked the dagger from her side, twirling it in her fingers. Her uniform began to turn darker as her blood stained it. It didn't seem like the wound fazed her at all, no trace of pain on her face.

Nyx couldn't understand her, and she gasped hard, shuddering breaths shaking her as she pulled herself back from the woman. There was one thing that was clear. This woman intended to kill her. She raised her arms to defend herself when the woman descended on her again, murder in her eyes.